A DANGEROUS RIDDLE OF CHANCE

FLYING

The Book Guild Ltd

First published in Great Britain in 2021 by
The Book Guild Ltd
9 Priory Business Park
Wistow Road, Kibworth
Leicestershire, LE8 0RX
Freephone: 0800 999 2982
www.bookguild.co.uk
Email: info@bookguild.co.uk
Twitter: @bookguild

Typeset in 12pt Minion Pro

Printed and bound by CPI Group (UK) Ltd, Croydon, CR0 4YY

ISBN 978 1913551 988

British Library Cataloguing in Publication Data.
A catalogue record for this book is available from the British Library.

To Tanya for giving me Chance – as well as Henry de Poisson, Davinia Angelica Plum and the rest of the characters. And for Caroline for teaching me to suspend disbelief in making the unbelievable, believable.

And not forgetting Saskia and Alexia – with their enduring belief in a world of fantasy, for they, like others at that age will be forever young.

CONTENTS

Author's Note   xi

Prologue   xv

Part I

Chapter 1   Two Heads Are Better Than None   3

Chapter 2   All Creatures Great and Small   13

Chapter 3   Tied Up in Knots   26

Chapter 4   Blink Blink It Makes You Think   36

Part II

Chapter 5   Under the Cloak of Darkness   45

Chapter 6   A Handsome Cab   52

Chapter 7   Snatched   60

Chapter 8   Out of the Frying Pan   64

Chapter 9	Into the Fire	72
Chapter 10	Wisendrama	93
Chapter 11	The Secret of Toe Hee Do	101
Chapter 12	That Long Wait Home	115

Part III

Chapter 13	Whilst They're Away, The Cat Will Play	127
Chapter 14	A Trip Down Memory Lane	134
Chapter 15	Rival Sentimentalists	141
Chapter 16	Dread	155
Chapter 17	The Pen Is Mightier Than the Sword	165
Chapter 18	A Stab in the Dark	177
Chapter 19	If Only	183

Part IV

Chapter 20	The Dodecahedron	193
Chapter 21	Lotte's Lot	202
Chapter 22	Feeding Tim's Dreams	212
Chapter 23	Wild Dreams and Amazing Gadgetry	219
Chapter 24	Hung Out to Dry	224
Chapter 25	A Rude Awakening	233
Chapter 26	Warnings	239

Part V

Chapter 27	Beware of the Eyes That Cried	259
Chapter 28	A Thieving Misdeed	277
Chapter 29	Patients and the Mysterious Dr De'Aff	291

| Chapter 30 | Flying Bedpans and Another Good Deed Indeed | 308 |
| Chapter 31 | Knocking at Death's Door | 325 |

Part VI

Chapter 32	Out of the Shadows	331
Chapter 33	Barnard and Barnard	336
Chapter 34	A Testy Rehearsal	345
Chapter 35	What a Performance!	357
Chapter 36	Truth or Lies?	367
Chapter 37	The Big Chance	379
Chapter 38	Another Dimension	402
Chapter 39	Acridcradaver	409
Chapter 40	B.C.D.	425
Chapter 41	The Caravan of Death	432
Chapter 42	The Oraco Dex Lo Paediac	451

Part VII

| Chapter 43 | Bare Bones of the Matter | 463 |
| Chapter 44 | Everything in Life Is a Riddle… A Riddle of Chance | 489 |

Epilogue	509
Acknowledgements	514
About the Author	516

AUTHOR'S NOTE

A PRE-EMINENT JOURNALIST ONCE said that there were only a finite number of plots based on human emotion or real-life situations that were available to use in writing: love lost, love regained; life and death; forgiveness and laughter; hate and redemption; grief and joy; good and evil and so on. But for me, it was relatively easy to start off with, say, using one of the latter: e.g., good versus evil. However, some writers may then struggle to find a character as a peg to hang their story around, as well as a theme of an idea on which to base their storyline.

I consider myself quite lucky, for such an idea literally fell into my lap from a real-life event. Because many moons ago, my daughter Tanya, as a student of art, happened to design and construct several life-size figures. Amongst them were a harlequin and a clown, (despite some people having coulrophobia – an irrational phobia about clowns!)

which she subsequently called Chance – a figure of fun and joy.

After all – "*Laughter – is the sweet music of the planet. The nectar of happiness... the universal language understood by all species and the elixir of all life!*"

At the end of term, whilst driving to the family home in her little old car, because it was raining, Tanya decided to leave the figure lying in the back seat under a lamppost until the following morning, until help could be summoned to carry the figure up the stairs. Well, certain things happened unexpectedly during the night, subsequently creating a train of surprising, and sometimes astonishing, events in its wake.

Furthermore, whilst constructing the timber frame for the harlequin, an unusual knot – the colour of rich amber – fell out of the wood. (True!). It provided the idea of a rare, prized gemstone that had unusual magical properties that endowed the owner of such with remarkable powers that could save his life.

Apart from Tanya (aka Saskia) – the young art student, the creator of Chance ("*A trick of light upon your face... wish you were part of the human race*"), Mudd the cat and Barnabas Quick (a pseudonym) – the local vicar, (who, incidentally, really did hold a service for all animals and pets) – the characters in the following story are entirely a work of fiction.

Herewith, a quote from the vicar's sermon: – "*Evil can only exist in the absence of good. Evil will only flourish where there is misery and unhappiness. So, root out this evil from our lives, then goodness and love will have a chance to live!*"

However, I have to admit satirising characters from real life, such as: Roland Bigglesworth, the eponymous hero –

the cabbie; Seth Ropely, the teenage thief; young Lotte Pert and Tim Needles with Ram the dog; Henry de Poisson, the gentleman sidekick of Chance; Nick Rossiter, newspaper reporter (*"Make the unbelievable, believable"*) the sinister Dr De'Aff and the tyrant Qnevilus-the-Terrible from the Alterworld, (*"Kill all good-doers and purveyors of joy from the face of the earth!"*).

And not forgetting Davinia Angelica Plum, the beautiful but cold-hearted woman who was left behind at the house whilst the others embarked on a dangerous quest – when Chance chases a riddle to extend his life on earth, so that he could unite the Three Kingdoms (i.e., the one of trees and flora, the one of creatures and animals as well as the one of humans) in a battle against the evil Custodians of Terror.

Furthermore, any resemblance to other actual persons living or dead is coincidental. Apart from the beginning of this tale, which happened to be true, the veracity of the rest – including places and events – is a fantasy, or purely by chance.

F L YING

PROLOGUE

I T WAS AFTER A bright new dawn that had promised
so much, when a sudden darkness fell as if it were
night. Like a deathly black shroud, it rapidly came. It
happened without warning; thick and impenetrable, as
if someone, somehow, had deliberately and mysteriously
created it at will with a slick snap of the fingers. A strange
foreboding hung in the air. It was one of dread and
expectation; something you could not grab hold of – or,
for that matter, stop in its tracks once it began… Because
just then, the events of a prophecy started to ominously
unfold…

On the other side of town, two large figures loomed out
of the shadows of an enormous tent recently pitched there.
They approached each other, whispering furtively behind
the backs of their hands, each casting glances suspiciously
over their shoulders in case they were being watched.

Pushing and pulling, they quickly threw their hoods over their faces for immediate camouflage.

'Does he know about us? Has he been told of the riddle?' hissed one, a rasp in his throat cutting the cool night air.

'Not yet,' replied the other one. Like a vulture, his head and body stooped low scraping the ground with his baying cry echoing all around him.

'*But how can you be certain he'll turn up?*'

Circling stealthily around the other, he felt the bridge of his nose with a gnarled finger that fumbled from a slit in his coat and snorted. 'Argh, in my mind's sight my sixth sense is never wrong. He *has* to take a chance. He can't keep away. He's a joker, the kind that loves the limelight – once he's tasted it. What's more, he's the type that loves all of life's creatures with a ready smile.'

He thrust a clenched fist angrily at the sky and continued to snarl, spitting through a gap in his hood. 'Moreover, methinks he's a goody-good, too-good-for-his-own-safety kind of fool. It's a matter of chance, you see. He hasn't any choice. He's bound to come and search for the answer. He *has got* to – to save his own life.'

The taller figure shuffled, dragging his feet stiffly towards the other, towering over him somewhat. Through his mask, he spat on the ground venomously and then stamped a heavy boot over the spot, grinding a hole beneath with murderous fury. 'So, he'll fall into the trap, then?'

'Oh, yeah, yeah. Yes!' sneered the other. Steam began to rise from beside his neck, as if he were boiling over with searing hatred. 'Yes, I'm absolutely certain of that. He'll be like a juicy, fat moth stupidly attracted to a fire.'

'But wouldn't that make him a martyr for those in the Kingdoms and cause an uprising in the Alterworld?'

'*No!* Not if I have anything to do with it.' There was a sinister swagger in his voice, as though he was extremely cocksure of himself.

'Ah hah, my friend: but will he have what we're looking for on him?' enquired the other with a nasal whine. He rubbed his hands together greedily, giving off an odd sound like a rattlesnake about to strike. The temperature of the night dropped noticeably several degrees as they confronted each other.

'Of course, we *need* to find out – with slow, cutting torture to break him, if we have to.' A horrific cackle, which was as frightening as it was merciless in its threat, signalled that a battle of terror was about to begin. And they revelled in it with sickening glee.

'Remember, the Mighty One, *the Supreme One*, expects us to deliver. Otherwise, you and I will pay the ultimate price if we fail!' His arrogance returned as he straightened up fast.

'*What!* You... you don't m... me-mean... do you?' asked the one with a whiny squeal, suddenly all of a stutter. His ugly body bent inwards with fear.

'Yes, I do *mean* that!' came the chilling reply. He sliced a shrivelled, but sharp edge of his hand across his throat and uttered a hoarse and terrifying '*Ge... Ger. Ger-rrk*' which slid from an ugly gash in his face from where his mouth should have been. No sooner had he said that than the ugly cockiness vanished abruptly from his stride.

'We should have killed him, the minute he arrived on

the earth!' He grimaced ruefully. Again, he spat on the ground, just missing his feet.

'How could we? Right from the first moment, he was protected so carefully by his creator. She brought him to life at her place of study. Surrounded by so many witnesses, she continued to watch over him like a mother hawk, as though he were a rare jewel – incredibly precious beyond compare!' retorted the other angrily. His face contorted with increasing rage.

Menacingly, his shoulders rose towards his ears as tension flew into the air between them – each trying to blame the other for not acting sooner when they had the chance.

The taller one started to bang his heels heavily on the ground, shifting from one foot to the other, impatient to get away. 'We were fools to miss the warning signs that flashed before us in the skies announcing his arrival at the beginning. You, of all people, should have recognised the significance of the light when it lit up the horizon.'

'You mean those strange comets that shot across the planet? There were three of them, one after the other.'

'What do you think, you numb-brain! Wasn't it obvious from those odd, dragon-like tails spreading from their bodies that something momentous was about to happen? And didn't it occur to you that these, were unusual… *different* from the last cluster that passed at the birth of the new millennium, when they last appeared?'

'B-but, how was I to know… I… I thought it was a call to arms to gather our followers from across the globe. And then, when those fireballs exploded and set off almighty bell-blasts from belfries and towers across the land, all hell broke loose, so I naturally assumed that it was our *Grand Master* – the Supreme One – giving us a signal,' blustered the other one as he attempted to cover for his mistake.

'*Well, nevertheless, we should have killed him when we had the chance!*' the taller one repeated sullenly, as if unwilling to forgive and forget.

The figure then stepped back further into the shadows and shivered as though frozen. And yet, strangely, the grass beneath his feet suddenly turned yellow, as if it had begun to die due to a mysterious heat of some phenomenal power.

'But… but can I ask what happens to the boy, the girl, and the other unsuspecting ones he meets on the journey?' asked the other, his whiny voice squealing worse than ever.

'They'll have to take their chances to save their own skins like everyone else in the Kingdoms. If they are foolish enough to get in the way, then of course they will suffer the consequences. And what's more, the naïve, stupid little fools, they should have stayed at home – safely tucked up in bed like most others… and not take the risks. If they thought that this would be just another innocent adventure – a harmless bit of fun – then they've got a nasty big surprise coming!' His cold voice said it all by its tone of indifference which made it that more terrible.

Silently, he sidled up to his companion, shrugged heavily and stared into thin air, as though to curb his impatience. 'And we must remember it's *him* that we're after. So, my friend, we'll just have to bide our time. And when it comes, he will be led like a stunned lamb meekly to the slaughter. We can wait. We've got all the time in the world.'

With a chilling laugh, they gloated into each other's faces and shook hands. Then, immediately, they faded into the background, melting into the safety of the pitch-black darkness but leaving a sense of menace hanging in the air behind them…

Part I

A trick of light upon your face,
I wish you were a part of the Human race.

Chapter 1

TWO HEADS ARE BETTER THAN NONE

I N A SPRAWLING SUBURB on the outskirts of south-west London where the river wound its way past the reaches of Richmond and Ham, the local fire station had received its first emergency call-out of the day. Reports came in of a massive explosion which had rocked an old Victorian building near the town centre, housing its local college which was once famous for providing props for stage and screen. Immediately, three adrenaline-charged fire crews rushed at the double to the scene.

At first, the chief fire officer thought that it might have been a latent earthquake not yet recorded on the Richter scale. Or was it perhaps a secret cache of gunpowder exploding? However, this was not the case. On arrival at the site, it was discovered that one of the students, a Miss Saskia Goodall, had left a head... Well, let's qualify that... a sculptured head in one of the kilns, which had apparently, due to a miscalculation, exploded. It had, in turn, blown off the oven door, which, together with the head, shot upwards like a rocket-like missile carving a neat concentric hole two feet in diameter in the roof of the ancient building. As it happened, no one was hurt as most of the students and staff had left early for the spring break. Within minutes the fire brigade had rapidly put out the fire, containing it in the workroom.

'He's my whole year's work!' wailed Sassy (her nickname), increasingly distraught when questioned by the attending police and emergency services. 'I was just putting the final touches to his body when this happened...' she added tearfully. Trembling, she gripped her face in her hands.

'We'd better have a look at... er, you know... it... him... to see if he's all right. Just in case, Miss,' said one of the police officers, arching an eyebrow quizzically.

Sheepishly, Sassy led them to a corner of the room, which had been virtually untouched by the explosion. She opened a tall metal door from one of the lockers and slowly wheeled out a shrouded figure draped from top to toe in a white sheet.

Nervously, the officer peeled back the upper part of the sheet. He quickly recoiled as if he had just seen a corpse. 'Cor,' he gasped to his colleague breathlessly. 'It's headless... like one of those Frankenstein monsters!'

'Er. You know, Miss, for the records... what's happened to his head? Is he for a show or for one of those film studios or something?' asked the other police officer curiously.

'One of his heads has just been blown up by mistake!' exclaimed Sassy, ignoring the question. 'Anyway, he's a secret. He's going to be a harlequin, and a very, special one at that – to make the whole world laugh and to be happy,' she added mysteriously.

Just then, old Reg, the college caretaker, came shuffling in, having made a safety check of the premises. Overhearing the young student, he interrupted, 'Hold on. I thought you had made *two* heads, just in case!' Reg had not forgotten the incident last January when they had scared the life out of him the first time, he saw two of them sitting on a shelf, like warning trophies from centuries ago of people who had been decapitated for plotting against the Crown. Shrugging his shoulders, he smiled inwardly, knowing that the young student had a penchant for making figures – in fact, a couple of others, just as life-sized, had been transported back to her family home. 'What on earth do her parents think of this unusual hobby?' he murmured under his breath, thinking that most girls of that age would have taken up needlework or something equally harmless.

Slowly, his eyes swivelled around the damaged walls, the dust-covered workbench, the overturned stools, all now blackened, thick with soot. Raising his head towards the hole in the ceiling exposed to the open sky: 'Well, well! Now the local authorities *will* have a field day,' he said under his breath.

The police shrugged and decided that there was nothing more they could do. 'Well, Miss, since no one's hurt and no one's been killed or reported missing, we'd best be getting back to the station and file our report. Now, you mind how you go, Miss!'

Sassy nodded goodbye to old Reg and hurried home for an early night. Wearily, she turned the key in her front door. 'Anyone at home?' she shouted half-heartedly. Checking her watch, she just remembered that her parents had already left earlier for their holiday in France. And of course, it being Friday evening, Pilar, their devoted home help had gone home after feeding Mudd, her pet cat. She dumped her bag noisily on the hallway floor and slammed the door.

On hearing the commotion, the little black and white cat, whose markings were not unlike those of a mini panda, had stirred from her favourite sleeping place on top of the bathroom radiator. She stretched her limbs, then lifted her little black ears like sharp antennae and scurried downstairs to investigate.

'Hello, Muddie! Peaceful, isn't it, with Mum and Dad gone?' Sassy patted her on the head and gave her an affectionate stroke. She received a hefty butt from her head in return. A croaked meow, followed by a chirp from the back of the throat, was the next response. This was because of her jaw being lopsided following a road accident five years ago. Since then, she had been unable to close her mouth properly, and so she purred with a rusty singing voice – a bit off-key. The right side of her face, including her eye, was paralysed. Thanks to the brilliant skills of Mr Findlay Bird, the local vet, Mudd's life and limbs, but not her previous handsome looks, were saved.

'How's the gang upstairs, eh, Muddie? Behaving themselves, I hope?' continued Sassy, rubbing the cat's tummy vigorously. The cat rolled onto her back, thumping the floor loudly with her heavy black tail. She carried on the one-way conversation with her cat, half-hoping for a reply. 'I was hoping to bring back someone else who's rather special to keep you company, whilst I join Mum and Dad for the hols. Never mind, eh? When he's got over the accident where he was nearly blown up, I'll bring him back after the weekend. He's sure to make you smile.' She gave Mudd a sharp ruffle along her back. Then she added wryly as an afterthought, 'And keep the others in their place!'

'Oh, by the way, we mustn't forget that it's the All Pets and Creatures special service at St Swithin's on Sunday. That'll be fun, eh, Muddie? You'll enjoy that. Wonder if our friend Mr Bird will be there? Well, I'd better have an early night tonight. I'm exhausted!' she exclaimed. As she made her way upstairs, Mudd padded behind – intent on staking a claim at the foot of the bed.

***

Now, not long afterwards, the college precinct was soon deserted, as all the occupants had gone for the night. The empty building was in complete darkness, save for a dim light for security, bathing the entrance lobby and stairwell. Reg had decided to take the weekend off after checking all the doors and windows in case of thieves and vandals.

As it happened, at three minutes to midnight precisely – noted on the large round clock near the entrance hall – something strange and out of the ordinary happened... Suddenly, a thunderous noise broke out outside, filling the skies above. It sounded like a peal of bells. No, it was much more than that. It seemed that every single church, every kind of tower, every sort of building from all around, started to ring their bells. They unleashed a cacophony of metallic-bronze noise that was ear-shattering. It was enough to wake the dead. The noise seemed to filter from far and wide and spread like wildfire from the edge of the city. Fortunately, it did not disturb anyone at the college, because, as it was said, it was completely empty, save for the scores of mice hiding behind the holes in the floors and cupboards – and how could they, bear witness to what went on?

Whist inside the workroom, still blackened and smelly from the earlier explosion, Sassy's figure stood alone in the centre of the room, covered still from top to bottom in a white sheet, like the veritable ghost from a Christmas long since past. It stood in the exact spot where Sassy had left it for the night. It cut a lonely figure. As the noise from the bells rang out from the air outside, a bright light lit up the sky. Moments later, a clutch of comets started to streak across the star-filled sky. A thunderbolt crashed down as the heavens suddenly opened, rattling the slates of every roof of every building within its range. An enormous bolt of lightning sliced through the darkening sky and struck, with missile-guided accuracy, the ridge of the college roof. It trickled its way towards the rim of the neat hole that had been made in the roof, gobbling up everything in its path.

Through the large hole, the glow from the heavens appeared to radiate inside the room, illuminating the sheet that covered Sassy's sculpture. An electric charge enveloped the figure as it travelled down from its shoulders to its feet. It seemed to give it energy and give it warmth, making the whole thing glow in the dark. For three whole minutes, just as the clock began to strike midnight, everything in the room started to shudder and shake. Beneath the sheet, the figure appeared to vibrate and spin on its axis. Then, like a spin dryer, it juddered abruptly to a halt. It was just as well that no one was around to see this, as they would have had an almighty fit. And, particularly, it would have scared poor nervous Reg witless, who hadn't quite recovered from bumping into the headless figure in the dark last week.

***

At the exact time that this was happening – on the other side of town – in the centre of the great city, the persistent clanging of the bells and the light in the sky swelling woke Sassy up at home. Reluctantly, she dragged herself out of bed and stood beside her window. Mudd flew off the end of the duvet and curled at her feet, yawning.

Cursing the disturbance, Sassy peeled back the curtains, mystified. 'Oh well,' she grumbled, still half-awake, 'something funny's going on out there. Perhaps, it's some kind of celebration in the city taking place – anyway, it's nothing to do with me!'

The thunderstorm had suddenly stopped. As she looked out into the sky, three comets, tailing one another, shot across the dark horizon. At first sight, she thought that this was strange. But again, she had just remembered that a few years ago seeing a really, famous one – Halley's, named after its discoverer. She wondered, then, if that had returned, as it sometimes did from its journey around the sun… but she was wrong. If she had looked more closely, she would have noticed that these, now flying overhead, were not the same. The shape of their tails was strangely different. Being noticeably spliced down the middle, their bodies had also taken on a different colour. But it was too late at night to take it all in.

Tiredness now got the better of her. Drawing the curtains, she collapsed back in bed. With a deep yawn and a shrug, she mumbled to the cat, 'Ah well… can't think straight at the moment!'

Her thoughts drifted back to college. 'But, oh, I hope he's all right staying there by himself. He'll be safe, I'm sure. Nothing terrible can happen to him there.' Crossing her fingers, she closed her eyes. She dragged the duvet over her head, and soon she was sound asleep. She started to dream of an explosion of bells. Church spires and bell towers throughout the land collapsing, one by one as a murderous storm raged out of control.

***

Meanwhile, in the centre of the city, again, precisely at three minutes to midnight on that very same night, large crowds had gathered in Parliament Square. They were attracted by a sudden peal of bells from Westminster Abbey that went on and on, unabated, for over two hours. An expectation filled the air, that some profound announcement would be made, which would affect every single inhabitant of the country. The precise time all this was happening was noted by keen-eyed observers staring at Big Ben across the square, thinking that the famous clock had something to do with it.

People from overseas had also heard at exactly, the same time (but taking the time difference into account) a similar burst of deafening bells striking without warning in other cities throughout the continent. And, seemingly tilted by some mysterious hand controlling it, it magnified the mystery a hundred times over.

It happened in Paris at the cathedral of Notre Dame, the converted mosque in St Sophia, Istanbul (which was stranger still, since the bells had long been silent for the last five hundred years or so since it was last a church), and St Mark's Basilica in the centre of Venice. Simultaneously, the bells followed on in sequence as if there was an invisible force at play – manipulating it like clockwork.

Reports had also confirmed millions of people from all corners of the earth seeing the sky being lit up by three incredibly bright comets. It was as if at that precise moment, there was a worldwide event of some monumental importance taking place under their noses. And excitedly, as they waited huddled together en masse, they hoped for a momentous sign that never came. However, despite that, in many places across the globe, hundreds and thousands fell to their knees in shock and in amazement.

Desperately, the city authorities tried to explain it, dismissing it as a freak of nature or an incredible coincidence. But secretly, they were just as worried as the people in the streets. And especially so, as later-on in the news bulletins, reports came flooding in of unexplained gales being whipped up in the early hours of the morning after the cacophony of bells had stopped so abruptly.

No sooner had that happened, seas started to rise and pound the coastlines. Flocks of seabirds in their thousands migrated inland as gigantic hailstones, the size of golf balls, fell, denting cars and roofs, as if a violent typhoon had been gathering pace across the land. Whilst across the country, packs of wild foxes, rabbits, squirrels, field mice, magpies, crows and wood pigeons, to name but a few, fled into the towns and cities, adding to the hordes of wildlife already seeking shelter there. Furthermore, it was reported that the foxes began to howl at the moon like wolves long ago, adding to the mystery further.

Weather experts from far and wide tried to calm the population, who were getting increasingly anxious, by saying that global disruptions from others far away were to blame. And from central government, a statement was put out to say:

'No one needs to panic. After all, it's just typical of the unpredictable pattern of the climate at this time of the year...'

And that no strange phenomenon that the authorities did not know about would happen that would change the face of the planet.

But little did they know what was around the corner for every single creature on this planet Earth. Because, from that day onwards, nothing would be the same again... as all things from now would be left to chance...

Chapter 2

ALL CREATURES GREAT AND SMALL

T HE REVEREND BARNABAS QUICK was the proud vicar of St Swithin's. This was the local neighbourhood church at the end of Westhope Terrace, Paddington, where it sat nicely in a neat little square. Its quaint Gothic-style architecture contrasted dramatically with the backdrop of the brightly painted Victorian houses built in 1848 on one side of the square and a row of dilapidated lockup garages built in dull concrete on the other. The little grey-stone church was founded in 1852 in St Swithin's Square, which opened out at the north end of the terrace into a small communal garden.

St Swithin's was a pretty, little church with a robust congregation from all sides of the square, as well as the adjoining streets. It was an odd coincidence that it was named St Swithin's. It had some sort of microclimate of its own. If it rained on St Swithin's Day – and sometimes on special holidays – it would rain, would you believe it, for forty days and forty nights in St Swithin's Square, leaving the surrounding streets remarkably dry.

And, conversely, if the sun shone, it did so gloriously over the little church, lighting up its haughty spire with its large bronze bells and its pale, moonfaced clock, whilst simultaneously, buckets of rain would drench the adjacent neighbourhood for forty days and forty nights.

So as to suit the different nationalities of his congregation, Reverend Quick (though he preferred to be addressed as Father) would vary his Sunday services to make them happy. His experimental services, with their unusual themes, courted the accusation of eccentricity by the rival churches, which did not attract the numbers for worship that his did.

He wore a little round-cornered hat in black, ringed with a gold braid and crowned with a bright red bobble, so favoured in France and Spain. Furthermore, when dressed in his Sunday surplice with a purple and yellow sash over a plain white cassock, it conveniently disguised his face with its drooped eyelids and bloodhound-like expression.

Today's Sunday service was no different. But in fact, it was very, different. Today, St Swithin's was proudly holding a "SPECIAL CELEBRATORY MASS for the ANIMAL KINGDOM".

The congregation, which encompassed a wide area, was invited to bring along their pets – or any stray animal, for that matter. Fish came in jam jars. Stick insects, the size of frankfurters, came in cardboard boxes, rabbits in straw-filled rucksacks and tortoises squashed in plastic buckets.

Gerbils, hamsters, guinea pigs, birds in cages, cats and dogs of every description were commonplace. There was even the odd snake or two stuffed down their owners' coats.

Celia Darling, who taught music at the local school, sat bolt upright on her organ stool. At the nod from the vicar, the organ struck up the first few chords of the opening hymn, followed by the strains of the choir attempting to fill the church with the singing of their new composition, which they had written especially for the occasion:

'Lord, save us from these restless waves,
And violent storms, you try to save,
These lands so fair, beyond our gaze,
With man and creature caught in a daze.'

There was an air of wonderment and anticipation about the place. The pet owners took their places in the pews, holding on firmly to their animals. Sassy excitedly clasped Mudd, carefully perching the cat over her right shoulder. The little cat snuggled around her neck, trustingly, like a fur collar. Squashed next to the vet Mr Bird was Mr Freddie Perkins, the local firefighter, with Atilla, the voracious Doberman, straining at his leash. Meanwhile, Mudd, with her good eye, looked down anxiously from the safety of her vantage point high up on her owner's shoulder. Because in the same pew, squashed up to her, a young lad from the next street had brought his ferret, which never appeared completely in body, but peered out from the top of his owner's trousers with its beady, sultana-shaped eyes, watching sinisterly.

There seemed to be over one hundred and sixty people, animals and creatures in different shapes and sizes, colours and textures packed into the little church that Sunday. The choir sang alone, as no one else knew the new words to the next hymn. The vicar had recently rewritten the lyrics to the tune of "Fight the Good Fight", which, understandably, he did not think was appropriate in the circumstances.

'*We swim in waves of human face,*
Pretend a life of animal grace.
And reflect our deeds, the way we treat,
All life's creatures we think as meat.'

A two-minute silence followed, which seemed like a lifetime, broken only by the sound of barking, meowing, and twittering. Peace then descended on the congregation like a thick winter blanket. It was interrupted when the Reverend Quick ascended the lofty pulpit to deliver his sermon from a great height. He fished out his reading glasses in readiness...

'*Brethren, sisters and you noble creatures, great and small, I welcome you to St Swithin's. And today is a special day for* you – *our little creatures, for we welcome you in the name of your beloved patron saint, St Francis of Assisi, the blessed guardian of the animal kingdom, with whom we are celebrating today.*'

He crossed himself theatrically.

Adjusting the red bobble on his hat, his bloodhound-like eyes looked upwards to the roof of his church as if for inspiration from on high, and then they drooped downwards in slow motion towards his flock, looking at everyone in turn. Sassy was relieved that she was partially hidden behind a pillar. He fiddled with the bridge of his glasses, which started to slide off the tip of his nose due to increasing perspiration, and solemnly he began to read:

'Many others, the great and good before me – priests, world leaders, writers, and so on – have always preached about the battle between good and evil. My sermon today is no different, dear family, boys and girls. And I include your pets and all those in the wild. The challenge for survival in the face of evil, which faces each, and every one of us today, is no different... Thus, today's sermon is taken from the Book of the Ancient Philosophers – The Oraco Dex Lo Paediac written in 299 BC; chapter thirteen, paragraph three.'

There was a loud groan from the pews, so the vicar cleared his throat.

'Ahem – er... from this great tome of ancient wisdom, I quote a passage from one of the most famous philosophers of all time, Aristotle, who in 350 BC declared that the world was made up of Three Kingdoms...

'Firstly, the Kingdom of Man. Secondly, the Kingdom of Animals. And finally – the Kingdom of Plants... Such edicts were revolutionary, as the ancients held for thousands of years before that the world was dominated by man and animals, and nothing else. And even more controversial, was Aristotle's declaration that all animals and even plants had a living Soul...

Because before that, it was a long-held belief that the Soul was the sole prerogative of Man. This remained unchallenged for thousands of years. And so, you can see my friends. You were all created as our fellow creatures, to live as equal tenants on this mighty earth of ours – together in peace with us your fellow creature – man, hand in hand, and most important of all, Soul *to* Soul!'

The vicar wiped the steam he had generated in his passion off his tiny, round, rimless spectacles with the hem of his cassock. And then he began again. Wringing his hands noisily, his resounding voice boomed and wheezed through the loudspeakers.

'*Yes, I have to tell you, my friends, that our planet on which you and they live*' – he pointed to their pets – '*is under threat. It is crumbling away from the forces of evil. It is attacked by the evil power of man. Oh yes, we even attack one another with wickedness as we fight our neighbour for extra space to live in… We attack our fellow creatures in the animal kingdom and even attack and destroy the plants and trees in the other kingdom.*'

Gulping deeply, he hesitated for a moment, then wiped his hand across his face, as if he were about to sob.

'*For what, I may ask? …Oh yes. All for that nasty thing called money and greed! So, I say unto you, my flock, if this continues unabated, then whole rafts of species are in danger of being extinct. Future generations will never see them again. And the Three Kingdoms will be no more.*'

Deliberately he paused, giving it time to sink in. Then he went on, his voice quivering with impassioned excitement,

Quickening his tone, he gripped the edge of the pulpit. He took a sip of water, which made a gurgling sound down the microphone, as though he was cleaning his teeth.

'*Yea, my friends, I have this dream. A dream that one day, from species to species, there will be no barriers of language, or discrimination by colour or creed. We shall speak to the* trees. *The trees will speak to the plants. The lion will talk to the sheep. The cat will talk to the bird. Man shall converse with the dog.'*

'But we already do!' mouthed the dog owners in the audience – rather smugly.

'*Our dear feathered friends shall be kind to the insects and our four-legged pets shall be kind to the birds of the air. There will be no more hatred or strife. There will be—*'

Just then, a hubbub broke out in the middle of the fourth pew from the front. A pet brown hen had got loose from its cage and started to peck at a little girl's hamster next to it. 'Gerroff, you, 'orrible cannibal, you!' yelled the girl. 'Peck on someone yer own size!' She aimed a sharp kick at the chicken, which flapped in fright and flew four feet into the air and landed on Freddie Perkins' lap, waking him up.

The hitherto quiet calm and peace was now shattered. The fragile truce that had held patiently for the last twenty minutes suddenly, collapsed. All hell broke loose. A fat tabby cat in the next pew tore out of its owner's arms and began to chase the hen, salivating greedily.

Sensing that he was losing a grip on his audience, Reverend Quick turned up the volume on his microphone in an effort, to drown out the din. He closed his eyes, looking upwards, hoping for some sort of divine help as he clasped his hands tightly whilst nodding gently.

A pitiful howl went out from the back of the pews. 'What about the injured hamster, then?' Voices were raised. Tempers frayed. Murder was about to be committed.

By now, the vicar was shouting hoarsely above the voices, trying to ignore the heckler Dermot Mulday, who was the barman at the local pub, who stood up from the front pew and yelled, "Ere! Fadher, how do you propose we can fights dis load of evils you warns us about?'

The Reverend Quick fiddled with his glasses on the bridge of his nose and leant down pointedly towards Dermot. '*Evil, my good fellow, can only exist in the absence of good. Evil, my friend, will only flourish where there is misery and unhappiness. Therefore, if we root out unhappiness and misery from our lives, then surely goodness and love will have a chance to live.*'

A large blonde woman shouted from the back of the church whilst trying to control her daughter's white rabbit, which had burst out of its box, 'Tell us, Father, how can we, get rid of misery with so much sadness in the world? What can we do? What is the answer?'

'...*Well, the answer my friend, to conquer this evil, is to... laugh!*'

'To laugh? *What – to bloomin' well laugh!* You've got to be joking!' roared back the congregation, stunned by what he had just said. Incredulous mutterings buzzed around the church.

'I know, I know, my dear friends,' retorted the vicar, his eyes scanning the pews patiently. 'This is hard to believe. But believe me when I tell you,' he insisted, increasing his voice by several decibels to make himself heard, '*that laughter... yes, simple plain* laughter – *will be the ultimate weapon to banish all unhappiness from our land. And then evil will be vanquished forever.*'

'But Fadher, I don't understand,' said Dermot, scratching his head. 'Who will bring this laughter? I mean, there's nothing much to make us laugh anywhere nowadays

– on the TV, or in the papers. It's always blinkin' bad news, doom and gloom.'

A hum of approving murmurs echoed around the place with a display of nodding heads.

'*Yes, I understand where you're coming from. But be patient, my good friend, there will be a stranger amongst you – yes, indeed, whom we have been waiting for, for a truly long time.*'

'But… but… you don't mean *the* – you know… *t-h-e?!*' asked Dermot, fervently crossing himself. His jaw dropped open in astonishment, which he shut rapidly as his fillings began to show.

The Reverend Quick quickly closed his eyes and shook his head, trying to correct himself.

'*No. I did not mean you know* who! *From you know* where! *…Well,* not *just yet. No, what I meant was that soon, meanwhile, will come, a complete newcomer – a special messenger – a "Pied Piper", if you like, of happiness. He will bring us joy and laughter. His laughter will cure all divisions… Yes, by teaching us to laugh again, he will drive out all misery and evil from our midst. Laughter, real laughter, will smooth our troubles and soothe our planet. In such a way, the Three Kingdoms will come together, my solemn friends. And unite all that dwell in it.*'

'Hallelujah…!' shouted his churchwarden, stretching both arms to the heavens. Others leapt to their feet and followed suit.

A wry smile crossed the vicar's face as he beamed in gratitude at his churchwarden for her support. Unclasping his hands, he swayed back and forth in the pulpit, and took a deep breath as he surveyed the anxious faces of his flock.

'What will this perfect stranger, this so-called "*Messenger of Mirth*" look like, Father? How can we recognise him?' interrupted old Freddie Perkins. He was fully awake by now, thanks to the large brown hen that had landed on top of him. 'Will he have a narrow, solemn face, a pointed beard and floppy sandals?'

'My friend, I do not know precisely what shape or form he will take when he arrives. But...' he continued, getting rather flustered by so many probing questions from his parishioners, 'I see a vision in my mind's eye.' He took off his glasses and leant forwards on the edge of the pulpit towards Freddie Perkins to emphasise a point. He rubbed his eyes with his knuckles, half-closing them.

'Mm... in my mind's eye, I see a vision of a large, round figure. Yes, a rather, shall I say jolly, enormous figure with a round face, clean shaven. And, let me see... oh dear, surprise, surprise... a bright red mouth full of white, pearly teeth, bearing a grand, beaming smile from ear to ear. And wait a minute... portly. Um, yes, not much hair, I'm afraid.'

'But will he be dressed all in white?' asked the old parishioner, his mouth agape.

'No, I don't think so. I see him in baggy clothes of many dazzling colours.' The Reverend Quick then shut his eyes and squeezed them tightly in a momentary blink. 'Open-top sandals, my dear Mr Perkins? *Hardly, my friend!* I see large, boat-like, bright red boots – pointed at the ends with a bell attached.'

A buzz of astonishment mixed with sheer disbelief flew around the church as the congregation burst out in unison, '*Bright red boots with bells on them!* I don't believe it! He can't be serious!' An undertone of muttering spread around the people like wildfire.

As soon as Sassy heard this, she was astounded. '*This can't be... Surely, he can't mean...?*' she murmured, her mind returning to the half-finished figure of the harlequin at the college. Clinging on to her pet cat for support, she held on to the back of the pew tightly, thinking she might faint. 'Impossible!' she muttered.

Then, she dismissed the idea and immediately blanked it out of her mind.

The sermon droned on. Reverend Quick then fished out a large, creased handkerchief from beneath his cassock and earnestly dabbed his glistening forehead, his eyes narrowing with a blazing intensity.

'*Finally... I need to warn you, my dear people, that we must treat our planet with love and respect. We must never forget the salutary lesson from the same ancient texts, which tells of how our beloved planet with its many kingdoms was virtually destroyed three hundred thousand years ago, when a massive asteroid from outer space struck the earth with such devastating force. The horrendous impact caused volcanic eruptions of astronomical proportions, spewing up indescribable hellfire and ash into the sky. It wiped out the sun. The earth went cold. Gigantic tidal waves rose-up and drowned the land. Beasts and every living creature perished. All plant, tree and shrub life died. And the Three Kingdoms were no more...*'

No sooner had he said that than a large clap of thunder made a direct hit over the church roof with a tremendous rattle. The heavens opened. A thunderstorm burst, followed by a streak of lightning. A torrent of heavy rain poured down.

Reverend Quick looked up anxiously at his newly repaired roof. He shuddered visibly and rapidly declared that the sermon was now over.

Suddenly, complete chaos erupted. Feathers and fur began to fly. Dogs barked. Cats hissed. Birds screeched at a deafening pitch. Children started to fight each other. Arms, legs, and tails were grabbed at random. A thin snake escaped and slithered down the iron grills of the central heating on the floor of the aisle. Mr Bird, the gentle vet, was flattened to the ground in the ensuing mêlée as he tried to stop the fighting, imploring, 'Pets, my dear gentle little pets, please, please, *behave* yourselves!' His pleas were completely ignored as they tried to kill each other.

Meanwhile, the worried vicar, with a nod of his head, gave a signal to the organist Miss Darling, who started to play as loudly as possible an up-tempo version of "All Things Bright and Beautiful". In an effort, to bring the service to a close, he abruptly banged his book down in front of him and pleaded loudly, '*May peace reign down on you, I beg you, my children!*'

With his face black as thunder, he strode down the steps from the pulpit, hoping his expensive church roof wouldn't spring a leak. He retreated to the altar in silence, praying fervently that adverse publicity would not come to his church and that a miracle would come to his rescue.

Having been dismissed curtly, the congregation streamed out fast, extremely stunned. Dare it be said, but it was raining cats and dogs. Somewhat in daze, Sassy left just as quickly, with Mudd scrabbling furiously to escape. Out of the corner of her eye, she noticed a short, slim girl, with glasses, aged about thirteen with fair hair tied up in a ponytail, was leaving by the side door and holding on to the hand of a small, sandy-haired boy with freckles. A large black dog with a lion's-type mane padded silently besides them. She saw that the girl limped a little and was met by a woman with dark hair, presumably her mother, who handed her a single crutch.

Sassy thought nothing of it. When she looked again, the girl with the stiff leg and the boy were nowhere in sight.

As she hurried home from St Swithin's, the sun blazed down on her and Muddie, leaving the pandemonium at the church and its localised thunderstorm behind. *Hey, it can't be St Swithin's Day; well, not yet* she thought with Reverend Quick's sermon still ringing in her ears.

Chapter 3

TIED UP IN KNOTS

THE WEEKEND FLEW BY in a flash, and Monday arrived with its inevitable speed and mundane regularity. The sky was grey and overcast, but that did not dampen Sassy's mood as she returned to work with a vengeance.

'Now for the head,' Sassy muttered aloud to herself. She then secured the harlequin's head onto the shoulders of the skeletal frame that she had built so painstakingly in front of her. The finishing touches to her secret masterpiece were almost complete.

Pushing back a stool, she stood a few paces backwards to take a good look. She paused to reflect on the figure staring back at her, proud of her own hard work. The harlequin was nearly six-feet tall, much taller than his inventor.

'Yes, you're quite handsome in a funny sort of way. I wish you could say something,' she sighed wistfully. 'Go on, make us laugh. Cheer us up a bit!'

She gave the figure a gentle punch on the chest, more of a friendly gesture than a forceful blow. His newly constructed head was spherical, almost the size of a smooth pumpkin. His face was completely round and moon-shaped with rosy cheeks narrowing sharply to a pointed chin with a bulbous endearing nose, the size of a ping pong ball perched in the middle of the friendly face.

He had an enormous smiling mouth, heavily painted, ruby red in a fixed wide grin spreading from ear to ear. His mouth was full of pearly-white teeth with an endearing gap between the top two. His eyes seemed to roll about, highlighting their icy blueness.

Sassy ruffled his hair playfully. The figure did not have much of it. Just a few strands made out of wool and string, dyed a red sandy colour and attached to the top of his crown. And as she went to gently pat it with the tips of her fingers, suddenly, without warning, a crystal-clear image flashed vividly in front of her, forcing her to gasp, 'I don't believe this!' Then she stopped. Immediately she felt faint. She grabbed the nearest stool and sat down. A vision of yesterday's chaotic service at St Swithin's Church suddenly flooded back to her...

Again, the solemn words from Reverend Quick's sermon reverberated in her head – now, as it did then. '*I do not know precisely what shape or form he will take when he arrives... In my mind's eye, I see a vision of a large, round figure. Yes... a rather, shall I say jolly, enormous figure with a round face, clean shaven. And, let me see... oh dear, surprise, surprise... a bright red mouth full of white, pearly teeth, bearing a grand, beaming smile from ear to ear... And wait a minute... portly. Um, yes, not much hair...*'

'Hang on a minute… I wonder… if there's a mistake?' she cried, grabbing the harlequin's hand anxiously. Her heart pounded so loudly, she thought it would explode out of her chest.

She dabbed some perspiration off her forehead with a tissue, then deliberately breathed in deeply, pausing for a moment. She then let out a deep sigh. 'Now don't be stupid,' she shouted at herself in anger. 'You mustn't be carried away, Saskia Goodall, you idiot!'

She pinched the tip of her ear sharply. 'The coincidence's too stupid for words!'

As she got up, she grabbed the figure's arms and began to smooth out the wrinkles in his clothes. She had dressed him up in a pair of worn cobalt-blue dungarees previously discarded by her uncle. They were a size too large and bulged at the knees but frayed at the edges. A bright woollen sweater was emblazoned in a striking pattern of concentric diamond shapes in red, purple, and silver. A large, floppy bow tie in crimson and white polka dots was loosely tied around his neck like a scarf. She perched on his head a loosely, fitted bi-cornered hat in purple-crushed velvet, which she had previously found in a charity shop.

'I like your boots with a tinkling bell fixed at the toes!' she remarked admiringly. They were large red ones. 'They'll stop you falling over.' She chuckled to herself. She rubbed a duster over them until they shone like a mirror.

'Oh, I wonder if it's still there, safe from prying eyes?' she murmured. She then anxiously felt inside his trouser pocket. 'Ah there it is, thank heavens!'

Securely in her right hand between finger and thumb, Sassy held a diamond-shaped object, which looked like a piece of glass shot with resin. It glistened in the light of the fluorescent lamps overhead, shimmering with a mysterious glow that made it almost alive. It was elliptical in shape, two inches by one, translucent and faceted on one side that was polished vigorously. And yes, it could pass as a diamond with the purity of light that reflected from within. The other side, however, was dark and rough, shot with streaks of blood-red and golden amber like a fire burning inside.

The combined effect of the two sides was blinding. By examining it closely, Sassy could see distinct particles of what at first glance could be mistaken as embryonic seeds of something quite remarkable, never seen before by human eye. They were planted deep inside the core of this unusual, semiprecious object. They whirled around constantly as moving clusters of sensational colours of pure blue, green and red. So dazzling were they that she could only describe them as amazing crystals of sapphires, emeralds, and rubies. They were so iridescent, so incredibly motile, that the whole thing felt as if it was struggling to jump out of her hand. At the same time, they possessed a strange life force of some powerful energy that was bursting to flow out. And yet it was seemingly strangely hypnotic.

'*This is a dead secret,*' she whispered conspiratorially to the harlequin. Cautiously, her eyes scanned the room in case old Reg was around without her knowing.'

Well, what had happened was this... Three months ago, when she was building the wooden frame for her model, she was told by the timber merchant who had supplied the wood that it was a very, rare hardwood, from the depths of a South American jungle. The supplier said, with a deadpan face, that it came from a sacred tree that was thousands of years old. But she did not notice that he winked at the same time when she was paying his rather expensive bill.

Whilst cutting the timber, she noticed that one of the larger, darker knots had fallen out. She kept it aside because of its unusual shape with its natural configuration and its diamond-shaped facets. This, as well as its scintillating contents, made it uncannily different from the rest. And so, when she first examined it under the light, it appeared to her to be like all knots from wood. The centre was scored with particles or bubbles of sap encrusted over the years, darkened from the effects of heat, compression, and climatic changes over the ages. Of course, it intrigued her – once she had got over the initial shock.

A million thoughts came to Sassy. Instinctively, she sensed that she had to keep it to herself. It was a mysterious find, one that comes once in a blue moon... *But who on earth could I ask about it? Was this really a real gemstone that came out of a knot in the wood? And could it really be precious? Did it possess some mystic power or magic aura around it?* ...Or was this another example of her overactive imagination running away with her?

On discovering this unique object, she had hidden it away safely. 'It belongs to him,' she'd vowed. 'It is part and parcel of his skeleton. And when I have completed him, I shall make a necklace and locket to house it and hang it around his neck for luck.'

Yet, despite the hiccup at the start with his head exploding, Sassy had managed to finish the figure. She carefully administered the final touches, combing back his few strands of hair tidily. Stepping back, she surveyed her work with pride.

Immediately, her eyes were drawn to the harlequin's big feet with its bright-red boots and its tinkling bells attached. She stared and stared. It left her still wondering whether she had heard things correctly the first time whilst at the church last Sunday.

But however hard she tried to push it to the back of her mind, certain words from the church service kept coming back to haunt her – just as a song can keep echoing repeatedly in the brain, like an "earworm". '...*that soon, meanwhile, will come a complete newcomer – a special messenger – a "Pied Piper" if you like of happiness. He will bring us joy and happiness...*'

'Get a grip on yourself, Sassy, my girl, before you lose it!' she shouted aloud.

With a concerted effort, she put it out of her mind once and for all. Staring at the figure straight between the eyes, she slowly focused her mind back to the job in hand.

'Ah, I must say, floppy bow ties are very fashionable at the moment,' she said, giving his nose a friendly tweak. For a split second, she thought he blinked back in reply. But then, tossing her hair, she dismissed it once more as probably an illusion or a distortion of the light. She looked at him again and grinned. 'My, oh my. You do look smart in this fantastic costume!' She gave his hat a gentle flick. 'You know, you look almost real,' she added.

'Now, what shall I call you? Clancy? Dancy? Fancy? ... What about, erm, Pants? No. Better not. People may poke fun... I know, I'll call you just *Chance*! That's it, brilliant! – "*C-h-a-n-c-e*", as you came to me just by accident. Or, really, by some incredible chance! We'll soon breathe some life into you.'

Given Sassy's artistic skills, it didn't take her long to alter a silver necklace her mother had given her for her seventeenth birthday. It had a strong clasp, and with a pair of sharp pliers, she was able to adapt the locket easily for the precious stone that originated from the knot. As soon as this was done, she placed the chain with the new pendant around his neck.

'There you are, Mr Chance. This special gemstone belongs to you. It came from the same ancient tree that gave you life,' she told him. Immediately, rays of light shone out of the stone with a magical luminescence which scattered all around, lighting up his face. 'Mm, the glow of that will match your pearly teeth.' She laughed, now much happier. 'I must show my mates Josie and Dippity.' And apart from anything else, she would need their help to lift the figure into her little car, which was parked in the car park just outside the rear exit.

No sooner had Sassy just finished signing her design in the shape of a dragon on his ankle, which all artists often do, when Josie and Dippity returned, slamming the door noisily behind them. 'Hey, *Miss Clever Michaela Angelino,*' they greeted her. She was somewhat embarrassed by their coming in like that, surprising her all of a sudden.

'Good grief! Look, Josie, at this amazing harlequin!' yelled Dippity, staring at the figure six inches from its face. She examined him slowly from face to toe and back again.

'Oh, yes-yes. He's great – really very smart! And so dead cool,' responded Josie with enthusiasm. 'He's brilliant. I like his teeth and his shining dome of a head,' she said, giving it a rub. She walked around him slowly.

'Congrats, Sassy! You've finally finished him. He's really fabulous. But hey, what's that?' she asked, poking at the glittering chain and pendant that was just peeping out around his neck.

'Oh, it's nothing much, just a good-luck charm. I made it from Mum's present,' explained Sassy, playing down what she really thought of it. She pushed the pendant into the neck of his sweater and out of view.

'Look you guys, can you help me move Mister Chance to my car?'

'Missed a chance? *Chance?* Crikey. No kidding? Saskia Goodall! What a name!' Holding their sides, they began to laugh. But when it sunk in that she was serious, they stopped teasing her.

She got a strange look in return. But nevertheless, she continued, 'So c'mon, you lot, give us a break. It's the end of term, and there's so much to do before we break up. Please give me a hand,' pleaded Sassy. 'Jo, you hold on to his head. I'll lift the body. Dippity, you grab his feet, but hold on to his boots, they're a bit slippery.'

'Blimey!' Dippity commented with a deep puff. 'He's jolly heavy, like a dead weight.'

'But hey, what's this lump at the back of his head?' asked Josie. 'It feels like a large duck egg.'

'Oh, stop exaggerating,' snapped Sassy. 'We all – yes, that includes you two – have a bump at the back of our heads. It's called the *Inion* or the Hump of Knowledge.' (She had previously looked it up in a medical book in the library.)

Immediately the two girls began to feel behind the back of their heads, then grimaced with surprise.

'Well, I never.' Josie smiled. 'But my, gosh, he's blinking heavy for a pile of wooden bones.'

Puffing and panting, the three of them manoeuvred the solid figure out of the room and along the passage towards the exit.

'Heavy or not, don't you dare drop him!' warned Sassy. 'He's worth his weight in gold.'

'Another of your weird fancy family then?' Dave Fellows, one of her classmates, called over his shoulder as he passed close by.

'Ignore him. He's a prize idiot!' Dippity advised, catching her breath as they reached the car park. They meandered their way to Sassy's battered, ancient yellow VW Beetle with its distinctive wire coat-hanger sticking out of the base of the aerial together with bright purple violets painted all over the bonnet and doors.

Rolling back the front passenger seat, they put the figure down so that he was lying flat on his back, feet first, head resting on the back seat. They started to cover him with an old blanket, which Sassy kept in the car to protect her work from being damaged.

'Don't cover his head!' exclaimed Sassy. 'He won't be able to breathe!'

'Now, c'mon! Don't be absolutely ridiculous,' retorted Josie, now thinking that her pal was taking things a bit too far in this fantasy world of hers. *For crying out loud, it's only a wooden dummy*, she was about to add. But, patiently, she held her tongue.

Sassy ignored what was said to avoid an argument. 'Look, you two. I'll see you after the Easter hols. Okay?'

'Where are you off to?'

'Oh, I've got to join Mum and Dad. They've rented a place with friends in France,' she replied nonchalantly, pretending she was not keen to go.

'Lucky you, then,' the other two commented together, rather enviously.

Just then, Dave ran after her to wish her happy holidays. 'Hey, have you heard? There's a circus coming to town.'

Sassy raised an eyebrow quizzically as she got into her car.

'Mind your funny old mate doesn't go walkies at night, then.'

She looked horrified.

'Sorree… only kidding,' he said, backing off.

In an instant, Sassy flung an old oil-stained rag at him and started the car. The little yellow Volkswagen spluttered its way slowly out of the college grounds, weighed down by the extra load of its unusual passenger. The sound of the hollow noise from the VW's old exhaust pipe faded as the Beetle disappeared from view with its weary driver finally making her way home.

Chapter 4

BLINK BLINK
IT MAKES YOU THINK

T HE EVENING BY NOW was closing in rapidly. The sky was streaked with pallid shades of pinks and greys, now swollen with the threat of rain. Dodging the potholes in the road, Sassy drove homewards slowly to avoid shaking up her passenger. She glanced in the rear-view mirror. It was already dusk.

Approaching the main road, the chassis of the little old Beetle creaked and groaned along the surface of the uneven tarmac as it rolled over the traffic humps. *Crumbs! I hope the suspension will last until next term*, she thought with alarm. *The exhaust sounds as if it's about to fall off any minute now.* She pulled a face. Then she checked again in the mirror as she went over another traffic hump. *Whoops, more bumps.* She gulped as she was thrown off her seat for a second.

But when it happened again, the impact jerked the harlequin's head and torso forwards so violently that it jack-knifed. For half a moment, he sat up straight as a bolt before collapsing right back again, flat on his back. In that split second, Sassy was stunned. Did he blink or roll his eyes? A sudden, strange thought flashed through her mind – which she couldn't help…

Blink, blink… It makes you think!

'Could he be…?' she muttered aloud. She scratched her head. 'I'm imagining things. I must be really tired!' But still, a nagging doubt crept in. And so, she quickly pushed it to the back of her mind and focused on the road ahead.

As she stopped at the traffic lights, she twisted, looking over her shoulder to check on her passenger. She thought again that she *must* have been mistaken. The figure looked remarkably relaxed and still. Under the glare of the street-lamps, the face had not changed one bit.

The lights changed to green. She set off again and, without thinking, started to hum a tune which rolled subconsciously off her tongue.

'*A trick of light upon your face, I wish you were a part of the human race.*'

'Now don't be stupid! Where did that come from?' Ticking herself off, she pinched the side of her face. Just then, a car passed by in the opposite direction, blasting its horn as it swerved deliberately to avoid her.'

By the time she had parked outside her parents' house in Westhope Terrace, it was getting dark. She could not lift the figure out of the car by herself, she felt, without damaging it. It had started to drizzle. She didn't want to ruin his clothes.

'I know,' she said. 'I'll leave it until the morning. Pilar or someone from Dad's office can help. He'll be okay, safely wrapped up in a blanket tonight. It'll be nice and warm under the street-lamp. No one will want to steal a dented old car.' She shrugged hopefully. 'Thieves would be more interested in the shiny, newer ones around here, I'll bet.'

Sassy moved her Beetle across the road and parked it just under a well-lit lamppost, just outside number 13, one of her neighbours. She took a lingering and final look backwards to her car. And as she did, she thought of Dave's warning as she left college: *'There's a circus coming to town. Mind your funny old mate doesn't go walkies at night, then.'* Giving a vigorous shake of the head, she dismissed the idea as completely ludicrous. 'He'll be safe and sound overnight here. I'm sure of it. Who on earth would want to do him harm?' she murmured quietly.

After one more look around the car and giving the figure an affectionate wave of her hand, she strolled across to her house somewhat reluctantly and let herself in.

***

Just at that very moment, the curtains twitched at number 13. Peeping slyly between the gap of the net curtain, old Rosy Harker, Westhope Terrace's inquisitive neighbour (who took "Neighbourhood Watch" literally to extreme by watching everyone, every minute of the night and day), was woken up by the klunk of a car door slamming just outside her front gate. Cruelly, most of the residents called her Nosy Parker behind her back, pretending it was a Freudian slip of the tongue. But *nothing* escaped Rosy

Harker's predatory eagle eyes or boat-like ears. Tonight was no exception.

'Aha. It's that young slip of a girl from number 10 opposite. It must be the end of term with her carrying all those books.' She tried to suppress a yawn. 'Wonder why she kept on walking around her little old car, staring in, and trying the doors so many times?'

Using the edge of her sleeve, she wiped a gap on the condensation on her window to get a better look. 'Must go out and investigate!' she muttered under her breath. She fiddled impatiently with the rollers in her hair. However hard she tried, the anticipation and the waiting couldn't be contained much longer.

It was just past eleven, as the church bells finished striking, when Rosy Harker could not wait to unlatch her door. All was now quite dark at number 10 with the Goodall household all in bed. As she tiptoed out of her front garden silently in her slippers, she glanced furtively right, then left, down the street. Only at the distant end of the terrace and around the little square were a few dim bedroom lights still visible.

Carefully, she eased the front gate in case it squeaked at the rusty hinges. There was not a soul in sight. Holding her breath, she crept stealthily over to Sassy's little old car, which was parked close to the kerb right under the lamppost. The place was quiet as a graveyard. There was distinct chill in the night air as turgid grey clouds scudded back and forth across the face of the moon, hiding it somewhat, which, Rosy was quite pleased about – tonight of all nights.

Pulling her old dressing gown firmly around her

shoulders for some added warmth – at first, she tried to look through the windscreen, but it was obscured with dirt and streaky marks. Then she took a hard look at the passenger window on the side. Cupping her right hand over her forehead, she pressed her head against the glass to cut out the reflections dancing into the back of the car. Her teeth started to tingle with excitement as her curiosity reached boiling point.

'What was so precious that, that Goodall gal was so concerned about when locking up her battered old car? And I wonder why she waved at it?'

Carefully, she shuffled around the car, keeping a watchful eye on the house opposite. It was still dead to the night, save for Mudd, the little black cat with her half-paralysed face, who glared at Rosy suspiciously from the front bedroom window.

Then, through the back window of the car, Rosy saw something that made her heart leap. Adrenaline was now rushing through her body. She tried to focus. She wiped her glasses on the hem of her dressing gown, thinking it would help.

'Am I seeing things?' she exclaimed. But as her eyes attuned to the borrowed light in the interior of the vehicle, she noticed a figure laid out. It was fully stretched out – completely covered in a blanket, save for its face and a brightly-coloured floppy tie. In the amber light, the face, with its balding head, appeared to have a ghostly hue – tinged with a sickly yellow reflection from the streetlamp overhead. And moreover, the pearly teeth, which were set in a broad-fixed grin and framed with bright red lips, loomed right back at her.

'Oh, my gaw...d!' She stifled a scream. *'It's a body! A dead body with blood dripping all over its mouth!'*

Rosy rushed back into her house, charging through the gate like a bull seeing red. She slammed her front door with a bang and leant with her back against it for a moment, her heart thumping in her head. Quivering all over, she took off her glasses, now thick with sweat, and jammed her fist into her mouth to stop her being sick, now really frightened out of her skin.

'I'll... I'll phone the police. Yes. That's what I'll do! I wonder if it's that missing person found drowned last week near the river,' she uttered, terrified. Her teeth couldn't stop chattering.

'Ye... yes. Mus... must be the one reported in the news the other day – "BODY STOLEN FROM HOSPITAL MORGUE NEAR THE THAMES!" Yes, that's got to be it. They said he wore distinctive clothing and had thinning hair. Though, I wonder why he's still grinning his head off?'

With her hand still shaking, Rosy rapidly dialled 999. *'Emergency! ...Police? Please hurry! Hurry!'* A blob of perspiration dripped off the end of her nose.

'Oh. Is that Scotland Yard? London Central? Yes, oh... Thank heavens. I wish to report a stolen car,' she mumbled in a hurry – embellishing the story. *'There's a body...* Yes, Officer. I'm dead serious. Yes, of course I'm sure he's dead all right.' She retorted indignantly. *'What? How do I know?* Well, he's lying stiff as a stiff and rigid as a board in the back seat of this old car just outside my house for a start!'

The call had been answered at the central police station by the duty officer who had taken calls from Rosy Harker several times before, when she had complained of this and that. 'Okay. Madam, please repeat the details slowly, and we'll get someone over as soon as we can.' Cupping the phone so that she couldn't hear, the duty officer yelled over his shoulder, 'It's that Nosy Parker – Harker woman again from Westhope Terrace! Better get one of squad cars to investigate. Hope it's not another bloomin' waste of time like the last time!'

He remembered her extremely well; because just only three months ago, she had complained that a pack of ferocious wolves were attacking the cats in her street – when in fact, they happened to be urban foxes fighting with city squirrels over left-overs from the bins.

In the meantime, Rosy put on the kettle to make herself a cup of tea, adding a strong nightcap to calm her nerves. She switched on the television and collapsed onto the sofa to wait for the police. Being thoroughly exhausted from the nocturnal goings-on, she could barely keep her eyes open.

'Where the devil are those wretched police?' she cursed. After ten minutes or so, her jaw grew slack. It fell open, and soon she began to snore fitfully as her body slumped like a sack of potatoes over the edge of the sofa, now dead to the world.

Part II

Blink blink, it makes you think...

Chapter 5

UNDER THE CLOAK OF DARKNESS

THE GIANT FINGER ON the church clock hovered around the figure twelve about to strike midnight. One by one, the houses along Westhope Terrace put out their lights, then the street descended into a cloak of darkness. The cemetery-like silence was soon quietly broken by the squeaking sound of soft rubber soles creeping along the road. It came from a young lad walking noiselessly on his own.

A black padded bomber jacket and well-worn, dark blue jeans covered him from head to toe. A large, peaked baseball cap in an obscure dark colour added to his disguise. The squelch of a noise came from his new white trainers scuffing the ground as he lazily lifted his feet. He approached the parked cars each in turn, nonchalantly trying each door handle whilst carefully scanning the road calmly. Stealthily, he snaked along until he reached the street-lamp in the middle of the terrace. He stopped, then paused, thinking, *Wow. That old VW's a doddle! I can soon hotwire that!*

From the rear, he easily opened the bonnet of the old yellow Beetle. Within two minutes, he had started the car. He pulled up his jacket collar above his neck, tipped his baseball cap to cover his face, looked round quickly, then jumped in. With a roar and a splutter, he drove off, whistling his head off – and so extremely pleased with himself.

Seth Ropely was just seventeen years old, a local lad who was a bit of a loner from the north-west estate near King's Cross. He was not so much a "villain" but more of a "misdirected youth" according to the local magistrate. Seth had appeared before him on previous occasions for joyriding since he was fifteen. Those who pleaded his case said that everyone around him had failed him. Indeed, it was said in mitigation that Seth hadn't stood much of a chance in life with a hopeless mother and a wayward father. Both deserted him when he was just six years old. He had been fostered ever since by several different families.

His aunt Drusilla, his mother's half-sister, being his only remaining blood relative, lost contact with him shortly after he was born, even though she was said to be his legal guardian when he started primary school at the time. Then his moving home a dozen times, trailing from pillar to post, meant changing schools every few years, which played havoc with his schooling. Truancy happened as regular as clockwork.

Seth looked a modern youth – slim, fairly-tall with cropped sandy hair, a fresh face of a lad with pre-adult chin stubble, which was fashionable. 'Lean, mean and lanky', he often thought of himself. He was a chap of few words. His real name was Jeffrey. But as a child, he had an unfortunate lisp and would say, '*It's... S... Seth,*' instead of, '*It's... s... s... Jeff.*'

He was eight when a kindly foster mother, named Gwen Jenkins – who also happened to be a speech therapist – took an interest in him. Given patience and loving kindness, she helped him to overcome his speech impediment. But the name Seth stuck. He preferred it. It had a kind of "street cred", he reckoned.

Mrs Jenkins, her husband Noel, who was a farmer, and three other children, who were also in care, lived on a large rambling farm in the centre of Wales. Those two years on the Jenkins's farm were the happiest period of his young life. He adapted to the outdoor life with enthusiasm and vigour. His energy was sapped daily with physical tasks which kept him out of mischief. Avidly, he learnt as much as he could about nature and wildlife. Seth was happy beyond his wildest dreams.

Everyone thought he was a model well-behaved child. But his life suddenly, collapsed when Mrs Jenkins died tragically in a farming accident with a combine harvester. Farmer Noel could not cope. And so, Seth was forced to return to another foster home on the outskirts of London but ran away due to repeated cruelty.

His first formal punishment started when he came before a juvenile court aged fifteen for joyriding. Under a supervision order, he was sent to work at Lock and Tinkersley, a specialist lock factory on the borders of Essex, when it happened again. In that year, Seth became somewhat of an expert at picking locks with his long, nimble fingers. In hindsight, the choice of factory was a bit of a mistake.

At Lock and Tinkersley, his job was to polish the locks by hand – so much so, that the pads on the tips of his fingers began to wear out. He also had an irritating habit of continually drumming and rubbing his fingers on tables and other hard surfaces, making small circles, rather than engage in small talk. This nervous habit of his, combined with hand-polishing metal daily, contributed to a remarkable discovery of his. By the time he left, Seth had worn out most of his fingerprints. Saddled with this unusual anatomical feature, it was pretty, obvious what tempting and wicked ideas flew through his mind when he returned to London to fend for himself.

Reaching a crossroad in his life, he could have either slipped into a life of petty crime or stayed on the straight and narrow. He wasn't a malicious youth. There wasn't really an evil bone in his body. In fact, he had quite a soft spot for the underdog. This was something he could identify with. Often he would go out of his way to help little old ladies or the blind to cross the road. He would donate his last few pence to charity collectors and the homeless when others passed them by.

After joyriding, he would clean up the windscreen, lock up the car and then, when he could, he would often return it to the spot where he took it from, parking it carefully without damage.

Seth drove the ancient yellow Beetle in the direction of Paddington Station. He was still whistling to himself, enjoying being cocooned in a little world of his own –

which was a million worlds away from stern warnings from authority: *"You'll come to a sticky end, young man, one day, if you don't change your wicked ways,"* and so on.

'Cor. Strike me. This ol' banger's flippin' heavy. Gotta be at least twenty years old!' he protested loudly as it lurched around the corners lopsidedly. At that moment, he happened to twist round to look behind him. The bright lights from the street caught the shape of a passenger which he hadn't noticed before, as it had been previously well covered up on the lumpy old seat. But now the blanket had started to slip…

'Good grr… ief, there's a blinkin' body in the back!' Yelping with horror, he gripped the steering wheel tightly. Just then, a large black cat scurried across the road, slap in front of his dim headlights. He slammed on his brakes as hard as he could. There was a deafening screech of tyres ploughing the tarmac. The harlequin's body suddenly sat up with a violent jerk, throwing off its blanket. Seth's jaw dropped a mile as the dummy jack-knifed and fell backwards onto the seat with a sickening thud.

'Oh, my maiden aunt! What in 'eaven's name have I let myself into this time!' He quickly twisted to take another look. *'Yipes, it's a dead person. Murdered or something!'* He took another look and realised that he was mistaken. But by then, he felt that he mustn't be caught with a stolen figure at the back of the car.

He wiped the sweat off the palms of his hands onto his jacket to get a better grip on the wheel. With his mouth dry, he swallowed hard. His heart thumped in his ears, as if it were about to explode. 'Gotta keep cool! Must be dead calm now,' he muttered for courage. 'Got to drive extra carefully... mustn't attract attention from the Bill.' As it happened, a police squad car roared past with all its lights blazing and its sirens blaring, heading west in the direction from where he had just driven.

Rather shakily, Seth proceeded to a back street full of shops that were well and truly closed. Hurriedly, he stopped the car. With Herculean effort, he dragged the figure out of the VW. The nearest spot was a men's clothing shop, whose window display was partially lit to deter burglars. He quickly dumped the figure half-reclining in its darkened doorway, partly hidden by a large black litter bin which was overflowing with rubbish.

Thinking that it might be useful for the unfortunate homeless sleeping rough on the streets, he flung the old blanket out of the car window. It landed haphazardly on the figure, which was now lying semi-prone. Without daring a second glance, he drove off at speed, his tyres squealing at a shrieking pitch. 'Phew, that was a lucky escape!' Seth muttered, blowing hard. With the back of his hand, he brushed his forehead, now very relieved, though his heart was still jumping.

Approaching Marylebone, he spotted a gleaming silver MG sports car parked in a side street next to the town hall. *That's for me!* he thought. *This old heap's falling to bits.* Quickly, he parked the Beetle under a street-lamp, cleaned the windscreen and locked it up carefully. He scribbled one word on a scrap of paper – "Westhope" – and tucked it under one of the windscreen wipers. He did not bother to wipe off his fingerprints, as it was unnecessary.

He tackled the sports car without a hitch. 'Stupid fool of an idiot hasn't even bothered locking it to set the alarm,' he said, with a whistle of surprise. It took him under a minute to slip the catch under the soft hood and climb in. Using a skeleton master key from his Lock and Tinkersley days, he started the MG easily. It roared into life and he drove off happily, selecting the easy gears like a pro. 'Now this is the life!' Seth chortled to himself. He started to sing and whistle a little song he had just made up to calm his nerves, which were about to burst:

'*Whistle while you work,*
Some people are such nerks!
They leave their cars with doors ajar,
No wonder gifts us perks.
Some 'ave bin mislead,
Soon they'll lose their heads,
Their cars have gone instead.
Whistle while you work!'

Chapter 6

A HANDSOME CAB

DRIVING A BLACK TAXICAB around London was a job that Roland Bigglesworth didn't particularly like. But still, it was a *job*, after all. He would work his own hours whenever he wanted to or go off on holiday when he wanted to. In that respect, he considered himself quite lucky. Most nights of driving, if he was perfectly honest with himself, were often boring due to the routine of it. He longed for something exciting to happen.

Roland knew the streets of London like the lines on the back of his hand. He was a good and careful driver, having taken his advanced driving test two years ago when he was eighteen. Roland was fair and stocky, and hardly could be called handsome in the conventional way. But despite this, people thought there was a certain roguish charm about him.

Still, his shoulders were quite broad and rugged, tapering to a slim, flat waist, thanks to a "Gym-at-Home

Machine" that he had bought by mail order from a Sunday magazine. Whilst leaning forwards towards his reflection in the bathroom mirror, he would flick his hair, which was cut close to the scalp in the modern "laddish" look with his open fingers, which he often did as a matter of ritual. His right arm developed over the years two inches longer than his left with a powerful fist the size of a large mango, from reaching out and backwards whilst still sitting in his cabin seat when opening the passenger door. He only actually got out of his cab for little old grannies, children, and beautiful women.

It didn't help matters when the occasional girl took a liking to him. With some embarrassment, he would have to explain, going slightly hot under the collar that, 'I… um… er… live with my… erm… er… old gran.'

Granny Purvis was a formidable little old lady, some seventy or so years old. She stood less than five feet tall in her stockinged feet. Now in the autumn of her years, a slight stoop became noticeable, which she did her best to disguise by forcing herself upright, remembering the old days of deportment training at school to improve posture by balancing a book on her head when walking around.

She looked every bit a typical granny. Her snowy-white hair with its central parting, was tied up in a tiny bun on top of her head. It was held securely in place by a polished tortoiseshell comb that Roland had bought her from a market stall near to the Portobello. She balanced a pair of small, rimless glasses, which were hexagonal-shaped with silver sides, on the edge of her thin, birdlike nose, highlighting her rosy cheeks.

Out of old habit she would go round in a matching twin set – a baby blue cardigan worn over a sweater and decorated with a row of pearls. These she treasured from her wedding day; they were a gift from Francis, her late husband, a RAF pilot killed in action towards the end of the Second World War.

Granny Purvis was a typical, kindly grandmama. Roland had known no other adult since he was four years old. His father Leonard emigrated to Australia after Molly, his mother, had sadly died of some terrible illness that was never mentioned. Len never returned to England. Apparently, he remarried with a new young family. Roland never heard from him again after the last Christmas when he was six. Granny Purvis, out of duty and love for her late daughter Molly, brought up young Roland as her own.

Granny Purvis – well, young Sybil Rawlings, as she was then – was a bright, enthusiastic twenty-year-old secretary in 1940, a year after the war started. Being well trained in Pitman's shorthand, by some quirk of fate she landed a job in the War Office – later known as the Ministry of Defence. One of her superiors suggested to Sybil that her meticulous skills with her discreet manner might be suited for training in the military intelligence network at Station ZQ – a secret government site at Blipton Park in East Anglia – to help the war effort. She had, of course, signed the Official Secrets Act and, as a fiercely loyal patriot, would not reveal exactly what she did with the team at Station ZQ, although she was debriefed many years ago.

Whenever Roland got home to Fulham, where they lived in a small, but pretty two-up, two-down terraced house built at the turn of the century, she would greet him with, 'Don't forget to change your socks tonight, Roland. And don't forget to clean your teeth as well, dear.'

'Yes, Gran,' he would reply automatically to make her happy.

'Look, Gran,' he would reply wearily, 'I'm nearly twenty-one now, you know.'

Roland would smile wryly to himself, recalling their last verbal jousting, but it didn't make one jot of difference. 'Oh, anything to keep the little old lady happy,' he would concede reluctantly. Then he would switch on his iPad and bury his head in the sports page of the evening paper while she prepared his dinner, humming contently to himself.

Now, as it happened, Roland had been driving aimlessly around central London for almost twenty minutes without picking up a fare. He often worked at nights. He preferred the darkness, which made most things anonymous with the pallid glow of the city bathed in sodium yellow from the street lighting overhead. He liked the relative peace and quiet, when most of the shops had closed for the day with the offices, dead as a morgue, and most of the people had gone home to bed: or so they should have done.

At night, the traffic was easier, being less stressful than the gridlock of the bumper-to-bumper traffic during the day. This way, he avoided the wrath of irate motorists dodging between the bus lanes, as well as the hordes of shoppers falling off the kerb to a deafening chorus of shrieking car horns. Indeed, it felt much cosier when the nights drew in. The ugliness of the strewn litter from fast food shops, and the awful graffiti smudged indelibly on the sides of buses, walls, and lampposts, seemed to melt away in the darkness.

'Um… Mm. I need to pick up a passenger soon. I'm wasting diesel. Bit boring,' he muttered to himself. He leant over and checked that he had the orange 'Taxi for Hire' sign switched on. 'Nope, that's not the problem,' he reasoned. 'Funny, the whole of the town centre is deserted tonight – strange, before the holidays.'

'Ah well...' Murmuring and scratching his head, he drove on, staring straight ahead.

As Roland headed slowly towards the back of Marble Arch, his eyes searching the empty streets, he happened to glance to his left at a men's clothiers, whose lights in their shop window flickered on and off as if from a faulty switch. He slowed right down, his foot dragging the brake. In the doorway, half-hidden by a black litter bin overflowing with rubbish, he noticed a strange, large figure. Half sitting up, it was partly covered in an old blanket.

It's probably one of those unfortunates or someone homeless, he thought grimly. He was about to accelerate away when he realised that there was something odd about it. The angled light of his headlamps caught the face of a dark, bulky figure lying there, as if stone dead. Grinning bizarrely, an outsize mouth outlined by bright red lips stuffed with a row of prominent white teeth greeted him by the reflection. This startled him, and his heart missed a beat. His mouth went dry. He licked his lower lip as curiosity overcame his fear.

He stopped his taxi and pulled up the handbrake. But he left the engine running in case he needed a quick getaway. Getting out of his cab, he cautiously approached the doorway with a torch. The shaft of light from its beam caught the grinning face of a large harlequin with its shiny forehead glinting squarely in the glare under a lopsided hat.

'Well, strike me dead. Where's he come from?' he muttered.

With trepidation, he poked the blanket with the end of his torch, standing back at arm's length cagily, in case the figure leapt up at him.

'No! Now, don't be daft. It can't bite! It's only a model – a dead dummy of some sorts,' mumbled Roland trying to reassure himself, though his pulse raced like mad.

'Well, well, oh my... he's in good nick, I must say!' he said as he took in the bright costume, pulling away the blanket. Gently, he prodded the underside of the harlequin's upturned boot with a tiny kick. 'Mm... now, I wonder if someone's dumped it in the bin.' He recalled once finding a stuffed alligator in a builder's skip.

'No way! Can't be right... looks too new to me.'

Roland looked up and down the street in vain, hoping to spot its owner. On the other hand, he thought it might have dropped off a circus lorry by accident or something like that. Scratching his chin thoughtfully, he then changed his mind. 'Bet it's been stolen from Madame Rousseau's! That's got to be it! The waxworks just up the road from here.' Pleased with his deduction, he started to drag the figure from the doorway. It began to drizzle as rain clouds threatened.

'Okay, better get it back to its rightful owners, dead pronto. They'll know what to do with it,' he concluded. He threw the old blanket back into the gloom of the doorway. 'Some poor devil sleeping rough will appreciate that!'

Now it was just as well that Roland was an extremely fit young man with all his keep-fit exercises. He knew how to lift bulky weights properly without damaging his back.

But carrying the dummy into his taxi without help proved no easy task.

'Well, stone me!' he panted. 'It's *really* heavy! Wonder what it's made of?' He puffed with exertion. Beads of sweat added to the drops of rain sitting on his nose. Eventually, the figure was secured sitting upright in the rear passenger seat. And to stop it falling over, Roland strapped it firmly into the seat using a seatbelt. 'In case we're stopped by the law!' He laughed dryly.

He drove carefully along the Edgware Road. Within a few minutes, Roland's taxi turned into the night porter's entrance on the side road to Madame Rousseau's.

Bert Brumble, the night porter was half-asleep, sprawled in a heap at the security desk, when Roland pressed the bell. He woke up with a start as the noise clanged next to his ear. There was a curse, followed by, 'What the blazes in the name of…! What the devil do you want?'

Aggressively, he glared at Roland, baring his stained, uneven teeth under a pair of red nostrils.

He was a rather round and dour-faced man with a short black moustache hiding a thin upper lip, which was fixed in a sneer. His bad temper was in keeping with his officious-looking dark uniform of officialdom, the sombre look of which was lightened only by some strips of silver braid and mock brass buttons.

If looks could kill, thought Roland, taken aback. 'Sorry, Mister, to trouble you at this time of night, but I think this dummy may have been stolen in transit from your depot,' explained Roland breathlessly, after dragging the thing into his office. He held on to it for dear life with it propped against his own body.

'Oh, stick the blitherin' thing in the office near the goods lift!' growled the night porter dismissively. Without getting out of his chair, he jabbed his thumb in the direction of a corridor to his right. 'Ned'll take it up to the exhibits floor on the next shift in an hour or so's time. I've done enough for the night!' He yawned unpleasantly.

Roland struggled on alone. He part-wheeled the dummy into the next office as the sullen porter looked on, totally unconcerned. The porter pushed his peaked cap aside, then got up lazily to put the kettle on to make himself some tea.

'Don't I get a reward? Say, a free ticket to the waxworks?' muttered Roland, cursing under his breath. He climbed, somewhat exhausted into his cab, his muscles aching all over from the night's exertions. 'Not even a wretched thank you or something? Now that's gratitude for you!' he grumbled as he drove away wearily back to work.

Chapter 7

SNATCHED

THEN, NO SOONER HAD the light of dawn begun to break than the smattering of rain during the night started to dry. The neighbourhood had begun to awake, ready to start a new day. Mudd the cat began to stir at number 10 Westhope Terrace. She leapt onto her mistress's bed.

Sassy woke up to a loud, drill-like purring in her ear. Feeling a bit cold, she suddenly realised that the duvet had been half-dragged off her shoulders by her cat clawing furiously at her bedclothes. 'Oh, buzz off, Muddie, it's not time to get up yet. It's not even seven!' groaned Sassy, still half-asleep. Annoyed, she slammed the alarm clock flat onto its face so as not to remind her.

Stubbornly the cat persisted. Her purring grew louder as she nuzzled against her owner's chin, giving it a hefty butt. 'Oh, all right then,' Sassy grumbled. 'You've woken me up now, you dreadful creature!' She flung the warm duvet off onto the floor, forcing the cat to fly off the bed like a bullet.

'Yarrh... um. I wonder what sort of day it is?' Sassy gave a wide yawn. She stretched her arms and body simultaneously. She drew back the curtains and instinctively looked into the street. 'Hey. Muddie, it's been raining in the night. Hope my little old car is okay, as it leaks when it's heavy. Oh, and let's hope our friend Chance has survived the night.'

Expectantly, she glanced across the road to where she had left her car the previous night, just under the lamppost. Then, suddenly... 'Oh my go...!' she cried, as her heart leapt to her mouth. 'It's gone... *It's not there!*' She looked again, this time rubbing her eyes hard. Frantically she searched through the open window in case she was mistaken the first time around. For between the cars under the lamppost, where she had left hers the previous night, there was a wide, obvious gap.

Panic-stricken, she rushed to the telephone. Immediately, she dialled for the police. 'Hello... hello? Thank goodness... My car, my little old car, it's gone! Yes, Officer. It's been stolen from outside our road. Yes... with a figure of... a... harlequin. Yes. A bit like a clown.

But it's – he's special. He's a harlequin... No, officer, not driving! He's a passenger in the car!'

The duty officer cupped the end of phone, joking with his colleague, 'Heh, Sarge, got a report of yet another one of those bloomin' clowns driving around town!'

Increasingly agitated, Saskia started to shout down the phone: 'I left him on the passenger seat covered up last night. I made him at college. It's for something very, important, as part of my course!' Whereupon she gave a description of the VW Beetle, giving its registration, then hurriedly went on to describe its passenger in detail. She had to repeat it twice, to an astounded station duty officer, who had a job jotting down the word "harlequin" for fear of ridicule from his superiors.

'Yes, Miss. We've got it now. Yes… all the details. We'll circulate West Central and City for the missing vehicle. Yes, Miss. Sure… As soon as we have news, we'll contact you. Give me your number again. Don't worry, Miss, it sounds like an opportunist joyrider to me… Doubt if your vehicle – with due respect, Miss – would be used in a robbery for a getaway. Villains usually nick newer and faster motors. Sure, we'll let you know, when we know… Yes, now, don't worry about a thing, Miss. Our officers will be on alert for a… er-erm, you state, a… hah… har… *h-a-r-l-e-q-u-i-n*, in a beaten-up yellow Beetle.'

With a heavy heart, Sassy put the telephone down and began to fret. As time slowly ticked by, she became distraught and numb. Not only had her little old car had been stolen during the night but, worst of all, Chance, her precious new friend had disappeared into thin air with it. She was getting more and more frantic by the minute. But for now, all she could do was to sit by the telephone and wait for news.

Sassy wearily propped her head into her hands, her elbows firmly, fixed on the table. Dazed and gutted, she stared vacantly into space. Terrible thoughts whirled through her mind. *Will I see my Chance again? Will he be chopped up for firewood and melted down for wax, or glue, by some mindless lunatic?* Such horrific thoughts didn't bear thinking about. She let out a little shudder. Then she got up and wandered over to the front window to stare forlornly at the empty street below.

Devastated: her precious harlequin had now been snatched… and there was very little she could do about it.

Chapter 8

OUT OF THE FRYING PAN

A BLANKET-LIKE SILENCE CREPT through the building of this world-famous waxworks. It contrasted starkly with the bustling activity of the never-sleeping city that continued relentlessly outside of it. The silence within was only broken at the change of the night shift. A sturdy trolley took the figure of the harlequin up to the second floor by the more amenable night porter Ned, who carefully positioned it on a raised platform between the wax figures of Napoleon Bonaparte and Houdini.

Old Ned, so rumour had it, once worked for one of the direct descendants of the celebrated Madame Rousseau in the 1930s. Ned was born so long ago that he had forgotten exactly when. In fact, he was due for retirement long ago, but the museum kept him on as his stories from his extensive memories fascinated and entertained all those he came in contact with.

When members of the Royal Family came to visit Rousseau's to view their waxen effigies, Ned kept them suitably amused with tales from the past. Unabashed, he told them that one of his favourite figures from the royal collection was the Queen's pet corgi, Kelpie. This went down rather well with Her Majesty.

'There yer are, me matey,' said Ned gruffly as he propped up the figure on the stand. 'Luckily, we really do need an actual figure of fun for the new show. Paliacci and Coco are nowhere to be found. Methinks these clowns were melted down last year and remoulded into some president or other, or maybe, I think, a prime minister of some sorts,' added old Ned, straight-faced.

Then he scratched the top of his nose and thought again. 'Bah! ...*Politicians? Dummies!* Heck! *What's the difference anyway?*' Raucously, he started to laugh to himself – so much so that he almost gave himself a stitch in the process.

'That'll keep yer all company. Now, see that yer don't run away, my friend!' he joked. He wagged his finger sternly at Chance and his two companions, one on either side of him. Then he ambled off slowly due to his arthritic knees to his desk on the ground floor, mumbling to himself.

The exhibition room had a fake grandeur to it – copying a grand hall or a ballroom of an opulent time from some glorious period in history – anything from the fifteenth to the eighteenth century. Its plain black walls were softened by rich drapes of burgundy-coloured velvet illuminated sparsely by imitation chandeliers filled with low voltage electric bulbs, shaped as mock candles, flickering on and off.

Each exhibit was lit by a pool of spotlight, giving each waxwork an eerie glow that added to the realism of the clever detail of their historical costumes and facial expression. Positioned strategically all around the room, casting shadows with other pieces of furniture, were reproduction antique chairs with maroon-velour upholstery and painted bowed legs in gold patina.

Seated in the chairs or standing near the tables, the figures assumed a life-like bearing, so realistic as to be almost frightening. Only Cleopatra eating a bunch of grapes, so it seemed, was half-lying down – semi-reclining on a type of 'chaise longue'. Whereas poor tired old, Rip Van Winkle was flat out... cosily hidden under his bedclothes, hibernating in a magnificent four-poster bed.

The room, in its synthetic magnificence, was airless. Its stuffy, suffocating atmosphere was filled oppressively with the smell of hot wax, faintly sickly sweet, reminiscent of an embalmer's chamber. There were no windows in sight. Shafts of refracted light borrowed from the corridors were bent inwards in the direction of the exhibits after bouncing off the shiny surfaces. A slither of light fell onto the face of the harlequin, whose expression, hitherto one of optimism and joy, had now changed to one of bewilderment and gloom.

'Monsieur, are *vous* awake?' asked Napoleon in his pidgin English.

'Oh, don't be dim!' retorted Houdini. 'He can't talk. He's only a wooden dummy. And a dumb dummy at that!'

To their astonishment, the reaction provoked by this final insult was nothing short of amazing. It began with a minute twitch of the mouth and rolling of the eyes. A tiny tremble and shiver on the harlequin's face soon turned into a violent shake of the head and neck. This began to grow in ferocity and force as his limbs started to vibrate from the top of the arms to the tips of his fingers. The flapping escalated. Chance's body shook dramatically. The movement spread to his legs and feet, which were now stamping like thunder, his big red boots marching relentlessly on the spot.

Napoleon and Houdini could only stand and stare. Both were bolted to the ground, their jaws gaped wide open.

'*Mon dieu. Sacre bleu!*'

'*Oh, my heavens!*'

The whole platform where they were standing rocked about, as if a mini earthquake had hit it. It seemed that an explosive energy of life had just taken over the network of nerves in the harlequin's structure… Had the dead suddenly come to life? Had the dummy just come out of deep hibernation? Whatever it was, the transformation was quite extraordinary. The figure continued slapping the flat of his hands against the opposite sides of his body, exactly as one would do when coming in from an icy storm. The spectacle stunned his onlookers. They had never seen anything like this before, and certainly not at Madame Rousseau's, at any rate.

Cautiously, Napoleon sidled up to him, suggesting, rather timidly, but with his hand hovering over his sabre at his side in case he needed it, 'Monsieur, please, we mean no offence. But cannot vous say something? *Comment appellez vous?* …I repeat: what is your name? Can vous 'ear me? *Parlez vous Français ou Anglais…?*'

Chance fought for words. He was still disorientated and shaken up from what had happened to him since he was stolen and separated from his inventor, Miss Saskia, some time ago. He rolled his eyes leftwards, firstly towards Napoleon, and then secondly, to the right, towards Houdini.

'Gentlemen,' he boomed in a deep, resonant voice. 'Of course, I can *hear* you perfectly well. Like you, of course I can *talk* when it's absolutely necessary. But straight away, I have to say that it's vital that I return urgently to where I was going to, before I was, shall I say… erm – you know… *mislaid*. It's odd, but I feel that I have a mission to complete and so little time to do it in. I could swear it in my bones.'

Flustered and wobbling unsteadily, Houdini turned to face him and asked, 'Wh… Who are you?'

'My inventor, my guardian – Miss Saskia – called me… erm… er… Mister… Chance. Well, actually – just Chance.'

'Why in heaven's name are you in such a rush to leave, when you've only just arrived?'

'I have to get out of this place urgently. *Now!* Gentlemen, I implore you. I need your assistance, please,' urged Chance, trying to cajole them into action.

'By the iron chains of my ancestors, you can't desert us so soon! The hundreds of people coming to the exhibition will be gutted,' pleaded Houdini, getting more and more exasperated with every second.

Chance spread his hands helplessly. 'Sorry, chum. I can't explain now, but time is running out for me if I hang about.'

'*Regardez*: do remember, *mon ami*, vous are a strang… er…'ere in central London,' warned Napoleon. 'Vous cannot go wandering on your own around the streets. Vous will only get arrested by the police as an oddball wearing that fancy dress. And besides, the underground does not start until five in the morning!'

'And furthermore, my friend,' added Houdini, pulling up his chair. 'The waxworks is a massive building with a maze of hidden passages and rooms. You could easily get lost and end up in the basement dungeons of the Chamber of Horrors with that 'orrible murderer Dr Crippen, or maybe Dracula or even Frankenstein.'

Chance shuddered silently, not wishing to admit that he couldn't stand the sight or smell of blood and gore. He preferred wax, plaster and glue any day. So politely he replied, 'Thanks for the advice, but I have no choice in the matter. I've *simply* got to get back – otherwise Miss Saskia will be distraught. She wants me to meet some others at her house before she goes away on holiday.'

His voice dropped. Again, he implored them. 'Look, gentlemen, please, I need your help to get out of here. From what I've seen of that nasty night porter Bert Brumble, I'm certain the security here is quite tough. I think once you're trapped in here, you can only escape as a bucket of wax! Am I...ri...ght?' His words stuttered due to worry.

'Now, which way is out of here?'

'Can vous walk, for vous look quite steeff?' enquired Napoleon, gazing with half-raised eyebrows at the harlequin's large feet. A frown appeared from under his famous cockade hat.

'Oh yes, indeed. No problem,' said Chance. 'I can even float off the ground in an emergency. Just watch!'

This he demonstrated, by twiddling his nose anticlockwise with a finger and thumb. Suddenly there was a quiet whirring of sound, a sort of gushing noise of wind being compressed, when vertically, he rose one foot off the ground. Silently, he glided forwards and backwards, then in all directions like a miniature hovercraft, much to their astonishment. He even did a circular dance around his new friends to their amazement, spinning concentrically like a top.

As he gathered speed, faster and faster, over a hundred revolutions per minute, he disappeared from sight – faster than the speed of light, making him quite invisible.

'There you are, my friends, demonstration over,' he said as a pair of large red boots slowly came into view. Then, gracefully, his body descended back to the ground, like a helicopter landing back to earth. The harlequin hardly broke a sweat, never mind panting a little. His audience goggled at him with undisguised envy.

'Well, I never,' said Houdini, astonished, though secretly impressed, 'If you *must* leave, you go through that corridor.' He pointed to the back of the room. 'And you'll find a narrow stone staircase. This is for the staff only. Therefore, to avoid the night porter in case he nabs you, you must give the main entrance, as well as the front lift, a wide berth. Go right to the bottom floor, turn left and then second right. You pass a tall knight in shining armour near the refreshment kiosk. Look for a green door towards the rear marked "Emergency Exit". That will take you out of the tradesmen's entrance. Push the bar up quietly.' He indicated with a finger to his lips. 'But if it is locked, there's a code pad next to the door with letters and numbers on it. Press firmly. Now, would you believe it, the security code is: "X – I T".'

Houdini half-grinned at the obviousness. 'Once through the car park, turn left and you'll reach the main road, which will take you back towards Paddington. But you will have to wait until that Bert Brumble leaves for the night.'

Chapter 9

INTO THE FIRE

NOT LONG AFTERWARDS, HOUDINI had soon dropped off, his head flat in his lap. His arms had fallen like dead weights that hung at the sides of his knees. Around his wrists, the chains clanked and grated as they scuffed the floor besides his chair.

'Hey. Pssst. *Wake* up!' Chance hissed into his ear. He kicked the legs of his chair, scraping the floor with a teeth-jarring screech.

Startled, Houdini suddenly woke up. 'W-wh-wha... What?' He rubbed his eyes with his iron manacles.

'Can't I twist your arm and persuade you to run away from this suffocating place and escape with me?' asked Chance. 'Why stay here like living death amongst all these waxen statues, reminding you of the tragic parts of history you wish you could rewrite, or might prefer to forget? Aren't you both cheesed off having to stand rigid as a board, every hour of every day, to military attention? And being stared at by millions of tourists, poked at, made fun of – keeping dead still, not even daring to blow your nose or go to the loo?'

Napoleon and Houdini nodded to each other, grimly tightening their lips until the blood drained away.

'And did you realise – and I overheard this from old Ned the porter – that when they get fed up with you, and you've reached your sell-by date, they strip off your clothes, then melt you down in their factory at Wormley Scrubs, where they have gigantic vats of boiling wax?'

A look of horror crossed their faces.

'No wo-wond-wonder, zen,' stuttered Napoleon. 'C... c... could that be...?' Trembling, he removed his hand from his waistcoat and pointed shakily across the room to a stand opposite.

For perched on a pedestal, directly in view, was a crumpled pile of white robes with what looked like faded silver and gold edging on the fabric. Around the discarded material there appeared what seemed like a large mound of molten wax. The waxen mass had congealed well and truly into the fibres of a magnificent Persian carpet, now shrivelled up at the edges. A glistening pointed hat, decorated with clusters of bright red and blue jewels, and surrounded with shimmering silver tassels, sat on top of an opaque mountain of wax. Not only that, but a dented bronze oil lamp had been dumped besides this mysterious blubbery mass.

'What on earth is that?' Puzzled, Chance walked over to this curious pile of clothes. He bent down hesitatingly and picked up the end of the fabric.

His newly found companions looked depressed suddenly. Houdini spread his shackled palms outwards in despair, crying hoarsely, 'There was nothing much we could do about it. Two days ago, er… it… erm… that thing… that grey blob, was… Al… Aladdin.'

'What do you mean, that *was* Aladdin?'

'Yes, Mr Chance. That blob, *it*… him… that thingy-me-bob… that pile of blubber over there *was* our late friend Aladdin and no mistake.'

Houdini pointed, not daring to touch the lump as though it had just died from some contagious disease or something worse. He gave a small cough and cleared his throat. 'We heard that he was no longer a star attraction like in the old days. The public was no longer interested in him anymore. He was considered passé – too old-fashioned and far too tame. For heaven's sake, who reads about the adventures of Aladdin and a magic carpet these days?' he added sadly.

Dropping his shoulders, he sighed forlornly. 'The powers that be, apparently then decided to chop his head off and melt him down. They will re-use the wax to remould him into perhaps a famous pop singer or maybe some celebrity or other.'

'Huh. It appears you can be a star one day and a blob of wax the next,' added Chance dryly, thinking how being famous nowadays could be so shallow.

'Why yes, apparently,' agreed Houdini. He began to sweat profusely with the dreadful thought that it might happen to him one day. He told himself that being chained and drowned in a large tank of water, as in his last stunt, was much more, preferable.

Chance gave a crumpled smile in embarrassment.

Then, as they crouched cagily around the shapeless blob that was once Aladdin, Houdini grew extremely anxious. 'Poor old lad. He got into such a stew and a panic the night before that cold-hearted Bert Brumble came up to get him. When his blood pressure boiled over with the terrible worry of it all, his fabled Genie in the lamp failed to use its magic powers to save him. Like a coward, it deserted him and left him to his awful fate. And so, his body erupted in the heat, reducing him just to a mass of blubbery wax.'

'You know, I've heard of that weird phenomenon called "spontaneous combustion" that's defied all explanation. But what a horrible way to end!' said Chance, quivering like a lump of jelly.

Stiffly, Napoleon shuffled forward. He bent down to retrieve the wax-covered lamp. It had dents on its side from years of use, but the gold and bronze handle was not tarnished.

'It's useless! Now probably empty.' He shook it vigorously next to his ear. '*Regardez, mes amis!* Try it yourself. Notheeng 'appens.'

Passing it over, Houdini also tried in turn to rub and shake it. He rattled it against his chains enthusiastically. Again, nothing! 'You can have a go. G'won. Here, catch!' He tossed it to the harlequin, who suppressed the urge to giggle.

Scraping off the wax from the wick of the battered lamp, Chance rubbed it hard. They both craned over him expectantly. 'You see, gentlemen – *nothing!* It's absolutely empty!' He was about to throw it away in disgust when, suddenly, the lamp spluttered to life, shaking violently in his hand. He almost lost his grip when a spurt of flame shot out.

'Yipes almighty!' yelled Houdini. Fearing for his life, he yanked his head back out of range. Then, he screamed, 'It's possessed! It's possessed!'

Napoleon, meanwhile, had cowered behind Cleopatra's sofa, gripping his hat over his face in fear.

A wisp of grey smoke leapt five feet into the air. A narrow, ribbon-like figure appeared some ten inches wide, flattened into two dimensions, as if it had been wrung through a mangle. It was about five-foot in length, skinny and thin, with a narrow, ghostly white face. Though shaped like a diamond, it had a pointed chin trimmed with a wispy beard. The whole apparition shimmied and gyrated about in a rhythmic dance like an ascending kite wafting in the wind towards the vaulted ceiling. The figure seemed to be made of a mass of tiny dots, like millions of pixels that kept floating about. He looked extremely old. His paper-thin skin was pallid, drawn tight over a mass of wrinkles. An ancient round skullcap adorned his pointed head – his hooded eyelids curtained his hollowed-out eyes.

Much to their surprise, he started to speak in a staccato voice that echoed. It was disjointed from the way his lips moved – woodenly, rather like a ventriloquist's dummy.

'Greetings, my friend, I have been waiting for thee. I have travelled a long way from the past to warn yee of some terrible dangers that are lurking around the corner for thee.'

'Who, *me*?' Chance stuck his finger into his chest and gripped the lamp even more tightly, despite shaking like a leaf.

'Yea, *yee*, the fat, laughing one. Yes, yee, who has in thine possession a wondrous gem around thine person.'

The ghostly figure curled his face downwards, holding the harlequin's stare. The point of his head wiggled at the same time.

'Yea, it's a *sacred gem* that was formed within an ancient tree – a *Tree of Knowledge* – hundreds and thousands of years ago. It is so priceless and unique, so coveted by so many in times past, that hundreds have died trying to find it.'

Immediately, Chance felt inside his sweater, easing his bow tie a little. He whistled a sigh of relief. The precious gemstone was still tied safely around his neck. But he hadn't a clue what the ghostly spirit was talking about. As far as he knew, it was just a pretty piece of jewellery Miss Saskia had made – as a good-luck charm to decorate his sweater.

The skinny apparition did not take his eyes off the harlequin for one moment. It continued in the same eerie voice as if it were being strangled.

'Beware, my ever-smiling friend. Heed the omen that has already been written. Awful death and destruction await to trap thee when yee leave this museum of waxen spirits. Mark my words, my naïve-o joyful one.'

'But… but what do you mean?' asked Chance, sweating under his sweater.

'Yeah. Who'd want to kill a harmless figure like him?' added Houdini, joining in.

The shimmering figure did a dance along the ceiling and wiggled back to face them, sliding down the wall on its back. It opened its mouth extremely wide, yawning like an enormous flat fish in a tank.

'So be warned, o unsuspecting one. There is mortal danger from some beings called the Custodians of Terror, who are not only cunning, but faceless. Like phantoms, they come in many shapes and guises. They're after thine blood. They are utterly ruthless, and indescribably dangerous, now waiting for yee, somewhere... out there! They have been waiting for thee since the day yee arrived on earth in that blaze of light.'

'Cust... odians... Pha... Phant... Phantoms... Terr... Terror? What the devil do you mean? And why *me*, of all people? I just don't understand,' stammered Chance.

His eyes glazed over in a white, hazy mist at the very mention of the terrifying words '*Phantoms... Terror...*', that echoed ominously – worse, when spelt out slowly, and aloud for himself to hear.

Just then, he fell to his knees on to the edge of Aladdin's carpet. He couldn't help it. From afar, he thought he heard, the sound of a wailing violin screeching... It was way off-key and tore at his insides. He put his hands over his face, for he almost fainted. A frightening vision suddenly flashed in front of his eyes like a dreadful omen. He just could not stop it happening. Snippets from what seemed like a horrendous nightmare flooded his senses. He saw colossal tremors shaking the planet as meteorites and asteroids hit the earth with explosive forces. Massive volcanoes erupted, rising to the skies as blackened ash blocked out the sun. Tornadoes and mighty thunderstorms followed, which rolled across the stricken heavens, whipping the raging fires that consumed, unchallenged, on the surface of the land. Whirling winds of tremendous power hurled trees and rocks across the landscape in wholesale destruction.

And all living creatures therein perished in an inferno in front of his very eyes...

...After what seemed like an eternity, Chance slowly came to. He was hopelessly dazed. The wailing sounds and cries started to ebb away into the distance.

Extremely startled, Houdini quickly ran to his side and helped him to his feet, anxiously asking, 'What on earth happened? It looked as if you were hypnotised out of your skull. Was it something *he... it...* said? Are you all right now?'

'I... I... must have dropped off. Something very strange overcame my mind and threw me. It... it seemed that I had been transported back hundreds and thousands of years ago... to the beginning of time, when something horrendous happened to the earth... and... But... I'm okay now. Don't worry, please!'

Chance kept panting heavily. Gradually, colour came back to his cheeks.

He searched round to confront the ghostly figure that was still dancing in front of his face, though the tail of his body was still glued to the lamp.

'For pity's sake, please keep still for just one minute,' he demanded wearily.'

There was a pause. The ghostly figure flattened itself against the ceiling. It hovered in the smoke still oozing from the spout.

'Now tell me. Please. *What is happening to me?* And what was that mournful, eerie music I heard? Please tell us the truth. Of all the ones on earth, *why pick on me?* I don't understand. *And who the devil are, you?*' asked Chance.

He was still so mesmerised that he almost dropped the lamp in fright, nearly splitting the figure from its tail.

'O perplexed one. Firstly, let me say, *do not fear me*. I am a friend from the past who has come to tell yee of the future. For it is *yee*, who has been chosen to seek the holy grail of life, joy, and laughter in order to do good in the present.'

'But hang on, my skinny, wafer-thin friend, as the harlequin says, *who are you?* And what the devil is your name?' asked Houdini, swinging his chains in front of him provocatively.

The wispy figure coughed nervously. 'Hurrh-umph. Well. Some mortals call me Cecil-the-Thin.'

'I can see that!' Houdini piped up. 'You're as flat as a pancake, skinny as a rake and need a jolly good meal to fatten you up.'

Feeling now braver, he beckoned to Napoleon that it was now safe to leave his hiding place from behind Cleopatra's sofa.

'Pardon. Come again?' said Chance, inviting another reply with the crook of his finger. 'What do you mean? Explain yourself – *who are you?* Again, *please…* What happened to me when I passed out just then?'

There was an exasperated sigh. 'I repeat, my name again is Cecil… *Cecil-the-Thin*. I bring thee truths. Do believe me. I am the wisest soothsayer in the land,' replied the skinny-one hurriedly.

He fixed Chance with a cold, strange stare and said, 'Yes, my rotund friend of fun, yee saw the truth of the earth that passed before in your head. The sound yee heard was a song of evil. So thus, when yee next hear the strains of a phantom violin again that accompanies the terror, it is, my friend, the warning of impending doom and death to all within its sights!'

His stare bore straight through the silence that followed.

The three of them stared at him open-mouthed, their eyes glued to the wriggling figure. Even Cleopatra half-opened an eye with lazy curiosity.

'...Now, from the depths of history, there is a prediction we are told, that yee... *yes, yee* with the happy, round face have been chosen to fulfil a special task on this planet to help to rescue *the Three Kingdoms.'*

'What do you mean by that?' asked Chance, scratching his head, completely stumped.

Cecil-the-Thin continued, in a droll, deadpan voice, 'As thee may know, this planet is made up of *three* worlds – kingdoms, if yee like...

'*Firstly*, one of Plants and Trees...

'*Secondly*, one of Creatures and Animals...

'And *finally*, that of Humans.'

He stopped, to draw in more breath.

'Each one is fighting for air to breathe, space to live in and food to survive. Now let me explain a bit further... In the kingdom inhabited by man, since time on earth began, there exist powerful forces at work, both good and evil. Not surprisingly, they pull in opposite directions. The good therein want to protect the other kingdoms, so that they can survive – to continue to live and coexist in harmony with each other. But as history has shown, evil forces lurking there are continually hell bent on destroying everything around them – not only from their *own* kingdom, but also from the *other* two.'

'But why? And for what reason?' asked Chance.

The ghostly soothsayer stared solemnly into space, then paused, as if to swallow some fresh air. His wriggling about was getting more intense the more he got animated with every sentence.

'For greed, power and evil,' he hissed. 'Now, out of these three, *evil* is the most dangerous, the most destructive. Evil destroys for the sake of destroying. Evil, yee must understand, kills for the sake of killing. It persecutes for the sadistic pleasure of persecution. It enslaves the free in its lust for greed and misuses its power to destroy the good that stands in its way.'

'But that is insanity. Madness,' said Houdini. 'One world cannot exist without the other!'

'Precisely. Yes. Yee tell 'em about it!' cried Cecil, squirming horribly.

'Yee see – evil in the world is contagious. Once started, it spreads like the plague. It suffocates and kills those who want peace, freedom, and happiness. And that is why, my friends, we have bloody conflict and constant battles between good and evil since time began.'

Chance was staggered by what he had just heard. Heavily, he balanced his rotund frame, perching on the edge of Cleopatra's sofa, mopping his brow, and almost flattened her bowl of grapes.

'Mm. Just look here, my skinny-wise visitor, what's it *got* to do with me? Me – I'm just a humble, simple one, who's just arrived purely by chance,' protested Chance, not quite realising the pun of it before it was too late.

The old ghostly soothsayer slid up the wall, shrugged and waggled his beard, protesting vehemently, 'Whoa! Wait... my funny, rotund friend. Do not curse or try to attack me. I am merely the messenger. All that I know, is that it is as I have declared – thee, yes, *yee*, have been chosen according to the prediction. And it is now down to thee to try to stop the march of this terrible evil.

For I repeat, it is thee…yes, only thee who is the embodiment of goodness, purity and happiness can unite those in the kingdoms, so that they can rise up one day, so that together, yee stand a chance to defeat the threat of the Custodians of Terror and its evil!'

'Okay. I get the message. I'm all ears,' Chance replied irritably. He shifted uncomfortably from one foot to the other. 'Then tell me more about what you have described as those dangerous… you know… *phan-toms*.'

He swallowed hard. You know… 'Those Custodians… of-of… Terr-Terror, I've got to watch out for!' Like a vice, he gripped the side of a nearby table to stop him from fainting again.

'Yeah,' interrupted Houdini haltingly. Sweat broke out on his lips. 'Tell our friend where he must look, so that he can best protect himself.'

As Cecil's eyes darted about, his grisly face drained whiter still. His lower lip trembled.

'*The Custodians of Terror*, I am told, may be *several entities* of the same evil that used to terrorise the Kingdoms from the beginning. But there again, I have to confess that I have heard rumours that they are perhaps actual embodiments of real beings, disciples and followers of this thing we call *evil*. According to rumour, they may be human; they may be creature.'

Complete silence followed, as Chance and his newly found friends tried to absorb it all.

Another deep breath followed.

'Now listen well, my friends. These evil entities, when they appear, can change in an instance – multiply or reduce to single creatures to fit the situation! I hear that they and their followers may have already infiltrated the population all over the planet in disguise. But... but, they are all under the control of *one supreme being!*'

Houdini was the first to react. 'Pardon... what do you mean... *one supreme being?*'

'There exists one, yes *one*, such being, right now waiting for the chance to emerge. He, I know, is just waiting for the right moment to rise with his powerful forces to take over the Kingdoms, and then to destroy all that is good which inhabits them. And when that happens, nothing, yea *nothing*, will stand in his way. For he, if not stopped, will go on to conquer and annihilate the planet, unleashing mass torture, whilst savagely oppressing all who live there.'

Chance gulped loudly his throat parched dry with nerves. Croaking, his voice rapidly faded. 'Who is this tyrant? Where can one find him? What does he look like?' he asked.

'All I can tell thee, is that it is said that he is faceless, and hides behind a mask... *a mask of evil.* But yee have to seek him out. It is thine chosen task to find him. All I know is that for centuries he has been protected in a hidden kingdom, out of sight – in an Alterworld, if yee like. There have been so many myths about his exact origins, or where he came from. But on thine journey, yee will discover all these things. For clues and help will be given to thee by friendly persons and amiable creatures along the way.'

'Mask? Faceless?...What do vous mean? O wisest Monsieur soothsayer,' demanded Napoleon, finding his voice at last.

Cecil waggled his beard in his direction. 'Everyone on earth hides behind a mask in some guise or other when it suits them. It is to disguise one's real feelings and identity. For instance, thousands of years ago, the players in Greek theatre always used masks on stage so that they can flit seamlessly from one character to another. Thee, and even your rotund-good friend of goodness and fun wears a mask to distract attention from his real persona when on view!'

Open mouthed, Houdini and Napoleon stared at each other in turn, curiously scrutinising each other's faces – trying to analyse if they were genuine faces or not. Chance began to tug at his chin and nose – questioning his own cheerful demeanour of fixed smiles as others saw him.

'But, 'Idden... 'Idden Kingdom? O wisen-one,' said Napoleon . 'What eez zat? Et comment s'appelle? And what eez zee name of this evil-one?'

The figure of Cecil floated over their heads, his skinny body having just separated from the spout of the lamp, and then managed to skim the top of Bonaparte's hat.

Then he hissed softly, 'All I know is that he goes by the strange name of Qnevilus. In fact – a supreme ruler, Qnevilus-the-Terrible: a self-appointed, jumped-up tyrant, who dares to ascribe himself as from royal blood – the equivalent to a king. Yee can see that even his name is inextricably woven with the meaning of evil!'

Chance's complexion paled at once. Houdini stared questioningly at Bonaparte, who spat at the floor at the very mention of a ruler... Bonaparte detested anyone that could have threatened *his* role as *king* for purporting to be of royal blood, however remote.

'Legend has it that from the beginning of the human kingdom, this most evil one killed the rightful ruler of one of the most peaceful kingdoms in the land and then usurped his throne,' continued Cecil, pretending not to notice the disgusting habit of spitting. 'Successive claimants to the throne were murdered one by one or were secretly assassinated so as to keep the Crown.'

'But where is he now?' Chance asked, with a nervous shake of the head.

Cecil shrugged violently, almost decapitating himself in the process.

'All I can tell thee is that some almighty calamity happened to the earth at that time, and his kingdom fell off the face of it, sank into the oceans and then resurfaced. And yet remarkably it somehow survived. Henceforth, it was lost and then became known as the Hidden Kingdom where for a very, long time this evil one sat, seethed, and raged, whilst plotting his revenge against the other kingdoms.'

'But let me remind thee, that the legend has it, that *yee* has a duty to seek out this evil one... this Qnevilus, then ultimately to kill him in order to save the Kingdoms. *Kill him*, my friend, and the Three Kingdoms will have a chance to reunite in peace one day!'

A wail leapt from Chance's mouth. 'I don't believe what I'm hearing! What! ...*You what! You mean I, have to find, and... and then, t-to... ki-kill this... being?*'

Houdini and Bonaparte were momentarily struck dumb.

'Yes, my sceptical, round-friend. It is thine job. *It is written.* But I warn thee again: remember, this evil one is all-powerful, ruthless – protected and surrounded by his followers... and is extremely dangerous. He will stop at nothing. Killing thee first will be nothing to him. To him, it would be like swatting a troublesome fly! He has no conscience to prick. So yee must strike first. *Kill or be killed!* That is the prophecy.'

'Isn't there any other way?' asked Chance hopefully.

'I'm afraid not,' said Cecil. 'Yee cannot change what has already been written, if yee want to live.'

By now, Chance was almost on his knees with worry but didn't dare to admit it in front of Houdini and Napoleon, who were watching closely.

'Tell me then. What do I have to do to help those in the Kingdoms? Mind you, I may not agree to it, although it seems I have very little choice in the matter. And anyhow, how can I best protect myself from these dangerous forces and this madman, or his followers when the time comes?'

While all this was going on, Cecil by now was getting thinner and thinner with his voice running dry. He was becoming more nasal by the minute.

'Soon after yee start thine incredible journey in search of those who need thee, yee must first seek all that fountain of knowledge to help thee in the task. That precious gemstone yee already possess around thine body will reveal some of the secrets to it and help thee on thy way.'

Then, in the very next minute, Cecil appeared suddenly evasive, as he twisted his torso away, hesitating, as if holding back.

'Is there something else that's on your mind that you need to tell our pal Chancy here?' asked Houdini perceptively.

Alarmingly, Cecil rolled his eyes around in tiny circles and then tugged hard at the brim of his skullcap.

'Do thee want the good news first, or the bad?'

Chance shrugged and splayed out his hands in a helpless gesture.

'Oh well, my friend, legend has it that yee has got forty days and forty nights in which to live on this planet. And at the end of this, thee will disintegrate in a puff of smoke!'

'What? Forty – a miserly forty! *You what!* …You can't be serious?!' Chance exploded as he crumpled to the floor. 'Then, what's the good news?' he whispered desperately.

'Yeah. Please tell our pal here, something more hopeful to look forward to so that he can live!' echoed Houdini as he helped Chance to his feet.

'If yee sorts out the riddles that's been set before thee as a task on thine journey, yee may survive to gain some extra time – erm… providing, of course, that yee have not been killed off by the Terrors in the meantime!'

'Riddle… *Sacre bleu!* …*Ridd… les?* What do *vous* mean?' asked Napoleon, gesticulating accusingly at the wavering face of Cecil-the-Thin. 'And how much *extra* time?'

'Ah. Hrrh… aherm… hrrh!' He gave a rasping cough to clear his throat.

'I have to tell yee all – meanwhile, there is a series of riddles our harlequin friend *has* to solve if he wants to extend his life on earth. Perhaps meanwhile, if it helps, he can gain a reprieve of, say, an extra ninety-nine days… but *only* under certain conditions. It is a test of his resolve and determination to go on with the quest. Thus, for instance, to start off with:

'Three good deeds will gain thee time,
For ninety-nine days will suit the task,
Thee part of tree, but in a mask.
Henceforth, what's more might settle the score,
O words of wisdom – survives legends in time.
It's a test of will, that'll solve questions of thine'.

'What the devil do you mean?' spluttered Chance, his face draining white with worry. 'That's just a sop to keep me quiet. But it's simply *not* enough! All I want is three score years and ten. The same as most people on this earth!'

In vain, Houdini tried to grab hold of the ghostly soothsayer. 'Can you explain about these things called – you know... *riddles*? Because what do you mean by *words* of *wisdom* to keep him alive? And then... good *deeds* to gain him time... does that mean...?!'

Cecil merely shrugged savagely – so much so that his skullcap nearly fell off his pointed head. 'That is all I can reveal to thee, o waxen friends. It is written from the beginning of time. It is up to thee to sort out the riddle if thine friend wants to live long enough and to help the Kingdoms!'

He then pointed to the pendant around the harlequin's neck with the tip of his beard.

'Next; to live months – even years – longer than the prescribed time that yee have already been allotted in single days, yee must seek and obtain the Secret of Life in order that thee may live long enough – even perhaps, forever on this planet to complete thine chosen tasks.'

'Where's the, *Secret of Life* then? We would all like a bit of that now, wouldn't we, Emperor Bonaparte?' joked Houdini cynically.

Napoleon nodded approvingly.

Cecil frowned so severely that his cap fell over his eyebrows and hid his eyelids. 'I believe the Secret of Life is held by a *second* precious stone, of which I presently have no further information as yet.'

He added, 'This, I am afraid, is a task of discovery *yee* have to perform to seek it out. But please be of good cheer. Use one of the most powerful weapons at thine disposal to protect thee from danger on thine travels.'

'What is that?' asked Chance.

'Laughter. Yea, plain, simple, and amazing *laughter*!

…*Laughter,* my friend, is described as the sweet music of the planet, the nectar of happiness, the common language understood by all species. And what is more, it is the elixir of all life.

And furthermore, yee should have unlimited reserves of laughter, haven't thee? A funny figure, such as thee should be full of joy, and one who should bring happiness to all he comes across. Joy and laughter will drive out misery from every corner of the globe, don't yee think? Who would fight? Who would kill, if yee made them laugh?'

Then, fixing Chance with a deadpan stare, he added solemnly,

'Armed with these three things – *knowledge, life* and *laughter* – these three gifts will go a long, long way to protect thee, and to enable thee to fight off adversity that chooses to harm thee.'

'*Pardon. Mon ami. Comment...* What 'appens if the harlequin... 'ere, say, fails, or refuses to 'elp... and just wants to save only his own skin?' interrupted Napoleon.

Whereupon Cecil wafted so close to Napoleon's face that they were almost touching, when he shrilled begrudgingly,

'Monsieur, o Emperor Bonaparte, as yee have experienced in thine own short life, there is *not* much time left on this planet of ours... This earth, and every single living species on it will be destroyed, if those evil forces are not opposed. And once *they* run riot, the Kingdoms, and all who live in them, will perish in confusion and chaos. Pestilence, disease, misery, and death will follow! ... Forgive the pun, but yee only have *one*... chance!'

'I don't believe you! We only have your word for it. Prove it!' challenged Houdini sceptically. 'Anyway, what's the big deal over a few odd flowers, miserly weeds and trees if they perish? What's so important about animals and creatures if they disappeared? Surely, we, the human race, *are*, after all, the more precious, the most vital element above all others. It is *we* who keep the world alive with our superior wit and knowledge. It is only *we,* who must live in order to renew all that is good for the earth.'

He rattled his chains noisily to make his point.

At which Cecil retorted angrily as the velvet drapes across the room shook dangerously.

'Do not mock me, my manacled friend. The impending doom – when it comes, is something even *thee,* cannot escape from. Oh yea. Plant and animal life on this planet, I must remind thee, have an equal right to survive as much as man, and others living... *For each Kingdom depends inextricably on one another!'*

Cecil's voice was getting more and more agitated by the minute. His squashed, wafer-thin body wobbled up and down, skidding around the ceiling of this great room like slippery eel. Then looking around, he spied a large bronze bust of the great Greek philosopher, Aristotle, sitting still on a tall marble plinth by the side of the door. 'Ah ha... that's what I'm looking for!' he exclaimed.

He then flew over to it, dragging the others with him. 'Now, what does it say under the shoulders of that statue then?' he challenged. No sooner had he said that, than he suddenly flew around the room, making a rude slurping noise of exasperation.

Quickly, Chance grabbed the bust and tipped it on its head as they all leant forward to take a peep. For written on a brass plaque underneath the base of the neck, it simply said:

'Respect with care. Be it at your peril...
For all living creatures and every species of plant on
*   this earth,*
All possess a living soul.'

Aristotle, 350 BC

Chapter 10

WISENDRAMA

FOR A COUPLE OF minutes or so, Houdini and Napoleon went extremely quiet as they tried to work out what the harlequin was thinking. Chance began to chew things over on what to do for the best... Then, suddenly, he threw his hands into the air, which startled them.

'Okay, Mr Ghostly Thin. Okay,' he conceded, 'I give up! I can't run away. Well, anyhow, not just yet. And so, for the moment... you might as well win! For I might – *just might* – try to help. Now. No definite promises, mind you!'

The other two turned and stared at this sudden change of heart.

He wagged his finger in front of him.

'So now, please explain how I can defend myself from these terrible forces of evil you've just described, which are waiting for me on the outside? Remember, I'm not used to all this heroic stuff. And don't forget that I'm just an ordinary, simple soul just wanting to mind my own business. I got stolen by a joyrider from Miss Saskia's little old car, then got lost, and finally ended up here by courtesy of some kind young cabbie.'

Frustration tightened across his face. 'Really, I just want to go home! And therefore, you must try to help me now. For instance, you say the best weapon is – *laughter*? But surely, that's only *one* thing. But how the blazes can that help when face to face with a murderous attacker hell-bent on strangling you?'

Hovering like a kite, Cecil continued to stare pointedly at the stone around the harlequin's neck.

'For a start, as I have said before, that gemstone yee have – *yes, that one!*'

He pointed again, gesticulating wildly. 'It will give thee the wearer the power within, through its all-powerful knowledge from the ancient tree it came from. Its wondrous properties will have been bestowed upon thee. Tap into its wisdom. It will guide thee in thine mission. Guard it well, my friend with thine life, as without it, thee will surely wither and fail.'

'Then, what next?' asked Chance. 'I'm all eyes and ears.'

'Next,' said Cecil, without wobbling about, 'I thus impart all mine worldly wisdom of bodily defence, and all my knowledge of self-preservation, down to thee.'

He looked at him straight in the eye. 'Now, remember this well that the spindly branch of the willow tree, however thin, bends ever so easily with the weight of snow upon it – unlike the oak which is inflexible! And because the willow is strong, but nevertheless, so incredibly supple that it

flexes without snapping, even in the mightiest of storms…
and what is more…'

Bit by bit, Chance and his comrades became more and
more impressed by what the skinny old soothsayer had to
say.

'Thee will be pliable like that of the willow so far
described, yet *awesome* in power, enabling thee to deflect
deadly missiles at the supple flick of thine wrists and feet.
Harness this with the power of knowledge from that gem. No
enemy, however dangerous, will be able to touch thee then!'

To emphasise the point, Cecil started to wiggle about
again, as if in a war dance.

'Thus, practise well, o figure of laughter, the immovable
but tricky stance of riding a wild stallion. Those big boots,'
– pointing with the tip of his chin – 'Yee must imagine to be
as heavy as lead, sticking tenaciously like glue to the bowels
of the earth. No force on earth, however big, will shift thee
then. Not even a two-ton truck or a colossal tornado can
knock thee down!

But again, a word of caution, my friend, use this power
only in the defence of the weak or for thine own self-
protection. I further lend yee this advice and give thee a clue:

Speed and guile will make thee smile.
Brute strength and curse will make things worse:
A jumping beast will teach thee first,
His flexible frame has one big purse.'

There were hundreds of questions Chance wanted to ask,
if only the figure would keep still for once and stop talking
in riddles…

Bonaparte's face clouded with a scowl. He simply could not believe his ears.

'*Excusez moi, mes amis*, what incredible non-sense!' Just then, he exploded with rage and began rattling the sabre at his side in frustration. 'Ow can *vous* fight the battles with only naked arms and legs? We are not insects! The French Cavalry 'ad to fight with muskets, sabres and beeg, beeg cannons. Zey could not manage without them! So where did *vous* dig these fictional stories from, *mon* fanciful *ami*?'

Cecil quivered drunkenly in and out of the mouth of the lamp and replied tartly, 'Ah, my doubting Thomas, me old bony-face, then let me explain…'

Intrigued, everyone in the room stopped to listen. Napoleon flopped down on the nearest chair, his scepticism unmoved, but nevertheless, he was all ears.

'…About five thousand years ago an ancient sage called Wisendrama-the-Cunning crossed the frontiers from Tibet to China. He taught the monks of the ancient temples of the north the secrets of an all-powerful and scientific fighting art of self-defence against bandits and marauders. He taught them inner strength of good health and longevity. He himself was reputed to be over 160 years old and still fighting like a young tiger.'

He paused for a second to let it sink in.

'These martial skills were based on years of observing how animals in the wild fought to protect themselves and their young. The cunning Wisendrama, however, would study and practise meticulously *all* the methods and predatory skills from *every* single animal and bird he observed in the wild. Use of claws, paws, wings, trunk, tail, body, head, jaws, beaks and so on, combined with the guile and cunning of man, were paramount. He distilled this into an amazing secret weapon of defence. It was an incredible and unique system of the fighting arts, only known to a chosen few who passed it down through the ages in secret. With it, thee only had to utilise the minimum of energy with the tiniest bit of force, to achieve the maximum impact with the most devastating results.'

Their mouths fell open as they hung on to his every word.

Excitedly, old Cecil went on. 'Moreover, in the right hands, it was delivered so fast that the enemy never saw what was coming. They swore that just before they died from the blow, they were struck by an invisible force. So thus, remember this, my friendly one:

The stance of a wild horse will blow them off course.
Wings of a bat are powerful as the might of a wild
tomcat.
The tail of a dragon can sweep away wagons.
Yet claws of lion are stronger than iron.
A beak of a crow will bend even the strong bow.
But the vision of man will defeat all he can:
By guile of his cunning, his enemies will go running!'

Silence fell throughout the room. They were completely lost for words.

Cecil wriggled and weaved all over the room, wiggling in and out between the wax effigies pretending he was trying to fight off an invisible enemy using his pointed head and his shrivelled fingers. Cleopatra, though, wasn't a bit impressed. Contemptuously, she yawned in front of him in disgust.

Then, towering over the harlequin, he offered, 'Do not fret. Yee will be granted the awesome power I have so described, and such phenomenal strength that thee will be able to move mountains with thine little finger, if yee wish or dare to.'

'Oh yeah! Pull the other one!' commented Houdini sourly, just a little bit jealous.

The skinny old ghost seemed restless, wanting to fly away. He kept criss-crossing the room, creating a draught about their heads.

'But wait! I repeat. There's an important warning for thee, o round purveyor-of-fun,' he cautioned. 'Tread warily on the journey. Beware on thine life the faceless, mysterious ones. For thine evil enemies have put a curse on thee and all those that try to do good…So remember this advice wisely.'

'But… but hold on. I have to know… what does that, you know… those… erm… *phan… phantoms* look like, and the other ghastly thing…?'

Chance couldn't finish what he was saying without shivering. And so, he just spat the words out quickly.

The ghostly figure tapped the lobe of his ear and touched his eyes in turn without blinking as though he had been suddenly struck deaf and dumb – or seemingly didn't want to talk about it anymore.

Instead, he said, 'A final warning, my funny friend. *Neglect not, the Three Kingdoms.* And again, remember these three things… *knowledge, life* and *laughter.*

'…And oh, I *almost* forgot – and the *power* and *skills* of Wisendrama. That's all thee needs to know in life!'

Sharply, Cecil turned away and subconsciously began to hum the words of the strange riddle again: '...*Brute strength and curse will...*'

His voice was beginning to fade rapidly. The lines of the figure started to blur at the edges with the dots melting fast away.

Panicking, Chance tried to stop the figure rushing back through the spout of the lamp. He cupped his hand over it with a slap and started to yell in frustration,

'But... Cecil... Thin... Soothsayer! *Please*, you haven't explained how I'm to... I also need to find out more about, you know... the riddle of words and the other thing...'

His agitation grew by the minute.

'And where is this teacher who can show me how I am to protect myself – with, you know, this secret weapon called...? Oh, blast it, so many things you didn't tell me about! There are millions of things I need to know. Wait... *Please wait!* Because maybe it will soon be too late...'

Before he had time to complete his sentence, the gossamer wisp of the figure faded. It flew away suddenly like a deflated balloon and disappeared through a crack under the door with an accompanying crude rasp of wind. The rude sound disturbed Cleopatra from her slumbers. Whilst Rip Van Winkle behind her in his four-poster bed – true to form – slept on, snoring, and was completely oblivious to the whole drama that had gone on.

Without saying a word, Houdini stooped down and stuck his nose under the door, searching in vain.

'But our mangled old Cecil seems to be really troubled about your future wellbeing, Mr Chance, I must say. He appears to have risked a lot of trouble to return from the past to deliver you a message about the future, both terrifying and chilling though it is!'

'*Oui*, more like a blunt warning, about murder and evil. 'Ope it's useful to protect *vous* then, *mon ami!*' added Bonaparte.

Increasingly drained and ashen-faced, Chance drawled slowly, 'Well, we'll have to see. He's scared the living daylights out of me, you can be sure. But I wonder what he means? For instance, that riddle's puzzling.' Without thinking, he scratched his scalp and nervously fiddled with the pendant around his neck.

Sighing deeply, he raised his shoulders to his ears, and then dropped them anxiously. The threats of torture and death had made him jittery. Since the college, his journey had taken him like a roller coaster from a scalding-hot frying pan into a scorch of a fire. And, not unsurprisingly, he began to feel a bit terrified because of it. Oh, how like now, he wished that he was safely back in the care of Miss Saskia, his inventor and protector.

And what of his promises to Cecil-the-Thin? Could he break them now, to save his own skin – but then be accused of awful cowardice? Could he live with himself if he did? But there again, what obligations did he truly have to those in the Three Kingdoms, of whom he knew almost nothing? So, whatever was waiting for him around the corner as Cecil had warned was perhaps a dreadful and fateful disaster waiting to happen, and about which he could do incredibly little. And the worst part of it was being stuck here like the veritable sitting duck of a dummy.

Chapter 11

THE SECRET OF TOE HEE DO

BEFORE THEY HAD TIME to recover their breath, they heard a sharp hiss coming from the passage outside the room.

'Ssh. Hush. Listen!' Houdini warned the others. He held his finger to his lips. 'Sounds like the lift is working. Someone's coming up!'

An uneven thud came from an ungainly step moving along the passage.

'Quick. Freeze. It's old Ned doing the night rounds. I can tell from his creaky old knees.'

The heavy door squeaked open. Old Ned shuffled in across the threshold carrying a large torch. 'Funny. Could 'ave sworn I 'eard a noise from 'ere,' he growled under his breath. He flicked the beam around the large room, darting the light into the corners as well as up the walls. Then he sniffed the air suspiciously. The remains of a strange smell from a dank mist still hung hazily in the air like a ghost train rattling through a tunnel.

'Funny. That's odd!' Ned snorted noisily like an old cart horse baring his nostrils. The beam from his torch caught the figure of Napoleon with his hat back to front, half-crouched behind the model of Joan of Arc. Puzzled, his torchlight then scanned the room, carefully searching. The sharp beam then fell onto Houdini's face, whose startled expression suddenly froze with a forefinger glued to his lips. Whereas the harlequin he had brought up just hours before, was now stuck halfway across the room with the late Aladdin's discarded old oil lamp gripped in his outstretched hand.

Ned shook his old head and polished his glasses on the front of his old woollen pullover. 'Must be seeing things in my old age. It's really peculiar, though. Must ask Bert if 'e moved things round before 'e left for the night.'

Abruptly, he stopped in his tracks. Then he thought again, shaking his head. 'Mm, now, I wonder if... those things on their own can...?' He looked across the room, holding his breath. 'Nah! Scary! Impossible! It doesn't bear thinking about.'

Still shaking his head like an old sheepdog drying its coat, he ambled slowly out of the room, his old, worn knees creaking worse than ever. He shuffled at a snail's pace down the passage towards the gates of the lift, mumbling under his breath. Halfway along the hall, a dull thump was heard. It sounded as if he had opened and slammed the door of a cupboard in rapid succession. Soon afterwards, the heavy, uneven footsteps faded and the whoosh of the lift in motion signalled that the old night porter had returned to the ground floor.

'Phew. Blimey. That was a close shave, folks!' blurted Houdini, now daring to breathe again. His finger from his lips slid down with relief.

'There isn't much time left. Can you two help to explain the ghostly soothsayer's riddle?' implored Chance.

'Well, let's go over it again, carefully,' said Houdini, scratching his skull with his manacles. 'Now what did that skinny old Cecil say…?

Speed and guile will make thee smile,
Brute strength and curse will make things worse.
A jumping beast will teach thee first.
His flexible frame has one big purse.'

'Now, could 'ee 'ave meant a monk? Perhaps, guile means wisdom?' suggested Napoleon helpfully. He stroked his chin slowly.

'Doubt it,' said Chance thoughtfully. 'A monk – so wise? Yes, perhaps. But… mm. Though, even if he were one: impossible! Having *one big purse* and all that. So no, that can't be right. Most monks become impoverished purposely, having given away all their worldly goods to the poor!'

'And they can't jump for toffee, and they tend to crawl along in a trance,' added Houdini.

Perplexed, the three of them sat on one of the long benches meant for visitors. They tried to puzzle it out, furiously jogging their brains. Napoleon straightened his hat and hoped for a quick brainwave to emerge from beneath it.

Getting now increasingly annoyed with himself, Chance

kicked the old bronze lamp under the bench with the heel of his foot. He repeated out aloud, '*Mm… a jumping beast will teach thee first—*'

'Um. Er. I wonder…' interrupted Napoleon, furrowing his brow in deep concentration. 'His flexible frame 'as one big purse? …Jumping? Flex-ible? …Big, beeg purse? Does 'ee mean, a prize fighter of some sort?'

No sooner had he said that then there was a massive yelp from Houdini, as if a lightbulb had suddenly been switched on in his head. Excitedly, he then leapt up, punching the air. 'Got it! By golly, I've got it! Yee gods, rattle me shackles, I think I've *got* it! I'm dead sure that Cecil must have meant something like *that* young furry Aussie beast that was sent here by mistake, which was originally en route to the London Metropolitan Zoo Museum.'

They all looked at him as if he were stark raving bonkers or something equally mad.

'Listen, you two. Why, Napoleon, my dear fellow, *you* should remember what happened last week with all the drama, when that nasty Bert tried to wrestle with that big hairy thing which fought with Ned through the door.'

Napoleon's blank look suddenly faded, like a penny had just dropped. 'Arrh. Of course, *mon ami*. It was that enormous kangaroo struggling with old Ned. Got a big kick in zee 'ead for all his troubles!'

Houdini pointed down the passage, savagely grimacing as he recounted the tale. 'Yes. It's a darn big furry Antipodean marsupial – they glibly call a *regular kangaroo* down under. Old Ned had a job stuffing it in the broom cupboard at the end of the hall for safekeeping, I can tell you! Let's go and have a peep at him. I'm sure he fits the bill.'

Blindly, they followed as he clanged and clattered his way out of the room and down the hallway, his shackled right hand firmly on Chance's shoulder.

'Hey, my dear emperor, can you remember what old Ned called this animal?' asked Houdini.

'*Il s'appelle "Oopla"* or something like that,' replied Napoleon, shoving his hand back into his waistcoat, which he often did out of habit.

'This is it!' Houdini bashed the door of the broom cupboard with his wrist chains. 'Hey... *Hoopla... Hoopy!* Are you awake? Oi, shake a leg! You haven't snuffed it, have you?' He knocked again and gave the bottom of the door a sharp kick with the irons on his feet. The noise was enough to wake the dead.

A muffled reply was heard: "Ere. Let me out, matey, and I'll soon tell ya!'

'Stand well back, folks. This could well be hazardous!' warned Houdini. Cautiously, he then unlocked the cupboard door.

'*A-whoosh... Ba-ang... Kerr-ash... Wallop!*'

The door flew wide open, half off its hinges with an explosive roar. A pile of brushes, brooms, mops, and buckets flew out, clattering to the floor. A large, whirling, furry figure somersaulted out of the cupboard with a thunderous crash, scattering dustpans, vacuum cleaners, and packets of cleaning powder in its wake. It knocked Napoleon down for six, pinning him against the wall. It then spun in a flash along the passage and into the room at an astonishing speed.

Houdini, Chance, and an extremely winded French emperor – clutching his hat for dear life – chased after the whirling dervish.

'Uh-huh... *Mon sacre dieu!*' exclaimed Napoleon breathlessly. 'It's that marsupial! *Je suis comprendez* now. *Purse... Pouch... Flexible.* Oh yes, *mes amis*, it's a very big jumping beast – indeed, *mais oui!*'

For standing in the doorway, with his right arm leaning nonchalantly against the frame of the door, with his left knee casually crooked over the right, was the largest kangaroo wearing bright red boxing gloves they had ever seen.

'Hi there, me ol' mateys! Am I glad you pommies came along,' it said happily. The furry brown animal began to shake some white washing powder off its ears, making Chance sneeze violently.

'*A-a-ah... Atch-OOO!* And what the blazes is *THAT* ?!' yelled Chance, stunned out of his wits. Together, they ducked in amazement under the animal's outstretched arm to reach the safety of the room.

Then nonplussed, Houdini announced, 'Folks, meet Hoopy Hoopla, the Aussie Kick-Flick Boxing Champion of South East Asia. This here is the famous *Hoopy* – King Golden Gloves of the South Pacific – old Ned was bragging about capturing the other day!'

The kangaroo flexed his bulging biceps and bowed to the ground theatrically, the tips of his ears kissing the floor. 'Pleased to meet ya, folkies! So good on yah!'

'Er... Hoopy,' said Houdini. 'We're told on good authority that you, being a world expert in Far Eastern fisticuffs, could teach our harlequin chum here a thing or two on how to look after himself. Chancy here has got the knowledge, and even a bit of power, but not much else.'

They told him of Cecil-the-Thin's visit via Aladdin's empty lamp.

'Ah,' said Hoopy, scratching his nose with the back of his glove. 'You mean the secrets of the ancient Chinese art of Toe Hee Do?'

'*Toe Hee*... what? Sounds like an oriental chiropodist or something equally as daft,' Chance repeated, wondering if he heard correctly in the first place.

'Yup... *Toe Hee Do!* Me old sporty. Nuffing to it, matey. It's like falling out of a blooming tree backwards. Anyhow, since yer asked, I fink it means *The Ultimate Way of the Wriggling Fist*... or summat like that!' the animal quickly explained.

'No kidding! But whatever it's called, can you teach me the basic skills of the art of its science?' pleaded Chance imploringly.

'Maybe, me ol' pommy. But what's in it for me?' The kangaroo began to jump and bounce, heeling and toeing on the spot like a human yo-yo about to warm up in the gym.

'Well, we can keep you out of the broom cupboard for a start. And help you to escape out of the clutches of the porters if you like,' replied Houdini temptingly. 'And oh, you can have a pile of these as well for starters.' Scooping a handful of nuts and grapes from Cleopatra's bowl, Houdini thrust them into Hoopy's open gloves.

'Okey dokey. One's easily persuaded. You've twisted me arm so to speak, me ol' cobber!' The kangaroo took off his gloves and popped some of the nuts into his mouth and stuffed the rest of the food down into his pouch. Using his lithe and powerful limbs, he started to clear a space for his demonstration. He kicked a couple of the long benches aside with his massive rudder-like feet, as if he were merely flicking away an irritating insect. 'Hey, gimmee yer hand, Mr Harleyfriend!'

Trustingly, Chance stuck out his right hand towards the animal.

Suddenly, there was an explosive *ker-aash!* – followed by a thundering *whaam!* ... Then a dull, leaden thud, as if the roof had caved in. Faster than a streak of lightning, Chance was thrown high into the air. He somersaulted twice and then was dumped unceremoniously onto his backside, landing with an almighty bang at the foot of Rip Van Winkle's four-poster bed.

Houdini and Napoleon were quite impressed and gave a little round of applause. Joan of Arc, deeply irritated at being disturbed, hissed at them to be quiet, whereas Cleopatra nonchalantly carried on snoozing regardless.

'Never, never... *never ever,*' tut-tutted Hoopy Hoopla, as he sternly shook his fingers from side to side in front of the harlequin's dazed face. 'Yer must never, ever give ya hand naively to a stranger you've only just met!' he lectured sternly. 'That's... vital lesson *number one!*'

Acutely embarrassed, Chance was helped up to his feet by Houdini and Napoleon, each pulling an arm. Red-faced, he straightened up his crumpled clothes. Sheepishly, he stared into space, his eyes half-glazed.

He stared at his feet, po-faced and a little ashamed.

'So, whatever ya do, never forget this!' lectured Hoopy.

'*One: the power of the mind is more powerful than the body.*

Two: the power of belief, that yar can do it, is much more powerful than one of self-doubt.

And finally, three: cunning and speed are always much more devastating than simple brute strength.'

'Oh! Silly ol' me, nearly forgot. If this doesn't work, then *cheat!*' he added with a smirk. 'Now stand well back, and watch me very carefully, me ol' pommy old pals...!'

In a space of fifty minutes or so, Hoopy Hoopla went through a whole range of amazing steps, holds, kicks, punches (even a powerful 'half-inch' push) and devastating trick-flips with his head, tail, body, and limbs. Masterfully, he gave them a remarkable demonstration of his ability, agility and prowess in the fighting arts, known to its chosen exponents as *Toe Hee Do*, handed down through centuries by the grandmaster of it all, Wisendrama-the-Cunning. Examples of his dynamic skills were shown to be awesome. His mastery of every trick in the book to confound an opponent was supreme. It was not hard to see why Hoopy Hoopla won championships in Korea, Japan, Thailand and even on Australia's Bondi Beach with such consummate ease.

Once they had gathered their wits, he spent the next couple of hours teaching Chance the subtle, further intricacies of these incredible skills.

After a little while, Hoopy said, 'Now. Look closely at me right hand, me ol' cobber?' An outstretched paw was offered, stuck right under his nose.

Chance kept his eye firmly on it but resisted to take it, thinking, *If he thinks I'm going to fall for this one a second time, he must think me extremely stupid or born just yesterday.*

Carefully, he watched the kangaroo's paws without letting them out of his sight. Then, without warning: '*whaam! Wallop. Thwack!*' Chance's legs were knocked clean from beneath him by a sweep of Hoopy's powerful hind legs, which spun close to the ground at a phenomenal speed without his even noticing them.

'Tut-tut. No! *No*... Never *ever*... And I stress the importance of lesson *number two*, me ol' matey... *never* just concentrate solely on *one* part of your opponent's anatomy!'

Hoopy spat a pile of nutshells out of his mouth with disgust. They rattled across the floor, echoing all over the room.

Now absolutely, furious with himself for falling into the trap for a second time, Chance slapped the floor with the flat of his hands angrily. With grim determination to prove himself this time, he picked himself up and braced his body – *ready*.

'Now show me what you can do, Mr Fancy Chancy!' challenged Hoopy, swishing his tail like a dangerous python. Effortlessly the kangaroo rushed at him, bouncing up into the air, almost grazing the ceiling. His powerfully strong back legs and truncheon-like tail came flailing at him thirteen to the dozen with an incredibly loud *boing... bo-ang*, finishing with an explosive *twang!* that would have normally concussed a raging bull spotting a red rag.

Dextrously, Chance dodged him with split-second timing. He side-stepped the flying kangaroo, missing him by a whisker. Flipping in a tailspin six foot into the air, he knocked Hoopy down with a massive crack, spinning in full flight. Then he descended, floating gracefully to the ground feet first.

'Ooh. Ah! Well done, me ol' sporty. That's goo... good on ya!' gasped Hoopy, breathless with excitement. 'Congrats, ol' Harley! I'm dead impressed. The pupil can now teach the teacher!' Without letting up, he threw himself at Chance head-on with the power of a rhino charging when riled, which in normal circumstances would have flattened a fifty-stone sumo wrestler in the ring.

Chance held firm like an immovable rock, his boots glued to the floor. Immediately, he twiddled his nose rapidly anticlockwise. Then his body rose two feet off the ground. His outstretched hands grew wide as shovels, met Hoopy halfway off the ground, who had flown at him at over a hundred miles per hour like a mammalian-guided missile.

An ear-wrenching bang was heard as their bodies collided. Hoopy bounced off him, as if there was a brick wall built invisibly in the air. Flung backwards from the impact, he landed almost on top of a shocked and surprised Cleopatra.

'Holy crocs! By heck, that's brill, man... you've got it. By me ol' granny's back teeth, you've got it!' Hoopy gulped in buckets of air, taking in massive gasps with each breath. 'Huh. Uh-uh... Yer see, it's dead simple if ya know how.

'Well, that's it, folks. Lesson over! You've got it. By Sheila, you've got it!' Ruefully Hoopy rubbed his head. 'Yup siree... Okey pokey. Speed and guile will make ya smile...!' He grinned laconically at the harlequin. Then he began to smooth his ruffled fur. 'Ya can now buzz off and try to save the blinkin' world if ya want to now me ol' matey!'

Chance shrugged helplessly, rolling his eyes.

'Ah ha, yer know, there ya go. You'll be okay. Yer got the *knowledge*. Yer got the *power*. If yer got the *wit*... you've got the *guile*. And even better, matey, *you've got the smile!*' Glancingly, Hoopy gave Chance a friendly slap on the back, which almost sent him flying across the hallway. His grin broadened while he pointed to the harlequin's face, as he gave him his final instructions. 'What's more, all the world loves a funny joker. So sock it to 'em, pal. Make 'em laugh! And they'll all laugh with ya! So good luck on ya, cobber... *I'm off*, before that bumbling Brumble tries to take me prisoner, ol' sport!'

Hoopy Hoopla hopped and somersaulted out of the room, leaving in its trail total chaos with Napoleon spread-eagled flat against the wall. He bounced and spun along the passage and down the stairs towards the exit, giving the broom cupboard a derisory kick in passing.

Chance could not wait a minute more to make his escape. His newly found friends just hovered in the background, looking rather sad and dejected, but accepting the fact of their having to stay put.

'Wait a minute, I want to thank you for—!' shouted Chance, over his shoulder.'

'Hey. Hold on!' shouted Houdini after him as an afterthought. 'Oi, hey, stupid! That's the wrong way – you'll end up in the Chamber of Horrors!' Houdini's voice dwindled away.

Houdini started to inspect Aladdin's now-empty lamp, which had now been discarded under a bench. He sniffed at it. The faint smell left there reminded him of the wispy spirit of Cecil-the-Thin, who had long disappeared.

Then with that, he pleaded, 'Chance, my good friend, if, and when you discover the *"Secret of Life"* that skinny Cecil talked about, could you quickly return and help us to live again, please?' He rattled his manacles in front of Chance's nose in frustration to remind him.

'*Et mon ami*, don't forget us, please,' Napoleon reminded him urgently.

Chance crept quietly down the stairs, following Houdini's instructions to the letter. He managed to push open the emergency exit without a hitch and then rapidly ran into the street. At the first gulp of the fresh night air, he felt intoxicated with its crispness. It was in sharp contrast to the stifling smell of the wax and suffocating heat from the lights of the airless museum he had just left behind. His sturdy red boots with his giant strides carried him quickly to the main Cromwell Road. A cacophony of sound from the never-sleeping city greeted him. In the distance a siren of an ambulance wailed by. A couple of welcome drops of rain fell on to his upturned face.

The hum of steady traffic swelled the background noise, which was only interrupted by the odd car or shop alarm going off now and then. No sooner had his eyes got used to the sudden shock of being outside in adjusting to the battery of flashing signs above shops and advertising, when he heard a police car siren screaming as it approached. Instinctively, Chance jumped into the nearest doorway, which happened to be a betting shop whose windows were covered in blown-up pictures of horse racing. He froze like a statue with his back to the door and kept perfectly still, trying to melt into the background.

The police car passed the shop and suddenly stopped, its tyres squealing, leaving a chunk of rubber on the road. It abruptly reversed so that it was parallel with the doorway.

'Eh, Charlie, isn't that a statue or maybe a dead body or something?' the police officer in the passenger seat yelled to the driver. 'We'd better have a look.' They both got out of their vehicle, leaving its blue roof lights flashing.

''Ello... 'ello! Now what have we 'ere? ...Cor blimey, Charlie, it's a real proper model of a flipping clown – a harlequin or something. It's brand new and all!' He gave it a little kick on the boots as if testing it for signs of life.

Charlie, the police driver, replied with a gruff, 'Oh yeah. Better take it in to lost property down at the station before it scarpers.'

Together, they lifted the figure onto the back seat and drove away westwards towards Paddington at full speed.

'Reckon it's worth a few bob or two, this dummy, eh, Charlie? Do you think it's been nicked or something?'

His colleague replied in a dull, bored voice, 'Yeah. Probably. They'll nick anything these days, even your old grandmother, unless bolted to the floor.'

By the time the patrol car had reached its destination, the two officers had finished their duty for the night. The duty sergeant told them that the lost property office was closed for security until the morning, but they could stick the dummy in one of the cells for the time being for security.

'Yeah, Charlie, I reckon it's safer in one of the cells,' came the droll comment.

The heavy iron gates of the cell were slammed shut with a solitary clunk, giving an air of finality about it. It left the harlequin a lonely figure, now abandoned and lying flat on his back on a stark wooden bunk with only a smelly old blanket for company.

Chapter 12

THAT LONG WAIT HOME

IT HAD BEEN A long wait at home for Sassy. Agonisingly, the hours and minutes had dragged by slowly. With each second ticking by, her worry and distress over the theft of the harlequin increased to fever pitch. As yet, there was no news of him or of her car. She looked at the kitchen clock over the stove for the umpteenth time. Even Mudd the cat was getting restless, as she kept padding in and out of the cat flap, time and time again.

'Ring... Bur-ring... rr-ing... ring!' The telephone ringing all of a sudden startled her. Sassy rushed to pick up the handset, knocking it over in her hurry.

'Yes... yes. Who's that? Is that...? Oh, it's you, Eddie. No. No news yet. It's already ten past ten. Of course, I'll let you know... as soon as there's news. And thanks for the offer of your help with your van. Yes. I hope so too. Thanks. Bye.'

After breakfast, increasingly distraught, she had telephoned her father's office and had spoken to Eddie about the missing car and its occupant during the night. Loyal Eddie Boltinqs who had worked for her father Hubert for many, many years in charge of transport, had offered to drive Sassy to collect her car, whenever it was found.

Impatiently, she sat under the clock, willing the minute hand to move faster than it did. As it reached almost half past ten, the telephone rang again. She grabbed it quickly and answered urgently.

'Yes… speaking. Oh… what? You've found him. *What?* He's been at the police station at Paddington for half the night! Oh, thank you. Thank heavens! Yes, I'll bring a sketch of him for identity. I'll get there as soon as I can! Thanks again.'

Sassy was over the moon. The police had telephoned to say that they had located what they called her "lost property" at Paddington. But so far, they'd had no luck so far about her stolen car. She telephoned Eddie immediately, who sped over in a large white transit van. Together they raced off to collect her missing figure.

'Lucky you turned up, Miss,' said the duty officer. 'One of our patrol cars found your property stuck in a doorway of a turf accountant in the West End. Erm, I mean a betting shop!' Then he added quickly, 'They nearly took it to that waxworks place – you know, Madame thingy-me-bobs – thinking it belonged to them. But then, luckily for you, they changed their minds and brought it in here. Anyway, follow me, Miss. We've had to put it into one of the overnight cells as it was too big to fit inside one of the lost property cupboards.'

Her face creased with uncertainty thinking of the worst. Then with some trepidation, they followed the officer to the back of the station to the cell block. Sure enough, inside holding cell number one, laid out flat on one of the wooden benches was Chance, her harlequin. He cut a forlorn figure as Sassy peeped at him through the bars. 'Why have you locked him in?' she asked with dismay.

The duty officer started to unlock the cell door. 'Oh, it's just a precaution, Miss. Didn't really expect this "stiff" to hardly run away, if you know what I mean,' he replied with a laconic grin. 'It's just routine precaution – daren't take a chance, in case he's valuable.'

Carefully Sassy lifted the figure off the bench. And she was so overwhelmed that he had not been damaged or come to grief that she gave him a hug, much to the embarrassment of Eddie and the officer. 'Oh, he *is* extremely valuable, Officer, as you say,' she explained rapidly, ignoring their bemusement.

Sassy and Eddie manoeuvred the harlequin out of the narrow cell, each holding on to his arms.

After signing for the safe receipt of her property, Sassy and Eddie carefully placed the figure at the back of the van and then set off back to Sassy's home. She pleaded with Eddie to drive carefully to avoid shaking him up further to add to his recent ordeal.

'Look, Miss. Don't mind me saying so – I know he's so life-like – but with due respect, Miss, he's only a dummy model, you know.'

Sassy held her tongue, for she didn't want to get into an argument with Eddie, who had been so helpful. Just then, a broad smile broke across her face as their van turned into

Westhope Terrace. 'Well, Chance, old friend, home at last!' she murmured whilst opening the door to her family home. 'Thanks, Eddie, I don't know how I would have managed it on my own, especially with Dad and Mum being away.'

'It's okay, Miss. Glad to oblige.' Carefully, he lifted the figure into the hallway. 'Do you want some help to carry it upstairs?'

'Oh, would you, Eddie? I would really appreciate the help.' And so, between them, they bodily carried the figure up to the first floor via the long, steep Victorian staircase to the front bedroom.

'Oh, by the way, Miss, I don't know if you noticed, but one of your neighbours, opposite was staring at us out of her window with what looks like a tiny pair of binoculars or something – poking through the curtains!'

'Oh, ignore her, Eddie. She's the street's busybody... doesn't miss a thing. She's got nothing else to do but spy on everyone!'

'Cor. Strike me! Has he got lead in his boots? He's not half heavy, Miss,' said Eddie, puffing noisily through clenched teeth. He put the figure down feet first, then happened to glance across the room towards the bay. He thought he was seeing things. Because sitting there in front of the window was not just one, but *two* further life-size figures! His heart lurched into his mouth, which opened and shut like a giant toad. He had heard from his boss, Hubert Goodall, that his artistic daughter Saskia had a wild imagination, but this took the prize.

'Oh, by the way, meet the rest of the family,' joked Sassy with a mischievous grin filled with pride. 'This is Henry... *Henry de Poisson!*' She waved airily to the left.

The extremely smart figure was dressed immaculately in a black dinner jacket, black silk bow tie, over a crisp-starched, white dress shirt and winged collar. In his right eye, he gripped a monocle and a silver fob watch and chain in his waistcoat pocket. His long moustache glistened in the daylight with its waxed tips tapering, curled up at the ends. It matched his ginger-red hair, which was slickly parted down the middle with hair gel.

Mesmerised, Eddie went up to him and examined him closely. 'Is he supposed to be that person on the telly or someone or other, Miss? No, wait a mo'... I mean that stuffy butler fella, you know, what's-a-name?'

Sassy threw back her head, shook her hair and let out a laugh.

Playfully, he patted Henry de Poisson on the head.

'Yes, Eddie, I know exactly what *you* mean.' Sassy interrupted him before he got carried away. She managed to divert his attention by hurriedly pointing to the female figure sitting in a velvet-covered armchair next to Henry. 'And this is Henry's partner, Miss Davinia Angelica Plum,' she announced firmly.

For a relatively shy man, his reaction was rather out of character. 'Wow. Strike me! She's a bit of stunner...!' Eddie commented with a gulp and a whistle.

'If you don't mind my saying so, Miss, she's got a... er, smashing figure in that black evening gown! But where did she get this incredible jewellery from?' Getting carried away, he boldly fingered the glittering diamante necklace, earrings and bracelet draped around the beautifully made-up figure.

'Oh, my mother makes them. She's a jewellery designer,

you know. But the tiara is a fake – costume or junk jewellery!' Sassy fiddled nonchalantly with it on top of Davinia's rich auburn hair that had been impeccably styled with hairspray. Pausing for a moment, she gave the tiara a little polish with the end of her sleeve.

He moved nearer to the window so that he could take a closer, longer look at Davinia Plum's beautiful face. He stuck his nose quite close to hers, which was tiny, slim, and turned up pertly at the tip. Despite the brilliant makeup of long black eyeliner and highlights of blush on her high cheekbones, there was a cold, disdainful look about her. 'Hey, Miss,' he said, moving away. 'She looks a bit like that—'

'Don't tell me!' protested Sassy, interrupting, waving in the air dismissively.

Eddie stared on, transfixed by all this. It was surreal and somewhat overwhelming. Suddenly, he shook his head, as though to wake himself up from a trance. 'Must be getting along, Miss, as the office is extremely busy… and especially with your father being away on holiday. By the way, when are you going, Miss?'

'I'm actually off tonight by train through the tunnel. I should reach my folks' friend's place by the morning,' she sighed. 'You know I'm so lucky that they found my harlequin in time. Oh, Eddie, before I forget, thanks a million for all your help.'

He started to leave by the stairs, still in a bit of a daze. He spun round to face her and grinned. 'I'll let myself out… happy holidays then!' Immediately, he slammed the door shut.

Now that Eddie was out of the house, Sassy patted

the harlequin on the hand, gesturing in the direction of the rest of the figures in the bedroom. 'Now, Chance, my fancy Chance, meet the rest of the family!' she proudly exclaimed. 'Davinia, Henry, I want you to meet a brilliant newcomer to our home. This is Chance… *lucky Chance* – the best harlequin in the world!

'Oh, hello Muddie,' greeted Sassy as her pet cat bumped against her ankles. She gave her an affectionate stroke. Then she picked her up. 'We've got some more company. This is Chance – my favourite.' She rubbed the cat's nose against the harlequin's. They stared at each other with curiosity, the cat sniffing the air warily between them.

'Look. He's definitely rather special, don't you think?' Sassy pulled back the floppy tie around the figure's neck to expose the precious pendant she had made. Mudd chirped and let out a meow as if in agreement. Then she promptly leapt like a rocket out of Sassy's arms and landed as light as a feather at the harlequin's feet, whereupon she immediately intertwined herself between his legs, purring loudly.

'Pilar will look after you all, dear gang, while I'm away,' said Sassy with a sweep of the hand. 'She'll call every day to feed old Muddie.' She then tickled the cat's ears reassuringly.

'I know, I've got a brilliant idea!' Supressing a giggle, she turned the harlequin to face the front window. 'That'll stare that Nosy Parker to death while I'm away!'

No sooner had she said that than the telephone suddenly rang, interrupting her. The police had rung to let her know that her old car had been found and had been taken safely into the car pound. As this was less of a priority now that Chance had been recovered, she told them that she would collect it when she got back from France.

'Don't worry about a thing, Miss. You have a nice holiday. Your car will be well looked after till you get back,' came the reply. Reassured, she put the phone down.

Mudd rolled onto her back for her tummy to be tickled. Sassy did so obligingly, saying playfully, 'You bad cat. Of course, I'm going to miss you. But you mustn't hold me up. I've got to finish packing ready for the night train. It's a long journey to the Dordogne and I've got to change trains. So, don't worry your silly old head. Pilar will keep an eye on you, I promise. I'll see you soon.' She rubbed the cat's head, then abruptly turned on her heels and went to pack her bags.

At 7pm on the dot, a local taxi called to collect Sassy to take her to the Eurostar. She ran upstairs two treads at a time to say goodbye to Muddie and her friends. 'Bye, old gang. Do behave yourselves and look after Muddie for me, won't you?' As she brushed past the harlequin, she couldn't resist planting a kiss on his nose. A profound sense of relief came over her. Her favourite figure had been safely found. After all, he could have been dismembered by thieves and villains, then melted down for wax candles after his timber frame had been chopped up for firewood. She shivered at the gruesome thought.

Increasingly impatient, the taxi driver honked his horn in the street below.

'Hang on. I'm coming!' she yelled, sticking her head out of the window. As a final gesture, affectionately, she flicked the back of Chance's head and patted the stray bits of hair to one side. 'Now, be a good pal and don't go walkies!' She wagged her finger at him teasingly, repeating what Dave Fellows had said when leaving the college. Then she quickly added, 'You're safe as houses in here. It's a big, dark world outside and we don't want you lost again, do we, now? So bye bye, old chum. I'll miss you – I'll miss the whole lot of you.'

Quickly rushing, she grabbed her coat and picked up her bags. She closed the door and then jumped into the cab, which roared away impatiently to catch the evening train.

Part III

Whilst they're away, the cat will play.
Tomorrow's just another day.

Chapter 13

WHILST THEY'RE AWAY, THE CAT WILL PLAY

A NOTHER NIGHT FELL QUICKLY, quicker than most when strange things happen one after another in rapid succession. And so, it seemed at the Goodall household, where the very bricks and mortar of its hollow walls bore witness to extraordinary happenings since the house was erected some one hundred and fifty years ago. How many ghosts or spirits, whether benign, content or tortured, had passed through the doors, floors and ceilings of this ordinary family house from days gone by? If only walls could speak; they could tell an amazing story of unusual events that passed their lips before, to yet more incredible adventures of the present… and stranger yet to come.

This night should have been no different to the others that had gone before it, in its tales and secrets not yet told. But there again, nothing, and no one in his wildest dreams did bargain for the arrival of a figure by chance. And when it did, the most peculiar of things began to happen – *as it always does* – particularly during the night... and, of course, *especially* with the people of the house having just gone away.

Suddenly, a plaintive meow was heard. Mudd, curious as ever, brushed past the harlequin's big red boots. Her feline senses detected something stirring in the limbs of the newcomer to the house. The cat raised her tiny head and tried to attract his attention, blinking rapidly with her good left eye. But there was no reaction from the figure. Its steely eyes did not move a jot. Neither, in fact, did Mudd's eye on the right, twitch at all to life.

Sadly, the right side of her face had been paralysed in a road accident with a bus seven years ago, when, as a young foolhardy kitten, she wandered carelessly all over the streets of the area. And so as result of this fateful accident, she was left with a lopsided jaw and a reedy meow – more like a strangled chirp from the back of her throat whenever she opened her mouth. As previously mentioned, her broken pelvis and damaged hind legs were expertly repaired by the brilliant skills of Mr Findlay Bird, the popular vet from Paddington in a series of intricate operations. Mudd, the incredible survivor, had eight of her nine lives left to fight another day, also had a friend, who, strange to say, was one of the feathered kind. It was, in fact, a woodpecker – affectionately called Zoot, whom she had met whilst fighting over a stray field mouse in the garden a couple of summers ago.

Zoot the woodpecker was an exceedingly large green woodpecker indeed. He was over thirteen inches tall – in fact, the size of a large tomcat on the prowl. His splendid plumage was green above with some downy-yellow under his belly. His magnificent head was crowned in red feathers interspersed with jet-black streaks running down his nape surrounding his mouth, and so giving the impression of a fixed wide grin. He had a long sharp beak of silver-grey, with black and red beady eyes that protruded out like juicy, ripe blackcurrants dangling on a stalk, blinking rapidly.

Against the run of nature, it was of course, strange and unusual that a cat should make friends with a bird. But then, Mudd had never been able to catch them due to her twisted jaw and bandy legs. Therefore, it became more sensible that she befriended them instead... and so it was, especially with Zoot, of whom she was rather in awe. He appeared to be so worldly and wise; so knowledgeable about the life in the countryside, as well as so very streetwise in the cities around them. He seemed to be clued up about everything – well, almost everything.

'Tap-a-ter. Tap-a-ter. Tap. Tap. Tap!'

It was a bird's beak drumming loudly on a rigid surface, coming from the direction of the garden. In an instant, Mudd recognised the coded signal knocking on the cat flap in the kitchen door.

'Well. Hell-ew! Have they gone away? Is the coast all-clear?' Zoot came hopping in on one leg on to the tiles of the kitchen floor. Sadly, he was a bit of a cripple like the cat. Perhaps that was why in the unspoken code of the animal kingdom they became bosom pals – their having a bond of disability in common between them.

The woodpecker had unfortunately lost one of his legs in a pigeon cull, which had used instant sticky glue in a trap on one of the buildings around Trafalgar Square four summers ago. A flight back to the woods from whence he came, ended in disaster as he was hounded from tree to tree, pillar to post, by jays and magpies who picked on him as a freak. After fleeing the countryside, he lived for a while in a hollow of a decaying oak tree in the gardens of Kensington Palace and fed on tit bits from the Royal kitchens by a beautiful princess who once lived there. From there, he flew to Hyde Park, before settling in the sanctuary of a large elm tree in the communal gardens of Paddington behind Westhope Terrace, which became his new home.

Fresh grubs, fat insects and juicy berries were abundant in the well-stocked urban gardens. Dry shelter and food were plentiful. Zoot's present life could not be sweeter. He had literally fallen on his feet. Oh, but then in his case... on his *single, solitary* foot.

'I want to have a proper bird's-eye view of the newcomer to the house. I believe he's *different* to the rest of them,' he announced with a greeting of self-assurance. He gave the cat a friendly pat on the head with the tip of his wing as he fluttered by.

'He's wooden and dead rigid!' chorused the others from upstairs.

Zoot flew up the stairs landing with a crash on the harlequin's left shoulder. Mudd followed him into the room, the bell on her collar tinkling away. Zoot then attempted to peck into the harlequin's cheek without success. Then he tried his left leg, creeping up and down it, gripping with his razor-sharp claws as if it were a trunk of a tree. 'Oh, he's solid as oak all right!' he exclaimed, as his beak skidded off the harlequin's body.

'Ah-hah! Ancient… mm… most ancient old wood, I do believe. Could be a hundred, if not a thousand years old from a tiny taste of it,' he postulated to a very astounded cat who was hovering near the door. 'Strewth! No sap at all. Dry as old timber!' He spat it out, banging his beak against the harlequin's shoulder as though he had grubs stuck on it.

Chance's eyes spun to the left, glaring with hostility.

Increasingly curious, Zoot flapped his wings beating in time, whilst trying to keep his balance. He stuck his beak right in front of the harlequin's nose and gave him a nudge. 'I wonder if this dummy is really dead or alive.'

'Is he in some form of suspected allegation?' asked Mudd.

'Nope, you dopey, muddled cat! I think you mean *suspended animation!* But whoa! Hang on a mo! Now he *does* remind me of *something* I've heard of in the past from *someone*,' said Zoot, drumming his toes impatiently. 'Now let me think… erm… recently. Now… what was it? It's on the tip of my beak. It's something that is *vitally* important to us. Yes, for you and me, Muddie, and thousands of others like us. You see, this dummy couldn't have just been sent here by accident, could he now?'

Mudd tossed her head in agreement. 'No, of course not! Miss Sassy brought him here with that man, Eddie.'

'Oh, I know that you, furry little idiot. What I meant was that *he's* arrived here out of thin air for a reason. There's a kind of secret mystery about him, I'm sure. Now what the heck was it now…?' Zoot tried to scratch his head with the tip of his wing. Then he did a little dance around the harlequin's head, staring at him as if under a microscope…

'Um-er. Wait a minute. In the faint distant past, I do seem to recall a legend of sorts. I heard it when I was born. Erm… something like – *all living creatures around us were hoping and waiting for a sort of champion – a kind of leader – to… er… emerge…to band us together, and to save us from being wiped out.* But hold on. Can that be right? Or did they mean save the planet, or did they mean…? Oh, blast. It's gone again!'

In the meantime, Chance had kept extremely quiet and still as a frozen statue. His rosy cheeks began to puff out, ready to explode in frustration about being discussed so coldly like a slab of meat. He was tempted to take a swipe at the cocky woodpecker, who seemed to talk such a lot for a bird. But he bit his tongue and waited. Then he continued to stare out of the window.

Suddenly, a feather stood up like a beacon on top of Zoot's head in a flash of inspiration. He had just remembered his old pal Wise Black Crow, who lived in the countryside. 'Of course, stone the crows!' exclaimed Zoot, flapping his wings in excitement. 'He'd know just about *everything* there was to know about the way of the world and about the animal kingdom.' A grin broke out across his beak. 'Well, that's sorted, Muddie. We can always ask my old mate, young Black Crow, for his wise advice. I'm sure he can jog my memory about the missing gaps in the tale, which we were told when we were young. And even better still, perhaps he can tell us now how to defrost this stubborn statue!'

And so, the very mention of his old country friend stirred up a bout of nostalgia for joyous days long gone by. He suddenly went into a sort of dreamlike state – you could have sworn he was hypnotised. He tilted his magnificent red plumage on the crown of his head and plunged his beak into the downy-green feathers of his chest. Then he half-closed his eyes. Soon, he was lost in a warm, pleasant daydream down memory lane…

Chapter 14

A TRIP DOWN MEMORY LANE

'ARHH… Z-z-z-z…' THERE WAS a rasping sound like a drain rumbling from the woodpecker's throat. Zoot had been transported back in time. Wonderful memories of his previous carefree life in the country, hundreds of miles from the big city, at once flooded back to him with warmth and happiness.

He started to chuckle broadly to the bemused cat, who gaped up at him, completely thunderstruck. 'Gosh, those were the days, my furry four-legged friend!' he said patronisingly.

'What a glorious place it was, where I grew up, dear cat. *Pure paradise!* You know, I once lived in a lovely little hole in a large horse chestnut tree, cushioned by soft moss in a magical bluebell wood with my parents.' Zoot's eyelids started to blink, as he drifted in and out of a delirious dream.

'…In those long, hot summers, all around us were scores of cabbage white butterflies and golden-honeyed bumblebees with copper-tinted dragonflies buzzing away in the sunlight. Wild rabbits would carelessly romp around chasing their tails. Nosy badgers and chubby-cheeked dormice darted around the undergrowth safely playing happily. Whereas at the edge of the wood, families of hedgehogs would ferret for big juicy caterpillars and fat crispy beetles amongst the rugs of lemon-yellow primroses under the hedgerows.'

Soon, his eyes glazed over in pure nostalgia. 'Ah, but the best bit of it all, my dear city cat, was the incomparable smell of the fresh dew in the leafy dell after the rain from the night before on the leaves of the shrubs and wildflowers… *Invigorating. Unbeatable…*'

Impatiently, Mudd thumped her tail against the carpet as Zoot broke out in poetry. He was perched on the edge of the bed spouting forth. In a fit of pique, she dragged at the bed covers with her outstretched claws and pulled them to the floor. 'Hang on. How come you befriended a crow of *all* birds? I thought that *they* were your sworn enemy?… Being carrion – I heard that they were extremely vicious, such as eating other baby birds and stealing eggs from their nests and all that.'

Flapping about, Zoot hummed and hawed defensively. 'Well… You know, *he* wasn't like the rest of them. Young Black Crow was different. From an early age, he revealed remarkable wisdom: hence the nickname "*Wise*". He appeared to develop a kind of sixth bird sense.

'You see, the Crow family was a sort of neighbour of ours. Young Black Crow lived with his folks on top of the tallest tree in the forest next to the woods where we lived.

'It was there that our friendship really took off. But in the beginning, both sets of parents were dead against it.'

'What! Because you were both birds from different places?'

'No, you silly puss. It wasn't just that. Both our families were prejudiced, bigoted, old-fashioned fuddy-duddies.'

A puzzled look creased the cat's lopsided face.

Reluctantly, Zoot tried to explain. 'It was because we were from *different* species – *different* backgrounds and *different* colours, you see. For instance, I was red, green, and yellow, a patchwork of multicolours. Whereas young Crow was jet black, pure as glistening coal. We were racially judged on the colour of our feathers. Rather stupid and narrow-minded, don't you think?'

Suddenly, he was rudely interrupted. An irritating humming started near the window. Davinia Angelica Plum was singing aloud on purpose. She was tapping her fingers in tune against the glass trying to provoke him.

'Birds of a feather stick stupidly together.
Those of a kind are just as blind.
Birds like fowl are foul with words.
And crows or woodpeckers talking are just absurd.
Their wings to be clipped – being only fit to be shot,
Then de-feathered and boiled for supper in pots!'

Murderously, Zoot glared at her whilst trying to ignore her. 'We had a glorious time then. But all that soon changed by the time I left. Oh, what a calamity!' groaned Zoot miserably, as though the whole world had suddenly fallen on his tufted head.

'And how things changed in the glorious countryside of yesteryear! It was a shocking scandal. Hedgerows, bushes, and vast acres of forest were deliberately burnt or cut down to make bigger, flatter fields for easier, intensive farming. A whole variety of trees – the lungs of the earth, were felled to make way for roads and houses. And swathes of glorious countryside lost forever...'

His eyes began to swim with moisture by merely thinking about it.

But sentiment soon made way for anger. 'Bah. Awful, disgraceful industrial vandalism, I call it... Scores of different species of irreplaceable insects, microbes and grubs from the hedgerows and copses became scarce or extinct. Rare varieties of butterflies, such as the brush-footed peacock and the red admiral, and other unique colonies of insects, like the long-tailed hornet and the brilliantly coloured dragonfly, were wiped out. Their natural habitat, their supporting vegetation was destroyed by the killing use of hundreds of toxic chemicals, herbicides, pesticides, and other poisons. Our lovely woodland where we once lived was stripped and ruined in the name of modern progress. Even rivers, streams and ponds, the lifeblood of all amphibians, became choked with industrial pollutants and plastic waste, fouling all its natural water life, killing off its flora, micro-organisms and hundreds of aquatic creatures.'

Zoot groaned again horribly, as if a dagger had pierced his body in two. 'It was terrible to see. We all felt so helpless. It broke my folks' hearts to see their beautiful home, the peace and tranquillity of nature, so wantonly ripped apart by the greed and thoughtlessness of humans.'

There was a short shudder of helplessness from

Chance, as soon as he heard this, but what could he do in the circumstances?

'What happened after that?' asked Mudd quietly. She tilted her head gently at the woodpecker, who was getting really, distraught by then.

'Well, as soon as I had grown enough, I flew to the city to find food and shelter in the parks and gardens after my parents were shot by poachers. Though, to cap it all off, our home in the horse chestnut was struck by lightning and burnt to the ground.' His pain and anguish were so palpable that there was a deathly lull filling the room.

An awkward moment passed. Then Mudd suddenly leapt onto the bed and tried to distract him. 'No wonder, then, that foxes and other animals deserted the countryside and fled to the urban areas. And do you know, Zoot, that I saw a fox at the back of St Swithin's Church last Sunday, when I was taken there by Miss Saskia for the special animal service?'

'Well, can you blame them? The terrible destruction of the rural lands affected everyone. We are all doomed if this carries on mercilessly like this – unchecked,' added Zoot gravely. There was a huge pause which seemed like an eternity but was much more sombre.

After a length of time, there was a fit of coughing. It was Henry de Poisson trying to clear his throat.

'Does that mean the end of the world?' cried Mudd anxiously.

'*Only* when the sun burns itself out in billions of years from now. And, frankly, there's nothing we mere mortals can do about it!' Henry's terse voice boomed and projected across the room, startling them all.

The cat's fur stood up at the back of her neck. The feathers in the woodpecker's tail ruffled up in an instant. Stress was in the air.

'He's right,' said Zoot wearily with a shrug. 'Why dwell on all this awful doom and gloom that hangs over us in the far-distant future, something we have no control over – when there are more pressing dangers facing us in the here and now?'

'Yes! Hey, perhaps your new visitor, *Mr Precious Fancy Pants*, can help you out of your predicament if *he's* so preciously clever, as that Miss Saskia and you lot all think he is!' sneered Davinia Plum, trying to stir things.

Getting more and more exasperated, tempers were about to erupt. Murder was in the air. And so, Zoot flew over the harlequin's head twice and flicked a wisp of his hair into the air with his beak to serve as a warning for them all. But just then, he thought he saw a sudden flicker of movement in the figure's eyes, as if he had been listening to all that had been going on. So, he fluttered down in front of his face and stared intently... watching, waiting. Then he gave him a sharp peck on the side of his nose. Nothing happened. Then, just as he was about to say something else, they were interrupted by a sudden weird noise, as if something was twanging like a double bass strumming against the back wall of the garden.

Zoot shot downstairs to take a look. 'Phew. Must have got carried away... I almost forgot. It must be a message from Wise Black Crow trying to get through to me from the country by bush telegraph.'

The woodpecker flapped about with great excitement. 'Must hop out and speak to my old friend. Remind me, old puss, I've got to ask him about the ancient legend we talked about when we were little. Must remember to ask him what he would make of our new visitor, this funny old stranger in our midst… also, to see if he knows how to jolt him back to life. And likewise, to find out what he's doing here?'

'But, hey. You're not going to leave Muddie here alone and return to the country, are you, Zoot, my dear birdy-chum?' asked Mudd, in a state of panic.

'Nar! Don't worry your pretty little lopsided head, dear cat. I can speak to my pal Crow from the communal gardens at the back of the house by telegraph message.'

'…*Telegraph*… *T-e-l-e-g-r-a-p-h?* Is that like a "telegram" – like in the old days before computers and the like?' asked Mudd. (She remembered Mr Goodall talking to Miss Saskia about office days in times gone by, when they used telegrams, telexes, typewriters, and other archaic odd things.)

'No, stupid! "*Telegraph messaging*" means exactly what it says. We can speak to one another over long distances, by jumping up and down in variable rhythms on the telegraph wires overhead.'

Instructively, Zoot pointed out the window with the tip of his wing. 'You see, it's a bit like bungee-trampolining, but upside-up… a sort of aviary Morse code, if you like. Heh! I won't be long. Keep an eye on those dummies for me, and make sure they don't fight while I am gone.'

Then, with an enormous bang and a crash, Zoot flew out of the cat flap headfirst, butting it violently against its hinges. He headed for the gardens, nursing a splitting headache. But any old excuse for a chance to gossip to his old pal, Wise Black Crow, perched in the country will do. He looked forward to it.

Chapter 15

RIVAL SENTIMENTALISTS

Now Chance was in two minds whether to run away or stay. It struck him that he could try his luck now that the woodpecker was out of the way. But he would have a job dodging the sharp-eyed cat watching his every move. He thought about it. Then he told himself that it would be rather stupid, for it was pitch black outside. And where would he run to anyway in the dark?

To return to the waxworks would have meant certain death with that loathsome Bert Brumble waiting to catch escapees. It crossed his mind about his old friends, Napoleon and Houdini, and wondered if they had been melted down by now. How he missed their banter, which had kept him on his toes. Just then, he thought of Miss Saskia rather guiltily, and how she would be devastated if he went missing again.

And now, having heard some of the stories from the

woodpecker about the terrible things that were happening to the animal kingdom and the world around them, he thought he'd better stay put and put up with the crazy menagerie for a bit longer. Moreover, what Zoot had said chimed with many of the tales that skinny old Cecil had revealed. And this only added to his worries as to the special role in life that had been carved out for him.

He stuck his nose through the half-drawn curtains. A splinter of light from a weak crescent moon filtered through to bathe his face and lifted his spirits. As he stood motionless in the very same spot where Saskia and Eddie had placed him, a deep yawn began to creep over him. He was about to slip into a snooze, when Zoot came crashing through the cat flap with a thunderous thud. Though somewhat dazed, he flew upstairs nursing his head. Bits of fluff scattered in the air behind him.

'Sorr-ee it took so long. We had a lot to catch up on,' he gulped breathlessly. 'It's tiring jumping in Morse code on that wire with only one leg, you know!' Still, he was grinning from one end of his beak to the other, the red rim of feathers circling his mouth glowed with excitement.

'What did the wise crow say?' Mudd asked eagerly. She scratched her ear with her back paw, concentrating.

Zoot settled onto the harlequin's shoulder. 'Ah yes,' he said, 'he did tell me a story once – a very strange tale, mind you, one which was wrapped up in old folklore and mystique…'

The cat was all ears. Her lopsided tiny face stared agog at the woodpecker, as if he were some sort of feathered god.

'Well, according to him, there exists an ancient legend in the animal kingdom, that for thousands of years the inhabitants have been waiting and waiting for a special and unusual being to turn up as their champion...' said Zoot, quietly. '...You know, a special sort of being, if you like, to help and save them from being wiped off the face of the earth. This unique figure, we are told, would be created out of a plant, tree or something along those lines.'

'A kind of brave leader to stick up for them, do you mean?' asked Mudd.

'Well, yes... sort of. Though if this were true – well, according to my old wise pal, then it, or he, would have to be able to cross over the boundaries of *all* living species. And if this were so, it, or he should be able to communicate – speak in a common language – sort of speak, to those living in the different worlds of humans, animals, fish and insects and so on—'

'And birds?' asked Mudd, a bit concerned for her friend.

'*Naturally*, you, dear daft cat!' snapped Zoot crossly, giving her a sharp rebuke for interrupting. 'Of course, this unique being would have been given special gifts from the day he was created so that he could band them together as a united force to fight against all impending evils of the land that sought to destroy them. Then under his powerful leadership, they would be able to rise up bravely in times of crisis and survive.'

'Crisis...? *What... crisis?*' yowled Mudd, perplexed. A deep frown enveloped her face.

Solemnly, Zoot folded his wings across his chest. Shaking his head, he said, 'Wise Black Crow warned me that the crisis in the animal kingdom today is worse than it was yesterday. Right at this very moment as we speak, terrible dangers are creeping up on us at a frightening speed, threatening our homes and destroying our livelihood. This devastation won't just stop there confined to our own backyard I tell you. Tragically, this is happening all over the world.'

Zoot went quiet for a minute or so, digesting what he and the crow talked seriously about via the telegraph wire. His heart thumped away with his throat parched dry just thinking about it...

'And not only that, but he also reminded me that countless numbers of endangered species are being annihilated by the selfish and cruel hunting by man. For example, look at the horrific killing of the magnificent tiger in the Indian and Siberian subcontinents... as well as the slaughter of the beautiful leopard in Africa. Yes, members of *your* distant relatives, the *cat family*, my dear puss!'

Mudd shivered visibly at the very thought of it. And then went cold all at once, the fur stiffening on her back.

'It's all in the vanity of fashion to use their pelts as coats. And let's not forget the horrific practice of body parts for oriental medicine. This wilful decimation, I tell you, is not confined to just the land but also in our oceans. Many rare species of our whales are disappearing fast at an alarming rate in the name of so-called "scientific research". Yet, these are just a few of the horror stories I could tell you, dear cat. Oh woe betide us! We will all suffer one day... for we in the animal kingdom *cannot* survive this onslaught. If this continues, future generations on earth will never see the likes of these rare and valuable creatures again. *This cataclysmic destruction to our world cannot go on!*'

A solitary teardrop escaped from the Zoot's eye. He tried to suppress a sniffle but failed.

Mudd couldn't contain herself. 'Excuse me, Zoot, are you, by the way, one of those so-called... *drivel... I mean, rival... sentiment... a... lists?* ...Oh, you *must* know what I mean!' The cat got rather muddled with her words.

Zoot stared back vacantly, then launched into another lecture. 'You mean "*environ-ment-alists*", you dopey, four-legged creature! You what! ...Environment... *Environment?* Pah! Enough of that sentimental drivel! It is simple self-preservation to save our skins, as far as I'm concerned!' exclaimed Zoot.

Mudd thought for a moment licking her paw, puzzled. Then she jumped off the bed with a delicate thump.

Zoot continued. 'I know. I know what *you're* thinking. To cross over boundaries and to be able to communicate in a universal language with different species – how is that possible? Well, Muddie, me old friend, underneath the skin of every living organism – all plants, trees, animals, birds, insects, humans and *every* single form of life – *we are all the same!*'

The cat's mouth dropped open in simple amazement.

'And did you know that all living matter on this planet is made out of *identical* units of biological cells? These in turn are made out of smaller units called molecules, which are made of even smaller bits called atoms. Finally, the latter are divided into tiny, minute, electrically charged particles. That is, *negatively charged* electrons, *positively charged* positrons and *neutral* neutrons, all whizzing round each other in space as electricity. Ah, but not only that: all living creatures on earth are also made up of mainly water! In fact, over seventy per cent of their body weight!'

This made the cat gasp, making her chew her tail nervously.

'You and I are *no* different. Birds, cats, men and women, and not forgetting your owner Miss Saskia, her parents, the local vicar from the church at the end of the road, as well as the Prime Minister, the Pope and even Her Majesty the Queen, would you believe it… are all made out of just plain *electricity* and *water – simple*, common-garden electricity and water, and nothing else!'

Zoot was extremely pleased with this amazing scientific pronouncement of his.

Kerr… aack! A crackling sound suddenly rented the air. Just at that very moment, the end of his beak accidentally brushed the tip of the harlequin's ear just as Chance was about to open his mouth. An electric shock of static crackled like a shot and made him jump into the air. The feathers on the top of his head stared up with a bang, as though struck by lightning. And a wisp of hair on the crown of the harlequin stood up starkly, though the mouth clamped shut like a vice, as though a revelation had struck a chord.

Suddenly Mudd got extremely excited. A pile of words rushed out of her mouth, as she started to chatter uncontrollably.

'Wait. Wait. Zoot! I forgot to tell you. In the service last Sunday, the vicar told us that an extraordinary person would come to rescue us. He said he will bring us happiness, make us laugh, unite all forms of living life, and save our planet from disaster. Hey, do you think he meant the *same* one as in *your* story… you know, a champion saviour for our cause…?'

'Possibly? Possibly. But maybe that's just a coincidence!' replied Zoot dismissively, not wishing *her* – just a simple cat – to steal his thunder.

He took off from the harlequin's shoulder and flew in a circle around the room, doing a couple of acrobatic loops like the Red Arrows after flying like a corkscrew upside down.

'But what other secret things did Wise Black Crow tell you?' asked Mudd, now somewhat crushed.

Then, with a noisy plop, Zoot landed on Chance's balding pate, his open claws making him cringe in agony. Loftily, Zoot looked down at them all, as if he were in a pulpit.

'Yes, you're right,' he drawled. 'There's more to tell. My wise crow chum did remind me to tell you that when we were fledglings, we were taught a little poem. Well actually, more like a folksy birdsong that was handed down from generation to generation. We didn't pay much attention to the seriousness of the message in it at the time, being so young. Anyway, it was a sort of every creature's national anthem...'

He cleared his throat and puffed out his chest like an opera singer.

'*For thousands of years,*
We've waited in wait to decide our fate,
For a humble fun one, not man, nor ape,
Will evolve from a tree, no cynical ploy,
Bring happiness and peace with unconditional joy.
No fish, fowl, man or beast will eat each other in feast.
Though Mother Earth, so precious on loan,

Serenity at last, no longer will groan,
Thrust into our midst, oh timbered fat man,
We appeal to your power – help if you can!'

Chance was shaken to the core. His feet trembled in his boots, whereas Zoot's eyes kept blinking repeatedly like a Belisha beacon for a tune kept spinning around inside his head '*Oh timbered fat man… timbered fat man – help if you can!'*

'…*Man? Fat?* Timber – wood? Who or what the blazes does it mean? Hang about – not man nor ape…' thought Zoot aloud. 'Now wait a minute, *surely that…'*

In that instance, Zoot thought he had better examine the harlequin more closely. He hopped skilfully onto Chance's chest, clawing up the buttons on his shirt. Then he vigorously prodded behind the harlequin's bow tie as though digging for worms. With enormous glee, he emerged clutching a silver pendant firmly in his beak, displaying it like a newly won sports trophy. He squawked triumphantly. His eyes gleamed with hungry curiosity. What he found was an amazing gemstone. It took his breath away. It was made of tiny crystals of shimmering greens, blues and reds which glistened in the light. They looked like priceless, miniscule jewels set inside a body of what at first glance seemed made of glass. He examined it more scrupulously, propping it up against the bright feathers on his chest.

He sniffed at it with the holes in his beak. Then he tried to bite it but failed. He decided that it wasn't made of glass after all. It was something much more precious than that: a type of material that he had never seen before. The pendant was about two inches long and one inch wide, elliptical, and shaped like a teardrop with facets on one side, which was pure, ice-white, and uncannily cold against his beak. The light radiating from within was dazzling, so razor-sharp that his eyes could not look directly at it, fearing it would burn them out as if looking at the naked sun.

The other side was rougher, reddish-amber in colour and glowed with streaks of fire swirling within it, as if a volcano were erupting. It felt warm to touch at the side of his cheek. Intrigued, he tried to rub it, when the whole thing began to shake about like a jumping bean on a scalding hot griddle.

Carefully, he started to lift the pendant from over the head of the harlequin to show Muddie. It was heavier than he thought. It accidentally brushed against the harlequin's nose, tweaking it. Even though he was careful, the chain of the necklace rubbed against the back of the figure's head, snagging momentarily on the bump under the hairline where it joined the neck.

Then, without warning, as if there was an explosion like a thunderbolt from on high, the harlequin's figure suddenly twitched, as though it had a massive electric shock. The head and neck spun around, owl-like, both ways, slowly at first, as if just emerging from a deep trance. Alarmingly, Chance's eyes gaped wide. They shot up and down, side to side – like a pinball machine – startled, then stunned, and nearly fell out of their sockets.

The nostrils under his large red nose flared out twice their size, expelling hot air. A massive '*whoosh!*' followed by a deafening '*gerr-arrh*' rented the air, as he started to bare his pearly white teeth, gnashing them dangerously like tiny icebergs set in two perfect rows.

'Yikes! Oh, frights! Strike me down! It's alive. *It's alive!*' yelled Zoot. As if suddenly scalded, he immediately dropped the pendant back to where he originally found it around the harlequin's neck. And then for safety, he flew to the top of the wardrobe and hid. Although scared, and his face a sickly puce colour, he took another look.

A tremendous shudder rattled from the top of the head of the harlequin. It rippled in waves down towards his neck, making his Adam's Apple bob up and down like a yo yo. Then a cascade of shivering ripped through his torso, which spread to his arms and legs like wildfire. What started as a gentle twitch in the body, gradually escalated to a thundering judder, making the room shake in its wake, as if builders were using pneumatic drills under the house.

Chance stretched his long arms, doubling their length. He gave a massive yawn, as though he had just woken up from a long hibernation. Like sails of a windmill, he began to flay his arms. The blast of wind made the curtains flap wildly. It blew under the skirt of Davinia's smart evening dress, much to her embarrassment, and flattened her hair. Henry and Davinia were rooted to their seats, paralysed. Then, the harlequin's long legs leapt spontaneously into the air in a sort of Irish jig. Then, slapping his boots, toe to heel, he banged each foot in turn in a noisy tap dance.

Scared for her life, Mudd yowled in panic and flew out of harm's way to hide behind the legs of the dressing table, scarcely daring to peep as the drama unfolded.

Abruptly, the body tremors stopped like a switch that had suddenly been thrown. 'Ah, that's better!' Chance said with relief. 'I can feel my toes in my boots now!' just as his dancing finished

'Oh dear, Zoot, what have you done to make him jump and explode like that?' cried Mudd nervously.

'*What have you done indeed?*' boomed a deep voice in reply.

'So, you've found your voice at last, have you?' asked Zoot, safely from his vantage point high up.

'Yes, siree, indeed! I've been waiting for ages to say so, whilst you and that soppy cat have been discussing me as if I were a dead dummy. Well, you both can come out of your hiding places now. I won't bite you!' Chance signalled, curling his finger.

The woodpecker flew down and hopped on the bed keeping a cautious distance. Mudd slowly emerged from her hiding place.

'Tell me, how did you *suddenly* change so dramatically from one state to another, just like that?' asked Zoot, astounded. 'I mean, the chain of your pendant merely got stuck around that bump at the back of your skull. Is it something called the Hump of Knowledge?'

'Why, yes, my clever feathered friend. How did you guess? In medical books it's called the Inion. All human beings have one at the back of their scalps.'

Immediately, the woodpecker and the cat started to search at the back of the heads. But there was nothing there.

'But wait a minute,' moaned Zoot. 'How come you've got one and you're not even human!'

'Maybe that's why he's considered unique and different after all,' interrupted Henry, trying to help.

Chance beckoned them nearer to pay attention. He whispered conspiratorially, 'I'll let you in on a little secret.'

He raised one hand to the back of his head and the other to his face. 'You see, by rubbing my bump clockwise and my nose anticlockwise at the same time, the static energy in my body is converted straight away into a powerful kinetic type of energy. But the key to it all comes from this special pendant around my neck!'

He stabbed at it with his thumb, whilst pointing this out. 'For inside here, the precious stone is the *real* source of this phenomenal power. It apparently protects the wearer, giving him universal knowhow, together with some incredible power!'

Zoot arched an eyebrow sceptically, shaking his head.

'I don't know how. But it does. All I know is that it kickstarts you off in life!'

'Simply amazing,' said Mudd.

'Don't believe a word of it!' sniped Davinia cynically.

Zoot ignored her and nodded gently. There was so much he wanted to know about the harlequin and why he was deemed so different.

'I'm told by the cat that her mistress, Miss Saskia, thought that you were rather special, and that she called you, erm... Mister... Chance, is that correct?'

Chance nodded. 'Chance will do.'

'Well, my friend, confess: have you been listening to *all* what we have been talking about the last few hours whilst you were in, erm... shall we say... some sort of suspended animation?'

'Oh yes! Every single word has sunk in. So, please continue what you know about the workings of the world and all that are in it. And in exchange, I'll tell you about what happened to me before I was brought here, and the plans that are afoot for me in the grand scheme of things.'

'Okey dokey! It's a fair exchange. You start first, my friend,' said Zoot, as he hopped onto the dressing table.

'Well, it's a long story...' Chance then went on to describe how he started life at Miss Saskia's college, and how he got stolen in her little old car by a young joyrider and then eventually taken by a helpful cabbie to the waxworks.

When Chance then told them of meeting the ghostly soothsayer, Cecil-the-Thin, and the legend from the past that Chance had been chosen to save the Three Kingdoms with all the dangers that ensued, Zoot and Mudd's jaws fell open.

Then he told them of the riddles and being trained by Hoopy in self-defence. And when he mentioned the phantoms as well as the Custodians of Terror and the evil ruler who had set out to kill him, Zoot fell off his perch in horror.

'What... *What!* You've got to be joking!'

When Chance shuddered and shook with the enormity of the task ahead, and his vital role in it, they suddenly realised that he was deadly serious. And at the mention of a limit of forty days and forty nights (but could, however, be extended by ninety-nine by fulfilling certain good deeds) that he had been given on earth to achieve all these things, as well as to kill Qnevilus, the evil ruler, a stream of sweat from worry ran down his face.

Zoot became suddenly anxious. By using his toes to count, he worked out the number of days that Chance had had on earth already. 'Mm, oh dear, it seems that you have only thirty-eight days left, my friend, unless you find the gem of life in time to save your life before you disintegrate in a puff of smoke!

But let's see how we can help you, eh, Muddie? Meanwhile, now tell me about the riddle that might extend your life a bit more in the meantime.'

Chance cocked his head to one side in deep thought about what Cecil-the-Thin had told him at the waxworks:

'*Three good deeds will gain thee time,*
For ninety-nine days will suit the task.
Thee part of tree, but in a mask.
Henceforth, what's more, might settle the score.
O words of wisdom – survives legends in time.
It's a test of will, that'll solve questions of thine.'

Chapter 16

DREAD

JUST UP THE ROAD in St Swithin's Square, Father
Barnabas Quick woke up with a start. With great effort,
he lifted his heavy head off the pillow and, half-opening a
bleary eye, he saw from his bedside clock that it was still
only two in the morning. He let out a groan and a silent
curse, hoping that the Almighty did not overhear him. It
was still dark, of course, only interrupted by a shard of
yellow glare from the street-lamp just outside the vicarage.

Restlessly he tossed and turned and punched the pillow,
and then pulled it over his head hoping to block out the
chink of light. For the second night in a row, he had been
having awful nightmares. The bedclothes were crumpled
and drenched in sweat, as indeed were his pyjamas. His
throat was parched dry, rough like sandpaper.

He had been dreaming again – vividly too, as if it were
real. He tried to recall what it was all about. Then it came

back to him in fits and bursts. And as it did, his face broke out in beads of perspiration again, salting his lips.

He stretched out to grab a sip of water from the glass besides him. *That's a bit better*, he thought, swallowing hard. It was all coming back to him now in a sudden flood. For twenty-odd years or so, the Very Reverend Quick kept a secret, a very dark secret for most of his life that no one knew about. *No one* – not a single member of his congregation – ever suspected that their outward-going and apparently happy vicar of St Swithin's was burdened with some terrible guilt and anxiety all this time.

And what would his loyal churchwarden or his organist, the forever-timid-as-a-church-mouse Miss Celia Darling, make of it, if they had so much as a whiff of the scandal that once embroiled his family those many moons ago? But as a pious leading member of the church and a righteous pillar of the local community, he took it upon himself to hide it, though always fearing that one day the truth would come out. The very thought of it sent a shiver down his spine, making his hands clammy with worry.

Two days ago, just out of the blue, his worst nightmare became true. A visitor arrived unannounced at the vicarage. Luckily for Father Quick, no one was around at that time to witness the unwelcome visitor, for it was mid-afternoon. Though, as always, everyone, all and sundry, were always welcome to drop in to see the vicar. The door was never closed.

But this time, it was different. When he was reminded of it, Father Quick cringed and shuddered violently at the very thought. What did this person want with him after all this time? Father Quick barely recognised him at first. For over the years, the face had lined with age, shrivelled and dry as a stale peach, but now disguised in a mass of coarse beard.

'*Good afternoon, Father. Long time, no see. Still in the do-good business? Saving the world's wayward souls, eh?*' sneered a tobacco-filled voice.

Recalling it again, Father Quick squirmed at the awful memory of it. Struggling for words, rising indignation was only half of it. But the shock of it stayed with him, rocking him to the core. However, he tried his best to remain calm so that he could deal with him as quickly as possible and get rid of him before Olga, the cleaner turned up.

'Well, my son. What can I do for you this time?' Father Quick half-expected a plea for money. But oddly it wasn't. It was an extraordinary request. What he wanted was to examine the copy of an old book the vicar held in his possession. He thought at first that he meant the ancient Bible; but hardly, since he knew from the past that he was dismissive of the church from ages ago and detested all forms of religion.

It transpired that he wanted urgently to have a look at a copy of *The Oraco Dex Lo Paediac*, held under lock and key in the refectory library. This famous manuscript of the ancient philosophers written in 299 BC held the ancient, revelatory and abiding wisdoms of the world: some say it was even more profound than the *Eternal Almanac* that predated it. Myth had it, that apparently there were only five copies intact in existence left in the world. Two of them secure in museums: one in Moscow, another somewhere in East Asia. Apart from the copy held in trust by St Swithin's Church, it was rumoured that one other had found its way into an undisclosed private collection back in Britain, en route from America. And another copy had simply vanished off the face of the earth.

The spectre of it all came back to him now like a bad dream. Father Quick did not waste time in asking him questions of the whys and wherefores. He just wanted to be rid of him as rapidly as possible. And so reluctantly he left him in the library after unlocking the glass cabinet housing the old manuscript, urging him to be quick in his search. But nevertheless, bursting with curiosity, Father Quick had listened intently with one ear glued to the door, alternating in turn by peeping through the keyhole. What he saw puzzled him. The unpleasant man was thumbing through the pages of the old manuscript in some considerable panic, as if his very life depended on it. What the devil was he looking for? This time, Father Quick pressed his ear close to the keyhole. Mumbling greeted him. He could just about make it out, for some of the words were incoherent. It sounded like, '*Three, four-five… power, riches – gems and life.*'

A look of confusion then appeared on the man's face. This was followed by a torrent of abuse as the book was slammed down onto the nearest table, accompanied by an angry curse. '*A riddle? Blast and dam-mit!*' was the last thing Father Quick heard when the door flew open with a savage kick as the nasty, unpleasant character rushed out of the vicarage in a blazing temper.

Father Quick sat bolt upright in bed. He was now fully awake. He touched the swelling on his forehead, where the edge of the door hit him those two days ago. It still hurt badly and brought back the most horrific memories of that appalling visit on that dreadful afternoon. He closed his eyes and tried to go back to sleep. It was impossible, as his head was abuzz with hundreds of thoughts and questions.

What on earth was in the old book that drew so much curiosity? Of course: yes, he was familiar with some of its texts from certain chapters of the ancient manuscript, especially the works of Aristotle and Pompest the Elder. Why, yet only last Sunday, he had extracted from it the theme for his sermon for animals based on the Three Kingdoms and the indomitable "soul" that lived through plants, creatures and, of course, man. But surely it wasn't just that that his nasty visitor was interested in? He must have been hunting for something else. What the blazes was it now? Somehow, he had to find out…

Quickly, he climbed out of bed. He threw on a dressing gown and hurried down to the library. Fumbling for his key in the dark, he switched on the reading lamp and unlocked the cabinet. The book was heavier than he remembered, so he slid it out on its back by pulling on its cover. Avidly he began to leaf through the pages of the manuscript, only pausing briefly to pore through its ancient script. He pushed back his reading glasses from time to time, as they slipped down his nose, which was wet with moisture.

'Mm. Ah yes,' murmured Father Quick thoughtfully. He chewed at the end of a pencil, trying to concentrate. Certain pages had been turned down at the corners. *Disgusting habit*, he thought. *How dare they ruin a rare book like this? Now what's this? Ah yes, chapter thirteen –* from where he had taken the last sermon.

"…The perennial battle between good and evil… the challenge for survival through the ages between the kingdom of man, that of animals, and… the world of trees, plants… etc."

He started to flick through the chapters more quickly, passing through the recordings of old, when it mentioned that the planet was almost destroyed hundreds and thousands of years ago, when a massive asteroid collided with the earth. Of course, it all came back to him now. He had used a bit of the text and cleverly moulded it into a warning to his congregation. … *"Telling of the end of the world – if they did not change their selfish ways and so on…"*

But wait a minute, thought Father Quick. Where did he get the bit about *a fat, cheerful man coming to unite the Three Kingdoms by laughter?* He could not have made it up now, could he? He scratched his chin and then his head. It must have come to him in a vision. *Ah, that must be it,* he thought because it was so clear in his mind. He couldn't have been mistaken. As he shut his eyes, he could see the image of him even now: round, happy, jovial as a clown, grinning all over his face. He stirred again to purposely dislodge the image.

Towards the end of the book, his attention was immediately drawn to several pages folded in half. Most of them were quite frail and brittle, yellowed over the ages, with the odd corner broken away, as if a mouse had been nibbling. Carefully, he prised them apart. He looked closer…

At first glance, it seemed the pages were filled with a mass of indecipherable symbols, of which he could not make head or tail. *A load of mumbo-jumbo,* he thought. He trained the beam from the reading lamp closer onto the scribbles to get a clearer view. It made no difference. This section of the book appeared much older than the rest of the earlier chapters. The latter being written in ancient Greek, most of which he could translate, having been once a scholar in the ancient classics.

Now getting tired and rather fed up, he was about to throw in the towel and return to his bed, when, by a sheer fluke, the light caught one of the pages he was turning over at an angle. As it shone through, it cast an image onto the adjacent page, projecting parts of letters and even sections of words or phrases, from one page to the other like shadow puppets. Thereby, meaningful texts or hidden messages could be read that had been skilfully concealed on the previous page between the incomplete symbols… hidden, he assumed, for centuries and centuries.

Startled at the discovery, Father Quick's heart began to pound in his head. He grew giddy with excitement at finally cracking the code. Because, whoever devised this, when *The Oraco Dex Lo Paediac* was compiled out of collected ancient manuscripts over thousands of years, was quite cunning. To make legible sense of it all, you had to read from right to left, and from the bottom of the page upwards. And so, he scrutinised each page carefully in turn, passing a beam of light through the previous one.

He congratulated himself: 'Ah, yes – a pattern begins to emerge.' He analysed the next-to-last chapter.

Disjointed words began to appear…

"A mysterious mass containing a precious gemstone from the sky hitting the earth, hundreds and thousands of years ago… breaking up into several pieces… scattered… which held secrets of knowledge, power and…"

The words tailed off on that page. And so, he returned to the previous page, in case he missed something. Numbers appeared at random – "3... 4... 5..." – reading diagonally, interlacing with the words: "*Riddle...*"

So therefore, the explanation should be in the first few pages of the last chapter, he assumed. Immediately, he turned them over, this time very slowly and carefully. *Wait a minute*, thought Father Quick, his stomach gurgling – *there is something wrong here.*

He adjusted his glasses. He checked the numbering on the pages: "1334... then... 1337." He looked again. There was a gap. It then hit him between the eyes. Someone had ripped out the pages in the middle. He bent his face downwards, almost kissing the surface. Yes, there was a tiny remnant of the roots of the paper jutting up between the others. Fury began to boil up in him. That *someone* who had dared to savage this ancient, most precious book so callously could only have been that most ghastly man who had called on him recently. It was that terrible same someone he had been silently dreading for ages.

'How *dare* he, the dastardly creature!' he uttered in an unguarded moment. His mind turned over in turmoil. Against all odds, he hoped perhaps that the torn-out pages had been thrown away – somewhere nearby in a fit of pique to teach him a lesson for old time's sake. That is what he prayed for anyway. He lowered his eyes to scan the floor under the furniture, searching every inch. For a split second or so, his heart stopped beating as he held his breath. Because, screwed up under the leg of the desk towards the back of the room, his eyes caught sight of a piece of paper, freshly crumpled.

'Ah. That's it!' he cried wildly with excitement. Immediately, he crawled under the desk to scoop up the ball of paper. Quickly, he unfolded it, flattening it on the top of the desk with the palm of his hand, his heart quickening now to resume its normal rhythm. But then, after rising hopes, massive disappointment suddenly crushed him. It was not the missing pages that he dared hoped for after all, but a crumpled-up leaflet that had probably fallen out of the pocket of his nasty visitor. He gave it a cursory glance, swallowing hard. Then he hastily shoved it into his dressing gown pocket and pushed it to the back of his mind.

Now weary with emotion that had seesawed up and down, he placed the book carefully back into the cabinet and locked it safely away. Thoroughly exhausted after so much disappointment, Father Quick turned off the light and returned to his bed.

Soon, he fell into a fitful sleep, and the nightmares started again...

***

He dreamt that he was in the middle of a dark field at the foot of a mountain that appeared to reach the sky. He was surrounded by enormous creatures which had no faces and yet were trying to bite him. And then, they were trying to crush him with their massive wings.

Still in a dream, he was trying to hold on to a glistening piece of rock, which was glowing, alive, but wriggling about with strange humanoid faces embedded within it. Riding astride one of the monstrous-winged creatures was the one person he dreaded seeing. He was beckoning to him with a crooked finger, mouthing mockingly, 'Why don't you give in, Father, and join us? You'll never win. I'll show you the way to dreams of paradise and riches… Don't be a fool. We will show you how to really live!' Hopelessly, he tried to fight back, but he was rigid with fear.

Abruptly, the scene then changed. A crater opened under his feet filled with a massive swirling gorge of water. He felt he was drowning. But underneath the water, a large round man with a cheerful face started to push him up beneath his feet so that he could see the open sky again. He was able to gasp for air. Then, someone drenched in raw evil was trying to wrench the glistening piece of rock out of his hands… and he heard a voice cursing: 'the riddle goes on…'

***

Father Quick woke up again covered in sweat. He stared at his hands resting on top of his chest. Thunderstruck, he was startled to find that he was gripping an empty glass hard, which he must have grabbed during his sleep, but he had now emptied the contents of water all over himself.

It all came back to him now. Reluctantly, though he did not want to at first, he felt that he now had to find his unwelcome visitor by some means or other, and to confront him to demand the return of the stolen pages of the manuscript. But at the same time, he had to find out why he was so interested in the riddle. Deep in his heart he suspected the man's motives from experience of the past. But the realisation of it now filled him with awful dread.

Chapter 17

THE PEN IS MIGHTIER
THAN THE SWORD

Three good deeds will gain thee time,
For ninety-nine days will...
Thee part of tree...
Henceforth, what's more might...
O words of wisdom – survives legends in time.
It's a test of will, that'll solve questions of thine...

Zoot stared at Chance, dumbfounded. 'Mm. I wonder? This strange riddle you've been given appears to be the key on what's next in store for you, my friend. Mm... *Words of wisdom...?* And if we are lucky enough to unravel its secret, and then...'

The woodpecker flapped about and flew upside down as if to stimulate blood to his head. Then suddenly as a brainwave hit him between the eyes...

'I know: *words – wisdom!* I've got an idea! Mudd, you once told me that your owner's father, Mr Goodall, was a keen collector of unusual and rare books on history, including encyclopaedias and manuscripts on world secrets that go back aeons and so on.'

Mudd gave a conniving nod. 'Mr Goodall, though, keeps everything valuable well hidden in his study on the top floor.'

She shot up the next flight of stairs, followed by Chance and Zoot. Next to an open studio, where Daphne Goodall kept all her design tools and materials for jewellery-making, there was a narrow door.

'That's the study,' meowed Mudd, pointing with her whiskers. Chance tried the door, but it appeared to be locked. He gave it a tiny kick at the foot of it, but it was to no avail.

From downstairs, Henry shouted, 'I say, my man, try Madam's sewing box for the key.' In a few quick strides, Henry jogged up to join them on the landing. Brushing Zoot aside, he strode into Mrs Goodall's studio and pointed to a large sewing basket lying next to a sewing machine. 'I'd look there if I were you,' he said knowingly.

Chance carefully opened the lid of the basket and gently pushed aside the boxes of buttons, reels of cotton and swatches of materials. Right near the bottom, next to packets of needles and scissors, was a plastic pouch. In it was a large brass key and a small round object wrapped in tissue paper. On opening the pouch, the key fell into Chance's palm. When he unwrapped the round object, he delicately placed it on top of the bits of material. To his surprise, lying neatly on its side was a glistening antique thimble cast in bronze. Carved on one face of the thimble were prominent jagged whirls, rather like the impression of a fingerprint. Attached to this object was a sticky label with the intriguing words:

"Hubert G's study. Private – *keep out!*"

This intrigued them even more.

Zoot and Henry's eyes widened.

And so, Chance scooped up the thimble into his large hands and, followed by the others, he immediately opened the study door with the brass key. Inside, it looked like a library. It was packed with row upon row of books cramming every wall, the shelves rising to the ceiling.

'I wonder if some clues are hidden here?' said Zoot. He flew up and down scanning the shelves. Within seconds, his eagle-like eyes spotted on the top shelf, jammed between two large books – entitled, respectively, *Magical Hidden Treasures of the Ancient World* and *The Neanderthals' Diaries* – sat an imposing and massive tome of a book, much larger than the rest. It was about fifteen inches tall and five inches wide, bound in well-worn, though faded, brown leather. Inset around its covers were elaborate brass hinges and a strong metal clasp which was securely locked.

As he hovered near the ceiling, he read out the faint print of its title: *The Oraco Dex Lo Paediac.*

It was beautifully embossed in gilt letters, though worn over time. 'That could be *it*, I fancy. It stands out from the rest!' exclaimed Zoot with rising excitement. 'Can you reach up and get it for me?'

Using his long arms, Chance stretched up and grabbed the book safely. It was heavy, heavier than a block of wood. He blew off the dust from its cover, and together they carried it down into the bedroom and placed it carefully onto the bed. Zoot tried to open the lock on the clasp using his beak and his claws. It wouldn't open. He tried again using the bronze thimble he had snatched from Chance's hand by thrusting it into the lock as if it were a straightforward key. But again, it did not open.

'Look.' Chance laughed. 'You've got it upside down and back to front. It's similar to a fingerprint for personal security!' He stuck the thimble onto the end of his forefinger, and then pushed it into the U-shaped hole in the lock with the finger pattern foremost and pressed firmly. The lock snapped open with a loud click. Turning the pages over gingerly, Chance was anxious not to tear the old parchment, which was moth-eaten over the ages. They stared at it open-mouthed, agog at the realisation that they were looking at something so old, so mysterious and so full of ancient wisdom.

'Isn't it magnificent! Is it really old?' asked Mudd. She leapt up onto the bed beside it.

Chance nodded instinctively as if he knew already. 'I'm sure it is. It's extremely old. I mean. Just *look* at it! ... Touch it! Smell it!' He gasped in awe as his fingers danced reverently over its cover. 'Look! Just study the title again. Carefully! But this time, split the syllables.

'And run the letters with different spaces, but ignore the first three letters of the introduction, such as "*T-h-e*"... which is the definite article.

'Then look at the rest of it. For instance: ...*OR-A-CODEX-LO-PAEDIA-C*. Now try to decode it.'

Suddenly, Mudd joined in. 'Do you know, Zoot, that vicar in the church read from something like that and he also said…'

To shut her up, they gave a hard stare for interrupting.

Henry twisted his neck at odd angles. He almost strangled himself in the process to look at the title in trying to work it out. 'Mm. I wonder if…' he muttered aloud.

'The next part, you know… "O-R-A-C… O… D… E… X…?" '

Squinting with his monocle, he bent closer over the book and began to trace the beautifully embossed letters with his forefinger.

'Well, let's say, for the sake of argument, that if you drop the fifth letter, "O", and the sixth one, "D"… Then add the letter "L", as well as drop the eighth letter, "X", it would conveniently spell "oracle", wouldn't it?'

They glanced up and stared at each other, as though they were just thinking the same thing at the same time. 'And an oracle, my good friend, surely means a profound source of advice or prophecy,' said Chance.

'Ah, like the *Oracle at Delphi* in ancient Greece, you mean,' added Henry smugly, showing off again. 'That's such an indisputable fountain of knowledge!'

'But what about the end of the title… "*LO-PAEDIAC?*" ' asked Zoot suddenly, not wishing to be left out.

'By Jupiter!' exclaimed Henry. 'It could be a coded abbreviation for an encyclopaedia, could it not? That is a complete book of the world giving information on all subjects under the sun.'

'Bingo!' agreed Chance, smiling his head off, as if they had just won the lottery. 'But do look at the middle.

Particularly at the way the syllables could alter their meaning with different emphases on the punctuation. For example: "*Or... a... CODEX... lopaediac*".'

'Well, I never!' gushed Zoot. 'A... *codex!* ...I'm certain that means it's an authentic ancient manuscript... a panacea to unlock the mysterious codes of life.'

'Precisely!' said Chance.

'Is it valuable? Is it rare? What's a first edition?' asked Mudd.

They looked at her, as if she were stupid.

'Whatever it is, it must be a prized possession of Miss Saskia's father. But I wonder where he found it?' queried Henry, racking his brain.

'Never mind! Now let's get on with the job in hand. Try looking up the word... the clue... "*Legend* " ' suggested Zoot hopefully.

Chance replied that the index showed dozens and scores of legends, too many to sift through in a hurry. Though he surprised them by his fluent command of the language of the ancients in which the book was written. It must be the influence of the precious gem he had on him, they concluded, just a little enviously.

'Wait, my friends. I've got it!' offered Henry, suddenly inspired, as if he had just woken up from a daydream. 'Try Temples, Legends and Aristotle...'

'You what!' came back a chorus of disbelief.

'You'll see. You'll see,' said Henry, quite sure of himself. (Though he didn't let on that he had overheard Miss Saskia's father mention it once.)

'Aris... *Aris... tot-le!* What the blazes has *he* got to do with it?' they retorted. Chance then said that he had heard of him at the waxworks, where he came across a bust of the famous philosopher. Whereupon he went on to reiterate the encounter with the ghostly soothsayer from the past, Cecil-the-Thin, and all that he revealed.

Between them, it took a little while to work out the hidden messages encoded, between the pages numbered 1330 onwards. The mass of symbols towards the end of the book confused them at first. They could not make head or tail of it until Chance had an idea and shone a torch through the delicate pages. And lo and behold, the shadows of the broken script crystallised into legible words on the pages behind.

After a few minutes of searching, Zoot found what he was looking for. It was confirmation of the history, together with the origins of the truth of the story that had been told to him by Wise Black Crow and his forebears. The story had indeed been recorded in ancient Greek history by the great philosophers, such as the incomparable Aristotle. As he read excerpts from the ancient writings that had been handed down from generation to generation, his eyes grew like saucers. Would it throw light on what he already knew? He was hopeful. His voice quivered as he read out aloud…

'From the beginning, as far as it was known, the first time in history that this legend was heard of was from the lips of a wizened old wise man named Pompest the Elder on his deathbed. He had been poisoned by tea made from the black blood of serpents of death by rivals who objected to his campaign about the animal kingdom.

'This ancient mystic lived in ancient Greece in the year 325 BC. Known as an eccentric soothsayer, he was also a friend, as well as an academic colleague of Aristotle's at the

Temple of Enduring Wisdom. However, somewhat earlier in 350 BC, Aristotle achieved both notoriety and fame for declaring that all plants, trees, as well as all creatures on the planet, had a *soul*.

Now this was highly controversial at the time and led to angry clashes with the people. From their enemies came death threats. They objected to their preaching, saying it was blasphemy. Well, you can imagine the uproar it caused...'

Zoot continued haltingly: 'Pompest the Elder started to broadcast to the people, warning them that the end of the world was nigh if they did not mend their wicked ways. And what's more, they were also warned they had to change their arrogant and dismissive attitudes to the other world of animals, creatures and flora – or that they would perish.'

Solemnly, Zoot read on to a hushed audience. Even Davinia Plum kept unusually quiet.

'Furthermore, Pompest warned them that it had already happened before in history, when three hundred thousand years ago the planet was virtually wiped out following the impact of an asteroid from outer space. Due to this astronomical collision, awesome destruction followed. Horrendous fireballs lit up the earth. Vast volcanoes erupted and spewed high into the skies. Powerful tornadoes and cyclones raged out of control. And gigantic tidal waves rose-up and swamped the land which eventually fell into the sea. The moon totally eclipsed the sun and remained like that for what seemed like an eternity. The world was plunged into pitch-black darkness with no heat or light to sustain life. All living things, plants, creatures of every description, from prehistoric slugs to gargantuan mammals, such as the mammoths, were wiped from the surface of the earth, like the dinosaurs before them.

'You see, I was right. I told you so!' Zoot started to chortle in anticipation at the discovery.

'The people thought that Pompest the Elder was going insane when he recounted this legend of an asteroid smashing into the surface of the earth, carrying with it a priceless and rare gemstone, which was actually motile with an indestructible inner core. This contained a "living force of life and soul" from another planet – so he claimed, as perhaps a seed for the survival of man and creature to regenerate life again, in case the earth died due to an unmitigated disaster.'

Shaken at the revelations, Zoot swallowed hard. Chance's jaw dropped to the floor at hearing this but urged him to press on.

'...the myth goes on to say that this gemstone scattered into several pieces...'

Chance nodded slowly, as the gravity of the story sunk in.

'Now, according to the legend, one piece fell and embedded itself in a wizened ancient tree which later became known as the Sacred Tree of Knowledge, because of its considerable age from when life on earth began. It was also said that it held secret magical properties. Now this piece hardened, carbonised, and then crystallised over time with searing heat and compressive forces, which moulded it into a grainy knot, as the ancient tree grew around it, protecting its secret. Over the ages it was sought by many but discovered by no one... until...' recounted

Zoot enigmatically, as his eyes swivelled towards each of them in turn.

'A second piece fell into the Secret Tree of Life, similarly it was preserved and shaped over time. But a gigantic tidal wave due to a massive eruption under the seabed rose out of the waters and flooded the land, its sacred gem contained therein was lost and got buried under the oceans.'

'What happened to the other pieces?' asked Henry, stunned out of his head.

The woodpecker's eyes began to glaze over with the enormity of the tale. 'I'm really not sure...' He hesitated to say. 'But it says here that they survived. But they were scattered throughout different parts of the world, hidden from man and the living kingdom. Who knows?'

Pausing a minute to catch his breath, Zoot continued. Skipping over the pages from 1334 to 1337 about riches and power, he carefully and slowly turned to the next page.

'When all this was published at the time in ancient Greece, other ancient civilisations around the globe, including Rome, Egypt, China, and South America, were horrified. Their scholars simply refused to accept Aristotle's so-called fanciful theories. They thought it was heresy to say that animals and even common vegetation of the field all had "living souls" and thereby deserving of equal respect and love to man.

'And as for Pompest, to declare that an alien mass of rock from another planet fell out of the sky carrying with it a precious stone, the "seed of life" – that was the last straw. His enemies, including the priests and the gods, immediately plotted his death...

And so, on his deathbed, Pompest the Elder predicted that there would come a time when someone would emerge. Someone special had been chosen to seek out this stone one day in the future. That "someone" would be able to unite the pieces of gemstone which had shattered in the collision as a perfect complete jigsaw. And when that happened, that person would be endowed with the power to mobilise and bring together the *three kingdoms* – the one of animals, the next one of plants and the other of mankind. And by doing so would ensure the renewal of life to continue as it did before.'

Mudd was itching to interrupt again, saying that she had heard something like it at St Swithin's with Miss Saskia last Sunday. She bit her tongue and stayed silent. Pointedly, she stared at the harlequin as the penny dropped.

A solemn grimace crossed Chance's face as the implications of the story began to sink in. 'But what of the riddle to extend my life?' he asked, his voice breaking with emotion. 'Do I have to wait to find the Gem of Life in order to survive?' Immediately, his hand flew to his throat, looking quite concerned. He gripped the pendant for reassurance, but he was still unconvinced about what was revealed in *The Oraco Dex Lo Paediac*.

Zoot raised his shoulders to his ears with a great deal of sighing. 'I don't really know, my friend, but the information we have before us is indisputable as predicted from an oracle, as Henry has said. If any of you needed historical validation of the truth, it is written in the words of wisdom right here!' Gently, he tapped the cover of the ancient book with the tip of his wing.

'But according to the riddle, *"good deeds will give you"*… does that mean that our friend Chance here needs to carry out good deeds, say three or more, to gain a whole lot of extra days or so?' suggested Henry, trying to be helpful.

'Could be! …Could well be,' said Zoot encouragingly.

'But what about the meaning of *"henceforth, what's more"*…?'

Zoot shrugged this time, as if defeated. 'Look, folks, when the time comes, you may need to consult another wise Oracle!'

'But even if I managed to carry out those tasks of goodness, how will I know if I'm successful in gaining some extra time on earth?' grumbled Chance.

'Simple! There will be a momentous magical sign from you know where!' Zoot rolled his eyes mysteriously upwards, suppressing a snigger. Just then, a plant pot containing a cactus plant fell off the mantlepiece into the hearth with a crash.

'Oh yeah. Such as what?'

'It'll hit you like thunder between your eyes, your ears will burn like wildfire, your nose will glow like a halo and that precious gem of yours will jump about as if it's bewitched!'

Chance looked at the woodpecker askance, not knowing whether he was joking or not. And so, he let out a nervous laugh under his breath.

Suddenly, Henry suggested that they should all follow him into the kitchen for some refreshments.

'A good idea,' agreed Zoot. 'I don't know about you lot, but I'm simply famished!'

Chapter 18

A STAB IN THE DARK

IN A DISTANT PART of the west of the country, just thirteen miles south of Wedgemouth Ho, where the land begins to snake towards the sea, a strange dark cloud shaped like an enormous mushroom gathered overhead. It sat like a giant's hat over the outskirts of the endless suburbs which sprawled out of the city.

Daylight had yet to break, but a glimmer of dawn rose slowly over the ocean to the east. A row of brightly painted caravans and trailers stacked high with equipment was packing up, ready for the road. The field where they parked looked a sorry sight; the grass was now badly churned, having suffered the traffic of hundreds of visitors over the site – past witness to a large circus over the last seven days, which had just finished.

A heavily draped figure emerged from behind one of the larger vehicles, treading his feet cautiously, as if the mud had clogged up his boots from the recent rain… But it was really, more than that. Suspiciously, he darted his head side to side as well as backwards, as though scared of being discovered. Panicking, he dragged his collar high over his shoulders and suddenly reached out with his arm to grab a figure who was passing by.

'What the blazes!' screamed a terrified voice, as its owner shook off the grip of a hand that appeared from nowhere.

'Steady, my friend,' hissed the first figure into the other one's ear. 'It's only me, you fool!' he said, dragging him into the shadows. 'What took you so long to get back? I thought you had been caught in the act!'

Increasingly hostile, they glared at each other with blatant mistrust. 'The wretched train was late leaving Paddington,' came the angry reply. 'Signal failure as usual, curse and blast it!' His hand swept his face, tugging at his beard in weary frustration as his heart leapt a beat.

'Keep your voice down, fool, do you want the others to hear?!' The burly figure threw out his chest, raising his shoulders, which made him seem double in size. He kept glancing backwards, fearful of being seen. He need not have worried, for it was difficult to make out his face as a large fedora hat and a mass of hair covered most of it; though the slits beneath the brim where the eyes should have been glinted an odd deathly shade of white with blood-red sockets in the half-light.

He spoke again, a harsh, grating sound that seemed to come from a gash in his nose as if the upper half of his face was concealed in a kind of mask. 'Well, my friend, did you get the secret information you wanted?'

By now, the other felt angry at being bullied. For indeed in size, his own physique wasn't that small in comparison, but he shrank a little from being intimidated so much.

Wearily, he leant with his shoulder against the back of the nearest trailer, which was fortunately empty, and sighed. 'A waste of a journey! Everything was tied up in a stupid riddle! Worse still, the secret was hidden in a massive old book, which was difficult to steal and hide easily inside one's coat pocket. And furthermore, it's watched over like a hawk by a prickly and tiresome old man, who kept preaching at me and would attack anyone who got close, never mind actually being able to touch his wretched, precious old manuscript in the first place!'

He spat on the ground, just missing the other one's boot.

'Never mind that! We'll have to think of a way,' he snarled, grabbing hold of the other's lapels, spitting in his ear. 'More importantly still; what news of the fat, cheerful one? Where is he? Is he on his way?'

'Haven't you heard, then, that our jolly naïve friend has returned to the house where that student girl, his inventor – his "guardian angel" – lives?' A contemptuous leer broke over him.

The other pulled his hat further over his face and shook his body, still shifting side glances back and forth, seemingly worried that they might be caught being seen together.

'Pah! I thought you knew already. I assumed you had spies everywhere!' sneered the one with a beard, snorting derisively. 'Though I still maintain that we should have killed him the moment he arrived on the planet. We foolishly missed the chance! Even though there was so much noise and chaos created in the towns and cities around the globe when he was invented, we still could have got to him in time. It would have made life much easier.'

He continued to complain.

'*Well, if he came in with a bang of glory, then he'll go out with a bang of even greater glory!*' snarled the other viciously, trying to shift blame onto the other one's shoulders. '*It is still not too late!*' He glared at him disparagingly, moving menacingly towards him.

Just then, it seemed that the two of them might come to blows, when a sudden high-pitched scream from beneath the wheels of a nearby caravan split the air, as if someone had been mortally wounded, and made them stop. They whipped round, startled. Two large tomcats were baring their fangs, arching their backs, and hissing at each other – a not-uncommon cat fight. Uttering blood-chilling cries, which sounded like humans, they were trying to kill one another. Eventually, both animals disappeared into the surrounding bushes, still snarling in the undergrowth.

'Anyway, quickly, man, was *he* alone?' He carefully adjusted the top of his coat, pulling it yet even higher over his face. A spurt of mist sprang out in front of him from his chilled breath, for the early-morning air was still dank from the night before.

'Hardly,' came the reply. 'When I peeped through the letterbox and passed the window, there were voices from others with him.' Scratching his hairy chin, he added, 'As far as I could gather, I think there's also a strange, birdlike creature and another animal of some unusual intelligence hovering around for company. Maybe they were there for his protection, guarding him and preparing him for his journey. Who can tell? They were certainly giving him all sorts of information with advice and warnings about the future.'

'The future? *What future!* The idiotic fool hasn't got one, if we play our cards right! Can't you get it into your head, like all do-gooders of virtue, that's he's a born loser? You fumbling fool, you've now missed your chance. You should have got nearer and killed them all when you were searching for that blasted book nearby!'

The bearded-one shrank back at such torrent of abuse, wondering why the other one hated the emergence of a cheerful, jolly harlequin with so much murderous venom.

'Keep your voice down, my friend,' he urged the other to calm down. 'The others will soon be awake. What's the panic? There's plenty of time.' Stroking his beard thoughtfully, he pulled out a cigar from the top of his outer pocket and bit the end off it, as if to light it.

As the taller figure started to peel away, he choked as though spitting blood. 'Our master – *our grand noble master*, the Mighty One, as you should know, does *not* have plenty of time, you, incompetent numbskull!'

He uttered a curse under his breath. Then threateningly, he arched his back to thrust his face close to the other one, murmuring, 'Next time, I warn you, there will be *no,* second chance. There must be *no* mistakes. We have our orders, the fat, cheerful one must be stopped at all costs before he learns more about the legend and rallies support on his journey to the kingdoms.'

Putting away his unlit cigar, the other replied, 'Don't worry, my friend, we can wait when our quarry leaves the house – hopefully soon and alone. We daren't strike now. It will be too dangerous to come out into the open so soon. It will be like a blind stab in the dark!'

Hurriedly, the two of them separated and went their opposite ways – quietly tiptoeing stealthily using the shadows of the large vehicles to shield them from view. They were shivering from the tops of their heads to their toes, though not from the cold… but more from the adrenaline coursing their bodies; because now, a celebration of evil was about to begin.

Scarcely an hour passed, when daybreak arrived, and a most peculiar thing happened. The mushroom-like cloud overhead suddenly changed into a gigantic cigar-shaped mass – mysteriously hanging quite low. It was now purplish in colour as it drifted out from over the town towards the coast and into the distant horizon of the nearby sea. And as it did, a violent tornado whipped up. It raged for a couple of horrendous minutes, churning up the water like a mammoth whirlpool. It sucked up millions of fish and crushed a fishing boat in its path, whilst hurling everything high into the sky. A huge torrent of dead fish, seaweed and tons of black, sodden detritus then angrily rained down onto the tops of cars and the roofs of the town, smothering the streets.

It was said in the local paper the next day that the inhabitants of Wedgemouth Ho had never seen anything quite like it in a thousand years. And of course, it scared them no end having such mysterious and out-of-control happenings following such an ordinary, joyful event such as this – a harmless and happy visit of a family circus for children.

Chapter 19

IF ONLY

THEY DID NOT WASTE another minute, and so they began to raid the kitchen cupboards for food. Hungrily, they tucked-in, to their fill, lounging lazily around the kitchen table. Zoot confined himself to nuts and raisins and the leftovers of a leek and onion pie Saskia had left in the fridge. He shied away from bringing in worms and slugs knowing that his guests might not appreciate it at the table. Although Henry wasn't very hungry and stuck to fruit and biscuits.

'My, I really enjoyed the bananas and lemon cake,' said Chance. He smacked his lips noisily, suppressing a burp, whilst downing a jug of lemonade to quench his thirst. He hadn't realised how hungry he was.

As they were getting up from the table, Henry suddenly spoke up. 'Excuse me, my good man. May I come with you when you leave this house?'

'What on earth for, Mr de Poisson?' replied Chance.

'You will need help with the directions. I can be useful and assist. I've been here for a little while now and used to things. I'll serve you loyally, my dear sir.'

Chance thought about it for a minute or two. Then he nodded agreeably, for Henry's company in the outside world to help him on this dangerous quest would not only be welcome, but vital, if he was to survive.

'And what about me?' pleaded Davinia, suddenly realising that she was about to be to be deserted. 'Henry, you cad! You can't leave me here alone with that tiresome cat and that horrid... Please? I implore you.' But her pleas fell on deaf ears.

Refreshed and restored, Chance and Henry were now ready and itching to start on their epic journey. Although eager and full of anticipation, the actual thought of it now, and what they had to do, filled them increasingly with dread of the unknown. But the idea of challenges ahead of them in the outside world spurred them on, and adrenaline steeled their nerves. Mudd and Zoot were poised to accompany them to the front door, when, at the last minute, Chance hesitated, dragging his heels.

'By the way, Zoot, I almost forgot to ask you – the search for the missing pieces, what must we look out for to protect ourselves along the way? Cecil-the-Thin warned me about certain dangers, but he disappeared into thin air before he finished.'

'Ah, from what you told me, that skinny Cecil fellow seems a pessimistic old prophet of doom. Therefore, you had better watch out, as he said. Beware of this, and beware of that!' said Zoot, offering cautious advice. 'Sure, there will be many pitfalls for the unsuspecting along the way. Mortal danger may face you from different sources and from many unexpected directions. So be extremely careful, my cheerful friend. Let laughter and wisdom guide you! And don't forget to practise that oriental Toe Hee nonsense you told us about for self-defence!'

As they approached the threshold, Chance had another question. 'Oh, another thing, if we don't get back in time, when Miss Saskia returns from her trip, what happens then?'

The woodpecker flapped his wings impatiently, startling everyone. 'Look, my friend, I don't know everything. You'll have to trust your namesake and take a chance!' He started to guffaw at his own joke.

'Here, you'd better take this. It's a map showing major flight paths for us birds around the country. For speed, follow the direct route indicated – "As the crow flies!" And according to my good pal the crow, the best place to start is to look for a circus that's just come to town: they'd know all about animals and people. And when you reach the country, search out for Wise Black Crow for his help.'

Gratefully, without an argument, Chance folded the slim parchment into his pocket for safekeeping.

Then, deftly, Zoot unlatched the front door with his beak as if he owned the place. They clambered down the front steps to the garden gate, stepping confidently outside into the road.

Undaunted, Chance led the way, followed closely by Henry. From the bedroom upstairs, a loud wail and a sob could be heard as Davinia started to cry her heart out.

'Oh, let her stew. She'll get over it eventually,' said Henry, without a spark of emotion.

'We can only come with you to the bottom of the road. That's all,' suggested Zoot. 'Then you're on your own, I'm afraid.'

The figures walked briskly along the road, creating long shadows under the light of the stars from the pitch-black sky. The moon looked down auspiciously as swathes of thick grey cloud scudded in front of it. A backdrop of pure street theatre was created by the twilight – given the rich costume of the harlequin and that of Henry's, complete with a silver-tipped cane. This odd couple was escorted – so it seemed to outside eyes – bizarrely by an enormous green woodpecker fluttering over their heads and a slim black and white cat toddling at their heels like a pet dog following.

It was just as well that Rosy Harker from number 13 was snoring her head off, as the sight of such a thing would have given her a heart attack.

At the end of the road, Mudd stopped abruptly. She lifted her head and meowed with mixed feelings. Zoot flew low, calling in the crisp night air, 'Au revoir, old pals. Don't forget, you've only got thirty-seven days left for you to bring back the second lucky piece of that gem or, get a reprieve by fulfilling the riddle in the meantime. Failing that, then you'll have had your chips and you'll immediately disappear as a pile of dust!'

Chance turned and waved with his big, gloved hands. There was a tinge of sadness at saying goodbye to his newly found loquacious chum. 'We're going to miss you tremendously, my dear feathered friend. Aren't we, Henry?' said Chance. Tight-lipped, Henry nodded in agreement.

Mudd and Zoot wheeled away in a complete U-turn and headed home, quietly thinking that it would seem oddly empty and somewhat lonely without those two. But they would not stand in their way. The kingdom of animals and the humans on earth, not forgetting that of flora, depended on Chance to succeed for theirs and others' very own lives.

***

The next day, Pilar the daily help arrived for her work at the Goodall's house. A scene of chaos greeted her. At first, she thought a burglar had been. She was puzzled to find a pile of dirty plates in the sink and remnants of food on the kitchen table.

'I'm *sure* I washed and tidied up the other day,' she murmured with great consternation. She scratched her head and, with a dustpan and brush and a clucking of her tongue, she started to sweep up. She tutted, wondering what Mrs Goodall would say. Picking up the row of paperbacks that had fallen off the shelf in the lounge, Pilar began to tidy up, hoovering like mad. Mudd immediately leapt onto the sofa out of the way.

When she reached upstairs, she was flummoxed to find the bedrooms in a yet more chaotic state than downstairs. She rescued the plant that had spilled out of its pot, retrieving the soil that had been thrown over the hearth rug. Without a further murmur, she tidied up around her whilst keeping her opinions to herself.

But when she discovered that Mr Goodall's prized antique book – his treasured ancient encyclopaedia – had been left on top of the bed, she grew alarmed. Desperately hoping that it wasn't damaged, she placed it carefully back onto the shelf in the study. 'What on earth's been going on?' she asked herself. 'It's that naughty girl, Miss Saskia. She must have had a party the night before she left for holidays. I'll have to have a strict word with her when she gets back!' she vowed sternly.

The final straw was the discovery of the bronze-whirled thimble lying on top of the duvet cover. 'Careless girl! Probably sewing or mending a button at the last moment!' Pilar remarked loudly, scolding her in her absence. Always tidy and helpful, she placed the thimble into Mrs Goodall's sewing basket, hiding it amongst the needles and scissors for safety.

Given all these distractions, she did not properly take in that one of the figures, Henry, was in fact missing. But if she did, she might have assumed that he had been taken back to the college for an exhibition or something.

'Funny about those dirty plates, though,' she said ruefully. She rubbed her eyes with the edge of her apron and muttered, 'Still, who am I to say, eh? I just work here. Don't you agree, little old puss?' She gave Mudd a vigorous rub on top of her head.

With great effort, Mudd raised her eye at her curiously and promptly fell back asleep on one of her favourite places on top of the sofa, completely exhausted.

'Been up all night, hunting for mice again, eh, you naughty old puss?' Pilar scolded, wagging a finger. She restarted the vacuum cleaner. This time, Mudd held her ground... grinning secretly – *if only* she knew.

Singing at the top of her voice, Pilar started humming in tune with the thrum of the vacuum cleaner.

'*Whilst they're away, the cat will play.*
Ah tomorrow's just another day!
If only…?'

Part IV

Please, oh please, direct me true on what to do,
To meet the challenge of the dangers of life,
Or run the gauntlet to meet the strife.

Chapter 20

THE DODECAHEDRON

AIMLESSLY, THEY TRUDGED THE streets for what seemed like ages. Chance and Henry began to lose their sense of direction. They had been going round and round in circles getting nowhere. From what Zoot had told him, Chance thought it was simple to find the quickest route out of the city. *Somewhere along the Great South West Road*, he suddenly remembered. Confusingly, they kept being drawn back to the same spot.

Then, eventually, beyond a maze of narrow streets in front of them, it opened out at last into a large roundabout leading to an enormous green. Excited, Henry pointed out with his cane some road signs ahead of him which said, "THE GREEN... RAVENSWOOD... BUSH..."

His face lit up. 'Ah, some definite tell-tale signs! We *must* be heading in the right direction to the countryside after all – bushes, green and woods.' Unfortunately, he was miles out. Finding the whereabouts of "As the crow flies" was further away than ever.

Despite Henry's confidence that he could help, Chance didn't think much of his navigating even with the use of the woodpecker's map, although he was secretly glad of the company.

Dampness hung in the air, reflecting their mood. As they glanced up at the darkening sky, banks of black clouds began to ominously gather. Birds began to chatter, for daybreak couldn't be far behind. But then, the atmosphere grew suddenly oppressive. It got gloomier by the minute. A storm was brewing.

'Kerr-aak... Crack!' It suddenly broke. A thunderous crack rumbled directly overhead. A spark of daggered lightning followed, lighting up the horizon. It started to rain. A few drops at first. Soon this turned to vertical sheets of water. Then another mighty rumble pierced the sky.

'Uh-oh. Thunder and lightning! Blow it. That's all we need!' Henry cried with alarm. He pulled up his lapels and collar. It was all in vain. The rain soaked through.

'My boots will fill like buckets of water if it continues like this,' grumbled Chance. They tramped on more quickly. But his boots began to squelch like a pair of wet sponges.

'Look. Do look over there!' mouthed Henry in desperation. 'There's a block of buildings, perhaps they're flats. With a bit of luck, we might find shelter.' Optimistically, he pointed his cane in front of him. He spat out water that was running down his face. They hurried across a wide grass verge and ducked under the first porch they came to. Next to the porch was a broad, modern window filled with a soft, welcoming light. The narrow porch didn't offer much shelter. Relentlessly, the rain and wind drove in. Soaked to the skin, Henry exploded with a sneeze. His waxen moustache started to droop, uncurling itself rather sadly.

'I think we need help quickly. Otherwise, you'll catch a death of a cold,' Chance said desperately, now half-wishing that they hadn't left the warmth and dryness of the Goodall's house in the first place. Using the back of his glove, he tried to brush off the rain that plastered bits of his hair to his scalp. Just then, he felt anxiously inside his jacket collar, which was now sticking to the back of his neck.

'Ah,' he murmured with relief, 'thank heavens the gemstone is dry and safe.' He caressed it again for reassurance.

From the corner of his eye, Henry noticed that the harlequin was holding on to the precious pendant jealously with all his might. 'A blooming pity it can't control the rain from chucking it down, my friend,' Henry blurted out desperately. He dried his monocle with a handkerchief and banged his cane against the wall in frustration.

'How I wish!' said Chance. He tried to cheer Henry up.

Henry replied with a sneeze. 'Might be already too late by then,' he complained despondently.

'Henry, are you getting cold feet? Shall we turn back? It'll be nice and warm back in Miss Saskia's place with the others, and safe and dry as well. What do you think?' Chance asked, trying to tempt him as doubt began to fester.

'Look, you're the leader. You've got more to lose than me. And don't forget there's less than forty days left. Remember Zoot's warning,' replied Henry, banging his shoes to keep warm. 'Return back there? You'll die anyhow, just sitting there like a sitting duck waiting for the end. Then crumble into dust or get blown up in a waft of smoke. Remember?'

'Yes. But it's hardly a ball out here, though, is it, my friend?' Chance retorted, shouting at the sky. His face was troubled about the right thing to do. 'We could drown out here. Or we could save ourselves – get rescued now, to fight another rainy day.' He winced with the irony of what slipped out. 'But *if* we go on, Henry, we could be strung up, slaughtered at any time at the end of it by the terrible ghoul of a phantom, or other murderous maniacs that Cecil warned me about. So, what are the odds?'

Henry shook his head and flicked some water off his face. 'Ah, but at least you'll stand a fair chance for trying. It's maybe fifty-fifty. You could gain some extra time… an extra lease of life to live. You promised Zoot to try to find the missing pieces. Haven't you forgotten? Isn't it worth the gamble… the challenge?'

Chance stayed silent, giving little away.

'Look, my friend, it's up to you. I thought you gave your word to try to help him and the others in the Kingdoms. And by doing so, help me and also yourself,' Henry persisted, refusing to give up.

After a while, the force of the rain began to ease a little. But the dilemma etched on the harlequin's face remained the same. Henry's words stung his conscience. Then, suddenly, Henry pulled him brusquely to the back of the porch, shielding their backs from the hostile elements.

'Look, my good friend, if you cannot decide what to do next, perhaps this will help you…' Reaching inside his breast pocket, Henry fished out a mysterious lumpy object.

It was the size of a large walnut, three-dimensional, with many sides to it. These were flat, smooth, symmetrical and shiny.

'What on earth is that?' Chance stared, goggled-eyed, at the peculiar object in Henry's open palm.

'Well, it's a type of dice sort of thing – a kind of gizmo to help you make important decisions. It's no ordinary dice, I tell you. It is in fact... *twelve-sided* – called a dodecahedron. See for yourself.' Henry pointed his finger at it. The object was fascinating. It had twelve planes, exactly the same size, which were diamond-shaped. They were bonded together so that they appeared symmetrical from whatever angle you examined it.

'This may sway you one way or another,' added Henry solemnly. 'As you know, in one's lifetime you have to make momentous decisions. Such decisions will dictate which path you take. These life-or-death decisions will decide your fate.'

Chance asked Henry from where he had got it. He explained that it had fallen out of an unusual Christmas cracker which Miss Saskia's mother had bought from a magic shop in Soho last December. Pilar had found it rolling on the floor behind the sofa and thought it was a Christmas tree decoration and popped it into Henry's inside pocket for safekeeping, then promptly forgot about it.

'Well. What's so different about this then?' asked Chance, mystified. Sharply, he made a move to grab it out of Henry's hand.

'Wait. Don't touch it yet!' warned Henry, moving it aside. 'It's only just warming up to be alive! You see, the usual dice is a cube with six sides which has dots one to six painted in turn on each side. But this one is *different*. Again, please look closely.'

He stuck it just a few inches under the nose of his friend for closer examination. Chance had never seen anything like it before in his life. For indented into each face of each facet were almond-shaped eyes, each with beautiful, curly black eyelashes. There happen to be one to twelve of them on each side of its twelve-plane surfaces formed in sequence.

Henry then instructed, 'If we roll it along the ground, it will tell us what to do. For instance, if the eyes *close*, then it shows *disapproval...* and it's a no-go. If they remain wide *open*, it will indicate that it's okay. It thereby *approves* of any decision you have made. However, if they *blink*, then it shows *hesitation – it is unsure*. And therefore, you must throw the dodecahedron again. Furthermore, you must add up the numbers... the bigger the sum, the greater the persuasion.'

Chance's lips pursed silently in an arc like a porpoise breaking water. Resigned, his shoulders dropped to accept the inevitable. 'Okay, Henry. I agree. I'm stuck. I suppose I really don't know what to do for the best. Do I go on with the quest?'

'*Ask it!* Throw the dice. See what happens. *Throw it now!*' Henry replied encouragingly. He placed the dodecahedron into Chance's open hand. They both then squatted towards the ground facing the wall. Not overly convinced, Chance reluctantly threw it six inches into the air. It rolled crisply along the pavement. At first, it jumped into the air like a magic jumping bean. Then it came to a sudden stop, just in front of their feet. They leant over and peered anxiously as it came to a stop. It landed face upwards with eight of its eyes exposed. They bent their faces nearer to look more closely. It showed four eyes wide open and four of them firmly shut.

'Oh dear,' sighed Henry. 'That's a fat lot of use; it's neither one thing nor another. I'm afraid you've got to ask it again. But this time – *be more positive, as if your heart's really in it.* And command it loudly and clearly as you throw it. But wait – it works better if you instruct it with the following words:

Please, oh please, direct me true, on what to do,
To meet the challenge of the dangers of life,
Or run the gauntlet to meet the strife,
Oh, mystic dice, I need advice...'

This was met with an incredulous look.

'Now, my sceptical friend, repeat after me...'

This Chance did, though he felt a bit of a fool, but he threw the dodecahedron nevertheless, this time with a little more conviction. It rolled along the ground more smoothly on this occasion without a nervous twitch. As it hit the foot of the wall, it rolled onto its back, showing a figure of five – but with all its eyes blinking, hesitatingly.

'Oh *no*! Not again!' cried Chance in despair, holding his head in his hands.

'Hey. Wait a minute,' cautioned Henry, resting his hand on his friend's arm. 'It's not finished yet.'

To their immense relief, the dodecahedron spun slowly in its final momentum onto its side. It gave a crisp click to reveal quite plainly a figure of twelve… Its eyes were all now open. Its curly black eyelashes fluttered, stretched wide to the limits, and smiling broadly upwards at them.

'Well, there's your answer!' Henry exclaimed with relief. '*No contest*. That's it – it says yes… *yes!* We continue the journey. There's now no turning back.'

Chance nodded in agreement. Henry scooped up his precious gizmo and put it safely out of sight.

'Now let's get out of this damp hole of a place before we drown to death,' added Chance. 'We must find proper warmth and shelter soon, or we'll die before we even get to start on our way, and all that we have done so far will have been in vain.'

They got off their haunches and peered hopefully under the porch through a steamed-up window of the nearby flat. Pressing their noses against the cold, wet glass, they were relieved to find someone at home. Their eyes quickly took in the scene. Getting out of a well-worn sofa, pushing aside a woven tartan rug, was a young girl with fair hair, who could not have been more than thirteen or so. She cast aside a metal crutch, propping it against the end of the sofa, and walked rather hesitantly on her left leg to start off with towards the adjacent kitchen. She stretched her arms above her head, gave a wide yawn in the process and reached up to grab a glass from a shelf in the kitchen. She filled it with water from the tap and started to sip.

In the next room, through the ajar door, a young boy aged about nine or ten was soundly asleep. He was curled up on his side; his tousled, sandy brown hair flopped over his arm, which was tucked under his head. His mouth was slightly agape, perhaps even snoring. At his feet, guarding the threshold of the room, lay an enormous black woolly dog with a large square-shaped head – the size of a television set. The animal's nose was buried deep into its large shaggy paws, but with one eye open, half-cocked in case of danger.

Henry was about to tap the window with the tip of his cane to attract their attention when Chance stopped him halfway. Urgently, he whispered that they had better wait until past dawn when it was just a tiny bit lighter so as not to frighten them. 'Psst,' hissed Chance into Henry's ear, 'the girl looks half-awake. The boy and the dog seem fast asleep. Let's leave them for a bit longer so that we can speak to their parents.'

And so with heavy feet, they turned away and stood patiently under the porch entrance to shelter from the resuming drizzle. They stamped about to keep their feet from being numb. Dribbles of water squelched out from the insides of their shoes. They tucked their hands under their armpits and shook their bodies. To restore some feeling, they then slapped their arms around their waists. But it was to no avail, for their teeth continued to rattle remorselessly. They had to seek help, and pretty soon too, before it became too late…

Chapter 21

LOTTE'S LOT

L OTTE PERT LIVED AT number one, Ravenswood House, the Green Estate, in a pleasant part of the Bush in West London. It was a large block of flats situated on a well-managed estate of identically built buildings in square blocks which were ten stories high. Those on the ground floor had small, paved gardens at the back, whereas those on the upper levels had outside balconies. All were constructed in the same dull red brick with spacious plots of plain grass lawns between the buildings – typical of the sixties-type architecture that mushroomed all over the country at the time. A few tall, spindly ornamental trees were scattered here and there, with a small children's play area slap in the middle.

As it was, Lotte and her mother Shirley lived on the ground floor facing the open green. Theirs was a comfortable flat, plain, and relatively roomy. It was made attractive and homely by the furniture, pictures and ornaments brought from their former home, which was, as it happened, not that far away in North London near the Heath, where they used to live with Lotte's father Tom before Lotte's parents were divorced.

Lotte had been reading late into the night; a new book that had captured her imagination about an amazing invisible witch who haunted a village school. She had been unable to get to sleep that night. Perhaps it was partly to do with the adventures in the book, which were rather far-fetched and a bit unsettling. Or was it due to the thought of going to school camp the next morning and having to get up early to be collected? Whatever it was, it wasn't helped by her trying to sleep on the sofa full of lumps fully dressed. Because, generously, she had given up her bed to young Timothy Needles, who was also going to camp. In fact, Tim really lived next door with his father Joe at number two.

Through the early hours of the morning, she had been trying to keep awake, though her eyelids felt like lead. Without realising it, she had eventually fallen asleep, her book open, in mid-chapter resting on her pillow.

Not long afterwards, a sudden noise woke her up. She sat bolt upright and rubbed her eyes. Peering over the side the sofa, she noticed that her book had fallen onto the floor, knocking over the alarm clock. 'Blow it, I must have dozed off whilst reading,' she muttered crossly. Stretching like a cat, she leant sideways and parted the curtains. Using the hem of her blue sweater, she smudged a small patch in the damp film frosting the window and peeped expectantly outside. 'Ooh. It's been raining heavily during the night,' she murmured. 'Wonder what time it is?' She looked through the window with interest. Dawn had just begun. A band of gathering light started to spread across the rooftops. Little by little, the yellow street-lamps of the city faded, ushering in another day.

She bent down and picked up the clock. It read 6.35am. Pushing aside a tartan rug, she gently placed a grey metal crutch against the side of the sofa whilst she swung her legs out of the temporary bed. As she leant onto her left leg, her face winced a little as if expecting pain. She hobbled slightly at first, testing it cautiously. Then, with increasing confidence, she gradually put her full weight onto both her limbs.

Suppressing a yawn and stretching her arms, she made her way towards the kitchen to get a glass of water. But she did not notice two strange, wet faces peering sadly for a minute or two at the front window. Being slightly peckish, Lotte grabbed a biscuit from a tin near the bread bin and perched herself on a kitchen stool. Sticking out her sore leg, she sipped from the glass, deep in thought.

Quite suddenly, a rush of memories flooded back to her... She couldn't help it... The residual soreness in her left leg was a cruel reminder of the horror of the start of last term at school, when the dreaded Braggerleys, Liz and Hector had chased and threw her up in the air in the playground...

"*It couldn't be helped,*" they'd said, dropping her onto her left leg and fracturing her ankle. They swore to the deputy head that it was a pure accident from horsing around. But everyone else knew that it was deliberate, as Lotte had been the target of their systematic baiting ever since last year when she entered the school as a newcomer, having moved recently to the area.

Carefully rubbing the stiffness in her leg, Lotte thought of them with a shudder. Three weeks ago, the plaster cast had been cut and removed at the hospital. As she regained her mobility, the supporting crutch was now being used less and less. Chewing on another biscuit, she reflected ruefully on the last term. She was glad it was the holidays. And not to see the horrible Braggerleys again for nearly two weeks or so was an immense relief.

All at once, in the quiet stillness of the early morning, with her mother having just left for the airport on an overseas business trip, and with young Tim and Ram, his gigantic pet dog, still fast asleep next door, the flush of memories continued as the floodgates opened. She recalled all too well her parents splitting up two years ago and having to sell their family home where she grew up. The worst of it all was having to move schools, which disrupted her studies, as well as having to make new friends and get used to a strange new neighbourhood.

It was really a bit of a nightmare that never seemed to end…

***

On the face of it, Shirley Pert was quite remarkable after Tom left. She took on an extra job at the airport shops in the evenings and occasionally into the early hours of the mornings with extended shifts. With unwavering determination, she maintained her day job as a legal secretary at a busy firm of city solicitors at the same time.

She always turned up on time without fail, and drove herself relentlessly in order to make a new life for herself and Lotte.

Shirley sold her car to economise and moved into the flat at the Bush last year. 'I'm afraid we'll have to be careful, as money will be tight from now onwards, Lotte, my darling,' she explained apologetically to her beloved daughter as she hugged her tightly with a tearful face. 'I know the flat's a bit small and plain compared with our last house, but hopefully it won't be forever. And I hope you won't mind going to the local school now, my love?'

After a while, Lotte tried to get used to the idea. Anyway, Shirley had been told by friends and neighbours that Bowers Spence was one of the long-established state secondary schools in inner London. The headmaster, bedecked in his black academic gown, proudly boasted to the new parents that Bowers Spence was formerly a famous grammar school and had achieved many Oxbridge places in the past. Bowers Spence, announced the headmaster in the welcoming address to the parents of the newcomers, was an amalgamation of two famous schools in the past in 1710 in the Age of Reason and Enlightenment. But, as far as Lotte was concerned, the history meant very little to her. The consolation was that it was co-educational, rather than segregated – girls from boys. Being the only girl of a single mother, this was important to her.

But it was bad enough, grumbled Lotte on her first day at school, having to wear the traditional uniform. The outfit did little to flatter her petite, slim shape, her tiny, pert nose or her steel-grey eyes. When first meeting her, one would notice that she had an array of delicate freckles on her cheeks and a tiny gap between her top front teeth, something Lotte hated from the day she was born. Her mother thought it was endearingly cute, giving Lotte a cheeky grin, which would light up her face, even at times when she was really a bit down in the dumps.

Lotte's natural blonde hair was kept neat and tidy by Shirley, who tied it up in a simple ponytail. 'It's important, my love, to keep this unruly fringe under control – to stop it getting into your eyes,' said Shirley. 'And you really ought to wear your glasses more often,' she scolded gently.

Lotte hated the terrible Braggerleys, who had picked on her and other pupils, who, like her, were newcomers or perhaps came from a different background. With regards to Lotte, it was because her mother was divorced and was doing her best to make ends meet.

'Huh,' scathed Hector Braggerley to his classmates. 'She comes to school by bus, would you believe it! And for crying out loud, they don't even have a car!' The Braggerley parents could have sent their son and daughter to Kingfishers Independent if they wanted to. But Councillor Doddington Braggerley, however, for his own political reasons, chose to send the children to Bowers Spence instead, despite the protestations of his disgruntled wife Grace.

At first, Liz and Hector rebelled against this decision, but quickly settled down as they dominated the first three years both academically and in sports, being quite bright and physically strong. Rapidly they realised that there was an advantage in not being separated, being only eleven months apart in their ages. However, this in-built resentment at being sent to a school not of their choice boiled over in baiting, teasing, and bullying the shyer and the less well off. They were inseparable and equally insufferable. It happened to be made worse by their over-indulgent parents, who spoilt them rotten.

The Braggerleys' other cronies (which made up the notorious gang of five) – Phil Grimsmore, Kev Scratchley, as well as Tilly Crossley – would soon join in with the bullying whenever there was a chance. A scrawny young boy named Steven Stammers from her class was often a target because his ears protruded a little. Lotte would try to protect young Steven whenever this happened. 'Try to ignore them, Steven. They're just plain morons. Arrogant, stupid and dim ones, at that!' she shouted when it happened again, trying to help him to fight back. Shielding him from the gang, they at last retaliated with a defiant chant:

> '*Sticks and stones may break my bones,*
> *But words can never hurt me!*
> *Empty vessels make most noise,*
> *Ignoramuses have no poise,*
> *For only cowards can play pranks,*
> *Because they're thick as two short planks.*
> *And so, we don't care a jot or tuppence.*
> *One day soon, you'll get comeuppance!'*

Bolstered by sudden courage, Lotte and Steven then deliberately stuck their tongues out at their tormentors and pulled faces. Immediately, they then ran away as fast as they could to the safety of their classroom, slammed the door and wedged a chair against it, leaving the gang of five hissing and fuming outside.

'You'll pay for this. Just wait and see, Lotte Pert!' Liz Braggerley spat murderously. Some weeks later, having failed to maim Lotte on the hockey pitch by aiming for her shins, their wicked revenge did succeed. Just after the start of the Easter term, the gang had caught her in the playground and threw her up into the air, smashing her leg…

***

That horrible nightmare of the recent schooldays continued to haunt Lotte. A series of miserable events, compounded with the turmoil of the break-up of her family, flashed in a string of nightmares in front of her eyes. She rubbed her aching leg once more and poured herself a glass of milk from the fridge.

'Better wake Timmie and Ram soon,' she said quite loudly, hoping that they would hear. But Tim had tossed and turned, having pulled the blanket over his head to shield out the light. His dog continued to snore like rusty chainsaw; his large furry black tail, the size of a gigantic, hairy snake, thumped a couple of times heavily. He had coiled himself lazily around the foot of the bed as though guarding his young master with his very life.

Without thinking, Lotte tapped her teaspoon against the side of her coffee mug and wondered if Tim was dreaming of school as well.

'Ger-ring… Aar-ring!' Her alarm went off, shrieking in her ear, just as she was about to doze off again. 'Oh, bother!' she muttered, annoyed. With the heel of her hand, she flattened the alarm's off-button as if swatting a fly.

From the adjacent bedroom, a bout of sudden coughing caught her attention. She stretched her leg and eased herself towards the room to investigate. Before she reached the threshold of the doorway the coughing stopped, just as she was about to poke her head around the door. The pattern of breathing changed just then. Both the sleeping boy and the slumbering dog started to snore at a different pitch, but Tim was mumbling incoherently. Ram had left his enormous jaws half-opened; his gigantic head lolled unevenly to one side, resting on one paw.

Oh, it's only Timmie talking and spluttering in his sleep. I'll let him sleep for a little bit longer. I bet he didn't hear the alarm, Lotte thought to herself generously. *I bet he's been dreaming about wretched school like me! Maybe he's thinking about his dad, just getting up next door to go to work? Oh, let him doze on just a little bit more. He's only a kid,* she added thoughtfully. She tiptoed a few steps towards him ever so quietly. But the vivid dreams about school and the flashbacks about her parents still lingered.

She returned to the kitchen and began to lay the table for breakfast, deep in thought. There was an increasing lot on her mind as well as on her plate. 'Mm… I suppose, *this is my lot – poor little old Lotte's lot!* And so, I'll have to put up with it a bit longer,' she murmured with bemused irony. Then, in a hurry, she clattered the cutlery against the cups and plates to wake herself up.

***

But in the cold and damp just outside the front door, Henry was about to tap on the window when Chance hurriedly snatched at his wrist and stopped him. He told him to wait a little while longer as light was fast approaching. 'We've waited this long. Another few minutes won't kill us,' said Chance.

'Speak for yourself,' croaked Henry, about to lose his voice. He stared through the window longingly, then turned away in despair.

Chapter 22

FEEDING TIM'S DREAMS

CROCKERY AND CUTLERY CLATTERED noisily as Lotte busied herself by laying the table. But still, it did not wake young Tim or his dog. A tight smile crossed her face. She decided not to disturb him just yet. She knew from his father Joe that he suffered from nightmares and was a restless sleeper.

Tim was a delicate boy for his age of ten. He was born on Christmas Day, which in normal circumstances should have been a wonderful occasion each year. But instead, it meant he received only one set of presents. Thin and wiry, his grey flannel trousers, which always seemed a bit too long for him, luckily covered his spindly knees. He was born naturally left-handed but was forced to use his right since childhood.

'*Use your spoon in your right hand, dear, like normal children,*' his mother Gloria had chided when he was four years old. But just before his sixth birthday Gloria left home and ran off with the local bus inspector from the number 13 bus. It was quite a scandal on the estate at the time. Tim's last memory of his mother was of her planting a kiss on his forehead whilst he was eating his cornflakes four years ago. By the time he had come home from school with a neighbour, Gloria had packed her bags and vanished. She left a short note for Joe, who had just returned from a long trip from Germany in his lorry after delivering machine parts in Stuttgart.

The note said simply and curtly,

"I'm fed up with your long-distance driving and being on my own most of our married life. Make sure Timmie uses his right hand with his knife and fork. Don't try to find me. I'm moving up north."

After his mother left, Tim reverted to his old habit of using his left hand to write with, or cut up his dinner. For quite a while, young Tim didn't cry as he watched his father fret at having to put on a brave face at the shock of it all. Various people came to look after Tim until Lotte and her mother Shirley moved next door. The Perts took care of him whenever Joe had to make long trips away from home. It was a good arrangement and provided some extra housekeeping money for Shirley as well as giving Lotte some company.

Shirley kindly took him to the dentist so that his crooked teeth could be fitted with braces. Tim dreaded wearing the things, but the dentist took pity on him and made sure that the top row had a prominent pattern etched onto them. He was over the moon when he discovered that the metal braces lent a rather 'tough-guy' appearance to his grin, which frightened off a couple of the bigger lads on the estate who tended to victimise him. Therefore, by flapping his arms like a wild heron, he would narrow his eyes menacingly, then he'd snarl with his teeth of steel, which was often enough to see off his potential tormentors who would flee over the gardens to safety.

Whenever Joe saw Tim, which wasn't as often as he wished due to his job driving all over Europe, he would ask about school. Even before he had a chance to reply, Joe would lecture him loudly. 'Listen now, young Timmie. As I've said before, I want you to work hard at school. Education, me lad, is everything. You know, I wish I had me chance all over again. I want you to speak proper and be able to count your money when you grow up. You don't want to spend your life on the road driving lorries like yer dad. Do yer now?'

'But there's nothing wrong with that, Dad,' Tim would reply immediately.

'Promise me, son, you'll work hard at yer lessons. Don't drop yer haitches. I want you to make something of yer life, to be one of those upstanding citizens of society – a doctor or a teacher, or such like. Don't forget! It's only me and you left now son. So, promise me?' Joe would insist, suppressing a lump at the back of his throat with a cough and a sniff.

'Yes, Dad. I promise,' Tim would simply reply just to please his father. But he would cross his fingers behind his back, hoping God wouldn't strike him dead for telling a white lie. For all he dreamt of for the last few years, was that he would grow up to be an explorer in some faraway land and have some exciting adventures. Most of all, if he couldn't, then he would happily join a travelling circus and see the world.

Just then, Lotte heard him grinding his teeth. 'Cor. He's at it again. I'll leave him a bit longer,' she decided.

He felt so cosy and warm when tucked up in Shirley Pert's house that he didn't want to get up. The incredible weight of Ram, his pet dog climbing on the foot of his bed made the springs creak ominously. Without batting an eyelid, he sidled further up the bed, slyly creeping upwards towards Tim's head.

Ram also was lost in a bottomless dream. He would be chasing chickens on a farm or chewing his favourite mutton bones from the local butchers. The dog heaved a massive sigh between his gaping jaws. He licked his lips, drooling heavily on the duvet.

As a young dog, Ram had teeth like mini stalagmites and as hard as sharp nails. He was a strange mongrel mixture of part-sheepdog and wolfhound and some part unknown. But one thing was certain. One of his forebears must have been an extremely large animal, a very, large creature indeed – a bit like a lion, for Ram had inherited its mammoth frame… He was the size of a small pony with a black shaggy coat. His head was large and bulbous with a massive angular muzzle. His long bushy tail was as strong as an African cobra waiting to pounce. And when he wagged it, whether it was in joy or in excitement, he could knock down small trees like skittles in tenpin bowling.

How Ram came to join the Needles family was an incredible story. Or, as Shirley once put it succinctly, *"An unbelievable shaggy dog's tale…"*

Two and a half years ago, Joe, on one of his long journeys to Scotland to deliver a truckload of motor springs, had happened to stop at a roadside transport café for a cup of tea and a sandwich. On the next table near the window overlooking the trunk road sat a couple quarrelling in loud voices which everyone couldn't help but overhear. They were splitting up and going abroad. They grumbled that they couldn't afford to keep Samson the dog due to his massive appetite, and putting him down was the only option.

Samson – Sam (so the dog was previously named, due to his gargantuan strength in climbing trees and knocking over bikes) – a constantly ravenous animal though he was, a dim mutt of one he certainly was not. Sam wasn't that stupid. He happened to understand every word they said. Sam had sensed that he was not wanted by either party, now they had split up – and that jolly well hurt. Giving a plaintive whimper, he would avert his eyes and fix them dolefully on the large man at the adjoining table who had an open, friendly face and rolled-up no-nonsense sleeves. And what is more, a whopping big pile of chicken and ham sandwiches on his plate. And so with his soft, moist eyes popping out of their sockets, Sam started to lick Joe's hand, slopping his tongue like a large painter's brush, and inched nearer and nearer to the sandwiches. Sam swiped three of Joe's sandwiches off his plate, gulping them down in one go. Joe's shirtsleeve was caught in Sam's cavernous jaws trying to protect his lunch, but the voracious dog wolfed down the rest of his sandwiches in another fell swoop.

'Please, Mister, can you look after him? 'Ee's such sweet liddle ol' doggie! Please can you find him a home... preferably with a butcher or a poultry farmer?' implored the woman, as she and her husband started to leave the café in a hurry.

When Sam managed to reach Joe's parked lorry, he then jumped up instinctively into the driving cabin. Having imposed himself already with a gigantic thump onto Joe's old sweater on the passenger seat, he looked as if he belonged. That was two and half years ago. Since then, he had never left.

Joe renamed Sam to "Ram", for, as he would explain to his workmates, it was because Ram was part-sheepdog and loved chasing sheep. Nevertheless, the name would seem to be appropriate because of his unruly mane and the enormous strength in his large paws – the size of footballs. Ram could knock a fifteen-stone man down in full flight. He would drool and slobber over those he trusted and grew to adore (but attack anyone who threatened them), such as his new-found friends and family, particularly Lotte, Tim and Joe, to whom he was devoted – the latter, of course, having saved him from certain death.

But home life for Tim happened to be rather dull and lonely at times. He hankered for some excitement and more company to liven up his predictable routine. This being…

Get up. Wash. Breakfast.

Go to school. Come home.

Homework. Dinner.

Wash. Go to bed.

Get up. Wash. Breakfast.

Go to… and so on, and so on, day after day.

His father would always seem to be working. 'Sorry, son. But there's only me to bring in the wages. We have four mouths to feed, you know.'

'But, Dad,' protested Tim at once. 'There's only three of us, now Mum's left,' he'd add pointedly, thinking Joe had made a mistake.

'Nope, young 'un – I did mean *four*. Ram eats for two of us!'

And so, it went on as Tim's dream continued – feeding the dream and his imagination wildly...

Chapter 23

WILD DREAMS AND AMAZING GADGETRY

A MASSIVE GRIN SPREAD across Tim's sleep-filled face as his dream of joy ran riot...

Now, as it happened... Joe's older brother, Ray, and his wife Freda, who would visit once a year, were constantly critical about Joe trying to bring up Tim on his own. 'Your son, Timothy,' would proffer Aunt Freda in a know-it-all voice, 'has developed a nervous twitch and a stutter when that Gloria woman upped and left! You really ought to find another proper mother for your son.'

Of course, Joe, having to be in the here and now, would be trying to hold on to his job and earn enough money to keep Tim clothed and Ram fed, so couldn't remember if that was true. It seemed to him that his son had always stuttered as soon as he started to speak. Although his speech hesitation was eventually sorted out, he would still on occasion, when excited or nervous, make a mess of it...

And after what happened with Gloria, Joe had become extremely wary. Adding to that, he knew that his sister-in-law henpecked his brother mercilessly, nagging him constantly. In the end, Joe consoled himself that he happened to be better off with just Tim and Ram and the continuing arrangement of convenience with his neighbour, Shirley Pert and Lotte.

Although Tim would never let on, that having Lotte and her mum around made up somewhat for his missing bit of the family. Grabbing Ram around the neck, he'd nuzzle up to his pet and bury his head into the mass of fur and would whisper furtively into his ear, 'Well. Looks like me and you weren't wanted by our mothers, were we, Ram? At least, we've got my dad and them next door.'

Despite Tim's spindly knees, his coordination skills and balance had improved in leaps and bounds after Joe had bought him a special pair of unusual roller blades for his birthday. These were a special Supersonic-Concorde pair of blades, Mk III. They were unique in every design sense. They were cleverly moulded onto a pair of sparkling, silver-panther cross trainers and finished in astronaut-silver sheen with side gusset grips that required no laces. An incredible feature would allow them to shrink or expand to provide a universal fitting for eight-to sixteen-year-olds. And the pièce de resistance was that the whole boot, with its blades, underneath, could fold flat like a book and slip under his bomber jacket to hide them from view, for they were light as a feather.

The twenty high-tensile wheels edged in titanium steel had been polished to racetrack perfection by industrial diamonds. The undercarriage was attached to a finely tuned micro-driveshaft concealed in the sole of the trainer. When called upon, the self-lubricating wheels popped down ready for action like those under a supersonic jet at a push of a button seated at the back of the heel. Powered by four gears – slow, medium, fast, and supersonic – it was activated by bobbles on the side of the boot. Yet, when the wheels of the blades were retracted into the boot they would look and act like an ordinary pair of trainers to the unsuspecting eye.

These special Mk IIIs were the finest examples of the very latest model, a prototype of an invention from Japan. How Joe managed to get hold of a pair happened to be shrouded in secrecy. All he would say was that a good pal of his who was an importer in Berlin had connections with an exclusive factory in Tokyo, which had the cutting-edge in the newest technology. He was told that there were only three pairs of these special roller blades in existence in Europe. And Joe had one of them. However, he was warned that they could revolutionise travel. The owner could fly along the ground, sticking to the surface like glue, however rough or smooth, or in the wet or dry at speeds up to a terrifying forty-five miles per hour.

Within a week of Tim owning a pair of these supersonic roller blades he couldn't believe it when another fantastic surprise landed in his lap. He was literally lost for words when he happened to get an amazing catapult from his Uncle Ray for Christmas, instead of the usual boring book on English grammar or a dictionary – thinking that he had made a mistake…

It happened to be called the Eagle-Eye, Rocket-Machine – Type A. This catapult was truly, amazing. It boasted a twenty-twenty telescopic vision for both day and night vision and would give unerring accuracy with incredible velocity (so the copy from the manufacturers in China stated on the package). The sling and the elastic came from no ordinary material. They were made from strands of rare shark gut, the finest quality in the land.

It had an expanding telescopic lens with night vision found only in the military. The lightweight alloy body was Y-shaped, being the latest state of the art in fold-flat micro-tubing. This could fold slickly within itself in such a way that it could shrink into the size and thickness of a ballpoint pen. And having highly elasticated strands in its sling, it would slot nicely inside the barrel – ideal for concealing it secretly on one's body. To an outside observer it looked just like a nice fat, shiny pen. A flick of a tiny switch on the side would be all that would be needed to propel the folding mechanism back into a light, but sturdy Y-shaped catapult – ready for life-or-death emergencies.

From quite a distance, Tim managed to develop devastating accuracy by hitting bullseyes with ball bearings, stones and marbles at sixty feet or so whilst practising in his back garden. Astoundingly, with the help of a tail wind, the missile would fly with awesome precision to its target over one hundred feet across the combined back gardens of the Pert's and his dad's. Tim was convinced that he could hit a particular leaf on a tree at such a distance – at a speed of seventy-five miles per hour.

Naturally, he was thrilled to pieces with his Supersonic-Concorde roller blades and his can-never-miss Eagle-Eye,

Rocket-Machine. But he had to be extremely careful never to take them to school, even to show his friends, as they surely would be confiscated by his teacher. And so, he'd hang on to his proud treasures carefully, guarding them jealously with his life…

His slumbers continued uninterrupted as all these remarkable events of his home life and at school vividly unfolded in front of him. Tim turned over in bed, with Ram nearly smothering the life out of him. He fell into a gentle snore in time with the dog's dense breathing. The latter had stretched out his body with a large head denting the duvet, shoving his master aside. They slumbered on like Rip Van Winkle, dead to the world. Though one, of course, dreamt of food; the other one of yet *more* amazing gadgetry.

Chapter 24

HUNG OUT TO DRY

MORNING HAD NOW BROKEN. The watery sky from the night before had now been banished for another day. As Chance peeped desperately through the Pert's front window, it was well past seven. Henry by now was looking worse for wear. His dinner jacket had been battered in the torrential downpour, his dress shirt now completely soaked and sticking to his body.

'Enough of this,' groaned Chance, now at the end of his tether. 'My clothes will shrink in the driving rain. We'll catch a death of a cold if we don't dry out soon.'

Henry sneezed violently. 'I can't wait a minute longer! I've got an idea that might pave the way.' He snuffled and grunted through a half-blocked nose. From the inner pocket of his waistcoat, he unfolded a sheet of paper. He leant against the wall of the porch and started to scribble in large capital letters,

"Don't be afraid... We are friends... Lost and drowning...
SOS... We desperately need help... Please!"

Chance tapped the glass pane with the tip of Henry's cane, gently, as Henry held up the SOS against the window.

Lotte looked up with a start, thinking it was the wind and rain rattling the windows. Raising her head towards the front, she was startled and naturally frightened at first to see two unusual faces pressed against the glass which was smeared with condensation. 'Am I dreaming?' she asked aloud. She rubbed her eyes. No. She was definitely awake. Her heart skipped a beat. They tapped again with the knuckles of their hands – this time louder. Frantically they waved, pointing at the note for Lotte to read. They mouthed animatedly, gesticulating desperately.

"Please. We need yours and your folks' help, Miss – or we'll
drown to death!"

Lotte hesitated for a moment. *Should I ring Joe next door in an emergency?* she thought. Or press the emergency intercom Joe had wired between the flats linked to a panic-alarm? He'd dash over soon enough if she really needed him to, and that reassured her. Or equally, she'd just need to yell, *'Foe!'* and Ram would immediately leap to her side, ready to see off any potential danger with his ferocious teeth.

Squinting and narrowing her eyes at the note with its bearer, she hurriedly put on her glasses.

The scene at the window became clearer as she focused. 'I don't believe it! It's a harlequin or some sort of clown, with rain dripping down his chin, and a city gent in a sodden evening suit. I wonder where they're from?' she questioned. 'Have they been to a fancy-dress party? Have they been doing some stunts for that television studio near the Bush?'

Rainwater had taken its toll. They looked dejected and thoroughly miserable. Lotte felt sorry for them. *For no one, not even my worst enemy, not even the dreaded Braggerleys, should be left to drown like rats after such a storm,* she considered chivalrously. Pointing to the porch door on the left, she opened it a fraction, leaving it secured on the chain. Her hand hovered over the panic-button.

'Wha… What do you want?' she asked hesitantly.

'We are absolutely lost, soaked to the skin, as you can see. We are looking for the circus that's come to town' – thinking that it was the most obvious thing to say. 'Can you or your folks please help us, Miss?'

'Look. You'd better come in. Otherwise, you'll catch your death with pneumonia.' She unlatched the door and pointed to the gas fire and radiator on the wall. 'You'd better dry off a little.' Lotte handed them a large towel each from the bathroom. Gratefully Chance began to wipe the drips off his face whilst trying to control his chattering teeth.

Henry sneezed again. His head jerked violently as his monocle ricocheted forwards like a missile.

They followed Lotte into the kitchen, where she plugged in a hairdryer and they started to dry their clothes. Steam rose from their shirts and pools of water began to form on the tiles where they stood.

'Would you like a hot drink and some biscuits?' she asked politely. They nodded their heads gratefully in unison. Armed with large mugs of hot chocolate and ginger biscuits, the three of them huddled by the fire, letting the warmth trickle to their frozen hands and feet.

'What are your names?' asked Lotte, warming her hands around a steaming mug of chocolate.

'Er. It's Mister Chance. Well, actually, Miss Saskia called me simply – *Chance*,' he replied rather shyly. He gave a cautious grin, pointing. 'And this is my friend Henry.'

'Henry de Poisson at your service, ma'am,' said Henry formally with a sweeping bow, his hand still leaning on his cane theatrically.

Lotte suppressed a giggle at such English stuffiness, particularly from a gent with the name of fish. Fortunately, Henry was too busy propping the cane against the wall to notice.

'Who is Saskia?' she asked, puzzled, thinking it was a relative of theirs.

'Well, Miss. She's a student actually, a designer. We all live in the next neighbourhood, around Paddington,' said Chance immediately.

'Oh, I know. I've been there to an All Pets and Creatures service recently with the dog. It's near to a square by St Swithin's. And please, call me Lotte like everyone else. But did you lose your way from there?'

'Well, sort of, Miss. Sorry... I mean Lotte,' Henry apologised profusely. He tried to explain. 'Miss Saskia's family, the Goodalls, have gone away to friends in France, we believe. And Miss Saskia's gone to join them, and just as we started to leave—'

'Everyone I know seems to be going away for holidays,' said Lotte wistfully, interrupting. The very mention of the word "holidays" stirred up a memory of the last sunny

Mediterranean holiday she took with her parents two years ago before they split up. She shook her head immediately to dislodge the vision, which had suddenly turned sour. She was still clutching the mug of chocolate in her hand, both grip and contents now gone cold.

'Miss Lotte, what happened to your leg?' asked Henry, noticing that she limped slightly on her left ankle getting up from the chair.

'What. Er… pardon? Did you say something?' Lotte apologised, still in a daze.

'We noticed that your leg seemed a little stiff when you start moving on it,' Chance added, casting his glance towards the crutch across the sofa.

'Oh. It's a long story… it's really nothing. It was a bit of an accident,' she offered generously, wagging her head to the side. 'Bit of tomfoolery at school at the beginning of the new year. I'm often teased by Liz and Hector Braggerley. They're brother and sister, you know – in the fourth year.' Self-consciously, Lotte looked at the floor. Blushing wildly, she tried to explain. 'They chased me around the playground with handfuls of slimy slugs and worms to put down my neck, or worse.

'Mind you, I wasn't the only one. They tried it on Steven Stammers, who's a bit timid anyway. Anyhow, I stupidly tripped over my laces and got caught by some members of their gang – that large bully, Kev Scratchley, and that horrible Tilly Crossley. All four of them grabbed me, one on each arm and leg. I was thrown up and down in the air – a sort of "Initiation Ceremony", they said, for the newcomers. They were supposed to form a sort of fireman's safety blanket, interlinking their arms to stop me hitting the ground. Anyway, I must have slipped out of their grip and landed with a wallop on my leg! That's how I broke my ankle.'

On seeing Henry and Chance's horrified look, Lotte added hastily, 'The specialist at the hospital said it's much better now. It's just out of plaster, thank goodness, as it was just getting itchy and driving me crazy trying to scratch inside the cast with a knitting needle! I don't need the crutch, really now. I'm told just to exercise by wiggling my foot and walking.'

'Rotten little devils,' muttered Henry indignantly under his breath. 'They deserve to boil in oil.' He was getting hot under the collar like a volcanic geyser erupting. Then, stupidly, he realised that he had left the hairdryer on, which was stuffed down his shirt. Immediately, Chance rushed over and switched it off in a panic, as steam was now rising out from Henry's scalp.

'Shoosh… Hush. We'd better keep our voices down,' warned Lotte, holding a finger across her pursed lips.

'Yes. We had better be quiet,' agreed Chance. 'We don't want to wake up your folks.'

'Oh, don't worry. I only have a mum, Shirley, and she left earlier to fly off to a conference. But we better cool it a bit, as Tim is sound asleep next door.' Lotte motioned with her hand towards the adjoining room with its door slightly ajar. 'And we don't want to wake Ram, that's Timmie's dog. He's got an extremely snarling temper if woken too early! He protects us with his life.'

'Is the boy your brother?' asked Chance with natural curiosity. He gave a side glance lowering his head towards the bedroom.

'Come off it! Hardly!' retorted Lotte indignantly. 'Tim's a bit of a nuisance, really. He really lives next door at number two. He hasn't got a mother. His dad, Joe, is a long-distance lorry driver.'

They raised their eyebrows quizzically. A muffled thump was heard through the wall next door.

'That's Joe. He's getting ready to leave for Holland or somewhere, to deliver crates or something or other, I think. Anyway, that's what he told us last night at supper time. My mum looks after Tim sometimes. I've got to take him to a school activity camp for the hols after breakfast. Mum has arranged a taxi to take us to the place in Kent.' Lotte pulled a face. 'To be honest, I don't really want to go. It'll be the same boring things as last time. Boring old Mrs Chivers! Boring, stodgy farm food; boring living in bare, damp dormitories. And all those strange kids dumped there by busy parents. Urgh. And what's more, those freezing cold showers at six in the mornings. Worse than death… brrr!' She shivered at the mere thought of it and wriggled her shoulders uncontrollably.

'Then, sometimes, we have to sleep in draughty tents for boring old field trips. And all that rambling for miles on end in the countryside before breakfast! Horrible!'

Lotte shuddered dramatically and continued moaning. 'Mum says, as a good neighbour, I've got to keep an eye on young Timmie, for he's only a kid. So, you can see he's really nothing to do with me… 'cause I'm an only child!'

'You're lucky to have a surrogate brother then, Miss,' said Henry, as though to console her.

'What's that?' she asked.

'Well, it's a sort of "borrowed" or an "adopted" brother.'

'Hardly!' pouted Lotte. She tossed her hair backwards and shuffled noisily in her chair. She took another sip of her drink with a noisy slurp on purpose. 'Besides, I've always wanted a sister, not a silly kid brother. I *always* have to give up my bed when he stays!' Petulantly, she continued to grumble.

An icy moment passed, with Chance tactfully changing the subject. 'What's happened to Tim's mother then?'

'Oh. I've never met her. She left years ago, before we came here. I think she ran off with a bus inspector, or maybe it was a conductor or someone like that.'

He was about to ask about Lotte's mother, when just at that moment, Tim stirred in the next room. They couldn't help but hear a garbled, '*Ooh... aw-aarh – urrh.*'

Noisily, Tim tossed and turned. He was dreaming again of performing in a famous international circus in front of a large audience as a high-wire artist, just honing his skills.

He was travelling at speed on his special supersonic-roller blades across the high-wire, high up in the big top. At the same time, he was firing ball bearings at a hundred miles per hour from his Eagle-Eye, Rocket-Catapult Machine at a moving target somewhere above his head. Unfortunately, though, the tiny wheels of his supersonic blades suddenly got jammed in the middle of the wire and came to a juddering halt halfway across whilst he was suspended ninety feet up near the top of the tent. Disaster struck. He fell out of straps of his boots and began to fall from mid-air. The ground began to rush up at him at breakneck speed. Then a deafening and sickening crunch was heard as his body hit the floor of the ring, churning up a shower of sawdust...

Meanwhile, Tim pulled the pillow from over his head and tried to wake himself up from this terrifying and realistic nightmare...

Chapter 25

A RUDE AWAKENING

WHEN, SUDDENLY, THERE WAS an enormous thud, for Tim had fallen out of bed to a very rude awakening, and a very noisy one at that. Like a deadly arrow, the alarm clock flew off the shelf above and crashed down onto the sleepy dog's tail. Immediately, Ram woke up and yowled with a deafening roar.

Lotte and her visitors leapt from the kitchen table on hearing the din and knocked over their drinks.

'What the... was that?' asked Chance.

Lotte peered around the bedroom door. 'Oh, it's just Tim. I bet he's been dreaming again,' she said.

Tim started to disentangle himself from the duvet which had collapsed like a tent over him. Ruefully, he scratched his head yawning. The dog went to lick his face. Irritably he pushed him away. 'Gerroff, yer sloppy mutt,' he protested wildly.

As he rubbed his eyes, he looked towards the kitchen. He just could not take it in at first. He pinched himself. 'I must be dreaming,' he said. But he wasn't mistaken, because at the table sat a harlequin as large as life, beaming grandly. He was dressed in bright orange and blue with the biggest pair of boots he had ever seen, quite as big as lifeboats. He stared again – his eyes aflame.

Squashed next to the harlequin was a very smart-looking gentleman in a black dinner jacket and bow tie, complete with a monocle and cane (actually, he and his pals at school would call him a City Toff). And what's more, these two strangers were nonchalantly chatting to Lotte around the table. He prodded Ram, who had slumped back to the warmth of the bed. Half-heartedly, the dog raised one eye lazily and pretended to doze again.

As quickly as he could, Tim slipped on his jeans and sweater. But in his rush, his sweater ended up back to front. In bare feet, he cautiously padded into the kitchen to greet the visitors.

'Oi. Master Rip Van Winkle, so you're finally awake at last! About time too,' accused Lotte, shaking a finger at him. 'You've been snoring, yawning and dreaming like crazy for the last hour or two, just like that lazy dog of yours.'

Chance looked at Tim and politely nodded in his direction with a bemused grin.

'Er. Excuse me, Lotte, are they from the circus or something?' asked Tim.

'Well, sort of,' she hastened, just to shut him up. 'I'll explain later. So, if I were you, I'd get properly dressed and put on those shoes and socks. We're miles late and need to get a move on.'

Tim beat a hasty exit. He glanced anxiously over his shoulder at the visitors in case they vanished into thin air.

'Hey. And while you're at it, don't forget to clean your teeth and wash that face of yours,' she yelled after him bossily.

He scurried to the bathroom a bit miffed. He gave his face a quick flick with a damp flannel, hoping that would do. Dashing to the kitchen, he saw that Lotte had laid the table for the four of them. The sound of the tinkling of glasses, the plopping of orange juice being poured and the rustling of cornflakes signalled that breakfast was about to begin. Instinctively, Ram pricked up an ear and opened his eyes. Eventually realising that his master had got up, leaving no one to snuggle against, he leapt off the bed and padded into the kitchen, thumping the floor clumsily, as if an earthquake were threatening. Cutlery and crockery clattered and rattled all over the table because of it. Ram greeted Tim with a sloppy lick, soaking his outstretched hand. Quizzically, he pinned back his ears, sensing the presence of strangers. A low growl started to rumble from the depths of his throat with his teeth bared until Tim announced sternly, raising his finger – 'A friend!'

Chance and Henry looked up in earnest from their plates, waiting to be introduced.

Gradually, Tim sat down as if in slow motion, his eyes as wide as the table mats in front of him, transfixed at the scene. Not daring to let the guests out of his sight for a single second, he subconsciously picked up a banana from the fruit bowl in the middle of the table and dropped it, unpeeled, into his cereal bowl. He began to pour milk over it. The bowl overflowed and dripped over the edges of the table, spilling into Ram's wide, welcoming mouth.

'For heaven's sake, Timothy Needles, *look* at what you're doing! Concentrate. Wake up. And look, you idiot, you haven't even tied your laces!' Lotte pointed to his trainers. 'You'll trip over your feet, you know.'

Tim waggled his head side to side as if to clear the foggy mist that still sat between his ears. 'Er... sorr-ee! Yeah. Sorry, Lotte. Wasn't thinking.' He patted Ram's bulbous head, now damp with milk, as the dog squeezed his bulky body between Tim and Henry's chair legs.

'Oh – Tim. This, by the way, is Mr Chance and Mr Henry de Poisson. They came to dry off from the storm.' Lotte introduced them, flicking her head towards the window.

The torrential rain had long since passed. With the world outside beginning to dry, the air began to lift into a better mood.

Chance gave a broad smile and nodded gratefully. He swallowed a piece of toast with a large gulp. Henry got up stiffly, swiftly removing his glove, then offered his hand, bowing formally. 'I'm pleased to meet you, young man... Heard a lot about you from your sis... Um, I beg your pardon... friend, Lotte.' He hesitated, for Lotte sent "daggers" murderously across the table.'

Shyly, Tim gave a gruff 'Hiya' in return. There was a minute's awkward silence. Then Tim could not contain his curiosity any longer. 'Excuse me. Are you in a carnival parade or something?' he quickly spurted out.

Henry and Chance stared at each other and shrugged, perplexed at the question.

'Are you really a harlequin – a kind of clown... you know special... Mr Chance?'

'Yes, siree. Full-blooded, one hundred per cent pedigree figure of fun at your service, young sir,' Chance replied flippantly. 'And I'm the one to make you and the rest of the world smile and be really happy!' And as he proudly said it, he got up from the table, stepped backwards, then did a backward flip, holding his cup in his hand without spilling a drop. Whilst rubbing his nose, he rose one foot off the ground, hovered smoothly around the room and then floated back to his chair to impress young Tim.

Lotte was too flabbergasted to say a thing.

'He's only showing off, you know,' commented Henry acidly. So as not to be outdone, he boasted, 'At least I've got an unusual cane in my possession.' Henry pushed back his chair and went to retrieve his cane, which was leaning against the wall near the door. Lotte and Tim noticed that it was beautifully polished, the body in shiny ebony and crowned with a glistening silver top.

From where he stood, Henry flung it across the room over their heads like a harpoon. And as he did, the silver tip flew off, revealing a thin length of silver wire that shot out from the end of it, which he quickly grabbed hold of. It unravelled itself, growing longer and longer by the second as it spun into the next room, its length seemingly never-ending. Then it sped towards a large, plumped-up cushion and speared it square in its belly with a sickening sharp *ker-dunk-like* noise. Using a quick flick of his wrist, he tugged it backwards. It cracked like a whip and recoiled itself into the body of the cane, which flew back into his grip like a frisbee...

'Now that's what I call something useful – a harpoon cane,' boasted Henry proudly, 'which doubles as a frisbee!'

'Now who's showing off now?' Chance laughed as they all sat down at the table again.

Ram let out a small whimper. Then he hid under the table, a bit scared. Tim stroked his tail to soothe him and said, 'Shush now, good boy. They're only tricks of the trade of magic. It's harmless, purely for fun. Nothing dangerous is going to happen.'

'Well, let's hope so,' murmured Lotte softly under her breath. 'I dearly hope so!' She was now wondering what she had let herself in for.

Chapter 26

WARNINGS

Whilst Lotte was chewing this over, the toaster popped up with a sudden ping. She sprang up and poured some fresh tea. Bemused, she watched the bantering that followed between Tim and the visitors, knowing full well his obsession with the circus.

'What are you two doing here then? Where did you come from? Were you born here in London? How did you…?' asked Tim, bursting with questions.

Chance stared hard and long at Henry. Henry narrowed his eyes at him, then looked at Lotte intently in turn. 'Well, it's really quite a story,' said Chance, sucking in his cheeks. He drew a sharp breath. 'You may not believe this, but just three days ago at Miss Saskia's college…'

Tim and Lotte were then told of Chance's incredible story of what happened – of how he came into being. And how Miss Saskia carved his structure out of timber which came from an ancient tree thousands of years old. Chance then described how he was stolen in Saskia's old car by a young thief named Seth. And how he was subsequently found propped up in a doorway by a mild-mannered taxi driver who took him to Madame Rousseau's waxworks, where he made friends with Napoleon and Houdini. He told them of his first encounter with a squashed ghostly spirit called Cecil-the-Thin, who had travelled back in back in time with a message for him in the form of a strange prophecy...

No sooner had he said that, he paused and gave a little shudder.

The children were mesmerised.

Studiously, Henry glanced at their faces. Their chins were frozen expressionless, propped up by their elbows on the table.

'Go on. Please!' begged Lotte, impatiently tapping the table-top with the tips of her fingers.

'Shush, will you! Don't interrupt,' growled Tim, a stern finger across his lips.

Then, as Chance started to describe what he had been told about the Three Kingdoms, Lotte interrupted again. 'What do you mean by the *Three Kingdoms*?' she asked blankly, her curiosity aroused.

Slowly, Chance pushed himself out of his chair and began to circle the room ponderously. Half-closing his eyes, he folded his arms as if to help him concentrate. 'Well, dear child, it's like this...' he drawled solemnly. 'You've heard of the Kingdom of Humans in which we live, haven't you?'

Both Lotte and Tim nodded hard.

'Well, there happens to be *two* other kingdoms: one of animals – fauna, and one of flora – plants and trees. These

Three Kingdoms – or worlds, if you like – make up the planet as we know it, and what's more…'

Their heads tilted again in agreement.

He paused briefly to study their faces. They were spellbound. Continuing, he went on to describe a time long ago on earth when there was a peaceful order of things, when all three kingdoms were in perfect harmony with one another – completely balanced with nature, as it were – happy and peaceful. But then, as time rolled by, he explained that this peaceful coexistence started to break down as food, fresh air and space grew scarce. The inhabitants, with their different species, began to kill one another on a massive scale. Genocide erupted. Chaos followed. Then a reign of terror spread throughout the land led by a ruthless evil being, who had grabbed power during the unrest. And the peace and tranquillity in the kingdoms were destroyed forever.

The children went extremely quiet, almost petrified. Even their dog froze quite still on the floor besides them as the harlequin continued his story. Calmly and slowly, he told them what Cecil had warned him about… of the terrible, evil forces whipped up by their leader, and which were now gathering in strength to strike at the kingdoms in readiness to invade this and other lands.

'Sounds terrifying,' gulped Tim. 'Who is this being… this leader? Why's he doing this? And what for?'

Chance shrugged helplessly and said gravely, 'I was told he is the Evil One, a ruthless tyrant that I was warned about. He goes by the name of Qnevilus-the-Terrible: a self-appointed ruler who set himself up as the monarch. I was further warned that he is nothing but a jumped-up dictator, an opportunist and a dangerous megalomaniac, who simply kills for greed, power and evil, and will assassinate anyone who dares to stand in his way.'

'How… how did this happen?' asked Lotte all of a stutter. Without thinking, she kept making shapes in the sugar bowl with her teaspoon, stirring it slowly.

Then Chance went on to describe how this terrible despot had survived through the ages and had murdered the rightful ruler of this – the first, and one of the most peaceful kingdoms in the land, to usurp his throne.

'According to legend,' said Chance, 'this kingdom – where every species spoke happily to one another in a universal language – was once happy, joyful and contented. It was once described as a paradise on earth… until this evil tyrant Qnevilus invaded the land – and stole the kingdom as his own. From that day onwards, he ruthlessly subjugated its inhabitants using torture and murder.'

'He sounds horrific. Really horrendous,' whispered Lotte hoarsely. 'Where is he now?'

Chance replied that as far as he knew, after some climatic disaster on the earth at that time, Qnevilus's kingdom simply vanished. And according to legend, it fell into the sea. But miraculously, it somehow survived and resurfaced as a hidden kingdom in the so-called "Alterworld", where to this very day, he rules his peoples by terror and fear.

Tim murmured that it sounded like the mythical lands that sank under the oceans, called Atlantis, or Oceanis, which he had heard of at school.

But Chance shook his head, saying it was neither of those or others that he had heard of before. It was something else that he had been told about, but just as mysterious and just as elusive. Restlessly, he continued to stride around the room looking tense.

The children's faces blanched noticeably as they sat rigid in their seats. Then quickly, Henry gestured to his friend to return to being seated, so that he could continue the story gently without scaring them witless.

Puzzled, Lotte wanted to know why Chance was involved in all this. He explained that he did not choose to be. But merely that Cecil, this ghostly spirit, had told him that *he* – the harlequin – was the "chosen one" who had fitted the prophecy of the ancient legend. And furthermore, it was he who had been chosen to help the Kingdoms fight back so that they could one day regain the peace and tranquillity that had now been lost.

Tim and Lotte shuffled about at the kitchen table pretending to nibble at their breakfast. They wanted to interrupt so many times. There was so much to ask. Chance simply held up his hand imploring them to be patient until he had finished.

Just then, Tim was about to ask him about something else, when he suddenly noticed how the glare from the kitchen light caught something glittering around the harlequin's neck. 'Sorry to interrupt, Mister, but what's that around your neck?'

'Ah, you mean this?' said Chance, pulling the pendant out from the top of his sweater. He held it between his finger and thumb and twiddled it so that it shimmered in the light. 'I was coming to that. I'll explain. It's all tied up in a riddle I've got to solve.'

'A riddle? What do you mean?' asked Lotte, her mouth full of toast that had gone a bit stale.

'Yes, a riddle. But, more about that in a minute. Firstly, this stone here.' Chance polished it carefully against the edge of his bow tie. 'This beautiful stone fell out of a knot from an extremely ancient tree I was made out of – which I have already told you about. Miss Saskia, my inventor, made it into a special pendant to hang inside my collar for safekeeping and to bring me luck. The glittering bit, according to skinny Cecil, is called the Sacred Gem of Knowledge.'

'Why is that?' asked Lotte, absolutely riveted.

'*Hold your horses*, I beg you, my young friends. I'll explain soon. Let me carry on with my story. There's so much to tell...'

Unwaveringly, Chance continued.

He described how he managed to escape from the waxworks and hid in a doorway off the Cromwell Road in the early hours of the morning. How he got "arrested" by the police and locked up in a cell for the rest of the night. Then how he was fortunately rescued by Miss Saskia and taken home to Westhope Terrace, where, he said, he met Henry and Davinia Plum, the other figures created and built by Saskia.

Henry nodded like mad in confirmation.

But seeing the look of disbelief on their faces, Chance repeated, again what he said. 'Yes, my young friends. Yes. All of us, all three of us, believe it or not, are unique inventions of Miss Saskia at her college.'

'Yup! But yours truly is the best and the cleverest,' growled Henry into his cereal bowl, as he puffed out his chest boastfully.

Lotte knocked over the bowl of sugar in her excitement, showering Ram's tail, which was sticking out. She spluttered incredulously. '*What! You what... all... three of you!* You can't mean... you two and that Davinia you mentioned were, er... I mean... all this time – unbeknown to the Goodalls, were *alive, well and kicking!* Didn't that Saskia girl know about it?'

Henry shuffled uncomfortably in his chair, pretending to sip from his cup, which was nearly empty. He stared awkwardly at Chance for help, wondering how on earth to reply. After a while, he said in barely a whisper, clearing his throat,

'Ah-erm... er... actually, I don't think Miss Saskia knew what we were up to when her back was turned, as most of the time we spent the night arguing amongst ourselves. Then we collapsed, wiped out and slept until morning, due to utter exhaustion. But that was only half the story. She couldn't have found out what her cat, the woodpecker and we got up to, because secretly they were equally devious and—'

'Henry! Can I *please* continue?' shouted Chance, increasingly annoyed as his hand slapped the table.

Chance picked up the story again and told them about Zoot, the bright old woodpecker from the garden square, and Mudd, the little family cat he met at the house. And how Zoot had said the same thing about the legend, the prediction and the riddle, and what Chance had to do in order sort out its secret.

'And importantly, what's more, Zoot had drummed it in,' explained Henry, 'that Chance – because of this, had been granted "*predetermined time limits*" on his life in order to carry out this quest. Such a time limit was to allow him to search for those in this hidden kingdom, and to confront the evil and his followers who were hiding there. He has no choice in the matter. Then he has got to flush them out and stop them dead before they have the chance to invade our lands.'

'*What!* Do you mean you have *no* choice in the matter?' asked Lotte, taken aback. Stunned, she started to rise out of her chair. But then she fell back again as if poleaxed.

'*Not if I want to continue to live,*' said Chance wearily. 'It appears that I have been given a deal – a contract if you like – on this planet so as to live. For instance, I have been given forty days to start off with to carry out specific tasks – although I could be granted an extra ninety-nine, by carrying out some good, kind deeds. But if I refuse, or if I fail, I was warned there'll be certain death. *So therefore, in that allotted time – it's find the one of evil, kill him or be killed.* I have no choice in the matter if I want to live.' This time he did not mince his words.

The children fell silent, now really frightened when they heard all this.

Henry coughed nervously. He tapped a spoon on the table at the mention again of the awful conditions attached to his friend's life. He knew only too well how these would have a direct effect on his life too. Lotte and Tim became extremely agitated on hearing this and urgently pushed for an explanation.

'Ah ha. Now!' said Chance. He leant across the table and grabbed hold of Henry's spoon to stop its irritating rattle. There was a gleam in his eye. 'Now, it's all down to this special gemstone and the secrets it holds...'

Carefully, he bent his head and slowly, removed the pendant from around his neck. He thrust it forwards under the bright light. Eagerly, their necks craned forward, their eyes coming to rest on the glittering stone nestling in the palm his hand.

Methodically, Chance then filled in the last bit of the story that Zoot had related… About how in legend, it was said where the gemstone came from. He described the time when, hundreds and thousands of years ago, an asteroid fell to earth carrying with it an amazing precious stone that fragmented into several pieces.

The first piece had fallen into an ancient Tree of Knowledge, a second piece, into a Tree of Life… and so on. He told them that the first piece was the very same piece he now held in his hands – the one called *the Sacred Gem of Knowledge*. 'The power within this beautiful stone will help me in my task ahead,' he added solemnly.

The children paused, their brains whirring like mad. Whether they fully understood or not, they accepted the harlequin's explanation as gospel, after lots of ums and ahs.

Chance pushed the stone closer to their noses, turning it over gently as if it were a living creature. He carried on.

Then, as though giving it a rest, Chance carefully returned the precious gem in its pendant back to where it belonged – securely hidden behind his collar. Lotte and Tim leant back into their chairs sipping the dregs of cold tea from their mugs whilst trying to take it all in.

Now, it was Henry's turn to pick up where Chance left off. He explained about the riddle's vital meaning – the way it unravelled. And how it ultimately controlled Chance's life by his having to follow the instructions in the riddle, if he wanted to live… He told them of the discovery of an ancient encyclopaedia in Mr Goodall's study and what its contents revealed. Furthermore, how everything in it confirmed the existence of the legend with its riddle, the prophecy and all about the kingdoms.

'Hold on a sec,' pleaded Lotte. 'You mentioned about the riddle being vital to Chance's life. How exactly—'

'That's enough for the moment, Henry,' interrupted Chance crossly. 'We don't want to scare them now. Let's save that explanation for later. If we live that long and are not killed off in the meantime.'

Then Chance told them of the dangers of being murdered by terrifying phantoms and faceless terrors called the Custodians, who were waiting for him on the journey. He was led to believe that they, like others, stood between him and Qnevilus, protecting the latter, as it were. No sooner had he mentioned the words *phantom*, *terror* and *Qnevilus*, the blood drained from his face. Gratefully, he took a gulp from a glass of water Lotte had hurriedly shoved under his face.

As the limits of time controlling the harlequin's life sunk in, Lotte became increasingly alarmed. 'But I don't understand,' said she, as she got up to refill their cups and mugs. 'What happens if you fail?'

Chance went incredibly silent. A deathly hush fell over the breakfast table.

Henry cleared his throat and fiddled with his monocle. He hesitated. 'Er... erm. Well, Chance here goes to meet his maker.'

'Whad'ya mean?' asked Tim, his mouth ajar.

'At the end of forty days – and remember, we've already had three – he's had his chips. He cops it. Dead! Disintegrates to dust!' said Henry gravely, without emotion. 'Unless, of course, he manages to get a reprieve of some extra days, or find the next missing piece in time: you know, the vital one of life...' His voice petered out, seemingly unsure.

Lotte tried to calm Tim down, who was by now fidgeting in his seat. He gulped down his breakfast at breakneck speed, throwing crumbs all over the table. They were stunned and flabbergasted. And the worry of it showed.

Chance swallowed hard. 'Look, youngsters, we've faced this threat before. The worry hanging over us is nothing new. But the gem might help to protect us.'

'We hope,' said Henry stiffly. 'The sooner we can get going to sort out the obligations of the riddle – *the better chance that you will live!*'

Lotte got up to clear the table and started to rinse the crockery under the tap. But then she got side-tracked and simply piled them high in the sink. She turned round to face them, still puzzled, her nose screwed up trying to work out something in her head. 'Funny, you know. The other Sunday at the church, the vicar went on about something to do with the Three Kingdoms or other. And I'm sure he mumbled something about an ancient book and waiting for someone special. Now what was it, Tim?'

'What are you on about then, Lotte?' snapped Tim, as he wiped his mouth with the back of his hand. He had been fiddling with his knife, slowly separating the peel from the marmalade on his plate.

'That's it! I remember now. Father Quick said that the world was waiting for a kind of Messenger of Mirth to save the Kingdoms. Didn't he, Tim?'

'I dunno, can't remember exactly. There was so much stuff going on at St Swithin's. I had a job trying to hang on to Ram and stop him from chasing the cats. And besides, your mum was in a bit of a hurry to collect us with your crutch and get us home in case your gammy ankle got tired.'

'It sounds like an amazing coincidence, don't you think, Mr de Poisson?' said Lotte.

Henry merely lifted his shoulders helplessly, whereas Chance stared vacantly through the window with a faraway look.

Tim pushed the rest of his breakfast away, got up and began to finish getting ready. Ram crawled out from under the table, his eyes following his beloved master around the room like a radar tracking device – never leaving him for a second.

As Tim started to throw a couple of things into his rucksack, he suddenly stopped. Turning to Chance and Henry, he asked, 'I mean… do… do you think, Mr Chance, Mr Henry… I mean, will it be all right, if me and Lotte could go on this adventure… er, I mean, this journey with you? Please…? You know, instead of going on to… you know… *Please?*' he begged.

'Tim! I'm sure they don't want kids in the way,' scolded Lotte. 'Do you now… I mean, do you… eh, Mr?' she added quickly with a hopeful glint in her eye. She sidled up to Tim and gave him a sly kick on his shin.

'We really don't want to go to that boring old camp at Mrs Chivers's again. Do we, Lotte? I mean your lot's adventure sounds much more up our street,' insisted Tim, hoping against hope.

Chance and Henry looked at each other long and thoughtfully. 'I'm not sure about it, young 'un. It could be a long way. Extremely tiring, and could be very, very dangerous,' said Chance, biting his bottom lip, trying his best to deter them.

'*Great!* Even better! The more danger there is... grr-eat! Wicked! Makes it even more exciting. Brill!' Tim started to get excited as soon as he said it. 'What's an adventure without a bit of danger? Doesn't scare me one bit!'

'Are you sure, young man? Absolutely certain?' Henry looked to Lotte for support.

But Tim just couldn't keep quiet. His legs kept jiggling about with excitement. 'I promise. Cross my heart... won't be in the way. Promise! We could even help you, you know. That phantom bloke you mentioned wouldn't dare touch you, if we came along. What with two kids and a dog – who can tear villains to pieces – it'll be a wicked disguise. If you know what I mean!'

Suddenly, Chance got up and started to pace the room to mull things over. He shook his head, full of doubt. 'No. I'm *really* not too sure. It could be incredibly dangerous. Even *we* don't know what is round the corner awaiting us. We would be naive fools if we failed to heed Cecil-the-Thin's warnings seriously. The deathly threat of the phantoms and the terrors sounds horrendously real enough. They could be one of the same, or perhaps even many more of them waiting to destroy me... us. There might be hundreds of them: who the devil knows? And finally, just as serious, we mustn't forget the evil ruler Qnevilus himself! Don't you agree, Henry?'

'Yes, I have to admit the journey is fraught with obstacles,' said Henry, nodding anxiously. 'Yes, there are tremendous dangers at every step along the way. The threat of evil over who tries to do good is as *real* as it is today, as it was since the beginning of time. But this time, the terror will kill! It vowed it would if Chance tries to follow the journey in chasing the riddle. And particularly, the threat of death over whosoever dares to seek the next piece of gem. I'm afraid, my young friends, it is no idle joke. And I must confess, it's really scary!' admitted Henry, stroking his moustache nervously.

'Ah. But hell's bells, I could flatten it with one shot of my special Eagle-Eye catapult in a flash!' boasted Tim. He grabbed his precious trophy from the side of his bed and tossed it into his rucksack. 'And Ram would guard us with his life now, won't you, doggie?' He ruffled the dog's head roughly. Ram bared his teeth and howled defiantly. 'So please, *please*, Mr Chance. Please, Mr Henry, let us come with you?' he pleaded once more.

Lotte nodded up and down supportively, hoping to persuade them. Behind her back she kept her fingers tightly crossed.

After some thought, Chance reluctantly agreed. 'Okay. Okay, you youngsters, you've twisted my arm. I give in. You can join us: but for the first part of the journey, mind, then we'll talk about it! But also, on the strict understanding that it's only for the duration of your school holidays – maximum! At the end of that time, you must return home regardless, whether we continue the quest ourselves, alone or not. Succeed or fail, both of you will return home to school. Henry and I will make sure of that. Okay? Do you agree the terms, Lotte? Tim? Then let's shake on it…

'Then, to our new, good friends and fellow travellers – welcome! And so, from now on, let us please drop this stuffy *Mister* business, shall we!'

They accepted Chance's outstretched hand. Tim let out a yell with an unrestrained screech. He leapt into the air, clenching his fist, shouting, '*Oh yes! Great. Wicked! Wowwee. Cheers!* ...Honest, we won't get in your way. Will we, Ram?'

The dog grunted noisily in agreement, whilst polishing off the toast that Tim had left on the table. He padded over towards Chance to curry favour and licked his hand.

'Do hurry up, Tim, and get dressed properly. And wash behind those ears!' As she ticked him off, her voice became a mixture of apprehension with excitement of the future unknown. 'We're going, you know, on a long mysterious journey. You never know whom we might meet!' Then she added a little laugh; but it was laced with nerves.

'Yup. We're off on a trip. An interesting adventure I'm sure it'll be. Won't it, doggy, me old pal?' Tim then bent down and gave Ram a hug. The very thought of following this amazing harlequin and his friend filled him with wild expectations, thrilling him to the core. *Magic!* he thought. *Pure blinking magic! And just wait till I tell my pals at school next term; they'll be dead sick with envy.*

He rushed into the bedroom to collect his precious trainers with their special supersonic-roller blades that he had folded flat and slipped them into the zip pocket of his rucksack for safety. In the other pocket, he put a bag of hardened glass marbles and steel ball bearings, the ammunition for his incredible catapult.

No sooner had Lotte started to tidy up the breakfast things than she remembered to grab Brush, her robotic mouse, which was her prized mascot. And this went everywhere with her, even to school, hidden from the prying eyes of her teachers and the others. When Joe had brought home the unusual present of the supersonic-roller blades for Tim, so as not to make Lotte feel left out of things, he gave her a robotic mouse, which she affectionately called "Brush". It had long white whiskers that bristled as antennae, which could sniff the air for any threat of danger from predators – be they animal or human. It had eyes that spun about 360 degrees, spying all around it, but could photograph distant objects from over eighty feet, better than any spy camera on the market.

It also had a curly tail that wriggled about in the air like an inquisitive worm emerging from a newly-mown lawn. The difference was that it had a micro-listening device cleverly hidden inside it and could record sounds, even conversation, from up to fifty feet or more, depending on the volume. In an emergency, it could even be used as an unusual phone – just by silently thinking out messages in secret, by stroking his tail – without anyone knowing.

Its head was segmented at its neck, which allowed it to move up and down, side to side. It could open and shut its tiny jaws to bare razor-sharp teeth and squeak disconcertingly loudly. Solar batteries were built into its tiny, pointed head, disguised by a rich carpet of grey fur all over. The pièce de resistance was that its four little feet could scurry in any given direction, commanded by specific voice-recognition by Lotte. By trial and error, it had been known that Brush could rush about at fantastic speeds and, hitherto unknown by living mice, could creep into the tiniest cracks, climb up furniture or, if told, hide up people's trouser legs undetected. 'What a find!' Joe had said, quite chuffed. 'Only the Russians could invent such a toy.'

Without wasting another minute, Lotte filled a large rucksack with packets of biscuits, a couple of fruit drinks from the fridge, some apples and bananas, and five bars of chocolate. *For emergency rations*, she reasoned thoughtfully. And, of course, not forgetting a large pack of dog biscuits for Ram. *Shall I take the crutch in case my leg gets tired?* she asked herself, just as she was about to collect it. She then changed her mind and decided to slip her silver fold-up scooter over the shoulder of her quilted jacket instead.

Tim was already packed and ready, itching to go. 'Okay, everyone. We're finally ready,' Lotte said. As they made their way to the door, she hesitated. She thought about whether to leave a note of explanation for her mum Shirley or not. She decided against it, preferring to work out a tactful way of how to tell her so as not to worry her unduly. Of course, she could always contact her through Brush by the time she came back in the holidays. Thinking of Shirley, she suddenly remembered something important. Her face went white for a second with alarm.

'What's up? Anything wrong, Miss Lotte?' asked Chance as they trooped past her through the door.

'Oh, blow! Bother!' she cursed, smacking her forehead. 'I almost forgot. My head's like a sieve. It slipped my mind with so much going on all at once. I promised Mum that we'd pop into the children's hospital to say hello to Shoona Canning, who's just had her appendix out. I said we'd call in on the way to Mrs Chivers's.'

'Who's this Shoona person, may I ask?' asked Henry with interest.

'She's at my school. Mum knows her mother. They work together at the airport shops.'

Lotte was the last to leave after shooing Ram to follow Tim. She locked the door after checking all the lights and windows.

'Hey. Haven't you forgotten something else, Lotte? You know, thingy-me-bob was supposed to collect us, to take us to Mrs C's. You know – at half past eight – arranged by your mum ages ago, don't you remember?' Tim called over his shoulder to remind her. By then, he was about halfway down the path followed by Ram, who had his tongue hanging out and was panting happily.

'Of course, I haven't forgotten, stupid!' she retorted, glaring at him. 'He's late. It's already nearly nine. He's had it! We'll get another cab if he can't get his act together.'

The morning light was clear and welcoming, bathing the roads with a clean, warm glow. At the end of the road, the rose blossom had suddenly bloomed. A hint of early spring was in the air. There was a little skip in Henry's step and an eager lilt in Chance's stride as they sauntered down the road with Ram glued to Tim's leg and young Lotte scooting along to save her ankle. They were full of exciting hopes and high expectations. Their incredible adventure was just beginning. If only they knew what was in store for them, perhaps they would have stayed at home – and heeded the warnings. Those terrible warnings from the past...

Part V

Beware of the eyes that have already died.

Chapter 27

BEWARE OF THE EYES THAT CRIED

A HUNDRED AND SEVENTY miles away in the ancient historical town of Glastonbury, the locals were getting ready for their annual festival of 'Spirit, Body and Light'. Madame Groszena Drizelda, the celebrated fortune teller, was preparing for the morning session of "palm and sole" readings with predictions by tea leaves and coffee grounds. She refused to use tea or coffee bags – be they round or square – as they simply did not work.

She had a special gift of reading the future with Tarrantulot cards, a sort of cross between common poker-playing cards, tarot and Happy Families. Crystal ball-gazing naturally was the mainstay of her trade. Occasionally, though, for bigger problems, she would employ the use of globe-like spheres borrowed from the tops of Belisha beacons from pedestrian crossings, either zebra or pelican – it didn't matter which. How they came into her possession without being pursued by the police for alleged theft is a mystery.

But according to a fellow fortune teller in the Glastonbury Mystic Circle, these large Perspex globes seemed to fall into her hands each time she attempted to cross the road when using the crossing soon after pressing the button on the lamppost. You can imagine her shock, the first time it happened four years ago when waiting to cross a busy junction on the high street. The light lit up signalling "WAIT". And so, she did, when a flashing globe fell into her surprised open hands. Since then, she regarded it as a good omen of the future, something she shouldn't ignore.

Madame Drizelda was descended from a long line of famous mystics. Her great-great-granduncle was the Great Percival Bellanoble, the renowned Gypsy King of fortune telling who was also a most-feared bare-knuckle fighter and a former champion of Europe. In 1861, after winning a fleet of caravans and horses following an extremely ill-tempered bout in Ireland, he fled to England chased by a mob who claimed he unfairly hypnotised their local champion, Dinty O'Loonergan, to fall asleep in the ring.

… and so, the story went.

Having such an illustrious background, it was small wonder that Madame Drizelda's reputation was held in some considerable awe by others, both far and wide. Apart from her natural gift at forecasting the future and her uncanny abilities to unravel the past for her clients, her strength was also in her no-nonsense manner with its steely resolve. And even more so, her iron grip, which stood her in good stead to extract money due from erring ungrateful clients who tried to swindle her. Such was the strength of her vice-like grip that she could have easily crushed the bones in the hands of particularly unpleasant individuals who deliberately tried to take advantage of a little old lady of an indeterminate age.

Her shop was in a side street veering up a wide slope, just off the high street, where it bent sharply on the way to Stonehenge. Giving directions by telephone, she would often say with a wicked sense of humour, 'I'm over the hill and around the bend.'

The shop front was painted a deep midnight blue with a bright yellow door with a picture of the sun in the centre panel.

A sandwich board was propped just outside the bay window on the cobbled part of the pavement. *"MADAME GROSZENA DRIZELDA - CLAIRVOYANT EXTRAORDINAIRE - BESPOKE FORTUNE TELLER"*, it said in prominent italics.

A similar colour scheme continued inside, though the walls were painted purple, edged with bright yellow skirting boards and architraves. The ceiling was sprayed jet black, but dotted with silver stars and moons all over it in relief. Although small, the shop was filled to the brim with glass cabinets and shelves full of thousands of different-coloured stones: jasper, amber and moonstones, together with slices of rare agates of translucent orange, indigo and sunset yellows. In a glass cage facing the door was a collection of precious and semiprecious stones: amethysts, sapphires, emeralds and so on.

Every sort of mystic prop and esoteric object to do with astrology, magic charms and psychic writings was packed into this tiny shop. Spiritual candles, incense, effigies of beasts cast in soapstone greeted the eye. Pathways to enlightenment, self-hypnosis books and other unusual books by the Alternative Press were stacked high up on the shelves. On a lower shelf, ideal for browsing, was an array of CDs, DVDs, audio tapes of animal and tree chants, sounds of the seas, whales and dolphins.

In a special display, under lock and key at the back of the shop, was an unusual collection of different glass jars containing shards of asteroid, bits of meteorite or reputedly moon dust. These were not for sale. Nor, indeed, was Madame Drizelda's treasured collection of dinosaur and serpent eggs.

Suspended on the wall behind the counter – out of reach of children – hung a cabinet full of miniature bottles containing magic toadstools and mystic potions, being elixirs for this, and cure-alls for that. Some claimed to soothe anger, some to stimulate humour for the miserably inclined, and others to sort out those with mixed emotions. Perhaps it was all in the mind of the beholder. But as usual, she did a roaring trade with the overseas tourists, especially at festival times.

Keeping her company was Oswald, an extremely large, longhaired white cat, who was the size of a baby panther. Oswald was a mixture of Persian and English tabby but had inherited the permanently cross-looking features of the former from his father and the laziness of the latter from his mother. His sharp-green eyes constantly shifted slyly across the shop or they would dart out into the street, taking in the scene whenever he could. He was a lazy old cat and spent most of the day and night dozing amongst the goods on display by nuzzling up to the semiprecious stones in the window, jade being his favourite.

Whilst in the back room, Drizelda's other friend was an old inky-black raven called Nero with strange silver eyes, bulbous and staring. Nero lived in a large battered old cage suspended on a metal stand next to the sink in the tiny kitchen. Though his wings were clipped, he was still able to flutter in and out whenever he so wished, for the cage was never locked. She had looked after him for five years or so after he retired from active duty in helping to guard the Crown Jewels in the Tower of London.

Groszena Drizelda was used to ravens, having spent many summers looking after these birds at the Tower, where she had a stepbrother, old Edbert Tuffnut, who was a Beefeater. Old Edbert was "Master of the Ravens", a kindly old chap who took great care of them and made sure that their wings were clipped regularly so that they could not fly away. For it was reported in folklore that once the ravens deserted the place, there would be an almighty calamity and the Tower of London would fall right down. And the Kingdom would collapse forever.

Such was Madame Drizelda's reputation as a fortune teller, and modern-day soothsayer, that people came from all over the world to have a reading. City financial analysts would consult her about the "futures" money markets. Lonely individuals would call to ask her to predict a suitable partner for them. Anxious parents would bring their children, hoping for a forecast of their exam results. Some days, she would get a really, bizarre request.

Today was one such day...

About an hour after she had opened the shop, having turned the Perspex sign around to "Open" on the front door, she started to tidy her green baize card table and polish her crystal ball. She then covered it up to rest a while to gather its mystic energy under a golden-coloured piece of silk in readiness for a reading.

Next, as part of her daily routine for work, she would go through a habitual ritual of superstition. She checked the calendar to make sure it was not the thirteenth. She checked on the astrological charts that her own stars were in the ascendancy. She stuck her head outside the door to check that the window cleaner had not left a ladder propped up anywhere in her street. Then she stroked the cat's tail and threw a pinch of salt over her left shoulder. Once all that was done, she would then be completely satisfied that she could begin.

She put the kettle on ready for the tea leaves and ground coffee and tucked her gypsy scarf of blue and white polka dots around her ears. And as she did that, it exposed a deathly-white complexion, which was a bit ghostly due to her ice-pale lips, though her dark violet eyes were heavily outlined by mascara. Her earrings you would expect to be big gold hoops; but surprisingly no. Rather unexpectedly, she dangled from her left ear a heavy cross made of jade, whereas from her right, swung an ornate Chinese dragon cast in gold, clutching a glistening white pearl in its mouth. A chunky necklace of golden amber clutched her throat, as though to disguise a purple birthmark shaped like a honeybee hidden just below her Adam's apple.

'*Ting-a-ling!*' There was sudden clang. Madame Drizelda jumped up with a start when the front door suddenly opened, tripping the miniature brass bell fixed on a spring over the top of the doorframe.

Suspiciously, Oswald raised his lazy head and let out a sleepy meow, only to lower it again. He covered his face with his paws and went back to sleep. In the semi-darkness, because of the shadows created by the dark interior and the piles of stock, Drizelda was startled to see a silhouette of a tall, imposing figure of a man. At first, it was difficult to make out his dress due to the bright sunshine outside the shop bathing the profile of his back. The doorway was filled with his massive frame as he stood impassively in front of the shop counter.

'…Ca… Can I help you?' Madame Drizelda ventured politely. There was no reply. 'May I help you, sir?' she repeated to the face that was shrouded in shadow.

But she was totally unprepared for the next surprise. An eerie staccato voice responded, but not from the lips, which did not move an inch. The sound began to ooze from his nose. A nasal, strangled squeal forced its way out, as if the voice and head were divorced from each other like in a ventriloquist's dummy, but minus the jaw movement.

'Madam, I need a reading. A psychic reading, urgently, in private,' he grated with a garbled voice, as though coming from a throat full of crushed marbles. It echoed eerily with the sound bouncing off the wooden floor.

Drizelda was not at all sure whether she should, for safety's sake, accept this customer or not. Under her purple silk blouse, her heart thumped like a rocket primed for lift-off. She pulled her knitted shawl tightly around her shoulders and fiddled anxiously with the wisps of hair under her scarf. She was now wishing that she hadn't opened the shop so soon.

Nervously, she asked, 'Sir, do you want a tea leaf reading or coffee grounds?'

'Never touch the stuff! Do you understand, woman? I want a crystal-clear picture of something extremely important. It's vital, to do with the future of the world,' he snapped back contemptuously.

'I'm afraid it's quite expensive, as I use only virgin crystal balls of the finest quality from Budapest,' she said, hoping to put him off – whilst thinking, *Uh-oh, we have an oddball here banging on about the planet.*

Undeterred, the stranger threw a fifty-pound note down on the glass counter with disdain. Reluctantly, she brushed aside the beaded curtain to the room at the back where she kept her reading table and gestured him to follow. This he did, scraping his left leg behind him as though he had a slight limp, but was attempting to disguise it.

She pointed to a well-worn rattan-backed chair across the table to hers. A dim bulb suspended from the ceiling enclosed in a deep crimson lampshade hung low between them. She then shifted uncomfortably to face him. At that very moment, how she wished that she had a window of some sort in this stuffy little room. Though it was a warm, dry day, she shivered a little. She hoped against hope that the stranger hadn't slipped the catch on the front door without her knowing. From the corner of her eye, she was extremely relieved to see that this was not so, or that he hadn't craftily turned the sign around to "Closed" without her noticing. With a bit of luck, she was hoping a customer or two would come in and browse so that the shop would not be so empty.

Drizelda glanced again at the stranger. To her surprise, he still wore dark sunglasses given the darkness of the room. With his large black fedora hat tilted well over his forehead, it was extremely difficult to make out a face as it was also covered in a jungle of a thick black beard... Despite it being twenty-five degrees outside and in, bizarrely he refused to take off his long, old-fashioned frock coat. Oddly enough, he wore open-top leather sandals, also in black. Being observant with an eye for detail, she noticed, as he crossed his knees when he leant back in the chair, that both big toes of his were missing.

Her eyes switched to his long, eagle-like hands, and, to her horror, the thumbs appeared to have been amputated and the fingers webbed between the remainder of the digits – the whole being covered in reptilian scales. Although longing to insist that he remove his dark glasses so as to lessen the sinister appearance, she couldn't think of a valid excuse, so she hesitated. Perhaps, she considered briefly, that he, like a lot of visitors to Glastonbury, wanted to look "modern, cool and with it". But in his case, she did not think that this was the real reason.

Removing the silk covering from her crystal ball, she crouched over it with both hands, cupping it as though to warm up her hands. Nothing happened for two long minutes. In the company of this oppressive visitor, it seemed like an eternity. Nervously she put on her reading glasses. These were oval-shaped, rimless. She balanced them, owl-like, at the end of her slim nose with some difficulty, for it was slippery due to her breaking out in drops of sweat.

'I'm looking for someone who has just been created on

this planet recently, growled the nasal voice, grating on a raw nerve.

'It's a baby then?' Drizelda asked. Then she thought, *Oh, my God, this is getting worse.*

Desperately, she looked anxiously beyond the front door towards the street, hoping that her local policeman would pop in for his weekly cuppa and free tea reading. But today, there was no such luck.

'He's not exactly human. But I need to know what to look for. He's a good-for-nothing, one of these self-righteous do-gooders that plague the earth. I have got to know *urgently* where to find him. Bah, blast and curses on these useless pious libertines. They are all the same. They are forever wanting to take over the world, telling us how to think and what to do in life. Have got to stop him – them, before they...'

He gave an evil cackle, simmering with hatred. But he did not finish his threat, for he suddenly realised that he might have given the game away by revealing too much already. But this was getting more and more bizarre by the minute.

From her crystal ball, a luminous glow began to emerge, and as it grew, it filled the void within it. Examining it more closely, she was surprised to see a scene of a happy circus full of laughing children and gleeful entertainers all enjoying themselves. The joyful scene faded away soon after it had started, because suddenly, out of the blue, a banner flashed across the crystal with a stark message in black and white.

"Beware of the eyes that cried... Pay heed to your great–great–granduncle, Percival Bellanoble!"

Two long moments passed. More perspiration dripped from her forehead. The warning message threw her, but sensibly she kept it to herself. She forced a false smile. 'I see a circus... lots of happy performers,' she read out. 'An audience full of giggling children and laughing parents... And now a black and white spotted dog has just run into the ring chased by a dwarf dressed in blue and yellow frills. And... oh. Oh – they're throwing water at each other. But... wait a minute. Custard... yes... and enormous custard pies at some of the audience in the front row... and—'

The dark stranger uncrossed his knees, adjusted his hat over his face and leant forward, towering over her crystal ball. He was about to grab it with his hands when Madame Drizelda stopped him in his tracks. Because *no one*, literally *nobody* – apart from her, was allowed to touch her precious crystal.

Then she got a shock of her life. His hands felt scaly, cold and clammy as a corpse. This really frightened her. The sudden jolt made his dark glasses slip towards the beak of his nose, but he quickly pushed them back onto the bridge. For in that split second, Drizelda noticed, to her absolute horror, that he had no eyes, as if he was wearing a mask. Instead, he had two empty grey sockets bored in the skull – just like two stick holes that had melted in the snow. To add to this, his nose had a slit with no septum in the middle. His mouth was a raw gash, without lips, visible teeth, or tongue. If only he had Dracula-white fangs or something like that – that at least would be some recognisable entity she could deal with by using her jade earring in the shape of a crucifix and a string of garlic from the kitchen. But horrors upon horrors, this was not in the textbooks she had studied as a student of mystics.

'*What* – a circus! *Where?*' His disjointed voice gasped with a bark. He recovered his posture and leant back again in his chair. 'Who's in it? Tell me, woman!' He grabbed her hand in earnest. Panic gripped her. Fear flew round the shop like wildfire.

Immediately, Oswald came flying in like a furry fireball to the rescue of his beloved owner. Hissing and spitting, he flung himself with open claws onto the visitor's leg. The latter merely brushed him aside with a cursory kick, and the poor cat retreated to the front window to nurse his wounds. Meanwhile, in extreme distress, Nero flew about in circles, banging at his cage and squawking at the top of his voice. Loose black feathers fluttered everywhere. Rattling the bars from top to bottom, he became hysterical.

Sharply turning around, the sinister stranger glared at the raven menacingly, pointed his right hand like a dagger at the bird's head and hissed under his breath, '*Sleep, like death, you mangy creature!*'

As if poleaxed, Nero fell abruptly onto his back, knocking over his bowl of water, and landed in his seed tray upside down. He was well and truly hypnotised with his feet dangling in the air, much to the distress of his mistress who was unable to help him.

'I repeat again, woman, *who is he?* Where is he now? You'd better tell me the truth if you know what's good for you!' He reiterated this with added venom without letting go of her hand.

Determined, she shook him off with her strong wrist. To play for time, she replied calmly, 'I'd have to look into a bigger picture using one of the larger beacon globes, as the small crystal has faded.'

From beneath a cupboard near to her washbasin, she pulled out a giant globe. This was one of her favourites which she had found after it had fallen into her outstretched hands from a Pelican Crossing near the London Planetarium last autumn, where she had been visiting to see a map of the night sky for a client. Bending over, she studiously peered into this balloon of a crystal ball, thinking she really ought to charge him more for this expanded consultation, but she didn't dare to suggest it in the circumstances. It was difficult to breathe, for she felt his hot, sullen breath just a mere foot away as he crouched over her menacingly.

'Why yes, it's the circus again,' she murmured, pretending to be calm. 'The performers in the ring are spinning around and around at top speed. I see a... an old, gnarled tree leaning from a jagged rock with something crystalline glistening from its branches. Oh dear. Oh no, I don't... the image has just dimmed. But wait a minute, I see an amazing harlequin – he's the star performer—'

'Describe him to me woman. *Quickly now!*' Impatiently, he growled with rising agitation.

'...Well, he's got a round, cheerful face with wisps of reddish hair plastered over his head. Oh, the audience love him. They are throwing flowers into the ring. The applause, it seems, is deafening. Oh my, he does seem to radiate happiness. But oh dear... uh-oh, there's a murky figure lurking in the background. I can just make him out. I think he's a sort of magician dressed in a swirling black and silver cape. It looks as if he's carrying something squirming close to his body... And... oh dear, it's gone again.'

Straight away, she sensed a murderous look that bored right through her, so she stopped. She wanted to give him as much information as possible. And as quickly as possible, in order to get rid of him as soon as she could. And yet, she had this morbid curiosity of wanting to find out why this terrifying and most hideous man was interested in a child's circus, of all things.

'Tell me quickly, madam, is he performing miraculous deeds? Where do I find him? Has he got a shiny stone on him? Maybe it's a pendant or some other sort of glittery object around his body?'

The hoarseness of his shrill voice was getting worse by the second.

'MIRACULOUS DEEDS? What the devil do you mean?' Drizelda's hand shot to her mouth. 'I don't understand you, sir. A circus is a circus, a place for entertaining children, and of course for adults who never grow up. It's for entertainment purely, and for nothing else. I think it's in London… on a large green, where they could pitch a big top.'

Keeping her eyes glued to the round screen, the enormous globe suddenly filled to the brim and began to wink brightly. A warning flashed up again. She stared at it in disbelief.

"Beware of the eyes that have already died."

She cupped her hands over it and squinted. More letters appeared strung together in a terse message…

"This is a life-and-death message from an alterworld. It is I, one of your trusted first ancestors, Pious the Meek – who headed the considerable family tree – that begat your great-

great-granduncle Percival. Therefore, listen well to us. Ignore our wisdom at your peril!"

She didn't want to let on about the warning from the past, and from such impeccable forebears. Her head was spinning. To distract the stranger from asking why she looked so dazed and bewildered, she added rapidly as a diversion,

'Look, sir, the pictures fizzled out. That's all I can tell you. I have got to stop the session now. Unless, of course, you want me to try to bring into focus, your past, your future… you know, your family… that sort of thing. Maybe discuss personal matters and so on. Sorry, sir, I'm getting tired now. I have to stop…'

Her voice tailed off quietly, exhausted by the effort.

However, his reply was vicious and to the point. '*Don't* you *even* think about it, woman! Don't you ever *dare* tell a single living soul about our session here today. Hah, what sort of *personal* matters were you thinking of talking about! And what is more, don't you ever *even* think of it, or try to check up on me, Madam clever-type, fortune teller – *if* you value your life!'

Venomously, he spat across the table, showering her precious globe with spittle. His featureless stare, icily radiating through his dark glasses, was enough to scare her numb. When he arched his back, she thought for one moment he was about to pounce on her. It was obvious that he did not want to be discovered. She was about to protest, but sensibly she thought otherwise so as not to provoke him more.

Pushing back his chair abruptly, it made a teeth-searing squeal on the lino floor. He suddenly got up, turned on his heels and rushed through the beaded curtain. Holding on to his hat, he ran through the front door and slammed it with all his might. The little brass bell above the doorjamb rocked to and fro, giving a concerto of tinkles and jangles. The sign freely oscillated from its metal chain on the windowpane with an angry clatter. Oswald jumped up with a start with his fur up on end, scattering the window display in the panic. Immediately, Drizelda chased after the visitor to tell him that he had forgotten his change from the large banknote he had left. But her real intention was to see where he had disappeared to.

She looked quickly in both directions up and down the road. But he was nowhere to be seen. He had literally vanished into thin air, leaving a wisp of blue smoke spiralling strangely upwards to the sky. She slammed the door with a bang and quickly slipped the catch. As she leant with her back heavily against the inside of the door panting to get her breath, she almost tripped over the post which had been delivered during her crystal ball-gazing. She bent down and picked up a copy of her trade paper, *The Spectral Ectoplasmic Weekly*, which had got tangled up in the doormat.

The headlines caught her eye:

"*A ghostly apparition of a phantom has been reported materialising in visual dimension in certain towns and cities around the country. The public is warned to be on high alert. Information is urgently requested about this psychic phenomenon – known as spectral vibrations, and furthermore…*"

She threw down the paper in terror. Feeling as if a coil of rough rope was twisting in her stomach, she rushed to the kitchen, holding her mouth. Hastily she grabbed a glass of water from the sink and swallowed it in large gulps. Simultaneously, she rinsed a face flannel and wiped the perspiration that streamed down her face, ruining her mascara. She stared at her reflection in the gilt mirror above the sink. Her face was a portrait of abject terror.

Drained with exhaustion, she decided to call it a day. She flipped the sign back showing "Closed" and locked the front door with a key. Her thoughts returned to the stark warnings by her ancient ancestors:

> *"Beware of the eyes that cried…*
> *Beware of the eyes that have already died."*

It preyed on her mind. Without thinking, she picked up a pencil and subconsciously tapped on her lower teeth. Which was it to be? What did it mean? Did it mean someone's eyes had been poked out? If it was so, why? She began to tremble and suddenly felt cold. She thought about it again. All that she was certain about, was that her guiding spirits of the past were trying to warn her of impending doom, danger and possibly death. And it was just as terrifying today, as it was before in the past. Oh, how she now wished that she had inherited the wisdom and strength of her foremost ancestor, Pious the Meek. And with it as well, the cunning and guile of her more recent great-great-granduncle Percival of Victorian times – then she would have felt much happier and safer for it.

Deep in thought, she returned to her reading table and covered her crystal ball and globe with its silk covering. Her body sank heavily into her chair. She pulled out a pack of Tarrantulot cards from a drawer besides her and shuffled them furiously in her hands. Then immediately, she dealt the cards in play on top of the seat of the chair where the obnoxious client had been sitting just a while ago... when a very peculiar thing happened as she stared at the deck of cards. As she dealt from the pack, the smiling faces of the Jester and the Ace of Hearts were abruptly swept aside by a picture of the Grim Reaper of Death with his skull and scythe. This happened three times, rapidly in succession.

Even worse, the Happy Family cards with Mr and Mrs Rabbit kept sliding off the chair onto the floor. They then skidded with a terrible squeal as they slid under the table to hide, whereupon they refused to return to the family pack. And however hard she tried to pick them up, they kept slithering out of her fingers as though coated with oil.

Drizelda shuddered uncontrollably. Her knees felt suddenly weak. The omens were not good. From them, she concluded that some indescribable terror lay ahead for someone important in life. That someone was now in mortal danger. Immediately, she felt that she must try to find out who it was, and where he was. Then try to warn him before it was too late.

Chapter 28

A THIEVING MISDEED

I T HAD BEEN A quiet and uneventful night for Roland Bigglesworth. For several hours, his cab had been trawling the empty streets without much luck. To kill time, he followed the river slowly. He drove wearily westwards as the morning light broadened over the stream of traffic jostling to get to work. By now, he was hoping that his luck would change in finding a fare.

No sooner had he drawn towards a set of traffic lights near to the Bush, the quiet lull was rudely shattered by a large leg suddenly jutting out into the road. A big red boot waggled at the end of it, forcing him to stop. His taxi screeched abruptly to a halt. Roland wound down his window and leant over towards the kerb. He was astonished to find a large, round face of a grinning harlequin leaning towards his window.

It was Chance followed by Henry. Poking his head

through the taxi window, Chance stood with his hand hovering over the door handle. 'Are you free, cabbie? Can you take my friends and me?' he asked.

Roland's jaw dropped to the floor. 'Su… Sure. Yeah,' he stuttered. He was so stunned that he forgot his usual sharp retort, that "nothing in life was free". 'Oh, hop in, mate,' he said without further comment, his instant wit having suddenly deserted him.

Chance turned his back to the cab. He stuck two fingers in his mouth and gave an almighty whistle between his teeth. From the shadow of a shop doorway, Lotte, Tim and Ram quickly emerged, one after another. As soon as they began to pile into the cab, there was another surprise to come…

Because then, as Roland's neck twisted around, his eyes jumped out in shock. 'Cor, I don't believe it! It's *you*, Miss Lotte and young Tim. Well, I never!' he said, flabbergasted.

Ram yelped in surprise and leapt into the passenger seat when sudden recognition hit them like a thunderbolt from on high. '*Why it's Roland, of all people!*' they gasped. 'Hey. You're miles late. You were supposed to collect us from home hours ago!' accused Lotte tersely. 'We thought you had forgotten us!'

'No, I didn't,' protested Roland, craning round, reddening like a beetroot. '*It's for tomorrow!* I arranged it weeks ago with your mother,' he insisted with certainty. 'I'm sure of it…'

'You're a day out, Roland… you've been daydreaming again!' groaned Tim, laying into him.

'Oh, forget it, you two. We've got a lift now. And at least with someone you know,' said Chance. He prodded Henry to quickly jump in.

Roland was about to ask the children about their unusual companions, when Henry interrupted. 'My man, can you take us to the children's hospital, straight away, please?'

'We've got to visit a friend there who's just had an operation,' explained Lotte, seeing the puzzled look.

As Roland carefully did a three-point turn in the road, the cab pulled smoothly away. He kept staring at them through the rear-view mirror as if they had just landed from another planet. More questions were bursting at the tip of his tongue. 'Aren't you going to Mrs Chivers's then, Miss Lotte?'

'No way!' answered Tim before Lotte could reply.

'No. We're going on an adventure… a trip of a lifetime with Chance and Henry. We'll tell you a bit more about it in a minute,' said Lotte firmly.

'How did you meet these two then?' Roland then asked. He jerked his head backwards to the passenger cabin as the taxi gathered speed, heading towards the centre of town.

'We'll explain later,' said Lotte impatiently.

Roland's eyes skimmed from the harlequin to Henry and then back again through the glass partition that divided them from him. Still loaded with questions, he continued to bombard Henry, though his gaze was now fixed on the harlequin.

'Hey, Mister! Hope you don't mind my saying, but your friend – your friend with the funny nose …been to a fancy-dress party or something or other, have you?' Then he hesitated a second, thinking aloud. 'Erm. You know what – he looks *so* familiar.' He scratched his head vigorously.

'I'd keep your eyes on the road ahead, cabbie, if I were you, or you'll get us all killed!' Henry snapped back as the taxi slewed and wobbled between the traffic.

Roland had been drumming the tips of his fingers on top of the dashboard, his brain furiously overworking. 'I know. Wait a minute. *That's it!* I think I've seen a figure dressed up like him before! It's just occurred to me. Blimey, of course!' The penny then dropped. '*Madame Rousseau's! The other night – in the doorway!*' He clicked his fingers, letting out a yell of triumph.

Chance stared back at him squarely. Having been taken aback by the strange coincidence, he swallowed hard. Then it all came out. How they had previously met by accident, after Chance had been taken in Saskia's stolen car, then dumped. And how Roland had found him and taken him to the waxworks.

Then it was Henry's turn to explain how he had met Chance back at Saskia's house – then how they had heard about the quest, the riddle and so on from Zoot…

Roland kept shaking his head, as though he just couldn't believe his ears. Lotte and Tim then told Roland that they had already made up their minds on the trip of mystery with Henry and Chance, instead of the activity camp… They then described the legend of the three good deeds which involved a riddle, and the pieces of the gemstone that had shattered and dispersed all over the earth, and Chance's journey to find them.

After they had told Roland the whole story, he went incredibly quiet for a while, trying to take it all in. Drawing in his breath, he cautioned, 'Well, you lot; if that's all real, then I'm gobsmacked. It sounds too incredible for words.

Besides, if it *is* true, then for you two youngsters, it sounds rather dangerous to me. Are you sure, now, you don't want me to turn back after your visit to your pal at the hospital and go on to Mrs Chivers's?'

'*No. No! Of course, not!*' fired back Lotte and Tim in unison, even more determined than ever. 'We don't want to go to that boring old camp again,' said Tim. 'We want to go on this incredible adventure. Ram will look after us, won't you, old doggo?' Tim ruffled the dog's coat fiercely, provoking a howl of approval from the animal.

'Besides, Chance will protect us,' added Lotte confidently. 'He's got special powers hidden in a pendant around his neck, you know.'

'Oh yeah. Pull the other one!' mused Roland sceptically. If you can believe that… then I've got a magic wand stuffed down my sock!'

'Sure, Henry and I will guard them with our lives. You can depend on that,' said Chance unwaveringly. Ignoring Roland's sarcasm, he even thought of mentioning the martial arts skills that Hoopy had taught him at the waxworks. But he decided to leave that for another time in case Roland wanted an actual demonstration right there and then. And in a moving London taxi, that would have been extremely difficult, if not extremely dangerous.

Holding up his hand, Roland then conceded, 'Okay. Okay, I give in. I'll think of something. I'll phone Mrs C to say we're going to a school sailing camp on the coast or something, and to tell Lotte's mum not to worry. We'll get you back well in time for the next school term. Cross my heart. I promise.'

'That's gr… great, Roland,' said Tim with relief.

'Thanks a million… you're an ace!' added Lotte.

Roland's face went pink with embarrassment, so he looked straight ahead, focusing on the road. Carefully, he manoeuvred his cab in and out of the bus lanes, dodging the double-decker buses.

Just as they turned a corner into Old Handover Street, Tim slid to the edge of his seat, when suddenly he shouted, 'Look. *Look*, Roland. Over there! Hey, what's all that commotion?'

'Where? What?' asked Lotte, staring out of the window.

'Further down on the right. Look over there, stupid… where my finger is!' Tim had wound the passenger window right down. The others then craned their necks over to where he was pointing. 'Look, you dim lot… it must be a robbery!'

He was right. In front of their very eyes, an ugly scene was unfolding. Two large figures were rushing out of a bank. They were dressed in shapeless black tracksuits, over which they wore bulky bomber jackets. Slung under his arm, one of them carried a battered old holdall; the other, large ominous-looking parcels, which looked like shotguns wrapped in plastic bags. Both wore a mask of a grinning clown over their faces with just slits for their eyes and holes for their mouths.

For immediately outside the bank, parked at the kerbside, was an old dark blue Rover. At the driving wheel was another figure dressed exactly as the other two. But he was leaning forwards, desperately trying to start the engine. '*Tut-ter-tut. Zroom. Phut-room… Splut!*' It gave a pathetic, hollow grunt. The ignition simply would not fire. The gang appeared to be cursing under their breath. One kicked the door in frustration, whilst his accomplice with his back to the car circled menacingly, forcing the people in the street to stand back.

No sooner had that happened, one of the bank staff, a thin sliver of a youth, ran out of the front door of the bank waving his arms in terror, crying, '*Help!* Someone, call the police!'

Utter chaos and pandemonium then broke out. The bank's alarm bell started to wail. The noise exploded in the street, shaking the windows of its very, expensive shops to their foundations. Next to the bank, to its right, was the exceedingly smart fashion store of Bonds and Broadwicks Ltd. Suddenly, scores of their customers came running out as fast as they could to investigate. Dropping their bags of shopping, they then fled down the street in a panic.

'For crying sakes. Get that blitherin' car started!' screamed the ringleader, the taller of the two, as they hysterically rounded on the driver. He then took a flying kick at the car bonnet, his face dripping with fury.

'*Do something. Oh, please do something! Quickly! Chance… Roland!*' urged Lotte at the edge of her seat. Roland didn't hesitate. He swung his cab right in front of the Rover and reversed sharply, jamming its front bumper. Chance, meanwhile, without waiting for Roland to stop, flung open the passenger door and hurled himself out onto the pavement. Using a rapid movement, he flicked his hand across his nose, skirting the pendant with a caress. Then, in a split second, he aimed his open hand, fingers apart, at the shop window of Bonds and Broadwicks…

As it happened, a wedding scene was serenely displayed on the left-hand side with life-size fashion mannequins. A beautiful figure of a blushing bride dressed in flowing white silk and satin was accompanied by a pair of coyly smiling bridesmaids clutching the train of a stunning wedding dress. By her side stood her handsome groom, smartly at ease in a starch-pressed morning suit. But as soon as Chance had wiggled his fingers at them, an astonishing thing happened: the figures on display all came to life and immediately leapt out of the store.

Unrestrained, they began to tear into the villains with gusto. The blushing bride, previously a figure of tranquillity, with her shy little bridesmaids started to grab at the gang's hair and stamped on their toes with lethal high heels. The groom tore off his top hat and flung it into the ringleader's face. Shell-shocked, the villains just froze on the pavement, motionless, their mouths snarling helplessly under their masks. Jostled and shoved, they were then savagely kicked in the shins by the mannequins, who danced hypnotically around them in a circle.

Meanwhile, Tim struggled to hold on to the collar of Ram, who was pulling frantically to join in.

In the meantime, hastily adjusting his monocle into focus, a thoroughly bemused Henry uttered softly between his teeth, 'I say. What a jolly good show!'

As the figures continued to wrestle with the robbers on the pavement, bags of money flew into the air. The ominous-looking bundles and the battered holdall were tossed to the ground. In a couple of giant strides, Chance leapt into the fray. Bodily grabbing the villains by the scruff of their necks, he tried to hold on to them, but they slipped out of his grasp. Shaken, beaten, and defeated, the villains quickly fled and jumped into their car, which, luckily for them, was now revving sweetly. Panicking, it reversed blindly but crashed, colliding into a police motorbike that had just arrived on the scene. The getaway car then swept sharply around Roland's taxi and accelerated desperately away. It flew down the street as fast as it possibly could. 'Quickly! Can you get their number?' yelled Lotte.

'Blow it! It's useless,' groaned Roland. 'It's covered in mud!'

Their mouths agog, they watched dumbstruck at what Chance did next. He closed his fist and flicked his wrist at the mannequins. As though responding to a magic signal, they returned to the store calmly and quietly. They took up their positions back in the window, static, dead as stone as if nothing had happened. The only clue to their recent adventure was that their wigs were slightly lopsided or back to front, and parts of their smart, beautiful dresses were now dirtied and skewed all over the place.

In a flash, Henry leapt out of the taxi to see if he could help. Chance stooped to the ground and scooped up the abandoned bundles wrapped tightly in newspaper and plastic bags. With one fell swoop, he swept up the bags of money scattered at his feet and threw them into the old holdall that had also been abandoned. He ordered Henry to stand watch outside the bank, whilst, with his hands full, he kicked open the front door and strode purposefully in.

The staff at the bank – two men and two women – cowered behind the glass partitions, hiding behind the broad mahogany counter. They were still trembling with fear. '*Oh, my heavens! Not another one!*' screamed the fairer of the female cashiers. She promptly collapsed behind the screen when she saw a large harlequin carrying, what seemed to her, sinister-looking weapons menacingly towards her. Undeterred, Chance tossed the bags of money with the old holdall onto the counter marked "Foreign Exchange".

Calmly, Chance looked quickly around him to make sure they were all paying close attention to what he did next. He then slowly, and with great deliberation, placed the large, bulky bundles abandoned by the robbers carefully on top of the counter. Cautiously, he started to unwrap them in front of the staff to find out what was hidden inside. The women let out a loud shriek of alarm and dived towards the floor for safety.

To everyone's shocked surprise, rolled up in the bundles of newspaper and falling out of the plastic bags were not vicious shotguns after all, but two very, large, fresh green cucumbers, which then rolled silently and harmlessly onto the top of the counter.

'We don't believe it… it *can't* be?' they muttered incredulously under their breath.

'We'd better go,' called Henry, sticking his head around the doorway. 'Hurry, now!' he urged impatiently. Abruptly, Chance turned on his heels and followed Henry, who had already jumped in the cab as Roland turned the ignition.

Now, as it happened by a remarkable coincidence, young Seth Ropely was cruising down Old Handover Street just at that time in a dented old red Mini, which he had recently "borrowed" from a car park. The hubbub of excitement outside the bank naturally attracted his eye. And so, he parked on the other side of the road with his engine still running and watched. Dumbstruck, he had managed to catch sight of several figures scuffling on the pavement with others, and then witnessed their sudden flight from the scene.

Just then, a large figure strode calmly out of the bank. Seth leant forward to get a better look. Something about him made him sit bolt upright. He whistled under his breath. 'Well, well, blow me… can't Adam and Eve it! It's that blooming old stiff I dumped out of that old crock of a Beetle the other night! And crikey – can't believe it! He's alive and kicking! But hey, what's that swinging outside his collar?'

For when Chance had climbed into the waiting taxi, bending his head a little, Seth's sharp eyes spotted something bright and sparkling that dangled around his neck. His eyes grew and grew to the size of pizza plates, as the stone in the pendant dazzled him, catching the light.

'*Wow! Blimey!*' He continued to marvel under his breath. '*What a dazzling corker of a gem! It's got to be bigger than the biggest diamond on earth… hundreds of carats in size! Bet it's priceless! Must get my sweaty little hands on it. It'll be the answer to all my dreams.*'

Hungrily, he licked his lips in anticipation at the mere thought of it. '*That old beauty of a sparkler surely must have some mystical powers about it to do all that – those figures brought to life, and all that magic stuff! I've simply got to have that shiny old rock in my possession now. Then I'll be rolling in it… filthy rich and all-powerful beyond my wildest dreams!*'

And whereupon, he fantasised more and more as he got carried away… He slipped the Mini into gear and began to tail the black taxi, murmuring to himself, 'What a stupid fool of an idiot I was to dump that figure in that doorway in the first place. Nearly lost me a fortune!' Seth continued to curse himself and slapped his face mockingly in punishment.

Roland's taxi gathered speed, though it didn't realise that it was being followed. 'Let's get out of here quickly before we get stopped,' said Roland to the others. 'The place will be swarming with the law any minute now. But at least those villains didn't get away with any loot.'

'Well done, Chance. You're a star. You've foiled a nasty robbery!' said Lotte, full of congratulations for his thwarting a thieving misdeed.

'Yeah, that's great. Awesome!' echoed Tim admiringly.

'Hey, you must have completed at least *one* good deed today already, my friend. Congrats!' added Henry sportingly. 'Tell me, is your nose glowing, and are your ears burning like fire? ...*For those are the signs of a good first achievement according to the legend.*' And so Henry hurriedly explained to the others about that happening – amongst other things.

Questioningly, they stared and glared at the harlequin's nose and ears. Rather self-consciously, Chance felt his nose and then his ears with the tips of his fingers and began to nod furiously. His face broke out into a massive grin.

'Well, isn't that dead wicked, Roland!' shouted Tim as he punched the air with glee. 'Wow-ee, Chance, do you feel anything else?'

The taxi swerved sharply around a bend, giving a wobbling cyclist a wide berth. Staring at his clothes, Chance felt frantically around his body to see if there was anything else that was different – when a tingling glow started to spread over him rapidly. And so, he blamed it on the legend and its riddle.

'Nar! Don't believe all you see at first glance,' replied Roland cynically. 'You see, probably right at this very moment, someone's saying nasty things about him – that's why his face is burning bright red!

'Now let's find that hospital...'

***

It did not take very, long before the air around the West End was filled with the screams of police sirens blaring which seemed to sour the fresh sunlight now bursting overhead. Effortlessly, two fast patrol cars zoomed to the area to reinforce the lone police motorcyclist, who had just stumbled, bruised, and battered into the bank. 'Get me an ambulance. *Quick!*' he gasped, nursing his sore head. 'The bike's all mangled up – completely useless!' he groaned. Then he fell into one of the armchairs near the front window – limp and lifeless as a jellyfish flung out of water.

Detective Inspector Geoff Bollins was one of the first from CID to arrive on the scene. He seemed in a foul mood. 'Now let me get this straight, sir,' addressing the red-faced bank manager, whose brow had broken out in purple blood vessels like fat worms.

'You state that you were held up by a couple of er... clowns wielding shotguns. Now, let's get this down, accurately shall we sir?'

Leaning authoritatively against the counter, he began to take down his statement with increasing incredulity.

'And after the clowns took the money, another one of them dressed like... erm... a harlequin came back and returned all the money to you – *every* single penny. And furthermore, you were held up by a pair of fresh green vegetables! Well, well, now! In all the years I served in the force, I thought I'd heard simply everything! Now, sir, let us go over this once more; very slowly now, just for the records...'

Chapter 29

PATIENTS AND THE MYSTERIOUS DR DE'AFF

NOON WAS FAST APPROACHING as Roland bobbed and weaved his way through the thick of the traffic, scattering stubborn flocks of dusty pigeons in his wake. Little did he realise that a battered old Mini had stuck tenaciously to his tail. Twenty minutes later, Roland's taxi drew up to the entrance of a children's hospital near the West End.

Seth's old car sidled up, well out of view. Having crawled behind a line of vehicles, he craftily parked well hidden behind a stationary ambulance in an emergency bay. 'Blow me. I wonder why they're going there?' he muttered. He scratched the tip of his chin, mystified. Immediately, he slid downwards behind the steering wheel, so that he wouldn't be spotted so easily.

Hurriedly, Chance, Henry, Lotte and Tim tumbled out

of the taxi in turn. 'You'd better stay here with Roland, Ram, me ol' chum,' ordered Tim, wagging a finger at his dog.

'Sit. Now *sit*! Good doggo,' commanded Roland, producing a chicken and coleslaw sandwich his granny had given him for lunch, and he hoped a piece of it would keep the dog happy. 'Look, you lot, I'll stay and keep him amused. But don't be too long.'

Lotte led the way, as she seemed familiar with the layout of the hospital. Coming to the first office at reception, she tapped on the window and said, 'Excuse me. We've come to visit Shoona Canning, who's just had an operation.'

The porter on duty left his television screen and shuffled to the security window. He slid it back, snapping begrudgingly, 'Yes? Can I help you, Miss? Oh, it's *you*, Missie,' he said, suddenly recognising her. 'How's your leg now?' He took off his glasses and peered out of the open hatch, suspiciously casting his eye over the other visitors.

'Er. It's much better, thank you,' Lotte replied hesitantly. 'Um. Oh, these are friends... erm... from the circus in town.' She held her breath, hoping a tiny white lie would avoid further explanations.

'Sure. A circus, eh? *Circus*? Well, I never... Shown a cat in, did you say?'

'No. *Shoona*... C-A-N-N-I-N-G!' Tim corrected him with a bellow.

'Well. Suppose that's all right then,' came the gruff reply. 'Sweet Peabody Ward. First floor – with a couple of kids from that Barnards, something or other. Look. See behind you, Missie... on the wall.' The porter jabbed a thumb in the direction of a notice board behind them. A large, colourful poster advertising a circus pitched at World's

End, Chelsea, stared back at them. Dead in the centre of the picture posed a clown grinning with a shiny red nose. Perched on his head sat a tiny black bowler hat, from which sprouted a bunch of daisies. In the background, a beautiful, slim trapeze artist was seen to be flying through the air – under the roof of a big top gripping a trapeze with her knees. Splashed across the poster in bold red and black lettering, it advertised…

"BARNARD & BARNARDS, THE WORLD-FAMOUS INTERNATIONAL CIRCUS. THRILLS! SPILLS! MAGIC! DAREDEVIL TRAPEZE AND HIGH-WIRE ACTS! BARRELS OF FUN AND LAUGHTER – WITH COSTELLO, GRIMBO, MIDGY AND CO... GUARANTEED!

ROLL UP! BOOK UP! BRING ALL THE FAMILY FOR A RIP-ROARING TIME. TICKETS FROM £5.50. ...NOW AT..."

'Well, gee, thanks, Mister,' said Tim, pushing his way to the front.

'Okay, Missie. Just take the lift in front of you or the stairs. First on the left, down the second corridor.'

Gratefully and without a further word, they streamed past the office as quickly as they could.

***

Now, without their realising it, their every move was being carefully spied on from the road. From the safety of his car, Seth had rapidly hatched a plan in his crafty mind. He thought he had better act soon before it was too late, if he were to stand a chance of snatching the precious pendant that he so desperately coveted. He pulled the peak of his baseball cap further over his face. Impassively, he then continued to sit and wait. He kept glancing out of the corner of his windscreen, his eye glued on the hospital entrance. Ambulances swiftly came and went. Patiently, he bided his time. Tapping his fingers on top of the steering column, he hummed to himself to pass the time…

'Whistle while you work, some people are such nerds.
When their guard's right down, they act like clowns.
Whistle while you work…'

***

Lotte dashed up the stairs a couple at a time. Tim followed closely on her heels. Using his gigantic stride, Chance took three steps all at once. But Henry tailed last, puffing a little with exertion. When they peered through the glazed doors of the ward, they counted nine children lying in opposite rows. They looked somewhat pale and tired.

Lotte pushed open the swing doors and waved to Shoona, whose bed was the nearest to the left. 'Hiya Shoona. How are you now?' Lotte said in greeting.

Shoona's face lit up like a beacon.

'These are my friends who've come to say hello as well.' With a plop, Lotte sat on the end of Shoona's bed, whilst Tim shyly perched on the edge of a chair next to the bedside cabinet.

'Oh, I'm all right, I guess, Lotte. Just a bit fed up and bored with the food, though,' said Shoona, pulling a face. 'Can't eat much yet, after they took out my appendix.' She grimaced and gently patted her tummy. 'Well, who's who then?'

'This is Timmie. Surely you remember. He lives next door to Mum and me. You met him once before, last summer, when you came round. You couldn't have forgotten? He's got that big woolly dog that pinched your dinner!'

Shoona blinked rapidly, suddenly remembering.

Tim smiled weakly, thinking, *Bloomin' girls. They're all the same!*

'And this is Chance, our new harlequin friend, and his best pal, Henry,' Lotte continued with the introductions.

'Pleased to meet you, Miss Shoona. Glad to hear you're getting better now.' Chance bobbed his head, grinning widely. Then, with a theatrical flourish, he produced a box of milk chocolates from the inside of his jacket and presented them to her.

Simultaneously, Henry made a low bow, sweeping his cane in front of him with one hand. And with the other, he draped his arm in a dramatic gesture across his waistcoat and whipped out a bunch of red and white carnations and thrust them towards Shoona, saying, 'Henry de Poisson at your service.' He bowed again, this time even more formally. 'Charmed to meet you, young ma'am.'

Fascinated, the rest of the ward looked on.

Shoona giggled uncontrollably, shyly accepting the gifts, then placed them on top of her bedcover. 'Ooh!' she commented. 'My word, he's a bit of a gent, isn't he?'

In the next bed sat another young girl. She had short black hair cut in a fringe. She looked a year or two older than Shoona and Lotte, and couldn't help staring at them. The look was rather glum. Opposite to them across the ward, a young boy with a wide, earnest expression, dark eyes, and Latin good looks waved self-consciously at Shoona with his left hand. His right arm was held in plaster from his wrist to his shoulder.

Lotte bounced up and down at the edge of Shoona's bed as though testing the springs and asked, 'Hey. Who's your new friends then Shoona?'

'They're both from Barnards Circus. Mimi here,' said Shoona, indicating to her left, 'is recovering from a nasty hernia operation. She's training as a dancer and trapeze artist like her mum – the world-famous Carrita... you know – that beautiful lady in all the posters. That's right, isn't it, Mimi?'

Mimi tilted her head rather self-consciously at Shoona and grimaced silently.

'Whereas Bonzo over there had his arm smashed in a multiple fracture in a somersault that went horribly wrong one night in the ring, ripping his back at the same time. Taking part in the clown troupe, he was just learning.'

Tim looked horrified and gripped his face.

'What happened?' asked Chance and Henry together.

'You'd better ask Bonzo yourself, I think.' Shoona lowered her voice as she stared at the floor nervously. Then she continued, 'Mimi's mother, Carrita, and Bonzo's uncle, Costello, who's one of the clowns, on their visit yesterday told us that there have been some strange goings-on at Barnards ever since a mysterious newcomer arrived at the circus.'

Bonzo immediately beckoned them over. He was longing to talk to someone. His uncle had visited him a couple of times and came once with a lanky giant of a clown called Grimbo. But the visits were few and far between. Bonzo, like the rest of the children there, was bored stiff and taking a long time to get better. They wore downcast expressions, being thoroughly miserable. And it showed.

'Hi. Ciao. Giorno. Are you-a show-biz... and do-a magic tricks?' Bonzo asked Chance in earnest in his broken English.

'Well, sort of,' replied Chance slowly, while Henry raised his eyebrows questioningly.

'Well, you'll understand what I'm about to tell-a you about what happened at the circus. Two weeks ago, on de last tour of de West Country, a mysterious masked stranger, calling himself the Mystic Dr Slatane De'Aff, arrived out of de blue. This stranger told-a de ringmaster, Mister Barnard, that de circus's main attraction, de Great Ziggarini... fire-eater, horse-whisperer and magician extraordinaire, would not be joining de London tour. He, so de story goes, had disappeared fast, back to Sicily because of a big problemo with his wife and de Mafiosi family...' Bonzo hesitated, reducing his voice to barely a whisper. 'Instead, he had asked this Dr De'Aff to take his place in de ring. Or so he said.'

By now, the whole ward, being in earshot was gripped. Speechless, Tim spent the time opening and shutting his mouth, frog-like. Lotte kept a tight hold of Shoona's hand.

Mimi kept trembling, murmuring quietly, 'Oh dear. How can we ever forget? That's right. Scary, nasty piece of work, he was. Scared the living daylights out of us, he did too.'

Listening impassively, Chance had perched himself on a chair next to Bonzo's bed. Henry, meanwhile, stood silently to attention, surreptitiously fiddling with the charts on a clipboard propped at the end of the bed, pretending to read.

'Hurr... urgh.' Chance cleared his throat. 'This mysterious stranger, this *Dr Slayer of Death*, if that's his name. What did he do?'

'No. No. You gotta all wrong. He maybe looks like-a *death*, sounds like-a *death*, perhaps even smells like-a *death*... but his name is Slatane... S-L-A-T-A-N-E... DE-A-F-F!'

Increasingly agitated, Bonzo carried on.

'Anyhow, we all had to admit that he was an unusual performer. He could make things like chairs, tables, even animals, fly through de air. Saw people in half, right in front of your very eyes. Stick big nails and daggers up his nose and down his mouth. Set-a water, yes, *water*, on fire by pointing a finger at it. He even could hypnotise anyone he wanted to... Yes *anyone*, including members of de circus. And even get some of de audience to do-a things that they would never normally do-a... like crawl-a through a hoop on fire, or make them jump into a bath of ice-cold water fully clothed.'

They all looked shell-shocked and didn't know what to say.

'Go on, Bonzo. Tell them about the last show, before we came to London. Tell them about your ghastly fall,' encouraged Mimi, jabbing a finger at him.

'I was about to ask you about your arm and shoulder,' asked Chance, tapping the thick plaster cast gently with his fingers.

'Well, when it happened, this De'Aff seemed to have muscled in on all de acts. All de performers seemed scared of him. Barnard the ringmaster appeared to just let him interfere. Don't know why,' said Bonzo dolefully. He tugged thoughtfully at his dressing gown.

'Well. Uncle Costello, Grimbo and Midgy – that's de star, dwarf clown – and me had rehearsed and performed this act a hundred times before without a problemo. We were in Wedgemouth Ho. And, after de usual warm-up intro of chucking de water around, followed by custard pies and buckets of paint at each other, I came on in de next act. There was a roll of de drums as de lights dimmed. Grimbo would jump on one end of de seesaw, which was a plank of wood over a beer barrel – with me being the lightest – apart from Midgy, that is – on de other end.'

Lotte stayed silent, perched at the end of Shoona's bed. She tried to make eye contact with Tim, who was staring into space, pretending – though not very convincingly – not to be listening.

Bonzo drew breath. 'Me-a. I would fly through de air and Costello would catch-a me as he hung upside down on de flying trapeze. Then he would throw me to de other side of de ring. And I would land safely onto a trampoline, then bounce off it to fly onto Midgy's shoulders, who would be riding around on his unicycle, and then...'

'Well. G'won. What happened then?' asked Lotte and Tim breathlessly.

Mimi answered instead.

'That horrible man De'Aff had climbed into the ring at the last moment of their act without the others knowing. He was showing off like crazy, twirling his cape like a matador. He then blew massive fireballs into the big top, setting the trampoline on fire. He said it was to help to dramatise the whole effect, adding that it would be perfectly safe for Bonzo to escape from, whilst promising that he could bounce out of it despite the flames… *Well. It didn't happen like that at all!* Poor Bonzo fell with a sickening crunch through the burning trampoline onto his shoulder and arm, smashing it to pieces, as you can see by the size of the plaster. The crowd booed and screamed at the acrobats and clowns to clear off. Missiles were hurled at poor old Costello. Poor, gentle Costello who wouldn't harm a living soul! Bonzo cried, like I've never seen before.'

Bonzo looked away, averting his face in recalling his shame.

'But that wasn't the end of it,' Mimi continued, her voice quavering. '*Everything's* gone wrong since *he's* turned up. And we can't get rid of him.'

'What do you mean?' asked Chance.

'Look. Many strange and awful things have happened since. Accidents now happen every day, whereas before it was extremely rare, maybe once in a blue moon. For instance, my mum Carrita swore that someone cut the high-wire and loosened the safety riggings just before one of the matinées.'

'Heavens. That's very dangerous,' said Henry.

'Tell me about it!' groaned Shoona. She, with Mimi, gathered sympathetically around Bonzo's bed in their dressing gowns as though to give some moral support.

Distraught, Bonzo sat bolt upright in bed, and eased his heavy plaster gently to one side, adding, 'He's evil, that man. Pure, one hundred per cent evil!' He spat into his left hand with venom.

'Yuk... Disgusting!' shrieked Mimi, pulling a face. Immediately she handed him a tissue, forgetting for a moment that he'd have a job wiping it off with his other arm stuck in plaster.

Solemnly, she then carried on. 'Do you know, there's a story going around that evil man keeps as a pet, a nasty bearded serpent in his caravan under the bed. Mum says that it was to stop anyone searching his place for clues, such as where he came from and why he is hiding under a mask. Furthermore, Midgy says that he once heard some eerie music coming from the caravan window. He said it sounded like a weird, ghostly musical instrument – he thinks an old, out-of-tune violin... you know, like bones scraping on cat gut that make your teeth go on edge. Midgy swears it was that De'Aff practising, making that serpent dance. Mind you, if anyone as much as approaches the door to try to peep in, it would let out a blood-curdling cry as if the monster was swallowing something alive.'

'A b-be-bearded serp... serpent,' gasped Lotte. 'You can't be serious!'

Several of the children had struggled out of bed by now, some in pyjamas, others in dressing gowns. They crept nearer so that they could hear this frightening tale better.

'Yup, hard to believe. But that's what Katrina told us. She saw it with her own eyes. The ghastly thing was curled up in a basket on the day *he* arrived.' Mimi gave a little shudder.

'Who's Katrina?' asked Chance.

'Oh, didn't we mention her? Katrina's a lovely girl – a Russian stunner,' said Mimi admiringly. 'She's been Ziggarini's assistant in all his magic acts for a year or two.

She's been devastated since he disappeared. But she's *had* to work for that horrible Slatane De'Aff on Mr Barnard's orders instead or get the sack. You see, she'd starve to death if she didn't have work.'

'Go on, Mimi. What's this about a bearded serpent then?' cajoled Shoona with a mixture of fright and fascination.

'Well, according to witnesses, this creature is a sort of long, creepy thing. I'm told it looks a bit like a slimy prehistoric dragon of sorts – like the giant Komodo dragon... alive today in Asia – crossed with a hairy python, but with scales and fat claws that hide under its belly. And apparently, just like its owner, it is difficult to see its eyes – just empty sockets, blood red, covered in hair. And the worst of it all... is that it squeals a greedy, high-pitched sound when it ogles small animals, like kittens, puppies and birds in its sight. Well, that's what I've heard anyhow.'

Lotte brushed her nose nervously.

'Katrina is convinced that this dreadful so-and-so, De'Aff was hiding something evil and sinister. She says she has an awful feeling that Ziggarini was dead, and that he didn't run off to Sicily as that De'Aff swore he did. And another thing, that worries us is the ever-present sense of terrible foreboding since he turned up. Something we cannot put our finger on. And he appears to be searching all the time for someone to harm. But we can't prove it. What's more, there is a terrible menace about the way he just creeps and prowls around. And especially in the dark, when he is heard to mumble weird words which sound like "Acrid-cradaver" or...'

Mimi shivered visibly, her voice draining away.

'Mimi's dead right,' added Bonzo dolefully.

'Whow. What a catalogue of misery, disaster and woe,' offered Chance sympathetically.

'But I haven't finished yet by a long chalk. That's only half the story,' complained Mimi. 'I mean, just look at this enormous scar from the operation on the painful hernia that ripped through my tummy. Mind you, it was worse before the stitches were taken out.' Demonstrating this, she peeled back the edge of her pyjama top to show Shoona and Lotte. Being real gentlemen, Chance and Henry tactfully averted their eyes.

'Someone greased the steel on the high-wire during rehearsals. It caused me to slide out of control doing the splits. I nearly fell thirty feet or so. Luckily, I managed to grab hold by the tips of my fingers in the nick of time. I could have been killed. Fortunately, Midgy was there and threw me a safety harness. The doctors said that the sudden hefty pull when I fell must have ruptured my tummy button, causing an abominable hernia. Or was it *abdominal*?'

Mimi paused to think. 'Well, anyway, whichever they said it was… it still flippin' well hurt!'

'Eeks! How 'orrible!' yelled Lotte. She jammed her fingers between her teeth.

Mimi grimaced. 'The list of sinister goings-on is endless. Why, just last week I heard, the night before they opened in Battersea Park, the Performing-Flea act had to be abandoned, as some ghastly person broke into the compound during the night and let them escape. In doing so at the same time, they threw a half-dead ferret into their box.'

'The Flea Grand Master was out of his mind with

worry. Well, you would not believe it, but if that wasn't a bad enough catastrophe for Barnards to deal with, there were dangerous mishaps after mishaps!'

'Did Barnards call the police?' asked Chance, trying to be helpful.

'Well, of course they did,' retorted Mimi irritably. 'By the time they arrived to investigate, they found someone had scrawled in enormous, spidery-shaped writing in the sawdust in the centre of the ring:

"HA HA HEE. YOU IDIOTS FREEZE. THE PHANTOM WAS HERE, SO IT CAN'T BE ME!"

'The police thought it must have been a hoax.' Mimi looked thoroughly depressed.

'Do you mean these strange happenings and unexplained goings-on... were...? Could it be, you know...?' Chance looked questioningly at the worried faces of Mimi and Bonzo. 'I mean. Could this phantom... what-yer-call-it-thing... of the circus, be that same nasty De'Aff bloke in a sort of sick joke disguise trying to scare the living pants out of all of you?'

Bonzo's jaw began to twitch uncontrollably. 'But hold-a on. We have not yet-a proof! Before we can accuse him, we have to catch-a him red-handed!'

Immediately, Mimi interrupted, struggling for words. 'B... But I've heard that Midgy's convinced that this De'Aff and this phantom are one and the same. He told Carrita that we've got to act now against this evil creature before something really fatal happens.'

Henry had remained silent until now, deep in thought.

He kept scratching the bottom of his cane gently against the foot of Mimi's bed. 'What could be worse than what had already happened so far, Miss Mimi?' he suddenly said.

'Oh, things *did* go from bad to worse, I can tell you. Anyway, that evening, the show was a total washout. A nightmare,' said Mimi. 'My mum Carrita nearly fell off the flying trapeze but saved herself with her hand at the last moment, and there were several other accidents, too many to mention...

'Then to cap it all, poor Katrina was almost killed in De'Aff's knife-throwing act. The flaming knives thrown at her were supposed to pierce the balloons pinned all around her body. Instead, several of the burning daggers missed completely and sliced through the top of her gown of pearls – one just narrowly missing her heart. Because of this fiasco, the performers fled out of the ring in tears. The crowd booed and screamed abuse, hurling insults like, "*Gerroff! What a load of cobblers*," and even worse.'

Mimi's voice dropped almost to a whisper.

'Wh... what happened next?' asked Lotte, swallowing hard.

'The clown troupe, Costello and co, tried to make up for it. They did their utmost to cheer up the audience and make them laugh a bit... But it didn't work. The booing and abuse just got worse. Popcorn, drink cartons and programmes were thrown into the ring. Many screamed for their money back. It was an appalling disaster!'

Mimi looked crestfallen as soon as she said it. 'No one, I mean *no one*, wants to work there anymore. They all swear that the circus is cursed, haunted by a terrifying phantom, and simply want none of it.'

'What does the boss, Barnard, say to all this?' asked Chance.

'He doesn't appear to care that much. It seems that loathsome De'Aff has him around his little finger. And now, this creature is strutting around the place arrogantly like nobody's business, getting in *every* act he can, as if he owns the place. You know, I don't trust him an inch. There something about him that's dangerous... *I hate him!*'

She choked with emotion. Tears stung her eyes just thinking of her poor mother, the Fabulous Carrita, running out of the big top crying her eyes out after being screamed at by the hostile crowd.

Just then, Bonzo cut in with a plea for help. He tried to move his back, which had stiffened up with the weight of his plaster across his body.

'*Per favore*. Look, Signor Chancer. Can you do-a us a favour, please, and help-a? Can you call on my Uncle Costello and help-a him out in the next show? You've heard what Mimi has said. Morale is bad at the circus. Everyone's so miserable now. *Everyone*... With-a your fresh new ideas, you-a could inspire them all. Grimbo, Midgy and the gang – they've lost a lot of confidence.'

He stared at Chance imploringly. '*Grazie. Prego*... You could at the same time help-a to check out this nasty creature De'Aff for us. See if you-a could find out some clues about him. Help-a the police. Find Uncle Costello. He'll help. He's a good and loyal man who's kind and would not-a hurt a fly. You can trust-a him with your life.'

'Look. I can't promise. But make laughter, fun and

other things, perhaps yes. Detective snooping work? …I'm really not sure! Anyway, I'll think about it,' replied Chance, trying to be helpful.

'Wait. Steady on, old boy,' quipped Henry. 'We may not have time. We've got to be on our way – as we have an urgent job to do to sort out the next vital part of the rid—'

He didn't quite finish, for Chance silenced him with a sharp hiss and gave a sudden kick at his shoe. Henry reddened. He snuffled loudly and collapsed into the nearest chair to nurse the side of his foot.

Chapter 30

FLYING BEDPANS AND ANOTHER GOOD DEED INDEED

WHILE HENRY CONTINUED TO examine his foot, Mimi climbed out of bed gingerly to avoid ripping the scar from her operation. She put on a dressing gown, pleading, 'Please. Please, both of you. We *need* your help. Stuck in here, there's no one else we can turn to. You and Henry, you look dead honest and clever. You seem to be able to do some extraordinary things – things we can't do, or even hope to do.'

Tim and Lotte nodded vigorously, adding their support.

'I mean, talking about all this sadness and unhappiness. Just look around you.' Mimi waved a hand and gave a tiny sniffle, tugging at their consciences. 'We're surrounded by misery. You don't have to look far. The ward's full of sick kids, all fed up and a bit depressed. Therefore, can't you do some funny tricks and make them laugh a bit?'

Undecided, Chance and Henry shrugged helplessly.

'Oh, come on!' pleaded Mimi, trying to prick their conscience. 'Cheer us up a little, please, before you go. *Please!* All of us, you know, could do with a bit of a giggle.'

Shoona and Bonzo joined in with an expectant smile.

Chance cocked his head to one side, pursing his lips in thought.

'Okay, folks. Why not? You've twisted my arm and my leg, so to speak!' He had been propping himself languidly against the end of the bed, when suddenly, like a Jack-in-the-box, he leapt up, flinging his arms into the air. From the inside of his jacket, he released a bunch of brightly coloured balloons. Dozens of them began to float around the beds, startling the children. He then whistled, forming a large circle between his lips. A stream of bubbles poured out, floating haphazardly to the ceiling. Forgetting her pains for a moment, Mimi climbed out of bed and chased after a couple of balloons with Shoona.

Henry was startled out of his chair as Chance stepped towards him, pointing deliberately to his face. At first, he didn't know what to expect. He jumped as his moustache started to twirl rapidly round and round, rather like a plastic windmill from a fairground. Bonzo, Lotte and Tim roared with laughter. Henry retaliated by leaning over and squeezed the pink carnation stuck in Chance's buttonhole, hoping to catch him by surprise. A sudden jet of water squirted out backwards instead, soaking Henry's face and monocle.

'Oh, drat! What the blazes was that?' gasped Henry, taken by surprise.

Chance creased up with laughter, slapping his knees hysterically. The rest of them joined in, shrieking with joy. Tears rolled down Mimi's face.

Towards the bottom end of the ward, the children screeched...

'More, yet more. There's loads of time for another encore!'

It stung Chance into action again. Quickly, he twirled his nose and stroked the gem around his collar. Suddenly, he rose a foot off the ground, and began to float horizontally in a whirring motion as he beamed towards them like a hover-mower with his big red boots suspended in the air.

They started to giggle in anticipation. 'Ooh, look. What's going to happen?' they exclaimed, pointing excitedly.

Stretching his arms out in front of him, as if blindly feeling the air, he started to waggle his fingers as though he were about to conduct an orchestra. To everyone's astonishment, scores of shiny steel bedpans began to clatter out from underneath the beds, whereas others started to burst out of the bedside cabinets nearby. They took off at low level, increasing their speed as they flew in circles into mid-air with a dense humming sound like UFOs in flight. Luckily for the patients' sake, most of the bedpans had been emptied and cleaned on the early-morning ward rounds.

A young boy with ginger hair at the end of the ward, who had just had his tonsils out, shouted hoarsely, 'Ooh, do look, everyone!' As he clutched the edge of his pillow he gasped, 'Wow! Flying saucers from space!' He stood on the bed and tried to catch his bedpan before it hit the ceiling.

A red-headed girl next door to him shrieked hysterically. She managed to down one of them with her pillow, which suddenly burst open, scattering a shower of feathers that sprinkled all over her bed.

By now, Chance had got into his stride. Somehow, he made the trolleys waltz about in the middle of the room in rhythm with the flying bedpans, which were still spinning in the air. Bed screens started to dance together, as he orchestrated them on by, seemingly conducting with an invisible baton. Effortlessly, they seemed to glide up and down the floor on their tiny castors. Their curtains of linen billowed in the wind whilst acting like sails on the open sea.

'Wicked! Incredible! …Grr… eat!' yelled Tim to Lotte, grinning uncontrollably as the hospital beds rose up and down in a kind of mechanised Mexican wave like one of the rides in a funfair.

This time Henry refused to be outdone. He reached under Mimi's pillow and scooped out a gigantic egg, which she thought came from an ostrich. But she was wrong. As he tapped the top of the egg with the tip of his cane, everyone craned their necks to watch, holding their breath. Suddenly the shell split open with a crack and out hopped a beautiful black rabbit with white paws, its fur all fluffed up. When it hopped in turn from one bed to another and skidded across the tops of the bedside cabinets on its bottom, the children squealed wildly.

The noise of heavy laughter with the clatter of the hospital furniture swirling about soon attracted the attention of the nursing staff. There was a large swoosh as the swing doors flew open. Staff Nurse Bernadette O'Fittergin came striding in without warning.

'For lawd's sake, children. Hush. Please! Please be quiet,' she urged in her soft, sugary drawl. '*What* on earth?!' she spluttered, her mouth agape. She ducked her head as bedpans flew narrowly over her. They then slid back into the cupboards and under the beds from where they came from. In an instant, like magic, the screens and trolleys stopped dancing. Immediately, Chance hid his hands behind his back rather guiltily.

'Begorra! What in heaven's name is dis?' The nurse was flabbergasted. In the meantime, the little black rabbit hopped down off the tops of the beds, scurried down the centre of the ward, then nonchalantly padded past her, and promptly disappeared into the bathroom near the door.

Straight away, Chance gave a low bow. He snapped his fingers in mid-air, then whipped out a single red rose from out of his pocket and pressed it into her hands. Henry then fumbled in his waistcoat and presented the nurse with a box of chocolate mints. It stopped her dead in her tracks before she could complain.

'Well, I'd never. Per-leeze, gentlemen. Noo more tricks. Cause otherwise methinks old Matron herself will have a fit, I'm sure!'

Tim, in the meantime, not wishing to miss out, had slipped on his special, silver-panther trainers with their supersonic-roller blades in the undercarriage. From a trouser pocket, he had pulled out his other prized possession… his special Rocket catapult, which he had flicked out from its pen-like body. Zigzagging on his blades, he immediately sped down the middle of the room at breakneck speed, dodging the furniture. Whizzing along, he snatched a handful of grapes from Shoona's bedside cabinet and a fistful of sweets from Mimi's without stopping.

Using his catapult, he took aim at three red balloons that were floating to the ceiling. *Ker-rack. Bang... Pop!* To a barrage of noisy cheers from the young patients, they burst with deadly accuracy and showered them with bits of plastic debris, which floated down from the air... As Tim spun backwards towards the door, he flipped the bobbles at the side of his boots to change gear to a slower speed. He went into reverse on one foot, did a backward somersault and landed on the other, then hit another floating target as it drifted downwards.

The children went wild, whooping uncontrollably at the top of their voices. Pillows and towels were flung into the air, as they shouted and clapped ecstatically. 'Wicked... Ger-reat. Dead cool!' roared the crowd, applauding.

Tim beamed at the adulation. Bursting with pride, he folded away his precious boots, retracting its mini wheels. His prized rocket-catapult was stowed into his pocket safely, folding it back into its original flat carcass.

In the heat of the moment, Lotte had nearly been carried away as well. For one split second, she thought of releasing Brush, her mini robotic mouse, to scurry over the floor. But almost instantly, she changed her mind, as it might have backfired and caused screams of fright. And so Brush remained put, its control switched off. Being now a bit peeved, she pulled Tim to one side and whispered tersely into his ear, 'Well, that's enough showing off for the day, Timothy Needles!'

As the noise quietened down, Nurse O'Fittergin glared up and down the row of beds with a frown of thunder. But as soon as she saw that all her young patients were smiling, she changed her tune. Happiness radiated from their faces.

Instead of a sickly pallor, there was a healthy glow to their cheeks. Their eyes gleamed with renewed zest and some fresh hope.

She turned to Chance and Henry, admitting, 'Ah… I'm wun over, my dear fellows, to what you've dun yourselves today. What clever men you be. What a handsome gud deed you've dun, begorra!' Then she mumbled her thanks for the gifts, sharply turned on her heels, and hurried to the bathroom in search of the black rabbit.

Handed such generous compliments, Chance's nose suddenly glowed brighter than ever. It lit up as a Belisha beacon, as if it had suddenly recognised that he, without realising it, had indeed achieved yet *another* kind deed. Simultaneously, the lobes of his ears boiled over – even his friends around him swore that they could almost feel the heat.

Lotte mouthed, 'Well done!' as the palms of his hands broke out in a sweat. He thought that he heard a quiet song humming in his ears… Then he suddenly recalled what his old chum Zoot had said to him back at the house, regarding a signal when goodness and kind deeds are carried out.

Tim gave him a thumbs-up sign, although Henry couldn't help feel just a little bit jealous, although he was convinced that his friend had a kind of glow – like a halo, bathing his head for that splinter of a second.

Automatically, Chance felt under his collar to check that his precious pendant was still safe. As the fuss died down, Henry stroked his upper lip to make sure that his prized moustache had not flown away in the excitement of the last trick. To bring his friends back to earth, he reminded them that they'd better get going soon, if they wanted to make the circus in time for rehearsals,

Somewhat reluctantly, Tim and Lotte got up from Shoona's bedside to catch up with Chance and Henry, who were already at the door.

'Bye, Shoona. Get better quickly and get home soon. I'll tell my mum to tell yours that we've seen you and you're looking good,' promised Lotte in earnest.

Tim looked over his shoulder on his way out and called, 'Bye, Mimi. Cheers, Bonzo. Get better soon.'

'*Prego. Grazie.* Please don't forget-a to see my Uncle Costello and give him-a hand. I promise that you-a can entrust your life in his hands, for he's a reliable and good man – one of the best!'

'Sure, I will,' Chance reassured young Bonzo. 'Don't worry about a thing. Henry and I will do our utmost to check out this mysterious creature, Dr De'Aff. We promise.'

'Tell Carrita, my mum, that I'm leaving hospital next week,' shouted Mimi. Theatrically, she blew a kiss into the air as Chance and Henry tugged at the swing doors to let Lotte and Tim leave ahead of them.

As they were closing the doors, by sheer chance, they almost collided with a vicar who was coming into the ward as they were leaving. By some strange quirk of fate, it was the Reverend Barnabas Quick, the vicar of St Swithin's. He had been doing the hospital rounds visiting sick patients in turn. By accident, he brushed past the harlequin within a hair's breadth.

'Oops. Sorry, Father... after you.' Chance apologised profusely. He stepped back to allow the vicar to pass him.

The Reverend Quick pulled up a chair besides Shoona and Mimi's bed. He started to greet them with, 'Hello, Shoona, Mimi... How are you getting on?' when his voice tailed off suddenly. His head then did a doubletake. It whipped round sharply after Chance had exited. But it was too late. The harlequin had disappeared completely out of sight.

'Oh, heavens above, now bless my soul!' exclaimed the Reverend Quick. His heart started thumping wildly like a bass drum booming. 'Oh dear, gracious me. Wait a minute. Wasn't that... *him* – a fat, jolly figure with a bright red mouth full of pearly white...? Surely, it can't...?'

His thoughts flew back to his last sermon at the church. *Smiling... oh... grinning from ear to ear. And yes... balding. Not much hair... Red... Was it, red wisps of hair?* He went extremely pale. Blood drained from his face. Increasingly flustered and confused, he began to question whether he had seen a ghost or a vision of someone like him in the past.

'Are you all right, Father?' Shoona asked anxiously.

'Got to sit down,' he conceded. He fell into a heap besides Mimi's bed. He fished out a large white handkerchief, fanned himself and blew his nose like a trumpet. Loosening his dog collar, he jerked a thumb towards the door, and then asked Mimi, haltingly, 'Was *that* a harlequin or a clown from the circus in town? I'm sure I've seen someone like him before!'

Her head shook firmly, saying, 'We've never seen him before until today. He came with Lotte. He's given us so much fun and entertained us like crazy. You know, Father, we feel so much better now!'

'Never laughed so much in our lives,' agreed Shoona. She was gripping a stitch that was developing on her side from all the giggling. 'Better than all the medicine we've been taking,' she added with a grin.

They all went rather quiet as Nurse O'Fittergin came storming back. 'Are you all right now dere, Fadther?' she enquired with concern. Instinctively, her hand shot out to touch his shoulder; then blushing, she quickly withdrew it suddenly remembering that he was a man of the cloth.

He was sunk well back in the chair, leaning heavily against the wall. He whipped off his spectacles, fiddling with them nervously. Furiously he wiped the sweat off his brow, breathing erratically. Straining with some effort, he tried to explain. 'I... I... er... thought I'd just seen an apparition of some sorts a few moments ago.'

'Pardon me. Do come again, Fadther. I don't understand.'

'That harlequin figure – you know, that one who's just left – after entertaining the youngsters. He seemed *identical* to someone I had seen in my mind's eye, a few times before. In fact, I described him in my sermon at the church – why, only recently, the other week. It was either *he* or a spitting image of him... you know, wandering around!' The Reverend Quick heaved a big sigh as he twiddled with his handkerchief, now sopping wet.

'Now whut in dear heaven's name do you mean, Fadther?' the nurse asked again.

Although completely flustered, he tried to explain further, dragging his words. 'I've said... I mean... I predicted to the congregation, that a being... a person will come to make the whole world laugh a bit and to cure the place of its misery. A Messenger – a Prophet of Mirth, if you like – will turn up one day. Rather like the figure I've just described – fat and jolly with a...'

He stopped and shook his head vigorously at the puzzled nurse and conceded wearily, '*No. I must have been mistaken.* It can't possibly be the one and the same. It'll be a miracle if his double is wandering around the hospitals doing the rounds before me. Ah. I must have dreamt it! But those dazzling multicoloured clothes...? *Those big red boots!'*

After that passing remark, she hurried on her heels and left the room sharply, grumbling to no one in particular. 'Now where's that wretched rabbit now? Just wait till I catch him. He'll end up in the Irish stew, even if I say so meself!'

***

Whilst all this was going on, Chance and his friends, being so absorbed with the excitement that they had just created, did not notice as they reached the main entrance, that a scrawny young man had been watching them from a car. By then, he had started to walk towards them. Staggering deliberately towards them, clutching his chest, was young Seth Ropely, struggling for air and coughing violently. He collapsed in a heap, prostrate on the tiled corridor in front of their feet. For a moment, he looked somewhat familiar. But as his body writhed in front of him, Chance wasn't at all sure.

'For gawd's sake. *Help!* Please help me,' came a desperate appeal. 'Get... a... doc-tor. Quickly!' he rasped. 'Can't breathe. It's me ticker... pains in my chest.' Both of his hands gripped his chest and stomach. Then clasping his throat, he gasped with his eyes half-closed, 'Quick, for pity's sake... I'm dying!'

They were so taken aback that they just gawped with shock. Chance recovered his wits and quickly barked at the top of his voice. '*Doctor... Get a doctor. Quickly! Hurry, please. Someone's having a heart attack!*'

Quickly, Lotte ran to get help. Henry and Tim rushed into the corridor to grab a trolley with a stretcher. They yelled for a hospital porter, who came running out with a nurse and a doctor.

With everyone's help, Seth was lifted bodily off the cold floor and placed on his back on the stretcher. He seemed to be agitated, calling for the harlequin. Concerned, Chance bent over to listen for his breathing, which was labouring under a whisper that sounded like, 'Thanks a bunch, you clown!' In that split second, Seth reached up and snatched the pendant that dangled from the harlequin's neck. Quickly, with deft sleight of a hand, he shoved it deep into his pocket and continued a moan, which was worsening by the second. The doctor and his staff rapidly wheeled the trolley into the emergency ward.

'We'll take over now. Thanks,' puffed the nurse, dismissing them curtly with a wave of her hands. To further dissuade them from following, a curtain was drawn abruptly across a screened-off cubicle right in front of their faces.

Outside the main doors, Lotte and Tim were waiting patiently.

'We can't do any more for him, poor chap,' exclaimed Chance, now joining them. However, it started him thinking, *Now, where have I seen him before...?*

'He's in good expert hands with those doctors now,' added a relieved Henry. 'Come on. Let's get back to Roland. He'll be worried. By the way, what was that young fellow trying to say to you back there?'

Chance was in a bit of a daze trying to work out where he had come across him before. Try hard as his might, it didn't come to him. He shook his head, dismissing it from his mind for the moment.

'Er... did you say something, Henry?' he asked blankly, still thinking.

'I said, why was that young chap asking for you? He was trying to say something to you. It seemed important.'

'I dunno, really,' Chance replied lamely, still trying to jog his memory. 'Can't work it out. It sounded like he was trying to thank me for our help... something like – thanks a bunch...'

'Well, that's really nice of him. After all, you saved his life. He ought to be grateful,' said Tim.

'Yeah. What a nice young man,' added Lotte.

On seeing them come out, Roland had drawn his cab up to the ambulance bay and shouted for them to jump in. He complained that Ram had flattened him with playing and running about. 'Walkies? You've got to be joking! Anyhow, what kept you lot?'

They began to explain all what had happened since they went to visit Lotte's friend.

'We'll explain a bit more on the way,' said Chance softly, now somewhat subdued.

Roland shrugged and began to drive away from the hospital with his foot firmly on the accelerator.

'Can you take us to the green at World's End, please, Roland?' asked Henry.

'We're going to the circus,' shouted Lotte and Tim with rising excitement, now jumping up and down in their seats. Laughing, they ruffled Ram's head back and forth.

'Why on earth there?' enquired Roland, half-turning round.

'We'll explain in a minute. There is such a lot to tell you. Don't worry, you'll find out soon enough,' said Chance, trying to reassure him. Suddenly, he remembered something very, important and stopped. Something was wrong. Frantically, he began to search under his collar, then felt behind his bow tie in earnest. He felt around his neck and under his sweater, scrabbling desperately. There was nothing there. *Nothing!* He was mortified. There was no mistaking it. *It had gone!*

The vital pendant with its precious gemstone was missing. Gutted, he slumped down in the seat and flopped sideways. He propped his head against the side window and closed his eyes. He suddenly, without warning, felt incredibly weak, as though a piece of him was missing… That single piece of gem, both unique and precious, that was given to him by Miss Saskia, had now been stolen. Gone. Lost forever. He felt suddenly sick in the pit of his stomach. He hit his forehead with his knuckles in frustration, trying to think back. Then of course, sickeningly, it started to sink home. Had it been stolen as he bent over that young fellow when trying to save his life?

Then, it slowly all began to come back to him like a bolt from above. Of course! …That young chap, the one that collapsed at the hospital. He had seen him once before! Miss Saskia's stolen car… of course! *Yes, it was definitely, him again, the dastardly, thieving wretch!* Silently, Chance began to curse his bad luck. A double whammy… a lightning strike twice! And now he'd fallen for a trick, a simple one at that – one of the oldest in the book. The fool! And again, he was simply furious with himself for his stupidity.

Immediately, a sense of dark foreboding crossed his mind as different thoughts whirled through his head. He fell into a half-slumber, lulled by the dull swaying of the taxi with its hypnotic hum of its tyres skirting the road. But his thoughts returned to what Bonzo and Mimi had told him: the mystery of the sudden disappearance of Ziggarini and the subsequent appearance of a sinister character named Dr Slatane De'Aff at Mimi's friends' circus. And how frightened they all were of him. Then the very mention of the terrible curse of a phantom of the circus now hovering there, left an inexplicable shiver that was icy cold and chilled his spine.

Chance became incredibly worried. He decided to keep it to himself so as not to worry young Lotte and Tim. But there was something strange going on there that he couldn't quite put his finger on. Could this Slatane De'Aff be one and the same as this phantom, flitting from one to the other? Mimi and Bonzo hinted as much yet admitted that they could not prove it.

Then furthermore, could this De'Aff, be also one of the embodiments of the figures of evil from the Custodians of Terror that Cecil-the-Thin had previously warned him about at Madame Rousseau's?

And another thing: could this same person be in some way connected with the evil-supreme of that faceless tyrant, Qnevilus-the-Terrible from an Alterworld that Cecil also mentioned at the waxworks? And if so then, by following this De'Aff be the way to track down this elusive, evil called Qnevilus?

Chance mulled it over. Perhaps it was a bit far-fetched; but after all the weird things that had happened to him so far, *anything* is possible? But if it were true, how could he now cope if he were to meet this evil, face to face who was bent on killing him? Could he protect himself? And, more to the point, could he protect his young friends for whom he was responsible?

Increasingly agitated and concerned, his mind skipped back to all the skills that Hoopy Hoopla the fighting kangaroo he met at the waxworks had taught him. But come the day, come the moment of truth, could his physical capabilities in the dynamic fighting arts of Toe Hee Do be good enough to deal with wispy ghosts or slippery phantoms you cannot even grab hold of, never mind, see?

Then a terrifying thought crossed his mind: say, for instance, the *many phantoms* were one and the same? Could its wicked force, when united, become magnified in strength? And if it were true, the reality then, would be too awful to contemplate. He therefore tried to blank it from his mind. As he grew silent, his friends became increasingly concerned.

'Are you all right, my friend?' Henry asked, anxiously peering at his ashen face.

'You're a bit quiet, Chance. You're not sick, are you?' added Lotte. 'You're normally so cheerful. It's not like you.'

'Hey, there's nothing wrong, is there?' asked Tim.

'Just a little tired from all the exertions back there,' came the reply, with Chance lying through his teeth. He daren't tell them the truth. And especially to the youngsters who thought of him as some sort of hero and, on the face of it, totally invincible.

'Please drive on, Roland. Thanks.' He sounded so weary, as if all the woes of the world had suddenly crashed down onto his head. Helplessly, he felt under his collar again. Without the precious pendant he felt so vulnerable. All sorts of worries now crowded in on him, thick and fast…

But however much he tried he just couldn't dismiss these morbid ideas out of his head from growing. Frightening images kept looming up in front of him… *Slatane De'Aff… the phantom of the circus… and the Custodians of Terror.* Though each name was an enigma, their images conjured up evil. And frankly, each nightmare they represented terrified him to death, although he did not dare to admit it. And the ironic joke was that, here he was on his way by taxi to confront them.

Chapter 31

KNOCKING AT DEATH'S DOOR

Before Seth had quite realised what had hit him, he had been wheeled into a cubicle in A&E surrounded by an emergency team. He raised his head off the plinth and swallowed hard, for facing him was the most impressive array of gleaming medical equipment that he had ever seen. The most modern, up-to-date cardiac monitors, ECG, resuscitation equipment, oxygen masks, red and green lights that flashed, dials and imposing screens from machines that lit up, surrounded his bed.

As the doctor approached him, Seth firmly pushed the cold stethoscope away from his chest and attempted to get up. He began to button up his shirt.

'Look, Doc. I feel okay now,' he announced unwaveringly. '...Just felt a little turn out there. You know what it's like – must have eaten something earlier that disagreed with me.

Yeah. That's it. I remember now. It must have been those dodgy sausages at that roadside caff!'

Desperately, the medics and the doctor in attendance tried to restrain him without much luck. The doctor stared at him gravely with the utmost concern. 'Young man, we ought to do an ECG on your heart. The consultant cardiologist is on his way. He's been paged. He will want to conduct an X-ray, a scan and other tests. It will only take a few hours or so.'

Increasingly worried, Seth began to sweat a little. 'Honest, Doc. Scouts 'onour. *Really*, I'm right as rain. Feel fit as a fiddle after that slap of cold water on my face, and that kind, pretty little nurse massaging my chest.'

As he spoke, Seth jumped off the plinth with remarkable agility for someone who was knocking at death's door a few minutes ago. 'I'm dead okay! Sorry, Doc. A false alarm! Blame those sausages,' he explained apologetically as he rapidly tied up his shoelaces.

'Well, I really don't know, young chap. We really ought to keep you here for observation, and...' The doctor fished out his watch from his white coat, stroked his chin thoughtfully and fiddled with his stethoscope that was dangling calmly around his neck. He looked round for something to write some notes on.

Seth was getting exasperated at the delaying tactics. 'Look. Honest, Doc. *Cross my heart, hope to die...!* Wait a minute. *You'd better scrub that!* Though thanks, but no thanks! I'm sure you've got more dead... oops – sorree, more sick people to see to, rather than me. I've never felt better in my whole life!' persuaded Seth with conviction. He felt inside his trouser pocket to make sure the gem and the pendant were still safely there. It was. He gave a triumphant smirk secretly to himself. 'Look 'ere. I can jump up and down, holding my breath whilst touching my toes, and run on the spot without snuffing it.' He gave a little demonstration. 'I can even jog without a problem. Swear on my blessed heart. *Look, Doc… Just watch!*'

Then, hurriedly, he brushed aside the curtain and tore out of the cubicle, almost colliding with a nurse who was just returning with a consent form for more specialist tests. Dumbstruck, the medical team was too flabbergasted and helpless to stop him. He sprinted down the corridor as fast as he could high on the rush of adrenaline.

'Got to rescue my car off those yellow lines,' he mouthed in panic. '…You know those wardens, they'd even ticket an ambulance, never mind a little ol' banger like mine, given half a chance!' A couple of onlookers flew out of the way as he rushed to his old car. Within minutes, he had leapt into his Mini and roared away fast, leaving a trail of blue smoke drifting in the ambulance bay behind him.

'Well, I'll be…!' commented the doctor in a state of shock. Then he immediately collapsed on the nearest trolley, pleading for water and a bottle of tranquillisers.

Brimming with self-congratulations, Seth was in seventh heaven. 'Wowee! Wicked, man! That was awesome. *I've done it!* Got it, you fools…' He pulled the pendant from his pocket and gave it a kiss. He smacked the top of the dashboard with the flat of his fist in glee. Then roaring with laughter, he held on to his body, which had doubled up in fits of hysterics. He was over the moon, so he burst out into song, tapping his feet in tune:

'*Whistle while you work, that fool is such a twerp.*
While his defence is down, he acts a clown,
Whistle while you work.'

Part VI

Oh, mocking curse, mocking curse, try not to catch me,
Too late, you're so stupid attempting to flee.

Chapter 32

OUT OF THE SHADOWS

I T WAS DURING THE night on the other side of town when
a secretive meeting took place... It had been dark now
for several hours. The site was fast asleep: dead to the world
outside. A sliver of starlight escaped through thick banks
of clouds that slowly scudded by. Some drizzle started to
moisten the dank night air, patchily at first. Chimes from
a church clock somewhere in the town struck solemnly in
the distance. It was three in the morning.

'Well. Is everything in place?' came a whisper. A tall,
lumbering figure crept from behind a tent, dragging his
feet stiffly as he scuffed the grass behind him. 'Is the coast
clear, my friend?' he growled, shielding his face with the
upturn of his cloak. A black fedora was dragged down over
his forehead, adding to the disguise.

'As far as I know,' hissed the other figure that had been
skulking in the shadows at the back of a large trailer. They

sharpened their eyes, glancing warily around them to see if they were being watched.

A mangy old fox darted just then across their path with a small animal wriggling in its jaws, and then disappeared into the darkness of the undergrowth.

'Hah. Thought that was a wolverine creature from the Alterworld come to look for us!' rasped the taller figure grimly. He spat after the animal's tracks. Then, wiping the remains of the spittle from his mouth with the back of his hand, he insisted, 'Here. Come closer, my friend. We don't want anyone – creature, human or otherwise – to see us now, do we?'

A gnarled hand crept from a wide sleeve, beckoning to the other. It was difficult to see. Bands of light from the night sky above rippled between sheets of darkness as the clouds thickened. It was a perfect dark night as far as they were concerned.

'Have you heard?' he asked, pausing heavily, as he jammed his face close to the other one's. The latter figure, though shorter, was just as bulky – but seemingly just as sinister – shrank back a little, repelled by the smell of stale garlic and decay.

'Wha… What do you mean?' he stuttered, averting his mouth.

'Have you heard that the *fat, cheerful one* is coming? He's on his way,' the taller one repeated. He placed his hand on the other one's sleeve, gripping vice-like, obviously concerned.

The shorter one tried to break free, but it was impossible. Together, as if as one, their bodies arched and swayed, spinning concentrically. Then a very strange thing happened, when a deep scorch mark began to form below their feet and ground a pattern in the grass beneath them.

'We have to stop him at all costs. The Worthy One… the Most Mighty One… expects it. There must be no mistakes. *None whatsoever!* We have been warned!'

'But… but… why now? Why not let him dangle a while, and then dupe him to lead us the way to the power and riches of the Kingdoms? After all, I've heard that he's sorted the first part of the riddle.'

'Oh, has he now?' sneered the taller one. 'He's far smarter than we thought. So, he's carrying on with the search, is he?'

No sooner had he broken away and stepped out of the shadows, when a gap opened in the clouds. The drizzle had stopped, but there was a lot of dew in the air that chilled it. The light was now less opaque, but still no facial features could be seen. He seemed to croak his words out of the side of his nose rather than where his mouth should have been.

'The comical fool has no choice… *if* he wants to live.'

These sinister words slid out in a threat that held no bounds…His crooked fingers twisted, one over the other, in sync with his writhing body as he continued to snarl. 'Ah, moreover, my friend, I'm told that he already has the first gem in his possession. We must get our hands on it before it leads him to the next. Then it will be extremely difficult to defeat him,' he warned. Automatically, he pushed his dark glasses upwards, as they had slipped down somewhat over his mask-like face due to moisture from the chilled night air.

'But he's already well on the way to fulfilling the first part of the quest, isn't he?' asked the other figure anxiously.

'Not quite. There's another part to complete,' came a vicious retort. 'As I said, we can stop him in his tracks. *Dead... here and now* – when he turns up! He will be completely unaware of a death trap arranged for him during one of my devil-tricks. This time, the time and place will be perfect. So, like a moth to the flame, let's tempt him in!'

'But he has friends with him... that boy and that girl. What shall we do with them?'

'We have *no* choice. Well, if they happen to be in the way – then...' He covered his mouth with his fist, the bare knuckles of his fingers tensed white.

The shorter figure raised and then lowered his shoulders, letting out a deep sigh. He kept shuffling on the spot impatiently, longing to get away.

'Still, I don't like it much to reveal our hand so soon. He's made so many friends, more and more as he goes on. He'll gain more and more popularity with support from the people, as well as creatures from the Kingdoms, if this goes on. He's no ordinary fool, although he plays the buffoon by spreading the message of joy wherever he goes.'

He tugged at his coat, yanking it higher to cover his nose.

'J... Jo... Joy! F... Fu... Fun! Happiness! Bah! Enough of that!' The other exploded. 'I *hate* those words – in *any* language. I detest them! Give me loads of misery, fear and loathing any time. These are much more powerful as weapons to control those in the Kingdoms than the other weaselly ones.'

There was so much vitriol in his voice that he almost choked.

'But what happens if we fail, and that cheerful fool gets away?'

There was a sharp rebuke from his co-conspirator. 'Fail? *Fail!* We simply cannot fail. *We dare not!*' he screeched through his cloak. 'The Worthy One... would... would...'

'You m-mean... We could be ki... killed!'

'Yes, my friend. There'll be no choice. It'll mean certain death for us all.' A shrivelled finger sliced across the front of his throat in a graphic demonstration.

They forced themselves to calm right down and spoke a little more quietly, fearing waking those asleep around them up.

'Again, I need to ask, is everything in place? We have got to stop him before he reaches those in the Alterworld and causes an uprising. And so, is everything ready?'

The other nodded and whispered out of the side of his face. 'The trap is set!'

The night clouded over completely. It became an impenetrable sky. The two figures shook hands, then turned on their heels, giving a sinister cackle before melting away into the pitch-black blackness that surrounded them.

The fox suddenly reappeared. He began to sniff the ground where the two had been. He stuck his snout into the air and let out a blood-curdling howl in anguish.

Chapter 33

BARNARD AND BARNARD

Barnard and Barnard's Circus had pitched its big top on the green at World's End at the bottom edge of Chelsea. The enormous bell-shaped tent of cream-coloured canvas appeared to rise out of the grass like a massive, round birthday cake belonging to a giant. Tall masts peeped out from a hole in the stretched roofline, one at each end like spindly chimneys. Attached to one of them fluttered a large flag of a snake curled around a top hat rippling in the breeze. In the centre of the flag, the family emblem of Theobald Barnard, founder of the illustrious circus in 1879, was proudly displayed.

Rows of brightly coloured bunting followed the contours of the tent. Several thick guy ropes, festooned with the national flags of every country under the sun, tethered the big top firmly to the ground.

Clustered around the big top were dozens of ornately

painted caravans, as well as garishly decorated trailers with their bold Baroque lettering gilded on the side panels. One of the vehicles looked extremely sad and forlorn. It belonged to the Great Ziggarini. It was parked behind the rear exit of the big top. The doors were now firmly locked and the windows heavily obscured with thick curtains and shutters, the place noticeably empty since his sudden disappearance some weeks ago.

A continuous hum from generators and a general clatter of noise rose in the air. Circus workers rushed about shouting hoarsely. Several dogs darted about, scurrying between the various tents and vehicles that were scattered haphazardly all over the muddy green site. Many of these would open later to sell refreshments, whilst others would operate as additional sideshows. Some of these bordered on the unusual, such as that from Madame Hilda Gloops. A large billboard propped against her tent proclaimed:

"GLOOPS'S ANCIENT MULTI-FINGERED REPTILES and STINGING ELECTRIC AMPHIBIANS DESCENDED FROM THE JURASSIC PERIOD."

(And so, she claimed. But as this was over 130 million years ago, this was barely credible. However, to most visiting the circus for a fun day out of fantasy, mere historical details were hardly foremost in their minds.)

"ROLL UP. ROLL UP. GET THE BIGGEST SHOCK OF YOUR LIFE. TICKLE THEM UNDER THEIR BELLIES. ONLY £4.50 A GO! ROLL UP!" ...and so the billboard read.

A blaze of light from clusters of electric bulbs bathed each trailer or sideshow like gigantic halos. The heat from the overhead lighting, together with the diesel fumes from the generators and the sweet vanilla smells from the candyfloss stalls, made a heady mix which cloyed the air.

Barnard's flag was still fluttering in the breeze, and the box office had just opened for business when Roland's taxi drew up in the car park next door.

Marcus Barnard was preening himself in front of a tall, oval-shaped mirror hung behind the door of his trailer, when he heard a loud knock on the door. Startled, he stroked the tufts on his coarse-cropped beard in irritation at being disturbed. Swishing the tails of his scarlet-red morning coat, he spun around angrily. Flinging open the door, he demanded, 'What the blazes do you want?'

Roland shrank back in surprise, pushing Chance ahead of him.

'My name's Chance. And these are my friends, and we'd like to—'

'Eh? Speak up, man! What the devil's sort of name is that? *Prance... Pants...* did you say?' The butt end of a partly smoked cigar lay smouldering in an ashtray behind him. A fug of Havana wafted out of the half-opened door and drifted lazily over their faces. 'So, what do you want?' demanded Barnard, as they stood unsure on the steps behind one another. 'Not *free* tickets, I hope? You're not collecting for charity or selling some rubbish – like those useless cleaning dusters, are you? Speak up!' He continued to bark menacingly.

'I'm called Chance. Just, plain *Chance*,' reiterated Chance, enunciating his words purposely. He deliberately kept eye contact with Barnard, thinking he could lip read. 'Our young friends and we, have just visited young Bonzo and Miss Mimi at the hospital and we—'

'...And we promised to call on you, to see if we can help, having been told that some of your performers had disappeared,' interrupted Henry.

The circus owner appeared unmoved. He glared at the visitors aggressively and scowled. 'If you're looking for a job, forget it! I've got loads of people already. Most of 'em dead useless!'

'Oh yeah,' shouted Roland, now boiling over. He gritted his teeth and tightened his fists. 'You're lucky, mate, for the offer. Mr Chance here is a brilliant performer – one of the best! And Mr Henry's a fantastic magician and conjurer. You ought to be grateful.'

Chance quietened Roland down with a glancing look. He smoothed his arm and held him back. 'Let's calm down, my friends. It's okay.' He just didn't want to rub the circus owner up the wrong way, for he needed to sidle his way into the inside to find out what's going on, having made a promise to Mimi and Bonzo.

'Look, Mr Barnard,' he repeated, 'we're offering you some *free* help while your circus is in a bit of a fix. But if you don't want our help... well then...'

They began to edge off the steps and wheel away when Barnard gestured them to come back. Gruffly he growled, 'Whoah! Hang on a mo! Hold it a minute, you folks. Look, sorry, gentlemen, young sir and young missie. The circus has been worrying me a lot recently. Been under a bit of a strain, you know, with people suddenly vamoosing in the middle of the night for no reason.'

He dragged the back of his hand across his face and sighed. 'You've probably heard that Ziggarini, the star of the show, has been wiped off the face of the earth. The animal acts have been cancelled. The top flea act in the country sabotaged. And one of the kiddies' favourites, Petton's dancing dogs, kidnapped. Now everyone's deserting us right left and centre on the flimsiest of excuses.'

Clearly rattled, he threw up his arms helplessly. 'Carrita now refuses to return to the high-wire, having lost her nerve... Not only that, but the jugglers kept dropping their blasted clubs on their toes. And you wouldn't credit it, but worst of all the wretched clowns – all of 'em kept being booed out of the ring night after night! Oh, I could go on... disasters, calamities, one after another.'

Barnard went silent for a moment, half-closing his eyes, as though wanting to clamp out the bad memory of it all. 'There have been so many unexplained and strange things happening here. It's like the circus is cursed or something,' he added in a half-whisper.

'Ah, come now. It can't be all that bad?' stirred Roland, trying to be upbeat. 'Surely there must be a bit of better news?'

Then Barnard went to grab another cigar from his top pocket, sniffed at it along its belly and stuck it unlit into the corner of his mouth, chomping loudly. 'Well, I suppose you're right. Yep, as it happens, now you ask. We do have a new performer who's just started. He's got star potential... made a big impact already.'

'What do you mean?' asked Chance probing.

The circus owner's face lit up. 'The night that Ziggarini disappeared, as luck would have it, this fellow turns up offering to take his place. Given the situation, I could hardly turn him down now, could I? He's caused quite a stir since he took over. Hundreds queue up nightly to see him perform – mostly out of curiosity, but who cares?'

'By what name does he go under?' asked Henry, feigning ignorance, recalling full well Bonzo's conversation at the hospital.

'He calls himself "The Great Mystic, Dr Slatane De'Aff,"' replied Barnard. 'A really great mystic he is too,' he added. 'Do you know, he's so amazing, so versatile, that he can levitate, as well as hypnotise all-comers, who melt like soppy kittens in his hands. Also, he can perform all kinds of tricks and magic that in all my years in the circus I have never seen done before. It's almost as if he's not human. Ziggarini's assistant young Katrina's been working with him.'

He omitted to say, *forced* into it, or threatened with the sack. 'She says he's *in… human* – no, sorry, I mean superhuman.' His lower lip trembled as if he were about to cry.

Roland thought he sounded a bit scared of this new performer and was holding something back.

Carefully wringing his hands, Barnard shuffled impatiently on the trailer threshold, his expression now blank as a mask. It was obvious that he didn't want to elaborate further on the mysterious Dr De'Aff. He cleared his throat with a grating rasp, which made the children jump and Ram bare his teeth.

'Well, how about our offer then?' Chance reminded him.

'Talk to Costello and Grimbo over there.' Barnard yanked his head towards the big top.

'Look,' he growled, 'I can't pay you. But if you can make the punters – I mean, audience – smile a bit again. No. *More than that…* I challenge you to make 'em kill themselves with laughter. Make 'em happy enough to come back again… even better still, to recommend the show and bring their friends.

'However, I might… well, just might, be able to reward you with a little bonus or something!' He rubbed his moustache deliberately as if still doubtful.

'Well, as long as my friends can have some free seats for the next show,' said Chance hopefully.

'Sure. That can be arranged. Tell Costello I sent you. You'll be just in time for the rehearsal. You'd better put your skates on, my friends, the show starts in an hour and a bit.'

Turning sharply, Barnard slid back through his doorway, tugged at his lapels tiresomely and slammed the door to his trailer with a bang. Out of habit, he immediately splashed his face with a fistful of a sickly-sweet aftershave and put a light to his cigar.

'Big deal!' muttered Tim to Lotte.

'Don't like him one bit,' grunted Roland, as he led the group away. 'The very arrogance of the man! He has no feelings whatsoever for his performers, or his staff. He's only interested in the box-office sales and nothing else.'

'Oh, come on, Roland. Be a bit kind. He has to keep the show on the road to avoid disappointing the paying public,' countered Henry generously.

'Well, I wouldn't trust my old granny with him,' declared Roland, unconvinced. 'Money! Filthy old lucre, that's all he's worried about!'

Whilst they were arguing, there was a rustling sound coming from behind Madame Gloop's tent just twenty feet away. Immediately, Lotte whipped round. She thought she saw a tail of a shadow darting away. Ram growled low from the back of his throat, crouching, ready to spring.

'Lotte, what's up?' asked Tim, seeing her agitated.

'I think someone's been spying on us,' whispered Lotte from the side of her mouth. 'Roland, did you see that?'

Roland narrowed his eyes in the direction they were staring. 'Nah. Can't see a thing,' he said. 'I think you're both tired and a bit jumpy.'

'I'm *sure* I saw something hiding there, whilst you were nattering to that man,' swore Lotte.

'Probably a dog or a cat,' offered Henry with a shrug. 'We can check it out if it'll make you happier.' Henry tugged at Chance's sleeve to follow him. They hurried towards Hilda Gloop's tent and trailer.

'Was it there, you thought you saw something, Lotte?' asked Chance, walking to the side of the vehicle. He jerked his head downwards.

Lotte nodded, pointing to behind the billboard. They pulled it out of the way and searched around it.

Kneeling on the grass besides it, Roland said, 'Can't see any trace of anything or anyone... But wait a min.' He hesitated. Then he carefully brushed the surface of the grass aside. A flattened indent caught his eye. It was different from the sharp, straight furrows caused by the weight of the feet of the board.

'Hang on,' he muttered. 'This is strange! It's a *single* imprint on its own. And it's splayed into a shape of an oval – frayed at the edges with indents like someone's big toes.'

'Is it a *human* footprint? Has it got claws?' asked Tim excitedly.

'Hard to tell,' replied Roland, still studying it closely. 'It could be an animal's?'

'It'll be a darn whopping big thing if it was,' offered Henry, '...slithering about on its foot.'

'You mean a big-footed creature, like the mysterious Yeti hopping about in the Himalayas?' asked Lotte. Her eyes widened, bordering on scared.

Chance bent down and had a closer look at the ground more carefully. He noticed a scuffmark besides the indentation. 'Hmm.' He scratched his chin thoughtfully and said, 'Perhaps something with a limp. Maybe a shorter limb?'

'Hey. Could it be a couple of one-legged creatures, arm in arm? Or even one of Gloop's old monsters that's got out!' suggested Tim, half-jokingly.

Lotte gave him a dirty look. Roland and Chance pulled each other up by the arms. Placing the board back where they found it, they shook their heads, still puzzled.

'There. I told you,' declared Lotte. 'My instincts were right then. I told you something *was* watching us after all. Crumbs, it's getting creepier by the minute.' She let out a shiver. Then she stroked Ram's head soothingly, for he was whimpering, sensing their fear.

'Never mind. Let's stick together. There's no time to lose,' said Chance softly as they peeled away towards the big top. 'Let's find that troupe of clowns for Bonzo's sake, before anything else strange happens...'

Chapter 34

A TESTY REHEARSAL

Meanwhile, Costello, Grimbo, Midgy and Willy were in the middle of a rehearsal, when Chance and Henry wandered into the big top unannounced. Roland and the children had left them to it and had taken Ram for a run to stretch his legs.

Willy Maestrom, known as the funny strongman, was trying out a new balancing act. Broad and beefy as a fighting bull, he aptly fitted his description. His hairy chest, half-revealed by a ragged leopard-skin toga, stuck out like a beer barrel, sprouting enormous hairy arms and legs like a trunk of a cactus tree.

Balanced precariously on his wide shoulders stood Grimbo – a giant at seven foot, he wore a long, pasty face that drooped over an ill-fitting suit in purple stripes. And he in turn was attempting to hang on to Midgy the dwarf, who sat on his head clutching his hair for dear life.

They were wobbling unsteadily as Willy stepped forwards and backwards to maintain his balance, which was made more difficult due to some cumbersome dumbbells, each some twenty-pound weight gripped in his hands.

'Hang on. Keep still, for pity's sake!' instructed Costello, a jovial-faced clown in a baggy-white two-piece covered in bright red pompoms. Costello darted around the human pyramid in circles trying to throw brightly coloured hula hoops over Midgy's head.

Gleefully, Willy danced about, kicking up the sawdust with his bare feet. Swaying his bottom, he spun a hoop around his ample waist. Suddenly, he dropped the weights from his grip, denting the ground with a grinding thud. 'Hey, gang! We have visitors,' he shouted a warning. Suspiciously, he looked up, arching his bushy eyebrows towards Chance and Henry.

Midgy and Grimbo then jumped off and somersaulted skilfully to the ground. They seemed extremely surprised to see the strangers, until Chance hastily passed on Bonzo's message. Henry explained why they were there, and why they wanted to help having seen Barnard.

'Oh yeah,' said Costello cynically. 'Pull the other one!' In one gigantic stride he turned to face them, his jaw jutting out testily. He thrust the back of his upturned fists into the sides of his body and waited.

'Show them. Demonstrate what you can do, Chance!' piped up Henry in encouragement. He sidled up to his friend and gave him a prod in the back. Chance did not budge.

'Come on, Grimbo. *You* show 'em how it's done!'

commanded Costello. He tapped his foot impatiently against the side of the ring.

On cue, Grimbo did a lolloping cartwheel three times. He reversed and back-flipped five times in quick succession with a balloon tied to each of his hands and his feet, and then landed onto Costello's shoulder without bursting a single, one of them. Spontaneously, Midgy and Willy burst into applause, yelling, 'Bravo! Brilliant!'

This stirred Chance into action.

He flicked his nose and, with supreme effort, leapt into the air. His body flew three feet off the ground. It made a sharp whirring noise as his large red boots spun rapidly in a circular motion like a high-speed fan, which blew wafts of wood shavings and sawdust from the surface of the ring. Like a helicopter, he took off at high speed, and zigzagged at forty miles an hour around the perimeter of the big top. On the way, he grabbed a glass of water that was parked on a tray at the ringside. Floating to the top of the tent, he continued to slurp from the glass without spilling a drop. A minute later, Chance slid down one of the tent poles and fell at Henry's feet with a clatter. He then handed over an empty glass for them all to see. Theatrically, he flung his arms wide and took a sweeping bow in the centre of the ring.

'Huh. We can better that!' boasted Midgy.

Playacting, he pretended to kick Costello up the backside. Costello then fell forwards to land on his head. Immediately, he began to spin upside down on a tiny bowler hat that was jammed on top of his head. Meanwhile, with one enormous hand, Willy the strongman picked up Midgy by the scruff of the neck, and threw him into the air. Costello caught him on his upturned boots. There the two of them stuck together like magnets, spinning as one, floating up and down the rows of seats like a hover-mower in full throttle.

All around the tent, the circus hands broke out in a frenzied bout of clapping and whistling. Without prompting, a couple of them ran into the ring and balanced a plank of wood over a side of a barrel, which they had rolled in, making a seesaw. A bucket of water was balanced at one end of it. At a signal from Willy, Costello, whilst still revolving upside down on his head, suddenly extended his knees and savagely kicked Midgy away from his upturned boots. The little clown rocketed across the ring and landed on the other end of the seesaw. As Midgy struck home, the bucket of water at the opposite end became airborne and flew into the path of Grimbo the giant, who was wobbling on stilts. In the nick of time, Grimbo managed to flip open a large umbrella as a torrent of water cascaded all over him.

But Costello hadn't yet finished. He cartwheeled towards the seesaw and landed heavily on the tip of it, sending the little clown spinning upwards like a spiralling corkscrew high into the tent. As he descended, Willy swiftly caught him on his shoulders. Another cheer burst out as Costello's troupe took a bow.

Somewhat stunned, Henry pulled Chance aside and whispered from the side of his mouth, 'Shall I show them our secret weapon, the harpoon-whizzing frisbee?' He was about to twist the top off his cane when Chance grabbed hold of his hand.

'Hang on,' warned Chance with a hiss. 'Keep the trick up your sleeve in case we need it later. They'll think we're showing off.' The back of his hand reached up to smother his words. 'Remember. We need their help to get into the performance and have a good look around for you know who... And what's more, we mustn't forget to sort out another bit of the riddle before we leave. We've simply got to. The clock of my life is running down fast!'

Then the rhyme returned to Henry's head. *"Three good deeds will gain thee time..."* The tension started to drain from his face.

Offering an outstretched arm, he forced a half-grin and shook the hand of Costello, who was now smiling. 'Congrats! That's brilliant,' Henry conceded generously.

'Yup. Let's drink to that. There's so much to talk about if you let us help,' offered Chance.

Grimbo and Midgy soon rustled up mugs of tea and ginger biscuits as they sat on the props around the ring. Nearby, over an upturned barrel, Costello firmly sat cross-legged and sipped his tea thirstily.

And then intriguingly, he said to Chance, 'Couldn't help noticing that you wanted to show us some more of your magic tricks. Eh? If I, were you two, I'd keep some of your special trade secrets to yourself. You'll never know when you might need them to save your skins.'

Chance gulped loudly. 'What do you mean?' he asked, dunking a biscuit into his tea, which sloshed over the edge of his sleeve.

Immediately, Costello moved closer within earshot and said, 'Didn't my nephew Bonzo warn you about this strange character who calls himself Dr Slatane De'Aff? Come now. He *must* have done.'

Chance and Henry nodded limply.

'You know, this sinister creature has gatecrashed into most of the acts at Barnards. He's virtually taken over the place.' Costello lowered his voice and glanced around the tent cautiously.

Grimbo then threw his stilts aside and joined in. 'We think he's got something to do with Ziggarini's unexplained disappearance.'

'Yeah. That devil's pure evil, he is. Gives us the creeps!' added Midgy.

'But your boss, Mr Barnard, didn't appear to mind this… what's-his-name… De'Aff fellow,' said Henry.

''Cause he's dead scared of him or something. That's why. He's got some powerful hold over him, I'm sure of it,' said Willy.

He began to flex his biceps with the dumbbells, toning up whilst he was talking. 'He's dead frightened that the crowds wouldn't turn up to see his act, even though it's pretty scary when you actually see it in the flesh.'

'*Strange thing is, people actually enjoy paying good money to be scared out of their wits*,' said Grimbo in disbelief. 'It's a peculiar human trait.'

Wearily, Costello brushed his hand over his heavily-painted face and said, 'Look, Mr Chance, all we know is that *everything's* gone crazy since that De'Aff bloke came to Barnards. We were all happy as Larry, once. The audiences loved us to bits. We couldn't put a foot wrong. There were never any mishaps.'

Then he stopped for a second to scratch his head. 'Well… apart from the odd accident, when a piranha bit a chunk out of one of the steward's hands during feeding time.'

'Ah, but don't forget the other accident a couple of years

ago, when someone got electrocuted walking the high-wire, when it was plugged into a generator by mistake,' said Grimbo, interrupting.

'Hmm, perhaps the idiot should've worn rubber boots for safety!' he added as an afterthought.'

As soon as Grimbo opened his mouth, Costello glared at him to shut him up. And so, he continued. 'But on the whole, life here was a bowl of sunshine. Not *now*, though. Today, *everyone's* miserable and on tenterhooks wondering what's going to happen next. Katrina cries herself to sleep every night worrying when the next disaster will strike. And you heard what happened to young Bonzo, didn't you?'

'...Smashed his arm and back in the ring, caused deliberately by that scumbag!' added Midgy angrily, suddenly interrupting.

'Ooh. Grrh. I could kill him!' raged Costello, now losing control. His face went red, then white again, ashen as it drained. 'Whosoever is behind this and these terrible things, we need to find the chief puppet-master, and... I'll... I'll... just wait till I get my hands on him!' His anger grew.

Meanwhile, Willy began to jump up and down on the trampoline. At the same time, he spluttered in rhythm, 'You... you must... have... heard from young... young Mimi and B-Bo-Bon... zo, that... *every*... time...somethi... thing... hap... happens... some... someone... or some... thing, then scrawls a threat... threaten... ing message in the sawdust... in the ri... ring.'

He jumped off the contraption and ambled over towards them breathlessly, puffing. 'Yeah. Smack in the centre of the ring was this creepy message, as if he was baiting us. What's it again, Midge?' he asked, trying to catch his breath.

In the meantime, Midgy had back-flipped onto Grimbo's head. He shouted down from a great height. 'Sure. How can I ever forget? It's printed in my little old brain…

"HA HA HEE. YOU IDIOTS FREEZE. THE PHANTOM WAS HERE. SO IT CAN'T BE ME!"

Stunned, Henry and Chance could only stare at each other. They began to realise now that things were getting worse, and probably out of control for them to intervene.

Despite that, Costello's face paled with shock. He trembled. 'Scary, isn't it? It happens every time after a disaster hits the circus – like one of the performers disappearing, or when Carrita fell off the high-wire,' said Costello, still fuming.

'It's more than a coincidence that all this happened the day that loathsome De'Aff came on the scene. It's all a bit frightening, I tell you,' said Grimbo.

'Pah. Blast 'im. May he rot in – you know where!' yelled Willy as he spat in the sawdust.

The little clown soon copied him by spitting into his hands. Then he slid off the barrel of a cannon that was parked at the side of the ring, somersaulted, and landed at Henry's feet. Henry was quite shocked with all this spitting, which he had only seen from time to time in football on the television.

Chance then looked Costello in the eye. 'Please explain. Wh… What do you mean, a phan… *phant… om*? Could it be this De'Aff character playing jokes on you all?' His voice went dry at the very mention of the word. The warnings from Cecil-the-Thin at Rousseau's came flooding back to him in a flash, which left him wondering…

But Costello stared at his feet and sighed, 'I don't think he's the type to do jokes. Besides, we don't have proof that he's one and the same. Maybe we're wrong, but wait till you see him this afternoon. You will see what I mean. Right now, some of the womenfolk think the place is now definitely haunted with a phantom of the circus like in history a hundred years ago. Mm, I really don't know. But relax, my friend, nothing will happen at this moment. There's safety in numbers!'

A cold sweat broke out on Chance's neck. The palms of his hands went clammy. An icy shiver crawled down his spine, just thinking about what he'd been told by others – apart from what Cecil-the-Thin had said. He felt slightly weak at the knees. There was a growing lump in his throat. The increasing dizziness enveloping him, he put down to his missing talisman – the sacred precious gem that had been stolen at the hospital. Somehow, he must get that back so that he could survive.

He paused to sit down at the foot of the cannon, thinking to himself about Zoot at Miss Saskia's house. He almost wished that he had *him* around to advise him right now. There again, at this moment, he missed his old pals Houdini and Napoleon. He was sure that they would know what to do in the face of adversity. After all, both in history proved that they could escape from the stickiest of situations… well, most of them… some of the time.

'Oi. Don't, for gawd's sake, sit on that cannon!' screeched Midgy at the top of his voice. 'It might go off and blast you to kingdom come!' The sudden warning jolted Chance out of his wishful thinking. He leapt to his feet and nervously ran his fingers through his hair.

They all laughed at Midgy's joke. But Henry grimaced tartly. It was too near the bone for comfort. He felt that they had had enough shocks for the time being since they left Miss Saskia's place. For a fleeting moment, he thought of Davinia Plum and wondered on how she was getting on without him. He rapidly dismissed it from his mind to concentrate on the tasks ahead.

As the final rehearsal came to end and with the testy tension now easing, they decided to leave the big top together. Costello put a friendly arm around Chance's shoulders, shepherding him towards the exit. 'After you, my friend,' he said politely, pushing him gently in front of him. 'We'll all need a break after this. We look forward to seeing you in the show.'

No sooner had Chance's hand reached forward to part the curtain aside, Midgy screamed out hysterically, '*Watch out!*'

In that very instant, Willy hurled his body forward in a rugby tackle and knocked Chance flying to one side. '*Kerr-runch... Ker-dunk!*' came a sickening, crunching sound of an enormous wooden stake that fell from above. It speared the exact spot just where Chance had been standing that split second before.

'What the blazes was *that!*' gasped Chance, as he tried to get up, still winded.

Panic-stricken, Costello and his friends cast their eyes upwards into the corner of the tent, which was obscured in darkness. A wooden pole had worked loose that had previously been secured to a platform next to the high-wire.

Midgy ran to help Henry pull Chance to his feet. 'Crumbs almighty! Yer dead lucky, Chance, me old pal. That would have made a minced kebab out of you, if I hadn't looked up in time!' said Midgy, extremely relieved.

Shaking his chin in disbelief and pulling up his toga, which had become bedraggled around his body, Willy levered the wooden pole out of the ground. It had embedded itself halfway up its shank like a lethal-thick javelin. As he examined it closely, he said solemnly, *'My, oh my* – Christmas crackers! This could have killed you, my friend. And no kidding, spliced with a massive stake straight through the heart as if you were a blood-thirsty vampire!'

'That's *never* happened before,' cried a startled Costello. He looked aghast, almost tearful. 'I'll never forgive myself if anything happened to a friend of Bonzo's.'

Charitably, Grimbo suggested that it was an accident. Midgy disagreed violently, shaking his head and muttered, 'It's that jinx upon us again.'

Henry became even more convinced than ever, that *something... someone* was following them around. And he was sure that, whatever it was, was trying to stop Chance dead in his tracks.

'Let's not mince words, Henry,' retorted Chance, as they reached the outside of the tent. 'It's too much of a coincidence. It's an obvious attempt to murder me, and whatever it is, won't stop now having failed this once.' When they stepped into the fresh air, Chance took in a lungful of it. As he glanced up at the harmless sky and gentle clouds, he felt somewhat better already. 'Let's find Roland and the kids so that they can join us at the show.' His calming voice began to soothe poor Henry, whose face was still twitching, not only from smelling the fear but from now having just tasted it... And secretly, that scared the living daylights out of him.

Chapter 35

WHAT A PERFORMANCE!

HALF PAST FIVE CAME quite quickly as the big top began to fill up with hundreds of excited children. Clutching bags of popcorn, fizzy drinks and programmes, they ran eagerly to their seats. The younger ones, chattering nineteen to the dozen, held on to balloons with one hand and their parents with the other; they streamed in more casually, their eyes wandering all over the place, noticeably agog.

Surrounding the wall to the ring, tiny shimmering lights like those adorning a Christmas tree twinkled on and off in time with the bass beat of the background music, which boomed from a small stage next to the performers' entrance. Bold pencil-like laser beams spun and twirled on vertical axes, criss-crossing the insides of the vast canvas creating a moving rainbow of colour.

The parade began as a trumpet sounded. Immediately skimming over the people's heads, in shot Midgy as a powerful wind machine propelled him in. He hung on to a gigantic bunch of balloons. On reaching the centre of the ring he suddenly let go. As the balloons flew up into the dome of the tent, he landed on his feet and somersaulted away. An expectant air of excitement began to stir.

As the stewards started to loosen the tie ropes on the trapeze to swing freely, the atmosphere grew to bursting point. The high-wire was tightened, primed into position ready for action. *Oohs* and *ahs* greeted the release of the safety net as it was dropped dramatically to the floor of the ring.

Having left Ram to snooze uninterrupted in the cab, Lotte, Tim and Roland had taken their places in the second row opposite the entrance. Sweepingly, they craned their necks all around them, taking in the spectacle.

Clowns of different shapes and sizes in assorted costumes skipped in and out, tripping purposely over one another. Water was thrown everywhere. As they slapped each other in the face, they pretended to scrub each other down with wet brushes and mops.

Whilst that was happening, Midgy spun in over tables and chairs that had been flung into the arena. He then started to jump on and off the shoulders of Grimbo, who wobbled in on stilts.

Perched on a unicycle sat Costello dressed in an oversized gorilla suit. Willy the strongman dragged him along using a long chain. Attached to their feet were gigantic hairy slippers whose toes squirted jets of water at each step.

Tim had fallen into a daze. He was daydreaming about joining the circus when Lotte dug sharply in his ribs. 'Oh, do look, Tim!' She laughed. 'Look at that cute little thing with a ballet tutu chasing after that gorilla!'

As the ringside lights dimmed and the piped music faded, a group of musicians climbed up onto the bandstand. A short, bulbous-shaped man wearing a tracksuit that was far too small for him squatted astride a large drum kit. He started to bash at the bass drum and cymbals roughly in time with the organist, who was rocking his head from side to side trying to put some rhythm into a tune that had noticeably fallen flat. A lone trombone wailed in the background. A worried-looking guitarist tried to unravel the leads to the amplifier, which had got tangled around his legs. From a machine underneath his feet, a purple haze of smoke belched out which started to whip up more excitement.

Then suddenly, the vast sea of faces turned upwards to a bustle at the top of the tent. Three handsome men and two beautiful girls, decorated from top to toe in gold and silver stripes, climbed up to position themselves along the high-wire and trapeze to a roll of drums.

'It's Dante's Aerial Acrobats!' gasped the audience, pointing upwards in excitement. Several more of the troupe began to shimmy up poles and rope ladders to join them.

Just at that moment, the lights went down. Several latecomers rushed self-consciously to their seats, ducking their heads so as not to block the view of others already seated. Five young teenagers scrambled noisily into the row behind Lotte and Tim. They yelled, raising their voices, calling to each other. 'Hey. Hurry up, Liz. Slow coach! Psst. C'mon, Hect... hurry, for Pete's sake. You'll miss the show!'

Lotte jerked her head back in the half-light, a reflex to the racket. Suddenly horrified, she realised even in the semidarkness that it was the dreadful Braggerleys, Liz and Hector, from her school. It was simply unbelievable that these two were sitting just behind her with their equally horrible gang – Tilly Crossley, Kev Scratchley and Phil Grimsmore.

'Don't look round, Tim!' hissed Lotte urgently, as she gripped his arm. 'It's the ghastly Braggerleys and their pals. Please...*Hope they won't notice us. Please...*' She crossed her fingers fervently.

Roland had been uncharacteristically quiet. Whilst his eyes feasted on the magical scene unfolding in front of him, he was preoccupied deep in thought. They were with his newly found friends – Chance and Henry, who were now waiting in the wings, hidden behind a canvas flap waiting to come on. He hoped that they knew what they were doing. And hoped even more, that they had not, in a rash moment of enthusiasm, taken on more than they could chew – once having made promises to young Bonzo and Mimi. He had been told that they had agreed to find out more about the frightening De'Aff and the mysterious phantom that had been haunting the place; but at what danger to his young friends. At least, Henry and Chance would be safe with the trusty Costello – and so he assumed, from what he had heard from the others. Popping a peppermint into his mouth, he rocked back on his heels. Making himself comfortable, he patiently waited for the show to begin in earnest.

Now remarkably, sitting calmly in the back row, half-hidden by one of poles of the tent, was a small, birdlike figure of a woman dressed completely in dark blue. A baggy cardigan had been pulled tightly around her shoulders. Covered in a polka-dot scarf, her head moved slowly up and down as she nonchalantly munched from a packet of biscuits. Her dark eyes scanned the scene, completely absorbed. It was Madame Groszena Drizelda, the celebrated fortune teller on a day trip from Glastonbury.

For as it happened, she was coming up to London to visit her stepbrother, Edbert Tuffnut, at the Tower of London. At Paddington Station, she had been given a voucher for a ticket at half price to Barnards' Circus in an offer with her Saver's Day excursion. As she had time to kill, this seemed a wonderful chance – something not to be sniffed at – to visit the circus, which she had not been to since she was a child.

Madame Drizelda began to search through her bag in earnest. Hungrily, she started on a bar of chocolate having missed out on lunch due to rushing for the 12.45 to London. She finished off her snack with a sip of tea – now gone tepid – which she had bought at the station. Slipping on a pair of round spectacles, she focused like the rest of the crowd on the acrobatic troupe assembling high above her, noting with interest from the programme that the Fabulous Carrita was indisposed through an unfortunate accident. Spellbound, she concentrated on the show, digesting her lunch.

Two minutes later, there was a sudden fanfare of trumpets from the artistes' entrance. The large flap of canvas flew open and in strode the Grand Ringmaster, Marcus Barnard himself no less, into the glaring limelight. In his bleached-white jodhpurs and shiny-black riding boots, over which he wore a bright crimson jacket and tails trimmed with a black velvet collar and cuffs, he made a striking figure. Instantly like magic, the grand parade of performers melted away.

Snatching a microphone in one hand, he cracked a bullwhip in the other and called for attention.

'Ladies and gentlemen, boys and girls, welcome to Barnard and Barnard's, the best... the most *a-m-a-z-ing*, the most *mag-nif-ic-ent* circus in the land! Welcome to you all – especially to you naughty latecomers!' He wagged a finger mockingly at the stragglers, who clambered self-consciously into their seats as the spotlight cruelly followed them in.

And then by a remarkable coincidence, young Seth Ropely using a free ticket he had found in the last car he had "borrowed", skulked in surreptitiously at the last moment and tiptoed gingerly to his seat. Hoping that he wouldn't be noticed, he pulled the collar of his jacket high over his ears and tilted his baseball cap over his eyes.

Hissing and booing greeted him as he struggled to his place at the last moment. Gratefully, he sank down into the bench, hoping to be hidden by a large family of excited children munching their way through popcorn and crisps in front of him. Desperately, he tugged at his clothes to hide his face and slumped downwards into his seat, his knees thrust sloppily upwards.

The announcements continued:

'Oh yes, you luckee folks, Barnards are proud to present to you today, an amazing and a simply incredible fun-filled programme packed with thrills, spills and laughter. Yes, siree – despite the cancellation of some of our acts due to circumstances out of our control – you will be *entertained*. You will be *en-rap-tured* as never before with the daring skills of our acrobats, jugglers, and artistes of the flying trapeze. You will smile. You will be tickled… and you'll be certain to roar with laughter at the fun, stunts and tricks by our *FAN… TAST… ICAL* group of clowns this very afternoon. *You will laugh, as you have never laughed before!'*

A deliberate grin spread across his face. *'Yes, folks, I give you our v-e-r-r-ee own and funn-ee gang, led by the one and only… the GERR-EAT… Cost-ELLO!'*

He bowed theatrically and then backpedalled to the exit to some faint clapping. The band struck up. As the lights dimmed, Costello cartwheeled effortlessly into the ring. Clusters of fireworks attached to his hands and feet spun and exploded like an enormous Catherine wheel. Clenched between his teeth was a metal spindle rotating concentrically. Spiked at its ends, enormous Roman candles began to spin. When they burst into flames, the auditorium became showered in a storm of tiny silver stars.

In that instant, Costello was enveloped dangerously in flames. Right on cue, Henry ran at him and blasted him with a fire extinguisher, covering him in foam from top to toe. He looked like a snowman that had been caught out smoking.

'Hey. Stop! That's enough… the fire's out! Pack it in,' spluttered Costello through gritted teeth. He scooped handfuls of foam from his eyes and mouth. But Henry had got carried away.

'That'll make 'em laugh, if nothing else will,' Henry mumbled hopefully. But an eerie silence greeted them.

Henry then whipped out a large hairdryer, the size of a trumpet, from the inside of his jacket and pretended to dry Costello.

'Just listen to that miserable lot. It's silent as a grave out there,' groaned Costello, dead worried. He stamped his foam-soaked boots and slapped his arms to shake off the wet.

Red-faced, Henry beat a hasty retreat, back to the wings to moan to Chance and the others.

Costello tried again. He peeled off his soaking wet outer suit – secretly fireproofed – hoping his inner costume, a white bony skeleton on black satin, would impress. But it didn't.

'That looks scary!' cried Tim aloud. Roland and Lotte nodded dumbly.

In desperation, Costello signalled for the rest of his troupe to follow him. He gave a sharp whistle. One by one, they tumbled in. A large, ungainly panto horse wobbled into view. Underneath its body sat Grimbo at its head. Wooden and square-jawed full of enormous teeth, it belched out fire and smoke. Facing backwards stood little Midgy under its tail, squirting a stream of bubbles out from beneath it as it cantered around the ring.

Immediately following them, a tiny bike with mini wheels rolled in barely off the ground. Hanging on precariously to the handlebars and saddle sat three brothers, known as the Zany Triplets, who were dressed alike in black and white pyjamas. They flung themselves on and off the bike, pirouetted and twirled. They fired water pistols at the audience whilst zigzagging under the horse's belly, which suddenly collapsed on top of them. A mock fight broke out. They sloshed each other with buckets of water and freshly baked custard pies thrown to them by Willy Maestrom from the edge of the ring.

Although there were a few half-hearted claps from one or two of the younger children, by and large, the audience was not amused. Peeping into the ring, Henry and Chance looked on anxiously.

'Oh, blast! What's gone wrong? Something awful is happening. They look thoroughly miserable. But why don't Grimbo and Costello try their stunts from rehearsal?' asked Henry, concerned.

'It's *too* late now. They just can't seem to lift the gloom that's hanging over the place, however hard they try,' agreed Chance.

'They're flogging a dead horse trying to get that lot even to grin a little,' added Henry. He got an odd stare in return from Chance, who wondered if Henry realised what he had just said. 'Then what hope in heck will we have when *we* go on?'

Costello tried for one more laugh. He pretended to push the horse backwards towards the exit. Willy then tried to pull at its tail. It ripped apart suddenly in his fingers, forcing him to trip over an upturned bike and fall into a bucket of water nearby, soaking Midgy.

Despite that, the response was still lukewarm... just a few sneering guffaws from a couple of noisy youths in the back row. ''Ere. Pull the other one, mate. Funny? ...You've gotta be joking! Seen better on telly!' they jeered.

'Rubbish. Fat lot of use! Gerroff!' added one of their girlfriends, flinging a packet of crisps towards the ring.

Straight away, Henry complained to Barnard that

something was wrong. The ringmaster rushed to the mic and announced with relief,

'Ladies and gentlemen, it's time for the interval. Get yer ice cream, burgers, popcorn and drinks while you see the fabulous sideshows… *Roll up. Roll up!*'

Abruptly, the floodlights went out. The band struck up a deafening volume to an upbeat tune to drown the awkward silence. Thoroughly demoralised, Costello and his troupe crawled off sheepishly. They were completely soaked to the skin and feeling like death, as well as feeling very, very foolish.

Chapter 36

TRUTH OR LIES?

THE REVEREND BARNABAS QUICK was just in time. He caught the bus to World's End. Alighting quickly, he hurried along to the green. It wasn't hard to find the circus. For in his hand, he firmly hung on to one of the flyers. Snug in his pocket, safe and sound, was a single complimentary ticket, a gift from Bonzo and Mimi.

The timing could not have been more perfect. It was barely into the break when the vicar caught sight of a distinctive figure striding across the grass. It was the ringmaster heading towards his trailer. Puffing somewhat, he accelerated into a trot. Just as the door to the vehicle swung open, he managed to catch up. At full stretch, he managed to grab the back of the man's elbow.

Startled, Barnard whipped round like a rocket. '*What the...* Why, it's *you* of all people! H... how the blazes did you get here?' he demanded, completely flummoxed.

'By the number 28 bus,' came the innocent reply. Without waiting to be invited, the Reverend Quick pushed past him and promptly sat at the edge of the sofa.

'I mean, *how* did you know where to find me?'

'Simple. You dropped this…' The vicar fished out a crumpled leaflet from the ball of his fist. 'It fell out of your pocket the other day!'

'Oh, so that's it then.' He scoffed mockingly. 'Huh. So, you fancy that you're a bit of a detective now, eh, Father?'

'Don't you dare *Father* me after all you've done!'

'Okay. Please yourself then, *old man*. Keep your collar on!' sneered Barnard. 'Now what in the world do you want with me?' He kicked the door shut with a vicious back heel. Provocatively, he arched his shoulders to tower over the vicar, who was now leaning forward, his arms casually folded in his lap.

Father Quick refused to be intimidated. He was used to hecklers and bullies in his line of work. Undeterred, he insisted, 'I want to know what you're up to. Why, for instance, did you butcher that antique manuscript at the vicarage the other day? A crime *so* heinous and such an abominable desecration that it's unforgivable! For heaven's sake… *why?*'

'You must be mistaken, *Father… old… man…*' taunted Barnard, still trying to rile him.

'You can cut that out for a start!'

'Sure, *Pop… Pater*, anything for old time's sake.' Barnard went into the kitchen and attempted to light a cigar. He glanced at his watch. The ten-minute break was shrinking fast.

Just passing the outside of the front door, Midgy was

on his way to change out of his wet clothes when angry voices from inside the trailer made him stop. Dead curious, he crept to the window and, on tiptoes, peered under the blinds. In the narrow light that escaped over the sill, he thought he saw two figures deep in argument. One of them he recognised as Marcus Barnard; the other had his back to the window, sitting down. Then, as the latter twisted around, he realised it was *a vicar... a holy man* whose face began to suddenly redden as if it were about to explode. Sidling to the edge of the door, Midgy glued his ear close to the gap beneath it. His eyes grew to the size of satellite dishes with what he overheard next.

'Don't you *ever* address me as *Father... Pop... or Pater*, or anything remotely like that ever again: *I... I forbid it!*' snapped the vicar angrily, who, in the next instant, got up, squared up to Barnard and prodded him in the chest. 'From this day on, I no longer recognise you as *my son*. May your dear mother – God bless her soul – may she forgive me.'

The little clown's ears leapt into the air. It did not register at first. *Then it sunk in.* His boss, the ringmaster, and that man of religion were part and parcel of the *same* family – related by blood! 'Well, I never. Just wait till I tell the others!' he murmured silently under his breath. 'What an amazing secret. Would you believe it? Marcus Barnard, a man of the circus – *his father* – *his dad* happened to be a holy reverend, a respected man of the church. One steeped in sawdust, the other in holy water!' He whistled through his teeth. Completely entranced, he jammed his eyes through the slit in the letterbox. Raised voices continued to be carried.

'Have it your own way then, you, stubborn old fool,' spat Barnard, vehemently. 'You were always preaching on at me. Even as a kid. You haven't changed a bit. *Do* this. *Don't* do that. Small wonder, then, that I ran away as soon as I could. Couldn't wait to join a place like this!'

He gave an extravagant sweep of his hands, gesturing in mid-air.

He stalked up and down and kept fiddling with his moustache, his temper smouldering. 'I mean, just look at you. Pompous... Pious... always in the right. You were so ashamed of us as a family. Circus folks were beneath you. You made it so obvious, calling them *travellers, nomads, caravan gypsies* and such like.'

The sneering continued; his face was rammed so close to the vicar's it was almost touching. 'Come on. What was it between you and the old fellow? You know. *Your old man* – old, Philly B. Barnard. I thought you would have been real proud of him, his carrying on the years of the tradition of the circus as he did in spite of ill health. C'mon. At least level with me now. You at least owe me some explanation!'

On hearing the name of the famous and great P.B. Barnard of the 1900s, Midgy broke out into a sweat of excitement. He couldn't believe his ears. The truth emerging was simply astounding. Because that holy reverend in there, standing arguing with the ringmaster – the two of them were *inextricably connected as father and son*. Not only that, but also the reverend, so it seemed, was *himself* related to the famous P.B. Barnard – a direct descendant of the founder of *Barnard and Barnard's* circus...

But how could that possibly be? Midgy thought. *A man of the cloth – dedicated to the church – having his origins in a circus? And a famous one at that!*

'But wait a moment,' he puzzled. 'That's funny.' He was sure that he had overheard that the Holy Father's name was "Quick". Without wasting another second, the little clown quickly stuck his eyes and ears closer to the door so as not to miss a thing.

Barnabas Quick began to get restless. He shuffled around, fidgeting. Seemingly, as if suddenly weary with the woes of the world closing in on him, he began to sigh deeply. He loosened his dog collar, which had grown too tight. The family secret about his dreadful son, Marcus, which he had managed to keep hidden from everyone and for so long, had now been blown. Moreover, over the years, he had grown tired of pretending about it all. Now, it was time for the truth, and no more lies.

His voice then began to waver, his hand clutching his throat. 'Your grand... grandfather, Phileus Bertram Barnard... er... adopted me. You see, I wasn't his real son – the same flesh and blood. My real father, Harold Quick, was a captain in the army. He lost his life in the Second World War.'

'So therefore, he was a great hero then? Bravely killed in action, was he?' asked Barnard, prodding.

Father Quick looked down on the floor, somewhat embarrassed. Haltingly, it all came out. 'Erm... well, not quite. His bike crashed into a tree as he pedalled in the fog to join his regiment. You see, the country was in an enforced blackout. It was everywhere. He never saw action. My mother couldn't cope with a young child at the start of the war. And so, I was left in an orphanage run by one of the religious orders.'

He stared vacantly into space, his voice cracking a bit.

'That's where Phileus Barnard found me. Because, you see, he only had a daughter to carry on the circus. He wanted a son to continue the tradition. But the truth was that I hated the place from the start. The way they made the animals work for their living. Poor dumb creatures: they're forever having to perform like monkeys against their nature. Just for man's selfish entertainment. I mean, was it really humane, for instance, to force tigers, cheetahs and other noble big cats to jump through hoops of fire? Or elephants manhandled to sit on tiny stools to sip tea with their trunks? And those poor, sad bears and apes, locked up in cages all day and night, going slowly mental... I could go on.'

He half-closed his eyes, as though haunted by the nightmare of it. His words drifted. 'I got out as soon as I was old enough.' His lower lip trembled. 'The kind brothers at the orphanage helped me to study and train for a new and gentler life. You were born a year after my first parish posting.'

Then, swiftly, his mood suddenly changed. He appeared angry and disillusioned all at once. 'But what a disappointment you turned out to be, always in trouble from day one. Stealing. Forever in trouble with the law. Playing truant. Running away. We often found you at fairgrounds or at a travelling circus. It broke your mother's heart.'

Barnard started choking. His cheeks went violent with rage. He spluttered. 'Don't you get it, even after all this time? You... you were always so goody-goody... overflowing with virtue. Nothing was ever good enough for you! Why you hated the circus so much, I shall never work it out. Animals are just animals. People are people.

You were forever ashamed of me! You never let me forget it. Even worse, you were ashamed of your background. Then furthermore, ashamed of the old man Philly Barnard, who rescued you…

'Then of course, you were dead scared, in case the neighbours, the community or the church, ever found out that you were brought up in a circus of all places. And as for a member of your family – your own son joining such a place; well, that really took the biscuit and got up your prim stuffy nose!'

Menacingly, Barnard advanced across the room. He shoved his nose into his father's face, forcing him to stumble against the door.

'Just let me tell you a few simple home truths, *Pop*,' insisted Barnard. 'I like it here. I'm proud to be part of this life. Not like you. I'm not ashamed of it… And another thing, whilst we're at it. Did you know that the folks of one of our prime ministers came from a circus! *He* wasn't at all embarrassed about his background, far from it. In fact, he wore it like a badge of honour. But even more so, it gave him a lot of clout on the street with the ordinary people.'

Beaten and defeated, Father Quick went quite still. With a heavy sigh, he said evenly, 'Okay. Calm down. I heard that after old P.B. Barnard died, his daughter took over. From memory, I think she was called Philomena or something like that. Later, I heard on the news that something terrible happened to her in suspicious circumstances. Do you know what happened exactly?' He gave him a searching look.

Barnard's cheeks blew up as if he were about to take off. His voice got shriller. 'Are you accusing *me*, old man? I tell you; it was an accident. Pure coincidence, it was. I told the police about it. A wooden stake worked loose from one of the platforms near the trapeze. It fell from the top of the tent as she came into the ring one night, just before a show.' His eyes blazed fire. 'It was a simple accident and nothing else! It's in the police report in black and white. Check it out if you like. I had only arrived to work here a couple of weeks before that happened.'

Seeing Barnabas Quick staring sharply at him, he quickly added, 'What's more, the reported arguments that were supposed to have happened between her and me were never proven. Some of the performers who had been here a long time resented my presence. That's all. Plain jealousy – when I returned to claim a share of what should have been mine.' He rolled his eyes to the ceiling angrily. 'You can understand, then, that I had no choice but to take over the place. The rest of the crew knew of the family connection with the old man. Naturally, for the sake of the circus, the show had to go on – regardless. Then later, changing my name by deed poll made my title much more official. *"Marcus Barnard"* has a much... *much* better ring to it than plain old *Quick*, don't you think?' A hollow laugh followed.

Father Quick felt a stream of bile creeping up his throat just listening, whilst trying to sort out the truth from the lies. He gave a grating cough. 'I've simply heard enough of this! Before I go, at least tell me the truth. Just *once* in your life. If not for me, then for the sake of your dear mother – heaven rest her soul.' He raised his eyes upwards and crossed himself fervently.

'I'm going to ask you once again. Why did you turn up at the vicarage after all these years? Surely, it wasn't just to have a chat or to renew family ties, now was it? And furthermore, most importantly, I want to know what you have done with the bits of manuscript you stole? And what's this ludicrous thing about a legend… a riddle and its riches?'

'What do you mean, manuscript? Do you mean that mouldy old book?' spat back Barnard.

'Mouldy old book!? You philistine! Let me tell you that *The Oraco Dex Lo Paediac* that you so mutilated and stole from, happens to be one of the most precious and rarest manuscripts on earth from ancient times!'

'Stole. Mutilate… *Stole?* How dare you! How dare you accuse me!' Barnard screamed, suddenly losing it. He thundered across the floor with his arms flailing in front of him, his hands aiming for his father's throat.

At that very instance, Midgy's legs were getting numb. In a flash, he shrank down, ducking his head, when he realised that murder was about to be committed. Panic rushed through his mind. Should he run and get Costello and the others…? Even the police? But by that time it would have been too late. Lifting his dead leg from crouching so long, he hobbled to the side of the trailer and hid out of sight.

Barnard's arms suddenly switched direction from the neck to the shoulders. Bodily, he lifted his father from under the armpits and frogmarched him to the door. At once, he kicked it open. Then he rammed his forehead into the old man's face. 'Look, Pop. What do you see?' he hissed, spitting in his face. 'Look. *Look*, old man… into these eyes! *Now!*'

Helplessly immobilised in a brutish armlock, Father Quick felt strangled, his strength ebbing away with each second. Barnard grabbed the back of the old man's head and twisted it closer to his. The old man's breath was being slowly squeezed out of him.

'Stare deeper old man. *Relax*, and you won't feel a thing. *Relax*, as I count to five.' The command was delivered in a hypnotic monotone, which made it the more chilling. Barnard continued to urge in the same way. 'When I count to five, you will forget all about our meeting today and all about my visit to you at the vicarage. *Relax*! Now – *one... two... three*. Relax... deeper still. *Four* – again, deeper... Now – *five*. You will forget *everything*. Your mind is now empty. It is feeling... *nothing*. Nothing at all.'

In an instant, the old man slumped into his body. Curling his head and neck forwards, his chin hit his chest. Abruptly, Barnard slackened his grip. Then he spun him around to face the steps and hurriedly pushed him down them onto the grass.

'Now, quickly, go back to the bus stop from where you came. Straight away, old man! Then I want you to hop on that wretched bus and return to your little old vicarage and forget that I ever existed!' instructed Barnard, calling after him callously.

Meekly, Father Quick shuffled across the green towards the road, retracing his steps, the fight squashed out of him.

Dusk was fast approaching. There was a distinct shiver in the air. A rustling sound at the edge of his trailer caught Barnard's ear as he turned to go in. He looked around him. From the corner of his eye, he thought he saw something small scurrying under the rear of the wheels. He shrugged and went to shut the door. He thought, *It's probably one of the cats out chasing mice.*

Just then, the tannoy announced that the show would restart in two minutes. He dusted himself off, flicking his sleeves with his hands. Straightening his jacket, he cleared his throat. Then he splashed on some more of his favourite aftershave, which was ironically called "B NICE".

Holding his breath, Midgy fled towards his caravan as fast as his little legs would carry him. Fearfully, he kept looking over his shoulder. He swore that he had heard a strange shuffling noise from the direction of the big top, which had been following him from the time he was crouching behind Barnard's trailer. It was so dark between the tents and the lorries that it was hard to tell what it was. He cursed himself for letting his imagination run riot.

Consumed by panic, he rushed at his door. He was surprised that it was left unlocked. Perhaps he had forgotten to lock it when he left in a rush earlier. Fumbling for the light switch on the inside of the door, he flicked it on. Nothing happened. He tried again. *Nothing!* 'Drat it!' he cursed. 'A bulb's gone.'

With his hands in front of his face, he felt his way into the darkness, heading towards the cupboard in the kitchen to look for a spare. He had left the front door ajar, hoping a chink of reflected light from the circus site would help him. But it was still dark and gloomy inside.

Suddenly, there was an almighty crash. He fell over a chair. 'Blast it!' he muttered, annoyed with himself. A split second later, there was no more time for any more muttering. A large, heavy figure collided into him. At the very same instance the front door swung back. Echoing, it slammed shut with a bang.

'Oh... my! Whaat... the dev...?' A terrified scream was stifled before it even left his lips. A pair of large, clammy hands grabbed him around the face as they fell across the room as one. Then it went quiet: exceedingly quiet. A deathly silence had fallen across the little dwarf's caravan. And there was nothing in the world he could do about it.

Chapter 37

THE BIG CHANCE

THE TWENTY-MINUTE BREAK MELTED away rapidly as the band restarted. The audience started to get restive wondering what was next in store. In the back row, a gang of noisy youths began to slow-hand clap and stamp their feet.

Behind the scenes, Barnard the ringmaster insisted that Costello and company return to the arena to try again. Henry and Chance listened in silence as they planned their next move. Reluctantly, Grimbo and Willy climbed into the ring carrying their props. Boos and hisses greeted them led by the gang of troublemakers at the back. 'Gerroff! Scram! Yer dead useless,' they yelled. Red-faced, the clowns fled as programmes, drink cartons and bits of food sailed over their heads. Pockets of chanting erupted. '*We want a proper show! We want our money's worth!*' The cry got noisier by the second. 'We want…' The remainder of the crowd took up the chant, joining in like sheep.

Panic-stricken, Barnard flew into the ring in an attempt to quell the unrest. Visibly nervous, Chance and Henry trailed in behind him. Raising his voice above the din, he shouted, 'Okay. *Ok… ay!* Now, ladies and gentlemen, please settle down. Yes, siree, we have indeed a treat… a mouth-watering treat in store for you—'

'Gerron with it!' scoffed a pasty-faced youth, springing up from the front row, shaking his fist.

'My friends… boys and girls, we have a special surprise for you at no extra charge!' Barnard shouted desperately, turning up the volume. 'We are lucky to have in our midst today, *a very special guest*. One of the greatest harlequins on the planet to entertain you – to make you laugh as you have never laughed before – at his one and only performance in the country! So, you luck… ee people. Please give him a big hand…'

Barnard started to retreat, motioning theatrically with his hands, 'The *very exceptional*… the *most stupendous* and the *truly inimitable*: I give you – the one and only… *Mist… er… Chance*, and his very funny butler… *Hen-er-ree de Poisson!*'

Out of the side of his mouth he spat in the direction of Henry and Chance. '*You'd better do something – if you know what's good for you!*' Furtively, he sliced a finger across his throat, then skipped backwards out of the spotlight, signalling to the band.

No sooner had that happened than the lights died, throwing the ring into pitch-black darkness. Suddenly, a clutch of laser beams in icy blue exploded from the corners of the big top. Strobe lights flashed in urgent starbursts in rhythm to the beat of the organ and drums.

Half-heartedly, some isolated clapping began.

'What a load of old pants!' yelled Kev Scratchley, cackling his head off, as he punched Hector Braggerley playfully on the shoulder.

'Something stinks of smelly old fish!' added Phil Grimsmore, joining in. Slapping each other on the backs, they roared at their own silly jokes. Liz Braggerley grinned maniacally, egging them on.

'Stupid show-offs,' muttered Willy under his breath, throwing filthy glances at them.

A hush then descended. Pencil-like laser beams shot across the arena, criss-crossing the shadows. Lights danced in tune, picking up the audience at random. Roland grinned nervously at Lotte, who grimaced, unsure of what to expect next.

'Just look at your teeth, Roland!' gasped Tim. 'They're glowing like pearls,' as streaks of ultra-violet swept over them.

A fanfare of trumpets wailed forlornly.

'Butler indeed!' seethed Henry through his teeth. He was longing to ram Barnard's words down his throat with the tip of his cane, but he didn't dare to in front of so many people.

'Oh, be quiet, Henry,' urged Chance. 'Cool it. This is our big chance. We've *got* to win them over. So, don't let me down, or I'll change you back into a dummy!'

At a certain signal from the wings, they sailed into their routine like the professional troupers they were. Jumping, spinning and somersaulting, they then floated energetically across the ring. Spewing from their open jackets, flowers and sweets were thrown like confetti into the audience to catch. Balloons in their scores cascaded down from the peak of the big top like blossom falling after a storm. One or two in the audience started to warm to the performance, giving a guarded half-smile. But in the main, they were largely unimpressed, remaining quietly bored as church mice on Sundays.

Just then, a cloud of dense-white smoke gushed across the floor of the ring, covering the auditorium like a thick November fog. And as it cleared, a mammoth football at least ten feet in diameter rolled in, pushed by Willy, huffing and blowing. As it rolled towards them, Chance stuck his foot out to stop it. Then, he invited Henry to stab it with the tip of his cane. It exploded with an enormous bang. Out flew Grimbo, propelled like an iron ball from a cannon. Spinning high over their heads, he collapsed in a heap on top of Willy, knocking him clean off his feet.

But no one laughed.

'Where's Midgy?' hissed Grimbo from the side of his mouth, as he picked himself up from the ground. '*He* was supposed to be inside that perishing thing, not me!'

'I dunno,' replied Willy, panting deeply to gather his breath. 'He didn't show up after the break. Just wait till I see him. I'll kill the little devil!' A mock fight followed. Grimbo and Willy started throwing buckets of water at each other, hoping to raise a laugh. But it was met with muted silence.

'Oh, what a calamity! What *do* we have to do to make them laugh?' groaned Henry, getting more disheartened by the second. Just then, a brainwave struck him. *Why not "audience participation?"* he thought from watching live TV.

He scanned the audience and hollered, 'Ladies and gentlemen, boys and girls. We want your help. Now, who do *you* think is the stronger of the two here in the ring? Willy Maestrom, our champion weightlifter, or Fancy Chance, our big-footed harlequin? *Now come on, kiddies. Who is the strongest?'*

There was an embarrassing silence. People continued to chat lazily amongst themselves, completely ignoring what he said.

Now just at that very moment, Chance, out of the corner of his eye, happened to notice in the next to last row on the right, near the main entrance, a familiar figure was trying to hide behind one of the large poles supporting the tent. It was Seth Ropely with a self-satisfied smirk across his face.

'Henry, Grimbo, quick! That young fella up there,' hissed Chance urgently between clenched teeth. 'Yes. *Him* up there – near the entrance! He's the one at the hospital. You know – the one that pretended to have a seizure. Yes, it's *definitely* him all right.' Chance pointed his nose upwards in Seth's direction. 'Next to the ice cream girl. He's got a dark blue baseball cap over his eyes – the little rat. He conned us all. He's stolen something of mine, something very valuable. I need it back, pronto. Quick, can you get him down here when we ask for volunteers?'

Instinctively, Henry realised the ploy. Grimbo didn't question it.

'Well, you nice people,' shouted Chance. 'I need an extremely smart volunteer to come down into the ring to help us in our very next stunt. C'mon now, you good folks!'

Invitingly, he continued. 'Yes, siree… a cheerful, strong and willing volunteer, who is not only brave but dares to join us to test his strength against Willy Maestrom and me in a very simple trick.'

Swivelling on his heels, his eyes darted around the audience. Tempting them, he said, 'If the plucky person wins, he or she will get not only free tickets to every show in town for the next three months or so, but *free* drinks, *free* popcorn and *free* ice cream! And furthermore, they will even get an autographed picture of Willy, the strongest weightlifting clown in the universe, lifting a horsebox onto his back barehanded! So come on now…!'

A tremendous groan greeted the challenge.

Henry and Grimbo, in the meantime, worked their way up the aisles looking for their volunteer. Powerful searchlights followed them as they crept up stealthily on either side of the unsuspecting Seth, who was cowering under the lights trying to melt into the background. He slipped further into his seat and pulled up his collar.

As the band struck up a tune, Henry and Grimbo, one on either side of Seth, reached over with their hands and tickled him under his armpits. His arms shot into the air, as though he had been bitten by a bloodthirsty mosquito, somewhere he didn't quite expect.

'Why, yes. Oh, *yes*, siree!' Chance exclaimed gratefully, pointing in Seth's direction. '*Indeed, yes, ladies and gentlemen… that brave young chap in the next-to-last row has agreed to join us!*'

'But… but… I… I didn't mean…' gasped Seth, protesting helplessly.

Bodily, Henry and Grimbo lifted him out of his seat

by his arms, though he struggled like a tiger. With his feet kicking aimlessly in the air, they frogmarched him straight down into the ring.

'Hey, Lotte. Isn't that the fella we bumped into at the hospital when he collapsed in front of us?' said Tim, giving her a nudge.

'Hush, Tim. You'll only draw attention to us. But you're right. It is him.' Lotte held a finger to her lips. 'But I wonder why…?'

'Ssh! Be quiet, you two! Chance and Henry know what they're doing. Just watch,' urged Roland.

Stunned and dazed, Seth stood meekly in the centre of the ring, face to face with Chance, Henry and the others. Bathed in the stark spotlight, his already pale face grew paler still when it suddenly hit him who it was standing right in front of him. Beads of sweat began to roll down the front of his sweatshirt.

Willy started to provoke the crowd. 'Poor little chap. He looks a bit hot and bothered, don't you think, eh, boys and girls? I think he needs a little bit of help to cool him down, don't you think, eh?'

People in the upper tiers started to clap. Seth began to quiver in his trainers.

Giving a huge wink at Grimbo, Willy grabbed hold of a mop and bucket from one of the stewards. He threw the mop to the ground and then proceeded to pour the contents of the bucket over Seth's head. Soapy water swimming in sawdust was sloshed over his cap and jacket soaking him to the waist.

'Mm. Well, that's better!' Chance gave a thin smile whilst some in the front row tried to suppress a snigger.

'I say. The audience is warming up a bit at last!' said Henry optimistically.

Then, suddenly, in one swift movement, Willy gave Seth a huge bear hug and lifted him straight off the ground. He placed him squarely on top of Grimbo's shoulders. Grimbo then climbed up onto a wooden bench, which had been placed in the middle of the ring. Firmly, he held on to Seth's knees as the latter tried to squirm free. Using the side of his foot, Willy then flicked the empty bucket high into the air. It landed with a rattling crash on top of Seth's head.

Then goading the audience once again, Chance announced that Willy would attempt to lift both Grimbo and Seth off the ground. Willy then squatted down with his knees bent in front of the human tower of Grimbo below, and the hapless Seth sandwiched in the middle like a piece of salami, the bucket on top of him. Sucking in a huge breath, which dented his ruddy cheeks, Willy's hairy chest expanded threefold like a mountain of gorse. Then, using his sausage-like fingers, he went to grip the underside of the bench under Grimbo's feet. His biceps bulged like watermelons expanding. He then tried to lift these two, one on top of the other, to the encouraging shouts of '*Heave!*' from the crowd.

At the first attempt, Willy only managed to ease the bench just a couple of inches off the ground, for his feet kept slipping backwards whilst trying to maintain his balance. His face glowed scarlet with the effort. Immediately, he dropped the bench back onto the ground, letting out a gasp... Seth nearly fainted from the shock, but Grimbo hung on to him in a vice-like grip.

'*Heave*. Give it a wellie! Heave!' yelled a large youth from the back row, gesticulating with his fists raised. Tim stared into the arena, keeping his fingers crossed, his chest fluttering with rising excitement.

Willy tried again. But this time, he shoved his shovel-like hands completely under the underbelly of the bench rather than just the edge of it and got closer to the bodies to save his back. Lifting with one tremendous effort, using all the strength he could muster, he hauled them up towards his knees. 'Arrh!' he growled explosively.

For a moment or two, he wobbled precariously to and fro with the load dangerously unbalanced. Then, finally extending his bulging arms, he lifted Grimbo and Seth, bench and all, high above his head. He stumbled at first, wobbled a bit, giving few steps backwards and then forwards. But then, carefully, he was able to strut around the ring like the giant Colossus of Rhodes, as though carrying the world on his shoulders.

When he lowered Grimbo and Seth slowly to the ground, he was greeted with a roar of approval, whistles and clapping. 'And now, boys and girls, for my next trick!' puffed Willy breathlessly. Wiping the sweat off his face using a mop thrust into his face by Henry, he gave a knowing wink at Chance. As Seth tried to escape from the ring – though his legs felt like lumps of jelly, Willy made a sudden dive at his ankles and lifted him upside down, swinging him like a cave bat. Vigorously, he shook him around and around in decreasing circles as the band played on. Guffaws and giggles rippled from the ringside.

Suddenly, lo and behold, the stolen pendant fell out of Seth's trouser pocket and flew into the air like a shuttlecock.

Immediately, Chance snatched it from mid-air and quickly pushed it into his jacket pocket for safety.

'Ah, thank heavens, that's back where it belongs!' muttered Henry, as the precious gem was returned to its rightful owner.

Immediately, a surge of indescribable energy rushed through Chance's body. He did not realise how really, weak he must have been from the time the gem was stolen at the hospital until now.

But Willy continued to keep an iron grip on Seth in his outstretched arms, dangling him like a limp rag doll. Using large steps, Willy stalked around Chance in a circle, inviting him to do something. Instantly, Chance bared his teeth and sucked in his cheeks like a pair of gigantic bellows. Then he suddenly let out a massive puff of air, which was aimed at Seth's midriff. As Willy relaxed his grip, the force of the wind threw Seth backwards at twenty miles per hour. It was as if he had sprouted wings; Seth flew like a bird, rising at first at a slight angle then dipping a little. And as he did, he rose windborne out of the middle of the ring, flying in a straight line in the direction of his seat in the penultimate row. Bedraggled and wet, Seth fell like a stone onto his backside on the bench, making a squelching, skidding noise.

Desperately, he clutched at his baseball cap, which had now spun back to front. And then he sank down well into his seat, too stunned to protest and too flattened to do anything else. Cursing his luck, there was nothing he could do but to close his eyes, exhausted. Thoroughly disconsolate, he felt as if he had just been soaked and tossed in a washing machine.

Right there and then, Seth made a silent vow to himself: *If I get out of this place alive, I will never, ever steal another VW Beetle again… and certainly not with a body in it, or especially anything remotely looking like a clown as a passenger.*

The crowd then rose to their feet. They roared with delight. They screamed at the top of their voices, 'More! More! Encore!' Seth's face changed from blue to bright red and back again. Grimbo and Willy chuckled quietly to themselves, a self-satisfied grin that split their faces from ear to ear. From out of the wings, Costello stuck his head out with a look of astonishment.

Barely had the excitement faded, when a sudden scuffle erupted from just behind where Roland, Lotte and Tim were sitting. Kev Scratchley had just bent down to tie his shoelaces when his head collided into the back of Lotte's shoulder. She whipped round in angry surprise.

'Well, I never! Look, Hect. Look who's here. Hey, gang!' Scratchley yelled at the top of his voice. 'Look. It's liddle ol' Lotte Pert and her pretend liddle bruvver – Tiddle Timmie Timidkins!' Deliberately, he prodded Lotte sharply in the back.

Liz Braggerley then made Tilly Crossley giggle. Provocatively, they stuck their thumbs up their noses and prodded Lotte in the back, who now blushed bright pink. Meanwhile, Phil Grimsmore snatched at Hector's bag of crisps and flung a handful down Lotte's neck. Tilly joined in and started to squirt some lemonade into Tim's hair.

'Now snotty Pert, enjoy the dirt.
You've had your lot, you stupid clot.

And lickle Timmie is just a dimmie
…The little weakling squirt!'

chanted the Braggerley gang, sailing into Lotte and Tim mercilessly.

'It's that horrible bunch from Lotte's school!' wailed Tim, trying to shake them off as they made a grab at the back of his collar.

Roland's eyes flashed murderously. He sprang to his feet, his fists clenched tightly. 'Ignore those stupid morons!' he urged Lotte and Tim under his breath. He wanted to flatten them there and then, but thought better of it. Several turned round to stare. Others shouted for them to be quiet.

Just then, Henry pointed in their direction. 'Hey, Chance. Up there.' He indicated with end of his cane. 'Those bullies attacking Lotte and Tim... I wonder if they are the same lot that Lotte mentioned who broke her leg at school? We've got to do something, and quickly, before it turns really nasty.'

Chance nodded. 'Let's take them down a peg or two!' Straight away, he went to the microphone. 'Now, boys and girls, for our next act, we still need some smart volunteers to help us. There is a big prize for them to pit their strength and brains against Willy here and me!'

'It's a fix. A blinkin' set-up. A trick!' hollered Hector, showing off still. He half got out of his seat to remonstrate.

Quickly, without further ado, Henry and Willy ran up the tiered steps and made their way towards Lotte and her tormentors.

'Oh, that well-built boy and that tall girl next to him... yes, that one with the brown hair. Yes, those two in the third row.' Chance indicated to Henry, pointing out Hector and his sister Liz. Suddenly they went quiet as mice, as Henry and Willy shepherded them down into the ring.

'And oh, I almost forgot,' shouted Chance, gesticulating again. 'Yes, and you – the one with short fair hair in the row in front of our brave new volunteers!' Lotte was singled out. She seemed startled to say the least, but Henry gave her a gentle smile. To reassure her, Roland gave her gentle squeeze on the arm, whispering that she would be safe with Chance and Henry.

'Now, let's give them a very big welcome,' said Chance with a big smile.

A burst of clapping followed as they entered the arena.

Blinking nervously under the spotlight, Lotte stood terrified next to Chance, who gave her a secret wink. Hector swaggered arrogantly into the ring with Liz, who giggled childishly all the way, whispering that they were going to belittle Lotte in front of everyone. 'Just wait, you snitch, it's all your fault!' they hissed murderously. 'We'll teach you and your stupid dummy pals!'

Menacingly, they towered over Lotte and slyly tried to crush her toes, though Chance quickly pushed them apart. Then, Henry asked them their names.

'This is a test of strength,' announced Chance to the audience. 'It's a competition to see who is also the cleverest!'

Placid-faced, Willy said nothing and just stood silently at the edge of the ring to prevent the Braggerleys from escaping, whereas Grimbo stood guard, his arms purposefully folded.

'Now, Hector – it is Hector, isn't it?' said Chance. 'This is a *very* simple task. Here are three buckets in the middle facing you; two are plastic and one is metal.' He pointed downwards at the floor quite close to their feet. 'As you can see, the first one's full of sand, the second one is filled with water and the third – the shiny, metal one – the one has feathers.'

Henry looked on knowingly with a half-smile.

Chance continued, 'We want you to lift each bucket in turn, starting with the first one. Then carry them to the edge of the ring so that the audience can examine what's inside. And then immediately run round to the other side of the ring with the bucket on your shoulder. Then hand it over to this young lady. She's your sister, Liz, so I'm told. Now am I right?' asked Chance with a pointed nod in her direction. Liz tilted her head with a surly reluctance, wondering what was next up his sleeve. 'If you can do this, young man, you'll be able to win a big box of book tokens, CDs or DVDs of your choice at the best shop in town!'

Chance stepped back. 'Now, are you ready?'

Hector then sauntered over to the buckets and their contents without a further thought. He rolled up his sleeves and flexed his biceps in the direction of his friends, boasting, 'It's a piece of cake. Dead easy! An idiot's game!'

'Oh, by the way…' cautioned Chance with a restraining hand on Hector's shoulder, 'I almost forgot to mention it – silly old me… There's a forfeit to pay – *if you fail to lift all three.*'

He glanced curiously at the harlequin's face, hesitating for a moment in his tracks.

'Well, the penalty – the punishment – I'm afraid, is that we will have to pour the contents of the buckets over your head!' said Chance, matter-of-factly.

Then with little effort, Hector managed to lift the ones with the water and the sand, and then strolled confidently around the perimeter of the ring, pointing in triumph to the crowd in the front row. He then handed the buckets over to Liz, who was startled but bemused by all what was going on.

But when Hector came to the bucket of feathers, he casually snatched at it with one hand, muttering, 'This is a doddle!' He got a shock of his life. It simply would not budge. He tried again, this time, using both hands, he tugged for all he was worth. Still the bucket would not move an inch. He went bright crimson, breaking out in a sweat.

Puzzled murmurings erupted from the audience.

'Having a little trouble with the feathers, my friend?' Chance enquired, concealing a smile.

Boos rippled across the circus. ''Ere! Can't a big strapping lad like you lift a few light feathers?' joked a large round lady sitting in the front row as she stuffed a half-eaten burger to her lips.

'I'll tell you what. You can have an extra couple of minutes, and whereupon you can also have the help of Liz… okay, Liz?' Chance offered generously.

Liz stumbled blindly towards her brother and joined her hands firmly next to his. And together, with fingers interlocking, they tried with all their might to ease the bucket of feathers off the floor of the ring. Three times they tried. Each time they failed. Crestfallen, their confident smirks rapidly slid off their faces.

'Heave! Lift, you wet weaklings!' screamed those in the back row.

For unbeknown to Liz and Hector, Chance had powerfully magnetised the bottom of the bucket to a metal ring hidden in a fixing under the sawdust. Power and cunning had returned to him with a vengeance, and he had his precious gemstone to thank for it. He caressed it gratefully under his collar.

Abruptly, Henry had another suggestion. 'I know, folks,' he announced through the mic. 'Why not let this young girl on her own standing next to us have a go!' Giving a broad wink at Chance, he nudged Lotte towards him.

'Ah yes. *Why not indeed?*' said Chance. 'It's Lotte, isn't it?' The inflection in his voice pretended surprise.

Begrudgingly, the Braggerleys stepped aside, growling, 'Bah, if *we* can't do it, then neither could a skinny, soft weakling like her!' They scowled at her poisonously and skulked to the side, simmering dangerously.

In inviting the crowd to show their approval, Henry stepped towards Lotte and lifted her hand. 'Shall we let young Lotte have a go?' he asked.

'*Ye-ess!* Yep. Great! Have a good go, Missie,' they yelled in encouragement.

Nervously, Lotte stepped towards the bucket of feathers. Then petrified, she looked around anxiously as if for help. Fixing her feet fair and square in front of it, she bent her knees and grasped the handle with both hands. She pulled upwards towards her body. The bucket would *not* move. She tried again, using all the strength that she could muster. It still wouldn't move. Panic set in. Straightening up, she twisted around, searching her friends' faces for help.

An oily smirk broke out across Hector's face. Liz waved to her friends with a 'told-you-so' guffaw. Grimsmore leant forwards in his seat and gave a thumbs-up sign, then leered at Lotte floundering in the arena.

Gripping the edge of his seat, Tim grew increasingly worried and upset. Roland became distraught and bit his nails.

'Now try again, *but this time with just one of your little fingers*, Miss Lotte,' advised Chance calmly. 'Also, this time, try to relax your shoulders.' The microphone picked up the unusual instructions, which echoed loudly around the big top. Surreptitiously, he rubbed the gem and crossed his fingers. Tim and Roland held their breath, each muttering a silent prayer, whilst Henry looked away, not daring to watch.

Then Lotte tried again; but this time crooking her little finger from her right hand firmly under the middle of the handle. To everyone's and to her astonishment, the bucket rose effortlessly off the ground. Triumphantly, she twirled it around at shoulder height for all the audience to see. She was so pleased with herself that she threw the bucket from one hand to another, as though it were a feather-light ball of cotton wool.

There was a gasp of silence to begin with. Then a thunder of applause exploded with shouts of, '*Well done! Congrats. Missie*,' from all corners of the arena.

The Braggerleys were gutted, their gang stunned into silence.

But then, from one quarter of the big top, there were cries of, '*Hey, what about the penalty?*' From another: '*Yeah, how about that!*'

'Hang on. Hold on, folks!' said Chance, trying to appease them. 'Let's give Liz and Hector a second chance. Don't you think that's reasonable?'

Henry joined in. 'I know,' he suggested brightly, 'If they can lift young Lotte clean off the ground and escort her back to her seat, then they will *not* be punished. Now, isn't that a fair deal?'

The audience went quiet, wondering what was going to happen next.

Hector and Liz's faces brightened noticeably. 'Easy peasy,' sniped Hector, from the corner of his mouth to his sister.

'We can get our own back. She's made us look such fools in front of everyone!' Liz hissed back, her voice fading into a whisper.

Grimsmore, meanwhile, cupping his hands shouted down, ''Ere, break her other leg!'

Immediately, Willy ran into the ring and skirted around the Braggerleys and Lotte, challenging them: 'G'won then. Show us how strong you two are!'

Terrifyingly, Lotte's anxiety returned with a vengeance. She felt extremely helpless now being faced with these two bullies again. All at once, it reminded her of school. Purposefully, both brother and sister strode menacingly towards her, one on each side of her. Viciously they gripped her arms, painfully wrenching her backwards.

'Hey, Hect. Teach her a lesson… smash her foot!' screamed Kev Scratchley sadistically as he stood tiptoed on his seat. Tilly Crossley nodded furiously in support. 'Dead easy. She's such a stupid paperweight!' she added nastily.

'*Now!*' urged Hector, yanking his head. Roughly, he and his sister cupped their arms under Lotte's shoulders as the two of them then tried to pull her upwards. To their astonishment, Lotte's body felt like a ton of lead. Try hard as they might, they could not lift her. Red-faced, they tried again. Again, her shoes appeared to be glued to the ground. Chance narrowed his eyes fixed at Lotte's feet, as if trying to hypnotise her legs. A rash of sniggers flew around the tent.

Swiftly, Liz rushed to Lotte's front and grabbed her around the waist. At the same time, Hector tried from the back, hooking his hands under both her arms. Repeatedly, they tried to lift her off the ground, kicking her ankles, but to no avail. Her feet simply refused to shift one iota.

Without their knowing it, Chance had magnetised Lotte's shoes to the ground. Sweat now poured down Liz and Hector's faces in frustration. Their pals hid their faces in their hands aghast.

The crowd started to slow-hand clap. They jeered and screamed, 'You useless wet weaklings! Can't the two of you shift that slip of a girl!' As soon as that happened, a cry was taken up: '*What about a penalty! Punishment! Pay the penalty!*' The chant spread like wildfire, rocking the arena like an explosion.

Incandescent with anger though Chance was – recalling Lotte's treatment at school at the hands of the Braggerleys – really vindictive and malicious he was not. And so, generously, he invited the audience to vote what they wanted to happen. Hector and Liz's fate would be decided by the people with a show of 'thumbs-up' or 'thumbs-down'.

Now as it happened, from the upper tier at the back, watching the proceedings with bated breath, Madame Drizelda shuffled uncomfortably in her seat. Things were getting out of hand in the arena, she thought. The fate of the two in the ring, she noted, was to be decided by the majority demonstrating their wishes by wielding their thumbs in voting. At once, it came back to her in a flash, as she closed her eyes momentarily. For that split moment or two, a vivid image transported her back to Ancient Rome, where nearly two thousand years ago similar life-or-death decisions were meted out in the same way in the arena. Now, in front of her very eyes, the auditorium of this circus before her was not unlike that of the ancient arena of the Colosseum. And what is more, the baying crowd, like a mob of lemmings, would use the same signal with the tips of their thumbs to decide the fate of those hapless persons down there. But, nevertheless, watching with nervous curiosity, Madame Drizelda reluctantly opened her eyes to see what the people had decided…

Unfortunately for Liz and Hector, the crowd had signalled overwhelmingly a vote of 'thumbs-down'.

So as to make it easier on her brother, Liz was invited to pour some sand, then water and a few feathers, over his head. She refused point blank and ran for cover to the side. Chivalrously, so did Lotte who backed away.

'*Pay the penalty. Dump the stuff all over 'im!*' screamed the crowd, hungry for blood. Repeatedly, they jeered and gesticulated, thrusting their thumbs downwards, towards the ground. Madame Drizelda shivered, her spine tingling all the way down to the soles of her feet.

However, without a jot of sentimentality, Grimbo flung himself towards Hector, scooped up a handful of sand and threw it into his hair. Immediately, Willy followed suit and tipped a bucket of water over the lad's head – finishing off with a pile of feathers, which he rubbed into his jacket. Soaked and splattered, some of it also drenched Liz as she looked on helplessly. Immediately, a rapturous cheer went up and a storm of laughter broke around the big top. Not only that, but a burst of applause greeted the clowns as they continued to throw water over each other whilst taking their bows.

Dishevelled and soaking wet, their clothes choking with clumps of sand and sodden feathers, sheepishly Hector and Liz crept their way back to their seats, snarling as they jostled past Lotte,

'Just wait till next term. You won't get away with this. *We don't just get evens... we get even better!'* they hissed chillingly. 'Just watch the *other* leg, Lotte snotty Pert, you swotty clever-clogs. And this time, you won't have your precious zombie pals there to protect you!'

Without stopping to pause, the audience clapped deliriously and threw things into the air. However immediately for safety, Roland and Tim were invited down to the front row to join Lotte to see the rest of the show. While this was happening, Grimbo spun about in the ring on a tiny unicycle and threw sweets into the audience. Willy strode around, happily juggling ten-pound dumbbells into the air. Chance and Henry did a little jig around each other whilst balancing buckets on their heads. At last, a feeling of joy spread around the place like fever.

'Ah ha, my friends – you've finally defrosted them!' admitted Costello, joining in the laughter.

'Congratulations are in order,' offered Grimbo, a bit dazed – grinning from ear to ear as one of Willy's dumbbells struck him at the side of his head.

The applause continued like peals of thunder. Chance bowed again and again. 'They're eating out of your hands at long last!' Henry smiled. *'But hang on… hey, you must have done the third and final good deed as required by the first part of the legend and its riddle by now!'*

As they made their way to the exits, Henry asked jokingly, 'Does your nose glow or your ears burn with heat and swell with pride – or any part of you feel different, for that matter?'

'Don't know yet, Henry, my friend,' replied Chance wearily. 'My face is definitely feeling red and burning hot from all that tension and exertion in there just now. Though, come to think of it, my feet do feel a bit tingly as well; but I better not take my shoes and socks off here to check just now in case they pong a bit! And so, for the moment, you'll just have to take my word for it.'

But before he had managed to finish speaking… just outside – not far in the distance – an explosion of thunder crashed suddenly across the sky. It was approaching fast. Inexplicably, the air felt thick and suddenly oppressive; you could swear you could cut it with a knife. As he opened his mouth to say something else, a tremendous shudder, like a bolt of electricity, rattled his body, making his hair stand on end. Then, uncontrollably, he started to shiver from top to toe, as if something strange had possessed his limbs.

Suddenly, he remembered what Zoot had told him, as to what would happen… *"As soon as the first part of the riddle was completed – there will come a momentous, magical sign from you know where… which will hit you like thunder between the eyes…"*

'Mm, now I wonder if…?' Chance was chewing this over, when… Just then, the gem in the pendant around his neck started to jump about like a mouse in a trap. It felt hot and alive under his fingers, as if trying to tell him something. Try as hard as he might, he couldn't quite explain it.

At once, his thoughts returned to his old friend Zoot and the mysterious and strange things that had happened before at Miss Saskia's house. 'Ah! Just as it had been predicted – the *crucial sign* from the legend giving me an extra ninety-nine days – the go-ahead to continue must have finally arrived,' murmured Chance gratefully. 'Of this I'm now certain. And this reprieve will now give me time to search for the next stage of the riddle...'

Pursing his lips and deliberately keeping his own counsel, he then strode quickly ahead of Henry as he dodged one of Willy's dumbbells which had just narrowly missed his ear.

As he glanced backwards, Henry noticed that the Braggerleys and their gang began to skulk off early – beaten, defeated, and shocked out of their skins, no doubt. Happily, moreover, some justice at least he felt had been done for young Lotte's sake; and he felt immensely proud of the part he had played in it.

What's more, the good news was that the first part of the riddle had been sorted; though the bad news was that they were no nearer to finding out about the phantom of the circus for Mimi and Bonzo as yet... And that scared and worried him to death. But nonetheless, he felt that the sooner they got out of this place, the better. Hopefully, things should go more smoothly now than before. Cautiously, he gave Chance a wary side glance and hoped that he hadn't spoken far too soon...

Chapter 38

ANOTHER DIMENSION

No sooner had they left the ring than Barnard barged into them in passing. Without a word of thanks for their efforts, he brusquely elbowed Chance and Henry out of the way as he rushed into the arena to announce the next and final act.

'My good people, boys and girls, Barnard and Barnard's are proud to present to you – the very, *very* special star with the most amazing act you have all been waiting for! …He is the world's greatest… He is the *most mystical* man of mysteries… He will *thrill* you… He will *chill* you… He will *scare* you out of your wits… He will perform the most amazing death-defying feats that have never been performed before…

'I give you – the most *incredible*, the most *indelible*, the most *inscrutable*… the *great mystic*… *Doc-tor… Slatane… De'aff!*'

The words had barely left his mouth when all the lights went out with a crash, pitching the big top into total darkness as if a main fuse had blown. The masts supporting the big tent started to tremble. The whole structure began to shake dangerously as a violent wind was whipped up. Outside, a sudden storm was exploding fast. Loose canvas not tied down began to slap about. Blades of forked lightning flew across the green, skimming the top of the big tent. Claps of thunder exploded overhead, rattling the riggings in its trail. Large chunks of ice fell from the skies as a welter of hailstones bounced off the outside of the tent like bullets, scaring the occupants witless within.

Shrieks and screams could be heard in the pitch-blackness as members of the audience grabbed each other in fright. Total strangers held on to their neighbours for comfort in the dark, not knowing what to expect next. Two long minutes passed, which seemed an eternity in the dark. A bank of emergency lighting was quickly switched on from behind the performers' wing, lending a hazy, but ghostly light to shine the way for those entering the arena.

Then suddenly in the dim light, striding arrogantly towards the middle of the ring, a tall, sinister figure enshrouded completely in black, brushed rudely past. Violently, he knocked Henry out of his path with the base of a large Gladstone bag. Pulling the rim of a wide-brimmed fedora down to hide his face, the figure tugged purposefully at a shoulder cape thrown over a black frock coat. Peering briefly over the top of his mirrored-tinted glasses, he threw a contemptuous look in Chance's direction, as if he expected him. It bore straight through him as though a red-hot poker had pierced his chest.

Cursing under his breath, the sinister figure then hissed like a snake as the fold of his cape flapped blindly into Chance's face. 'So that old witch from Glastonbury was right after all about the rendezvous with *you* here today ...Your destiny awaits you!' He spat through his teeth ominously.

Chilled to the bones, Chance shivered uncontrollably. Abruptly, it suddenly came back to him what Mimi and Bonzo at the hospital had warned him about... to be *extremely* careful and, moreover, to be on his strictest guard, when he comes across an odious and dangerous figure by the name of *Dr Slatane De'Aff...*

With a disdainful swagger that disguised a slight limp, the dark figure continued his entrance. He looked around him, squinting suspiciously in the bleak light that cast a ghostly glow around his head. He paused deliberately to make his presence felt. From the narrow slits in a black mask that covered his face, he cast an evil stare at the people in the audience. Terrified, most of them averted their eyes with fright.

Whilst some, summoning up Dutch courage, or just filled with brazen bravado, like the noisy gang of youths in the back row, looked up. As they did, they tried to scrutinise the features of this strange, frightening figure that dominated the centre stage...

Below his forehead, however hard they tried, they could not make out his eyes under the mask, even when his dark tinted glasses slipped a little off the bridge of his nose. But when they did, they were shocked to see what seemed like two empty sockets, blood-red and raw. There was a hole in the centre of the mask where a nose should have been. Horrifically, it appeared to have no septum, although much worse was yet to come. A wide narrow gash gaped just where the mouth should have emerged; the mask somewhat helped to hide it, but it was no less gruesome to the eye.

A deathly hush fell as De'Aff tossed his leather bag onto a table next to him. He opened the brass clasp with an ostentatious snap with his claw-like fingers, the overgrown nails scraping the edges of the leather. He reached into the depths of the bag and gurgled, 'Come on out, my dear little Delia… now, don't be shy, my precious little pet.' A guttural, rasping voice hissed out from behind the mask. The sound appeared to come from the back of the throat, yet it emerged via a raw hole in the nose.

Out of his bag, he pulled a gigantic, bearded serpent. It appeared to be over seven-feet long, a cross between a large hairy lizard and a snake. It started to uncoil itself.

Lotte managed to stifle a scream before it left her lips. Tim and Roland leant forwards on the edge of their seats with morbid fascination – scared, but still curious, nevertheless. Sobs of fear whispered around the arena.

The serpent's glistening muscular body slithered powerfully up his master's arm and intertwined around his neck. Its long, slimy tongue made up of three green prongs darted towards his face in a sinister kiss. With the serpent coiled around his arms, De'Aff then hoisted up his fingers towards the roof of the tent and screeched in a half-strangled cry, '*Let there be light upon my powerful genius, O Master, O Mighty One, O Supreme Keeper of Mysteries!*'

A large round lady in the front row immediately dropped her sandwich onto the floor, letting out a squeal of fright, her appetite suddenly forgotten.

'*For I am the indisputable, the unassailable, the magnificent, the Great Slatane De'Aff... Now let me show you the way to another dimension!*' he continued to cry.

A deafening roar of thunder suddenly rattled the big top like an earthquake tremor. A gale-force wind blew open the canvas flaps to the entrance, illuminating it from a shard of lightning that flashed as soon as he spoke. Instantaneously like magic, the main arc lights returned to the big top. A dust storm swirled around the ring and blew off De'Aff's hat, which flew across the floor, knocking off his glasses in the process. A halo of silver light bathed his face in an eerie glow. It emphasised the empty grey holes in his skull, which were sunken and bloodshot. Instinctively, he tried to cover his face with the palms of his hands, revealing his scaly hands with both thumbs missing, though a mass of coarse beard around his chin attempted a reasonable disguise. Desperately, he hung on to Delia, his pet serpent, as it slithered and slapped around his body with a rattling hiss.

At that precise moment, Madame Drizelda sat bolt upright in her seat. She opened her eyes with a rapid blink, having just about adjusted to the difference in light. Immediately, she noticed the thumbless hands and the burning holes in the mask that covered his face. Her stomach lurched with a sickening fear. 'Oh, my gawd! ...I can't believe it!' she mouthed silently. Her body shook. She tried to let out a scream, but nothing came out. She held up her hand to her open mouth with horror.

Could it be him… that sinister stranger who threatened my reading at Glastonbury seven days ago…? She thought quickly as her heart thudded in her head. *Could that be the same man with no eyes that preached hatred to anyone and everyone who wanted to make others happy…?* Yes, of course; she remembered now… *He did, after all, ask about a circus.*

By now De'Aff's rasping croak exploded across the auditorium at fever pitch. He scanned the audience up and down. '*Nothing can escape my eyes. Not even your inner thoughts! My eyes are all-seeing. They can read through your very soul,*' he cried, as he reached down to retrieve his glasses.

'Oh, my grief. Heavens help us!' she choked. '*It's definitely him…* those empty, evil eyes that haunt beyond the grave!' The warning earlier in her crystal ball came suddenly rushing back to her:

"Beware of the eyes that have died!"

A wave of nausea overcame her. She felt dizzy. She let out a scream. 'Argh! Watch out, you foolish, naïve clown of a harlequin. I don't fancy your chances…you must flee now…!' Helplessly she keeled over and toppled forwards into the seat in front of her; hitting her head, her arms flung out before her.

Two vigilant members of the St John's Ambulance Brigade, who happened to be on duty, rushed up between the aisles of seats to her prostrate body to administer first aid. Smelling salts were rapidly thrust under her nose. Then, the stricken figure of Drizelda was carried out by stretcher into the open air. The eye of the storm had just passed by. Speckles of fresh rain fell refreshingly onto her face, bringing her round.

'Please. Oh, please, I must get away from *him* in there,' she mumbled incoherently. 'Everything around him feels so oppressive... so suffocating.' Quivering, she raised her arm imploring,

'Please, I beg you, take me to the Tower of London; and quickly, my man!'

Astonished, the ambulance crew stopped abruptly what they were doing and hesitated a moment, for their jaws had fallen open. 'What! You can't mean, the... *the... tow-er?*' They assumed that she was still suffering from shock and losing her marbles. For in all their years in service, they had never had a peculiar request like this.

'Oh, don't just stand gawping, you fools! *Of course, I mean the Tower!* My stepbrother Edbert Tuffnut, a Beefeater, works there... so please hurry, man! Though I beg you, you've got to warn him – that harlequin in there... of the terrible dangers that are about to occur to...'

Agitated, she tried to raise her body onto her elbows, her hand pointing backwards towards the tent. But, trembling breathlessly without finishing what she wanted to say, she fell back onto the stretcher, calling for more smelling salts.

Chapter 39

ACRIDCRADAVER

IN THE MEANTIME, THE circus limelight had now been hogged completely by Slatane De'Aff. Menacingly, he strutted around, defying anyone to challenge him. With an extravagant swish, he swirled his cape back and forth at the petrified audience whilst stalking around relentlessly like a bullfighter in the ring pawing the ground. Nervous little children hid inside their parents' coats. A few who were a bit braver dared to peep out, squinting through spaced-out fingers trying to cover their faces. Although that did not disguise De'Aff's hideous face, which was contracting in and out like a distorted balloon sucking in air.

'Hey, look. He's got no mouth, nose or eyes worth talking about!' whispered Tim timidly to Lotte, who had averted her face, feeling sick to the gills.

'Huh, it's only a flippin' rubber mask with holes around

the nostrils and eye sockets!' said Roland bravely, as if that made it a whole lot better.

'But urgh… just look at the disgusting, slimy creature slobbering around his neck and shoulders,' added Lotte. Cagily, she twisted around to have a look.

Just then, an ugly staccato voice rang out to silence the mutterings. 'Now, all of you, I want you to pay attention!' De'Aff commanded. Defiant and deafening, he screamed,

'For my special trick, ladies and gentlemen, I will demonstrate to you my secret powers. I will demonstrate in front of your very eyes, the elusive power of wistful thinking of *a mysterious dimension* from an Alterworld. For it's *another visual dimension* that you have never ever experienced before!'

Slowly and purposefully, he then moved around the perimeter of the ring, arching his body in tune with the creature around his shoulders. 'For I am the greatest mystic in the whole of the planet,' he boasted. 'Only I, Dr Slatane De'Aff, possess the power to wist away objects and people into this untapped world. And I can do it, by merely *wistful thinking*, via the mind. *I can make them come. I can make them go…* All of them, merely at will!'

De'Aff adjusted the weight of his wriggling pet serpent around his neck. It slid down the front of his body, darting its tongue, and licked around his face affectionately.

'In this,' he announced, 'I will be assisted by the graceful young Katrina. Now, where is this beautiful creature?' he demanded impatiently. He switched his focus towards the performers' entrance… searching.

Katrina Belakova, Ziggarini's former assistant, had been waiting with trepidation in the wings. She was extremely reluctant to work with this mysterious and intimidating stranger Dr De'Aff, who had suddenly appeared from nowhere when Ziggarini disappeared. Slatane De'Aff, as far as she was concerned, had hijacked the circus, and had put the fear of God into everyone. But since Ziggarini didn't return, she was out of work. And there was no other role for her in any other of the acts. Willy, Grimbo and the others, fearful for her wellbeing, tried to dissuade her from assisting De'Aff. 'I simply have to work. I had no other choice,' she retorted with hopeless resignation. 'I'll admit that I'm still rather scared. And of course, I miss my dear friend and guardian Ziggarini.'

'Now hurry up, Katrina, you stupid girl! You're on! The Great Slatane needs you,' scolded Marcus Barnard. Cruelly, he gave her a sharp push in the back towards the ring. She stumbled barefooted into the glare of the arc lights and into the path of De'Aff with her heart in her mouth.

Her delicate beauty, with long black hair surrounding a pale heart-shaped face, gave Roland quite a jolt when he saw her. Given her flawless complexion, it could be justifiably described as pale as ivory and as delicate as porcelain. His pulse raced up a notch. 'Wow, now she's something!' He whistled admiringly before he could stop himself.

'Oh, go on with you, Roland – it's only a blinkin' girl!' scowled Lotte. Peeved, she kicked at his ankles testily.

De'Aff's scaly hands grabbed at Katrina's delicate wrist with a grip of steel. 'Welcome, my child. We have much work to do to entertain the paying public,' he spat scornfully through the slit in his mouth.

From the safety of the wings, Costello peeped out from the wings, looking on concerned. 'I don't like this one bit,' he said anxiously to Chance and Henry, who were waiting besides him. 'I promised Ziggarini I'd keep an eye on her.'

Meanwhile, Willy couldn't take any more excitement for the day and so he left hurriedly to look for his little friend Midgy.

Katrina fiddled nervously with her lilac-blue leotard, shuffling from foot to foot. Using the tips of her fingers, she swept her fringe away from her face.

'Music, my good maestro!' De'Aff commanded loudly with a screech. Hauntingly, the organ began to play, heightening the drama.

'*Now, let us summon up the other dimension. Let us bring it back from the depths of the past and project it into the future!*' In a deathly monotone, he droned on, swaying his head hypnotically to the dirge of the music.

Rigidly, he then stood with his feet apart and unclasped his claw-like hands towards the peak of the big top. As soon as he did that, a swirling mist of dense red smoke curled downwards from the top and enveloped his body dramatically like a gigantic cocoon. The serpent raised its ugly head in surprise and gave off a grating, noisy rattle. Deliberately, De'Aff stamped his foot on the floor in the middle of the ring three times. His boot struck the lid of a trapdoor half-concealed by sawdust, giving it a hollow thudding sound.

The audience remained dumbstruck. Simply scared to death, they didn't dare move. The central arc lights began to dim when the trapdoor suddenly flew open with a rusty squeal. Then, rising slowly out of the ground, an enormous mahogany casket with slits pierced in its sides creaked upwards, as though floating in mid-air. It hovered eerily for a moment or two, until two stewards rushed in to place a pair of steel trestles under its base to bear it aloft. Surrounding the side panels of the casket were placed six pairs of large, white church candles sitting in black metal holders that projected out from slits in the sides.

'Oh, *Master of Sight, let there be light!*' screamed De'Aff with rising hysteria.

He waved his arms around his body, flapping furiously like someone possessed. Blowing jets of fire from his mouth, he then instructed Katrina to light the candles using a torch of straw, which he produced with a flourish from under his coat.

'*Oh, precious forces of time, summon up the power which, by right, is mine,*' he continued hypnotically.

Then, agonisingly slowly, the lid of the casket opened. Gasps of surprise from the audience broke the silence. The bearded serpent began to slip off his master's body and started to slither in a zigzag fashion towards the mouth of the open casket. Puffs of blue smoke with yellow sparks flew out of its jaws as it slid lazily towards its goal.

From his coat pocket, De'Aff dragged out a tiny fluffy white kitten, who tried to in vain to wriggle out of his grip. It gave a pitiful meow.

'Ah, poor little thing,' cooed a family of children in the front row next to Lotte, though they sat petrified with fear.

Struggling, the kitten was placed into the open casket and the lid slammed shut. Just as the serpent reached its rim, De'Aff crooked his head to one side and leant breathlessly over the casket, stroking the top of it lovingly with his scaly fingers. Then he muttered something indiscernible –

words so terrifying that they brought a chill to those within earshot who managed to make out what he was saying…

> *'Acrid… cradaver…*
> *Acridcradaver,*
> *Dimension of darkness,*
> *To light my way,*
> *For this…'*

Just before he finished, the casket started to shake and rattle about on its trestles. At once, the burning candles surrounding it suddenly exploded. A mass of blue smoke bathing a clutch of bright orange flames burst beneath it, creating a cauldron of fire. Aghast, Katrina stifled a scream and leapt backwards away from the flames. De'Aff merely stared, mesmerised, into the belly of the fire with a kind of gruesome delight. Horrified, the audience was frozen into continuing numbed silence… not wanting to stay – or wanting to leave.

In deep concentration, De'Aff then snapped his fingers in the direction of the trapdoor besides his feet. The door flew open and a battered old violin floated upwards and out towards him. He stepped towards it and plucked it out of the air as it passed his face. Startled gasps were heard around the tent, splitting the silence. He placed the instrument onto his left shoulder and tucked it under his chin. Then with his right hand gripping the bow, he started to play a haunting melody that was so screeching and scraping that it made one's teeth stand painfully on edge. It was badly off-key; but to be generous, one could blame his thumbless hands if one were so inclined.

Peeping through a slit in the canvas curtain from the wings, Chance and Henry just then happened to catch a reflection of De'Aff's evil stare in the light of the flames, which danced about to the strange screech of the awful music.

Then, it all happened at once.

Chance didn't know what hit him next. Suddenly, without warning, a spasm of searing pain gripped his body. His hands grabbed hold of his stomach as he fell to the ground, doubled up, writhing in agony. He clapped his hands over his ears as he tried in vain to shut out the ghostly strain of the wailing cry from the violin. It screamed at such a terrible pitch from the raw strings that he felt that his eardrums would suddenly rupture.

Without wasting a second, Henry dropped to his knees, concerned. He lifted his friend carefully off the ground. Trembling with fear, Costello came to their aid. 'What is it, my friend?' asked Henry.

Chance's face had gone white as a sheet. 'It's difficult to describe – that dreadful music,' croaked Chance from the back of his throat. 'It's as if… as if a poor, defenceless creature is being slowly murdered. That… that screeching of strings scraping at your throat is, I am sure, the evil sound of a phantom violin… Remember, I told you about it, from Cecil-the-Thin's warning at the waxworks. *He said…*' gasped Chance, choking on his words, "*it is a song of evil. And when you hear it, it is a warning of impending doom!*"

Chance blacked out again, holding his face. He fell to his knees, his head crashing into Henry's waist. An awful nightmare flooded his senses. This happened once before at Madame Rousseau's…

Tornadoes and thunderstorms, seemingly from thousands of years before, filled the skies. Whilst untamed winds whipped up in an uncontrolled frenzy, uprooting trees, and hurling boulders across the landscape, colossal tremors shook the planet as meteorites and asteroids crashed to earth with a phenomenal force. Then as they did, volcanoes erupted rising to the heavens, their spewing ash blocking out the sun. And as gigantic waves rose-up in the oceans, all forms of life, however primitive, perished in the paths of these elements of unleashed fury.

But then, just as he thought it was all over, the nightmare started again...

Not far in the distance, a cloud of dense white mist came down and hurtled towards him like a deadly avalanche from which there was no escape. From its epicentre, an enormous figure covered in heavy black armour began to materialise in front of him. It grew and grew, until its gargantuan size almost reached the sky, sucking the earth towards it. It did not stay still, for it started to thunder towards him like a crazed prehistoric mammoth that had been wounded – but potentially much more dangerous.

Chance was gripped with indescribable fear...

Behind the figure, there was a blinding white light shrouding it. Narrowing his eyes, hoping to shut it out, it still lumbered towards him... relentlessly. Squinting hard, he could not make out whether it was human or beast. Whatever it was, it was still terrifying beyond all mortal imagination. Wielding a club-like limb in his direction, it beckoned him towards its massive, curved body with a crooked hairy finger. Chance tried to back away, but his feet became rooted to the earth. He clutched at his throat attempting to scream, but no sound came out. He fell to the ground as the suffocating figure caught up with him...

Chance opened his eyes again as Henry slapped his cheeks to wake him up. Desperately, he hauled him to his feet.

'That sound – that dreadful sound of anguish felt as if it were calling me from another place,' groaned Chance. 'And that... that horrific demonic sight coming for me! It felt like pure, unadulterated evil. I could feel it pulling at the insides of my stomach and shredding my brain... Death, so icy-cold travelled through my body, eating up my soul as if the world had come to an end. I can't help it. It fills me with awful dread.'

Sweat poured off his face.

As the moment passed, he stood up leaning on Henry's shoulder, gulping lungs full of fresh air, but he was still trembling.

'I... I'm pretty sure that I have just come face to face with that thing Cecil-the-Thin described as the embodiment of evil, *unadulterated terror and pure evil*.'

Chance's teeth were still rattling as he leant on his friend for support.

'Do you think it's what been described as the supreme evil one – Qnevilus-the-Terrible – you told us about?' asked Henry. 'Do you think that this terrifying creature De'Aff is somehow connected to this evil, like, say, a disciple, a follower – one of the Custodians? For after all, to begin with, just look what devastating effect he's had on you already!'

'I really don't know at this moment,' replied Chance wearily. 'I've got my suspicions, but we have to have some proof.

Inside the darkened arena, whilst this was happening, *oohs* and *ahs* greeted the scene of drama as it unfolded. 'Enough!' demanded De'Aff, casting the violin aside. He dismissed it with the back of his hand. And as he did, the lid of the casket creaked opened. Black smoke gushed out, billowing up into the tent as the flames died down.

'Katrina will check if the little creature is still intact...' he added with a slimy sneer. 'Now, please, dear girl...' He pushed her towards the open casket.

Tim and Lotte could bear the suspense no longer and pulled up their collars to hide their eyes. Katrina did what she was told. She walked towards it like in a trance, though she was crippled with fear. Cautiously, she put her hand inside the casket and felt all around the container. There was nothing there. Reluctantly, she stood on tiptoes to peer in. Her eyes searched round the inside, but it was completely empty. The white kitten had disappeared into thin air.

'Aha. Ah so!' uttered De'Aff triumphantly. '*Exactly as I thought. The little animal has successfully, like magic, journeyed to the other dimension!*'

He waited for applause, but none came. Immediately, he instructed Katrina to close the lid and stand well back. As he approached the top of it, he started to mumble, wringing his hands:

'*O Master of Light, O for a second sight,*
Acridcradaver... Acrid... cradaver...
Don't let it burn. I challenge you for its safe return.
Now, four, three, two... one!'

Falling into a deep trance, De'Aff rolled his head. A further puff of smoke with sparks greeted him, but they came from the fangs of his serpent, which had coiled itself around the base of the trestles. Immediately, De'Aff flung the casket wide open and put his hand inside. Then, with a flourish, he fished out the little white kitten by the scruff of its neck – looking extremely dishevelled. Clutching it at the ends of his fingers, he bowed several times in different directions towards the audience, hoping for applause. Cold-heartedly, he then stuffed the little creature back into his pocket, ignoring its mewing.

The people remained shell-shocked. A few attempted to clap, though more in relief to break the tension than in real appreciation.

'Now, ladies and gentlemen… the climax to my show!' De'Aff announced with a worsening smirk. 'Well, this time, I will demonstrate to you how a human being… yes, how an *actual person* can visit the other dimension using my phenomenal powers of wistful projection.' His gasping voice, filled with hysteria, began to slide more and more into becoming a madman's cry…

Now when he heard this, Seth, still sodden and bedraggled, became increasingly scared; in case he was press-ganged again against his wishes, he quickly slid downwards out of sight…

'Oh, yes. Yes, we do indeed have such a person… a very brave person indeed in our midst.' Fixing Katrina with a hypnotic stare, De'Aff gestured with a crooked finger, beckoning her towards him.

She backed away; her hands fluttered across her throat with fear. 'Oh no! Please… no… *No*…!'

'Oh *yes*, yes, my dear… don't worry. The Worthy One, the Master of Sight and the Supreme One of Light will help to protect you on your journey to the Alterworld. You will be safe, I promise… just like the little kitten. I shall bring you back. Trust me. For after all, I am the most powerful mystic on earth. They don't call me the Greatest Mystic, Dr De'Aff, for nothing!'

De'Aff appeared to hypnotise her. She moved towards the open casket like a zombie. She climbed in, trance-like. Her eyes, though wide open, were disturbingly stark with a vacant look.

Alarmed for her safety, Chance tried to rush into the ring, but Costello held him back, whispering him to wait. Everyone under the tent held his breath.

'Don't worry, my dear. Relax… *relax*.' De'Aff's sinister voice washed over her as she lay down and closed her eyes. 'So that you won't be lonely on your journey, I shall give you something full-blooded and alive for company. I shall lend you my precious Delia to accompany you. So therefore please, keep dead still, my dear, and you will come to no harm.'

Without a further word, he unravelled the body of the coiled serpent, gave it a kiss on the neck and thrust it into the casket besides the petrified girl, and then firmly slammed the lid shut.

Screams rang out as the crowd protested in vain. They sprang out of their seats. Roland leapt to his feet in helpless anger, shaking his fist. Henry started to rush to her aid when Barnard flung out an arm to prevent him. 'Oh my God,' protested Chance. 'The evil devil is trying to kill her!'

Then to add to the drama, De'Aff, without hesitating, pushed six swords, one by one, straight through the slits at the side of the casket. Next, he re-lit the candles adjacent to the gaps by breathing on them. The organ and drums from the band droned on in a groaning accompaniment. Boldly, the candles began to flicker. They then burst into flames, licking hungrily all around the sides of the container. Again, De'Aff's macabre chant began, but this time, with even more terrifying fervour than before:

'Acridcradaver. Acrid-cradaver.
O Master of Light and Purveyor of Sight.
Let it burn for its safe return.
Kill all of the tension…
And escort her to the other dimension!'

Smoke billowed out of his mouth as he blew at the container fanning the flames. Simultaneously, he wafted his arms upwards, stretching towards the top of the tent and high beyond it, as though in silent prayer.

Shouts of terror broke out from the startled crowd as the casket containing Katrina and the serpent broke away from the trestles. It rose steadily upwards into the air, as if carried by currents of hot vapour from the fire below. There it hung, suspended ten feet into the air for several minutes surrounded by a blanket of acrid smoke.

'You can't fool us,' whispered Tim, pretending he wasn't a bit scared. 'It's held up by invisible wires; it's a well-known trick. I've read about it in my circus-training manual for wannabe's!'

'Oh, do shut up, Tim!' gasped Lotte. She slid down into her jacket to hide her eyes.

Roland nodded miserably. He was pretending to pick

invisible bits of hair from his clothes, nervously wishing that he was somewhere else – but there, right at that very moment witnessing all this.

'*Acridcradaver... O Master of Might, levitate us to greater heights... Acrid...*' the garbled chant continued.

Then the casket slowly descended as the smoke and fire petered out. It fell with a crash back onto the trestles.

'*Levitation my foot!*' shouted Chance as he and Henry knocked Barnard forcibly aside and rushed into the ring.

In great panic, Henry pulled out the swords, which were now alight. And he then hurled them to the ground and stamped on them. Without waiting, Chance immediately prised opened the casket, searching frantically for Katrina. Seeing the terrified look on his face, Henry joined in. To their absolute horror, there was simply no sign of the girl. They tapped the sides and the bottom of the container with their bare knuckles in case there was a false panel. But alas, to their utter dismay, there was none. For all they found was the bearded serpent coiled up inside like a length of rope, stupefied and licking its lips.

When he saw what they were doing, De'Aff leapt towards them and savagely hurled Chance aside with a murderous glare. He quickly scooped up his beloved pet serpent into his arms and shrieked,

'*I'll get you for this... I'll ki... kill you for ruining my act, you... you interfering busybody!*' His body jerked uncontrollably. His features contorted, totally consumed by an indescribable loathing that had been smouldering for some time. '*You pious nobody of a joker! You think that in the Kingdoms you've got special gifts and that you're untouchable. Well, we've been keeping an eye on... on you...*'

De'aff gulped and swallowed his words, as if he had revealed too much.

Apoplectic with rage, steam started to rise from the top of his skull. He slammed down the lid of the casket, still ranting.

'*You and your clever snooping friends will pay dearly for this! You think you're so brilliant, think you're so funny.*' He spat out vehemently. Foaming saliva dripped down his beard.

'You think you can win everyone over and be loved by the people – you stupid clown of a fool,' he spluttered and spat. 'Nobody, I warn you... *no one* in his right mind dares tangle with me! Just wait and see!' Swaggering aggressively and swearing portentously, he screamed, '*I put a curse of death upon you all!*' choking with hysteria.

After aiming a kick at Henry's leg, he snatched up his hat from the side of the ring, wrapped his pet serpent around his neck like a long scarf and stormed out...

In that instant, Chance signalled to Costello and Grimbo, who were cringing with fear in the wings, and told them what had happened in the ring. 'You should have torn off that horrible mask off that evil face,' Grimbo said, 'when you had the chance.' He added that he was certain that De'Aff was the phantom of the circus, but now it was too late to prove it.

'Wait, you lot. Now, stop and *listen*! Katrina's gone *missing* – the young lass didn't get back in time!' wailed Henry, distraught, as the reality of what had happened a few minutes ago sunk in.

Gasps of horror echoed throughout the big top. Lotte held on to Tim and stifled a tear. Roland was thunderstruck as the dreadful news sunk home. Shock and fear hung over the entire place. Young children started to cry. Alarmed parents did their best to comfort them. People started to rush out, dazed by the terrifying events that had just been played out in front of them.

'How quickly in life, laughter suddenly changes to fear and sadness,' commented Chance cryptically. Because, one moment, he was happy and over the moon, then the very next moment, down in the dumps and in the depths of despair. And especially now more so, after meeting his demons.

Thankfully, Barnard immediately announced the end of the performance for the day, as the band wearily played out its dreary finale: 'The Party's Over'. 'Too true. Dead true,' added Henry flatly, too stunned to say any more. He escorted his friends out of the arena, his arm around Chance's shoulder, trying to console him. Chance seemed inconsolable. Devastated and demoralised. And sadly, for the two of them, there seemed at that moment… no way back.

Chapter 40

B.C.D.

IT DID NOT TAKE them long to push their way through the silent and sullen crowd. Although still dazed, Roland, Lotte and Tim hurried to seek out Chance and Henry, who were waiting outside, looking white and shaken.

'Costello and Grimbo have rushed off to find Willy and Midgy so that they can all join in the search for Katrina,' said Henry, still glum.

'Hang on. What do you mean?' asked Roland, completely thrown with what was just said. 'I thought, in there – she'd copped it, good and proper...'

'Sure, you may be right. But Grimbo told us that when Ziggarini last year performed a similar trick of sawing her in half in a sealed box at a show in Dublin, she later turned up safe and sound all in one piece – under a bed in her trailer,' explained Chance.

'It's a well-known trick by stage illusionists that had

been performed hundreds of times throughout the world,' added Henry, trying to remain positive.

'Ah, I bet it's through a false panel, via a trapdoor,' piped up Tim, as if he knew all about it. 'It's in one of my trick-of-the-eyes manuals for would-be conjurers.' Irritated by his showing off, Lotte gave him a sharp nudge in the side.

'Well, I dearly hope so, for her sake,' said Roland sceptically.

As they wheeled away from the big top, between the candyfloss stall and Madam Gloops' tent of stinging reptiles and electric fish, they immediately bumped into Grimbo and Costello with Willy in tow. They seemed out of breath and agitated.

Willy was the first to blurt out, 'We've just run back from Midgy's trailer. He's not answering the door. We think it's locked from the inside.'

Lotte glanced towards Chance and muttered hopefully, 'Perhaps he's having a good rest after all those energetic acrobatics in the ring.'

'Yeah, that's probably what's happened,' commented Chance reassuringly. But his eyes looked pained and quizzical, as though he was uncertain. 'Come on. Let's all go and have a proper look...'

Midgy's caravan, painted ice blue, was smaller than the rest. It had a bright yellow door with the door handle one foot off the top of the two wooden steps that leant against it. The keyhole and letterbox were also low down to allow the dwarf easy access. Without delay, Roland banged on the door and tried to turn the handle. The door was firmly locked. Henry kicked the foot of it several times as hard as he could, whilst Grimbo tried to peer in through the roller blinds which obscured the window.

Willy pushed them roughly aside, then stuck his mouth to the letterbox and yelled Midgy by name. 'Mid-g-y... Midge, old pal, can you hear me? I bet he's fallen asleep in the back room like he's done many times before,' suggested Willy. 'Midgy! Where are you?' he yelled again.

'Hang on – not so loud. You'll scare him to death!' cautioned Costello, raising a hand to his lips.

Some minutes passed, but there was no reply. 'Something's wrong,' said Roland anxiously. 'We'll have to knock the door down. There's nothing else for it...'

And so, Chance told them to stand well back. He ran at the door with the flat of his hands and hit it deftly with a flick of his wrists – recalling the technique of minimum force for maximum impact that Hoopy, the Aussie kangaroo, had taught him at the waxworks. The door flew off its hinges. Its locks burst to smithereens as though a stick of dynamite had hit it. Before the dust had settled, Willy was the first to rush in to look for his little friend. Grimbo and Costello followed closely behind.

Chance and Henry hovered by the gaping hole where the front door used to be. They tried to switch on the main light on the inside of the doorframe... But nothing happened. It seemed that a lightbulb had blown.

In the gloom at the end of the cabin, they were surprised to see a small portable television set flickering on and off. Facing it, but with his back to them, was the small figure of Midgy sitting in a chair in his dressing gown. He looked sound asleep, for he was oblivious to the visitors. Tearing up to him, Willy exclaimed with relief, 'There, I told you so. He often dozes off like this after a show! Hey, Midge, me old pal!' shouted Willy into the dwarf's ear. He shook Midgy's shoulder. The still figure of Midgy slipped and slumped sideways in the chair. Willy spun the chair round to face them. They gasped with sheer horror. 'Oh, my gawd…!' uttered Willy. '…He's… he's… Poor tiny Midgy's *dead!*'

The words ended in a hysterical scream which echoed eerily around the cabin of the caravan.

Straight away, Roland wisely stopped Tim and Lotte from entering the place and seeing the grotesque sight. The dwarf's lifeless face was ashen grey. His grease paint had been half-removed as though he had been interrupted suddenly, unawares. His eyes, still open, were glazed over with a look of terror. Slack-jawed, it revealed his tongue which was half sticking out.

Willy touched Midgy's cheek affectionately. It felt icy cold to the touch. The movement disturbed his little round head, which suddenly fell to one side. Then it slumped towards his chest, totally unsupported. Tactfully, he closed his friend's eyes with the tips of his finger and thumb.

'What on earth's happened?' Grimbo asked Costello incredulously. 'Who'd want to kill a helpless little bloke like that who had spent his life trying to make others happy?'

'Don't know… looks as if he'd been frightened to death by something terrifying,' offered Willy, his voice breaking with emotion.

Henry nodded at Roland, who looked stunned like the rest of them. Chance gulped loudly and swallowed hard as his chest banged noisily out of control. A sudden and frightening thought had crossed his mind. He immediately remembered Cecil-the-Thin's warning about the sound of a phantom violin. *When he heard it again* – as he had in the ring – *it would mean certain death*. And now it was all happening… thick and fast. With a shiver, he shook his head, for the truth was getting too close for comfort now…

Dragging his feet, Chance walked slowly and deliberately around the cabin, searching. A narrow door led from the end of it. Clenched fists at the ready, he cautiously pushed it open. It was a small dressing room. The others followed him through. It took a minute or so for their eyes to adjust to the dimly lit room. As their eyes looked in front of them towards the large vanity mirror, which was stuck on the wall above a narrow dressing table, they got a shock of their lives.

For scrawled in blood-red face-paint across the width of it, was a series of large letters which spelt "B.C.D.". Next to it were the words "OR-A-CODEX-LO-PAEDIAC".

'What the blazes is that!' uttered Grimbo and Willy together. 'What does it all mean?' They all looked at each other questioningly, worry compounding the thickening mystery.

'Perhaps it's a sinister message from the killer,' commented Henry. His mouth went dry as he tried to break the awful silence.

'Hang on. I think you're mistaken,' said Chance, as he immediately recognised the reference to an ancient manuscript, *The Oraco Dex Lo Paediac*, that he had come across in Mr Goodall's study with Zoot four days ago.

'Wait a minute,' said Henry, 'surely that middle bit – "*Codex*". Doesn't it mean an authentic manuscript, like the one we came across before at the house?'

Chance gave Henry a silent glare and put a finger to his lips, hoping that the others did not notice. He wanted to keep secret the significance of that rare text which told of the legend and the riddle, and now of his quest and his journey because of it. He then strode up to the mirror and pointed with his finger. 'Look. These letters are slurred all over the place, and then fading to a scrawl. I'm sure it's from Midgy under duress and his wanting to give us a clue as to the killer or killers. Now... *B*... *C*... *D*... mm... now, I wonder?'

Grimbo looked more closely. 'I believe you are right. It looks more like Midgy's writing. But what on earth does B.C.D. mean?'

Chance shrugged his shoulders, giving a vacant look.

'I'd better go and tell Barnard what's happened here, so that he can contact the police,' Willy offered. Under the strain, he started to withdraw wanting to do something practical in the circumstances. With a leaden heart, tears began to well up in his eyes. He snorted and sniffed and dragged the back of his hand across his nose, trying to maintain a tough man's appearance.

Protectively, Roland quickly ushered the children back towards the safety of his parked taxi, to be met by their rapturous dog. On the way, Roland explained to them what had happened, sensibly missing out the gory details. Then with gathering anxiety, they decided to wait in the car park for Chance and Henry to return.

Tim and Lotte just could not believe what they had just experienced in a matter of hours. One moment, they were laughing without a care in the world about their adventure with their newly found friends. Then, the very next moment, they were running scared due to the terrible events that started to unfold around their ears. However, little did they realise what they had really let themselves in for these last twenty-four hours. Perhaps if they had known, they might have chosen to go to Mrs Chivers's boring old school camp instead...

Chapter 41

THE CARAVAN OF DEATH

Detective Inspector Geoff Bollins had just completed his report on the fracas at Old Handover Street that morning, when he was called out to investigate an incident at Barnard and Barnard's Circus.

'If anyone else mentions another thing about *clowns*, I'll dump 'em in the flippin' Thames!' he barked, exploding at the desk sergeant as he made his way out of the station. He had woken up with a throbbing headache. His temper was on a short fuse. 'I've had it up to here!' he griped with increasing irritation, as his hand fluttered like a trapped butterfly under his chin.

With Detective Sergeant Rob Willingstone close on his heels, they soon reached Barnard's in no time at all in a fast squad car.

A stern-faced Marcus Barnard greeted them, wringing his hands, his leather bullwhip clenched tightly under his arm. 'Oh, thank heavens you're here, Inspector. We really don't know what's going on here. People suddenly disappearing. Animals vanishing into thin air. Performers running away. Acts cancelling right left and centre. And now Midgy, our little clown... murdered – dead!'

'Okay, sir. Don't worry. Now, please lead the way to the... er... *Caravan of Death*,' quipped DS Willingstone thoughtlessly. Murderously, DI Bollins glared at his colleague at the lack of tact, his headache worsening by the second.

At the crime scene, they came face to face with Costello, Willy and Grimbo, who were quietly whispering animatedly amongst themselves. Palpable anxiety filled the air.

Just inside the cabin of the caravan with their backs to the wall, Chance and Henry stood in silence, keeping their thoughts to themselves. But when they were asked how the front door was kicked in, Chance was the first to own up, explaining that it was locked and jammed securely from the inside.

Not long afterwards, Barnard excused himself, saying that he couldn't stand the sight of violence. 'You know where to find me,' he said curtly as he left them staring at the mess inside.

Ponderously, the officers crept round slowly, circling the chair. Using a gloved hand they prodded the lifeless body. 'Yeah, Gov. The little fella's dead all right. Dead as a blinkin' dodo! Looks to me he's snuffed it with sheer fright. Must have seen something dead horrible!' snorted the DS aloud.

'Mm, don't like this one bit, Sergeant,' continued DI Bollins under his breath. Slowly and carefully, he withdrew his hand from Midgy's sleeve and let the dwarf's hand drop leadenly to the side.

In stony silence, Costello and the others looked on, as the officers stared whilst examining the letters scrawled in grease paint on the dressing room mirror.

Just then, a tall young man, with short, dark, curly hair knocked on the door, which was hanging forlornly off its hinges. The visitor was fresh-faced, thin and gangly. Sporting a short, neat goatee beard and dark owlish glasses, it made him look older than he really was at nineteen. Over an ill-fitting sports jacket, he wore a thin waterproof anorak. Like an ungainly, overgrown bird out of its natural habitat, he hovered under the doorframe, hanging on to the underside with his hand. Because of his height and the low doorway, he was forced to duck his head, stooping his back. 'Hi! Hello. Can I come in, gentlemen?' the visitor asked confidently, stepping over the threshold.

'*You're already in!*' growled the DI with an unwelcome blast. 'Now, who the blazes are you? And what do you want!'

'Rossiter – Nick Rossiter, Inspector... *Chronicle and Times.*' He flashed his Press identity badge in the air, which could have been a bus pass for all the attention it was given.

'*Detective Sergeant!* Get the blasted Press out of 'ere!' bawled DI Bollins angrily, about to blow a blood vessel. 'How the devil did *he* get past security? I thought we threw a cordon around the site, and specifically imposed a Press blackout!' Searchingly he arched an eyebrow at the detective sergeant for assurance. The latter shrank back, nodding assiduously.

'Give us a break, Inspector. *Please*. It's my first job. I won't get in the way. Honest. God's truth. Just a couple of minutes… please – I swear it. There are no other reporters on site. I just happened to be reviewing the acts for the paper.' There was incredulity on the face of the CID as he glared back at the young reporter, whereas Chance and Henry just stared at him curiously.

'I mean, I saw the whole performance. You know, Inspector – there were some really, strange goings-on in there. Maybe I can help. You know, *exact* descriptions…'

He tapped the top of his camera encouragingly, which was slung around his neck, and winked, hinting broadly. 'You know, possible eyewitness accounts and so on, in case the circus lot won't help… they often look after their own, you know.' He proffered his hand invitingly. The officers chose to ignore the gesture. Costello threw the reporter a hostile look.

Pulling out a small notepad, Nick Rossiter quickly jotted down the letters scrawled on the mirror before anyone could stop him. ' "B.C.D. OR-A-CODEX-LO-PAEDIAC?" Mm… well, well. Now, that is very *interesting*,' he murmured under his breath. He scratched his head behind his ear with the end of his pen thoughtfully. The last group of letters somehow struck a chord in a distant part of his subconscious. Going over the letters silently and methodically in his mind, they seemed somewhat familiar. He couldn't quite place them from where, or when, he had heard of them before. After chewing it over, he decided to keep it to himself.

'Any theories, Inspector?' he asked, breaking the momentary silence. 'And how come the assailant got out of here, if it was jammed and bolted from the inside?' His eyes rested on the splintered door, whose locks had been shattered as though a bomb had hit it. Unable to control his avid curiosity, he then bent down and stared at the floor, about to point out something else that intrigued him. 'Well, now, what are those long, dirty marks streaking across the room towards the body?' he asked.

'And don't you dare touch a thing, young fella, or you'll be out on your ear, before you can say dead and buried!' Contemptuously, DI Bollins glared at him as he and his colleague began to take a closer look around the caravan. But like a magnet, their eyes kept being drawn back to the mysterious letters in blood-red so gruesomely etched on the mirror.

'Do you think it's a joke, Inspector? Er, this, er... B... C... D, and ORACO... DEXLO... thingy-me-what's-it, now?' asked the reporter.

'A sick load of mumbo-jumbo, if it is,' replied the DI grimly. He tightened his lips in disgust as the dreadful situation grew and soured his mouth.

Meanwhile, Chance, exchanging furtive looks with Henry, kept his theories close to his chest.

As DS Rob Willingstone continued his search around the cabin inch by inch, he almost tripped over Midgy's outstretched leg. Instinctively he looked down, his eyes skimming the floor behind the dwarf's feet.

'Hey, Gov. what's this?' From under Midgy's chair, he pulled out a small packet. As a precaution, after giving it a gentle rattle next to his ear, he opened it, peeling off the brown outer wrapping.

'What the...?' gasped the DS, taken aback. 'Look, Gov.

It looks like a box of some sort.' He indicated graphically with his finger, squaring the air as though taking part in a game of charades.

'Now, what on earth is this…? Cor! It smells like nothing on earth!' added the DS.

The others stood on tiptoes and arched forwards. But they soon quickly retracted their faces, repelled by a smell of decay.

'Urgh… look at this, Gov. It stinks to high heaven.' DS Willingstone gagged, with his hand over his mouth. He thrust the package under the nose of his boss, who was so appalled that he backed into Midgy's body. As they collided, Midgy's head suddenly lurched sideways. A dull thud was heard as something fell from the packet like a stone to the floor.

'What the devil was that!' yelled the DI as he whipped round accusingly at no one in particular.

'Not me, Gov. Honest,' retorted DS Willingstone. Thrusting his open hands in front of him, he retreated.

They both stared at the floor next to Midgy's chair leg.

'My god, it's a dead animal!' screamed the DS, shrinking back with fear.

Pretending to be unruffled, the inspector poked at it with the end of his foot, gingerly turning it over. It was a body of a dead bird, frozen and curled up in a ball.

Before anyone could stop him, Nick stooped down on his knees to examine it closely. 'Well, I never! This really is a strange-looking creature. It looks a bit like a thrush, but I don't think it's from this country. Now, I wonder if—'

From the back, leaning against a doorjamb to the bathroom, Chance finally broke his self-imposed silence.

Stretching forwards on his knees, he said revealingly, 'I think it's a type of exotic mockingbird, like the South American catbird family. I can tell by its long tail and those distinctive dark spots under its belly. They have something similar in the Galapagos Islands just off the coast of Ecuador...'

'Well, well, well, the Oracle has finally spoken!' snarled DI Bollins, increasingly irritated with all the interference on this, his latest murder inquiry. It had inevitably tipped him over the edge. So much so that he, on the slightest provocation, was ready to murder the next person who interfered, or offered another clever opinion...

'Okay, *Mister Know-It-All.* How come that this particular species from foreign parts happens to be lying conveniently right here, slap under our noses, then? Flown in by jet via Heathrow all the way from the New World, did it?' Sneeringly he mocked, as though the very mention of the word "mockingbird" had set off a train of thought that had begun to run away with him.

To defuse a possible fight, Henry immediately joined in to support his friend. 'For what it's worth, I think it's an old stuffed specimen, probably stolen from the London Metropolitan Zoo Museum.'

'Ah, *now* we have... *the veritable learned Sherlock Holmes Esquire in another guise*, I presume? Offering a probable hypothesis, have we now!' carped DS Willingstone, patronisingly.

Just then, Grimbo and Willy told them all to calm down. 'Heated arguments and conflicting rivalries will not get us anywhere in the search for the truth about the death of our friend Midgy,' they said whilst trying to impress upon them the real priorities. Costello nodded quietly in the background.

The detective sergeant swallowed and gulped. Then he straightened his tie, wriggling his bull-like neck awkwardly. 'Yeah. I suppose you're right. Let's cool it.' Guardedly, he shook his head, turning to his boss. 'You know, I don't like this, Gov. Don't like this one bit… Firstly, we've got a little clown's dead body on our hands… Secondly, a weird message daubed on the mirror. Next, we now find a foreign stuffed bird mocking at us!' He mopped his brow to dry the sweat that started to run over his eyes. 'And I tell you what, Gov, it's getting weirder by the minute!'

'Ah. Could it be the killer's calling card, baiting you with some gruesome but tantalising clues to entrap you?' volunteered Nick hopefully. 'Murderers often do this, you know, to throw you off the scent. It's happened many times before to test how clever you police are. Often, their warped, evil minds enjoy toying with you. It's a perverse and sinister game of cat and mouse to them!'

He skirted quietly around the dwarf's body, staring at it as though willing it back to life to act as witness. 'Again, also just look at those dirty marks embedded along the floor from the door to the victim. Could something greasy and slimy have recently slithered along there?'

They glowered at him poisonously, but their eyes cast downwards nevertheless to where he was pointing with the barrel of his pen. 'You've been watching too many Hollywood movies, my young whippersnapper!' growled DI Bollins.

'Sorry, Inspector. Just trying to help.' Nick shrugged apologetically and held up his hands in a conciliatory gesture.

Whilst the officers were in the middle of taking statements from Chance, Henry and the others, Willy was startled to see the young reporter push his face close up to that of the dead dwarf, as though to smell his breath. Before anyone could prevent him, Nick had swiftly prised open Midgy's lolling mouth with the tip of his pen. He pulled out a tightly rolled-up piece of paper. 'Ah ha. Now, what is this?' he announced triumphantly.

'*Evidence!* That's what it is. Vital, forensic police evidence!' exploded the Detective Sergeant, bristling with anger. In the same breath, he shot forwards and snatched the piece of paper from Nick's hand.

'Hey, I was… I was only just going to…' Nick protested. 'It's got writing or something on it…'

'What is it? What's in it?' asked Willy and Henry together.

DS Willingstone unrolled the piece of paper and studied it quietly for a minute, shielding it from prying eyes with his body. With considerable puzzlement, he turned the paper upside down and back to front, as if dissatisfied with what he saw.

'What's the matter, Sergeant? Something wrong?' asked his superior. He tried to peep over the other one's shoulder.

The DS appeared to hesitate, seemingly not quite sure of his facts. 'Erm… I can't quite fathom it, Gov. There's a load of gibberish written down here.' He rustled the piece of paper against the flat of his thigh, trying to unroll it at the same time, but the edges kept curling up again hopelessly. Scratching his head, he studied it again and again, and admitted, 'Doesn't make sense. I still stick to what I originally suggested... the deceased snuffed it by seeing something dead horrible. ...Died of fright. I'll still bet my life on it, Gov! It's more than likely that this scrunched-up bit of paper was stuffed down his throat to finish the poor devil off... and nothing to do with these fancy words written on it, I reckon.'

'That's enough wild speculation for the moment, Detective Sergeant! Let's leave *that* to the pathologist and the autopsy, shall we? Just read what's written down there; *if* you please, Sergeant!' The rebuke came sharp and fast with the DI scowling impatiently.

Rapidly going a vivid shade of raspberry pink, DS Rob Willingstone stood over Midgy's corpse and started to read out aloud, initially hesitantly, whilst Chance, Nick and the others looked on expectantly...

'*Oh, mocking curse, mocking curse, try not to catch me.*
Too late, you're so stupid, attempting to flee.
Per Chance you're so clever, always you think,
So desperate, not falter – return from the brink.

'*With oceans of treasure, so vast and so old,*
Temptation try hard to float all of its gold.
But, by Chance, you control the earth and the seas,
There are dangers that court you with fatal disease.

'*Though forbidden to danger, the Tree of All Life:*
All you will find is curse... death and strife.
Kill all your good laughter; it'll make your spine curl.
A watery grave awaits you to part from this world.

'Dare chase all life's dreams – a trail out of bounds.
Like fools follow the end, its death down to clowns!
Poke out all their lights that came quite by Chance,
Wipe out all the joy without conscience glance.

'Oh, mocking fool, mocking fool, why try to catch me,
You're too late – you're too feeble – desperate to flee.

'Signed... a... f... iend...'

But when they restudied the signatory, they noticed that the letter 'r', after the 'f' had been inadvertently or deliberately smudged out by a splurge of saliva – which only added to the macabre tone of the verse.

By the time the DS had finished reading, a stunned silence greeted him.

Henry was the first to say something. 'You know, is *he...* poking fun at us?' His voice wavered badly.

'I'm afraid it's much more sinister than that, Henry,' replied Chance gravely. 'He's goading us to follow... He's thrown down the gauntlet.' Chance grabbed a stool to sit down. He loosened his collar nervously to grab some air.

Concerned, Willy went over to him and asked softly, 'Is it a trap of some sort?'

Chance's weary nod said it all.

He put a hand on Chance's shoulder. 'Look, my friend, I think whosoever did this is trying to lure you. It's no coincidence that you've been mentioned by name several times. Though, to be honest, the rest of the message is a mystery to me. But whatever it is, or whatever it isn't, it sounds absolutely terrifying and extremely dangerous.'

On seeing the baffled looks from the two officers, Henry hurriedly tried to explain the succession of threats they both had endured, when trying to track down the unexplained things that had befallen them since they began this journey. However, over certain frightening details, Henry kept them to himself.

'Do you think it's the work of that mysterious phantom of the circus?' asked Grimbo. 'And I wonder if that sinister De'Aff bloke has got something to do with it?'

'I really don't know. It's now up to the police,' said Chance. He wiped his forehead with the back of his sleeve, breathing hard. He could hear his heartbeat rising loudly and wondered if the others could too. Before Chance had time to say any more, Nick Rossiter instantly latched on to what he had overheard, grilling them about the Phantom and De'Aff. And so, between them, Willy and Grimbo then described all the terrible incidents that had happened at the circus the last few weeks, soon after a character called Dr Slatane De'Aff had appeared on the scene. And then, soon afterwards, there had been sinister messages scrawled in the ring from someone claiming to be a phantom haunting the place. At the same time, performers suddenly disappeared without explanation – like that of Ziggarini. Animals kidnapped under mysterious circumstances. The trapeze and high-wire tampered with during the night. Near-fatal accidents that had taken place without warning, such as Bonzo smashing his arm and back, Mimi falling off the wire rupturing herself, and so on, and so on…

Meanwhile, Nick was furiously making notes, trying not to miss a thing, whilst at the same time quizzing them for extra details, however minute.

From the wall next to the window, Costello looked on grimly. He hadn't said much since the police had arrived on the scene. He appeared shell-shocked, like the rest of them.

After a minute or so, DS Willingstone piped up. 'You know, I really don't like this, Gov, one bit. Something 'ere smells dead evil and it stinks!' With heavy feet, he ambled across the floor of the caravan towards his boss. He handed over the rolled-up piece of paper extracted from Midgy's mouth and the package containing the stuffed mockingbird.

In deep thought, Nick tapped his pen against his bottom teeth and muttered aloud, 'Mm. I wonder... if that De'Aff's "Burning Casket" trick this afternoon and that missing girl has got anything to do with all this...?'

'Ah ha... seems we have a prime suspect in this De'Aff character!' suggested the DS smugly.

'Hold on. Wait a minute, Detective Sergeant,' interrupted the inspector. 'You can't just jump to conclusions – just like that...' He snapped his fingers noisily in the air. 'You just can't say that this phantom thingy-me-bob and this, what's-er-name, De-ath fellow are one of the same. From my experience, it's too obvious for words.'

He was immediately corrected that it was 'De'Aff', and not 'De-ath', even though it sounded like the same to the uninitiated.

'And do you mean to say that a girl performer *actually* vanished into thin air during this afternoon's performance?' asked the DI. His eyes and his ears grew bigger at each revelation.

'Oh crumbs, that's reminds us. We were on our way

to search for young Katrina,' said Grimbo with a sudden attack of guilt, 'when we came upon poor Midgy! Come on, Willy, let's look for Katrina. We can start with her caravan. Costello, you'd better see if that creature De'Aff has returned to his trailer. But something tells me, he's hoofed it pretty sharpish!'

The three of them brushed past the officers and, jumping down the steps, they hurriedly left the Caravan of Death.

'Oi, I nearly forgot, has anyone got a good description of this De'Aff character...?' asked DI Bollins, almost as an afterthought.

But it was too late: Costello and his friends were out of earshot.

Suddenly without thinking, Nick shot his hand into the air, forgetting at that instance that he had left school some years ago. 'Oh, I have. *I have*. I almost forgot,' he blurted out, all excited. 'I took a photo of his act with the levitating casket and that so-called "Other Dimension" thingy-me-jig this afternoon. It's in my instant polaroid camera,' Nick said brightly.

They all spun round to stare at him, both astonished and yet with rising hopes, all at once. Nick pressed a red button under his camera. After a minute or so, a square photograph slid out with a whirrh and a swish. Extremely pleased with himself, he handed it over to DI Bollins with a flourish.

A minute passed, when the DI suddenly choked and exploded. 'Hey... Oi... what's this then? You're having me on?' A reddening started to spread around his neck, seeping downwards like fire as he stormed towards Nick. He thrust the photo angrily in front of him. For in the middle of the picture, it was half-blank. The image of a casket came out all right, with that of young Katrina stepping into it. But where Slatane De'Aff was supposed to be standing, there was nothing there except for a thin red outline of a figure, but nothing more. This knocked them for six. Nick was staggered. He turned the picture upside down, examined it back to front and even rubbed it with his finger. It made no difference. The actual detailed image of the mysterious Dr De'Aff was missing; only a hazy silhouette remained.

'I... I... don't understand it,' spluttered Nick, perplexity etched all over his face like a rash. He pressed the red release button for the rest of the film. One by one, they came out. But this time, the photos were *completely* blank, save for a shimmering red glow around the ghostly shape of where De'Aff was supposed to be standing. Nick became speechless. He spread his hands helplessly in front of him.

As DI Bollins shook his head in annoyance and in frustration, Chance and Henry rapidly made their excuses to leave, saying that they had friends waiting for them in the car park.

'You'd better leave details of your whereabouts with the police on duty outside,' growled the DI tersely. He pressed his fist against his temple; his headache was banging away like a brass band inside his skull. He started to drum his fingers against the side of his head thoughtfully. For a fleeting moment or so, he thought that he had seen someone looking like Chance before. He shook his head and dismissed it abruptly, for he was getting extremely annoyed with himself for getting clowns and harlequins on the brain.

He began to mull things over again, when suddenly his thoughts were rudely interrupted by Nick jostling past him. He was the last to announce that he was leaving. 'See you around, gentlemen,' he said. 'Got to get back to the paper. You know where to find me. We're one of the last newspapers left now in Fleet Street.'

The DI was glad to have a bit of peace to collect his thoughts. He took the chance to grab a chair to get off his feet. Firstly, it was bank robbers, dressed like clowns, in the West End that morning. And now it was a macabre murder of a dwarf in a circus. Then he remembered that there was a report of a performer from the same circus called Ziggarini missing without trace some weeks ago.

And just now, in all probability, a young artiste named Katrina apparently had just simply vanished in the middle of the ring. On top of all this, there were reports of a ghostly phantom haunting the circus. Not only that, but there was the sudden appearance of a strange and sinister character, who called himself Dr De'Aff, who reputedly scared the living daylights of all he came across. And then by coincidence, *both these two* had vanished into thin air all of a sudden this very afternoon.

But if that wasn't enough, there were now eerie and very strange signs left at the scene of the murder: peculiar letters scrawled on the mirror, a dead stuffed bird and a strange poem which sounded as if it came from a madman. And to crown it all, now-haunted photographs that failed to come out. In thirty years in the force, Detective Inspector Bollins had never come across something as mystifying or as unbelievable as this.

In the meantime, the DS methodically continued his

search for clues at the scene of the crime now that the caravan was empty; except, of course, for the poor, sad little corpse of a dwarf.

∗∗

Five minutes later, Grimbo and Willy had returned, completely out of breath from running. Willy banged loudly on the side of Midgy's trailer, shaking the panels. 'Hey, steady on,' cautioned Grimbo. 'You're making enough noise to wake the dead!' Immediately, he clapped his fingers over his mouth, saying, 'Sorry, Willy, I didn't mean it,' for he noticed tears welling up in his eyes.

On hearing the racket, DS Willingstone stuck his head out around the gap of the door enquiringly.

'Officer, as we thought, Miss Katrina's trailer is completely empty. She's definitely gone missing. You see, after the burning casket act with De'Aff, she would normally reappear in her trailer from a secret passage, long before the crowds could spot her,' said Grimbo.

'Okay… you'd better give me a description of this De'Aff character then,' requested the DS, sounding very weary. 'Okay. Let me write this down… *has a black cape, black wide brim hat, dark reflective glasses*… His eyes – now let me get this straight…' He scribbled rapidly into a notebook.

'Mm… you say you've never seen his eyes… Pardon, do you mean to say, you think he hasn't got any?' DS Willingstone stared down his nose, fixed firstly at Grimbo, then at Willy. 'A mask…?' he then asked. His face then crumpled, extremely perplexed at his own question, only to receive nods of affirmation to it in return.

'I see,' drawled the DS, scratching his chin with the edge of his notepad, 'you, sir, also think that the subject in question may not have *even* a mouth or a nose. Now, gentlemen, let's go over this again. You say... *the subject... in... question... had just... er... a gash in the middle of his face, where the, er... sound came out...'*

He had a job writing this down, hoping others in the force – particularly his superiors – would believe what he was now hearing and now recording – verbatim...

A moment later, Costello had joined them at the foot of the steps to confirm that De'Aff's trailer was also found to be deserted and locked up.

DS Willingstone squatted down at the top of the stairs trying to take it all in. Using his notes, he fanned his face as he drew breath. He sighed deeply, as though trying to get his head around something, which was not quite in the usual run of things, particularly in his training manual, which he had kept from his days as a young raw recruit at police college. Glancing up at Willy, he continued to write, now furiously. 'Ah, yes. I've now got a good description of this person's pet serpent with three forked tongues... called, let me see if I've got this right... D-e-l-i-a... *Delia.* Well, now that's a nice name for a—'

'Detective Sergeant!' bawled the DI from inside the caravan. 'Stop digressing. We have much work to do!'

The DS went a bright shade of purple and buried his nose back into his notes. Then immediately, he started to read back what he had written.

'Erm. Well sirs, you say... *that a very tall person, dressed from top to toe in black with no face worth talking about – carrying a seven-foot-long, hairy serpent draped around his neck... absconded from the circus – under suspicious circumstances... disguised. And perhaps, using public transport... or... perhaps even... a... broomstick... Ha... Ha!'*

Carried away, he had started to add the last few words for a laugh. But then, he thought better of it – fearing that his boss might not have a sense of humour. And so, he crossed it out with a thick line through it.

'Well, now... sirs, the police forces around the country shouldn't have much trouble identifying the subject when trying to apprehend him, given all these brilliant eyewitness descriptions,' he said facetiously. 'Oh, before I forget, we're really indebted for your time, gentlemen.' Eventually, DS Rob Willingstone got up, stretched his body and rolled his eyes upwards. Whether it was in disbelief or in a silent prayer, it was hard to tell. He turned away abruptly to get on with the business in hand, as a team of forensic experts, disguised from their faces downwards in shiny white boiler suits – looking like astronauts landing from the moon – suddenly descended on the site to deal with poor Midgy's body.

Chapter 42

THE ORACO DEX LO PAEDIAC

B Y THE TIME NICK Rossiter drove his old blue Ford across Battersea Bridge in the direction of south of the river, the traffic had eased considerably. Dusk had barely arrived when the sun started to set over the skyline towards the west. After the day's sudden thunderstorm, the warm, sultry air promised a balmy night to come. Winding his car window right down, he soaked in the fresh breeze, which zipped past his car and cleared his head.

He was making his way home – back to the digs he shared with two other lodgers near the river. He was deep in thought. The words "Oraco Dex Lo Paediac" kept gnawing at his mind. Somewhere in the dim, but not too distant past, he had heard mention of it. Like a keen young reporter in his first job, he tried to remember every single news item, be they articles or breaking stories on TV, radio and even those from other publications.

He had just turned nineteen when he got the job at the *Chronicle and Times*. Using pure fearless charm, he talked his way into the job with the dour-faced editor Frank Thornsley, who assigned him to features. 'Get a scoop, young Rossiter, ahead of our rivals, and you've got yourself a promotion,' assured his boss.

Being a new young reporter full of fresh enthusiasm, he desperately wanted an exclusive of a story to make his name in journalism. Like many before him, he had always been a secret "closet scribbler", and one who desperately wanted to impress. Indeed, it was his stories and articles that he had penned at sixth-form college, which had persuaded the paper to take him on.

'Good, fertile imagination for fiction – perfect for journalism,' commented the personnel officer, who recommended him with tongue in cheek. *Blow to that*, thought Nick. 'Give me real-life drama, based on facts, anytime,' he vowed with determination when he landed the job. 'And to make believable, the unbelievable!' he added with enthusiastic conviction.

Out of habit, he had made meticulous notes of what he had seen at first hand at the "Caravan of Death". 'Hey! That's a brilliant news headline,' he murmured, slapping his knee. The car wobbled dangerously. But he straightened the wheel just in the nick of time to avoid a milk lorry head on.

Mm. Unusual pair, that harlequin, what's-his-name... Chance, and that toff-looking chap, he thought. 'I wonder if De Poisson was his real name. *Fishy lot...*' he mused as he stared through the windscreen. 'I'd better keep tabs on those two and follow them,' he said as an afterthought. 'I'm dead sure they're connected with this burgeoning mystery from what I heard earlier. Though I shouldn't have much trouble tracking them down. They stick out like sore thumbs.'

He tightened his lip and stroked the tip of his beard, reflecting.

His parents had retired early from teaching and moved to a small rural village just outside Norfolk. They didn't particularly like his job as a newspaper reporter but liked his sporting a beard even less. However, one thing he did learn from his father was that. '*For information, son, past or present, you can't beat the local reference library.*'

And so, he found his way to the local branch of the city reference library. He suddenly recalled that a couple of years or so ago, he saw a television documentary about an audacious theft from a bank vault in Zurich shortly after the Second World War, which had baffled international investigators for decades. The mystery deepened as it involved the death of one of the bank officials shortly afterwards who was found to be poisoned. Old masters and ancient artefacts, including valuable Russian icons and priceless ancient manuscripts dating back thousands of years, had simply vanished into thin air. It was the theft of the manuscripts that caught his eye. He was certain something phonetically sounding like *Oraco Dex Lo Paediac* was mentioned in the haul. Somehow, directly or indirectly, that perhaps held a clue to the same strange letters that he had witnessed scrawled on the mirror at the Caravan of Death, though of the other letters, 'B.C.D.', he was still in the dark.

The library reception desk was manned by a stern-looking librarian named Sidney Skillet, who seemed rather bored with his job. 'What can I do for you, young fellow?' asked Sidney Skillet gruffly, peering over the top of his bifocals.

Attempting to flatter him, Nick replied, 'I need your expert help, please.' Proceeding with a white lie, he said, 'I'm trying to trace an old news story about my late grandfather – a reporter, who was chasing some stolen works of art when he was killed in a mysterious accident. It was some time after the last world war...'

Sidney Skillet had a good filing system in his head. 'Um, ah yes. That'll be in the archive section of old newspapers. Over there, young fellow.' He directed him with a flick of his head. He pointed to a large bookcase in the third row near the window. 'Yes, that's it... shelves 45 to 49 in the Post-Second World War section.'

Immediately, Nick left the desk and strolled towards the window. Eagerly, he grabbed a pile of five enormous folders containing newspapers and articles, many of them brown with age. He placed them onto the nearest table, which was partly occupied by a studious-looking woman, who was reading some magazines in earnest. She glanced up at him curiously as he sat down, heaving a big sigh.

Nick rapidly thumbed through all the papers, one by one. It took him about thirty minutes to find out what he was looking for. In an old, faded copy of *The Telegraph Tribune* printed in 1947, he noticed a headline: "UFO Crash Mystery... Roswell, New Mexico".

Although that caught his eye, he read on. Because, on the next page of the same paper, another prominent headline captured his attention...

"*Audacious bank robbery... Zurich... major works of*

art stolen, priceless historical artefacts... Russian icons... irreplaceable ancient manuscripts – many going back thousands of years... Now vanished off the face of the earth... Bank official poisoned... Interpol called in..."

Reading the newspaper article, it was reported that amongst the collection of the manuscripts stolen was a unique copy of *The Oraco Dex Lo Paediac*. It was said that this famous manuscript of the ancient philosophers written in 299 BC held for the ancients profound and abiding wisdom of the world, not unlike the eternal Almanac of its time. Furthermore, rumour had it that only five copies existed throughout the world, some of them held by museums or universities, but seldom in private collections.

Nick suddenly also remembered that he had heard of this mystery more recently from a TV documentary made two years ago, when a valuable manuscript suddenly turned up as one of the lots in an international sale by Asherbys in New York. It had been placed for sale via a third party – an investment bank – acting for the estate of an unnamed client, who had suddenly died in dubious circumstances. The sale catalogue said that it was a rare copy of one of *The Oraco Dex Lo Paediacs* in existence. International art investigators acting on behalf of a major insurance company converged on the sale like flies. But they drew a blank as to how the owners came to have it in their possession, since there had been no trace of the whereabouts of the manuscript, or any of the other works of art that disappeared off the face of the earth following the heist in 1947.

Initially, there was a dispute over the provenance of the copy surfacing in the States at the time. Scholars and academics from around the world said it was a forgery. After arguments over the carbon dating which showed that the tiny sample from a page used in the test had at least authenticated its date, the sale proceeded. The copy was sold to an anonymous buyer, exceeding its reserve price by twenty-nine million dollars.

What puzzled Nick was how it came about that the letters "Oraco Dex Lo Paediac" came to be scrawled on the mirror in the caravan where the dwarf was murdered. Perhaps the victim had witnessed something about it, which led to his death? What was the connection, if any? *Perhaps there wasn't any...* thought Nick. Perhaps it was just a red herring, a strange coincidence and nothing more. Frankly, the more he thought about it, the more the mystery deepened.

Nick's brain was getting wound up, more and more, in amassing this strange information from the past. His excitement and curiosity escalated. To make sure that he didn't miss anything he swiftly flicked through old copies of the other papers, but returned to the original article of the '47 edition of *The Telegraph Tribune*.

What he gleaned was that:

"This ancient manuscript foretold of a legend and a riddle that was vital to the survival of the Three Kingdoms – the one of man, the other of animals and finally that of plants – and the role a Messenger of Mirth coming to unite the three. It told of three hundred thousand years ago when an asteroid collided with the earth causing devastation when all life in the kingdoms perished. Within the core of this asteroid a mysterious stone shattered into pieces: one fell into a Sacred Tree of Knowledge and another fell into a Secret Tree of Life.

It is believed that these were the vital seeds of a life force to enable life to begin again after the earth had died..."

Mesmerised, Nick read on.

Chewing thoughtfully on his ballpoint pen, Nick carefully folded up the newspaper article and placed it back in the folder but kept the report of the robbery in Zurich those decades ago, open at the edge of the table. He leant back in his chair to think. But before Nick left the library, he had an urge to steal the original copy of the article. But how could he do it surreptitiously without arousing suspicion? Then it came to him. He thought of a trick he had once seen in an old black and white movie from the '50s at the cinema. He quickly looked round at the librarian, Sidney Skillet. Fortunately, he appeared to be absorbed in a book.

Without a second thought, Nick pulled out a large tissue from his top pocket with his left hand. His right hand covered the feature in the paper with his forefinger and thumb, gripping the edge of the page in readiness. Then, pretending to sneeze, he did so violently. And as he did, he simultaneously ripped the article out of the page. The woman next to him scowled at him with visible disgust and promptly moved to the far end of the table.

Unfortunately, the force of blast from his exaggerated sneeze blew the piece of paper off the corner of the table before he could conceal it, and it flew underneath the table legs towards the heel of the frowning woman. Having a quick presence of mind, Nick deliberately – but making it look like an accident – knocked a pile of papers onto the floor.

'*Oops. Oh dear... clumsy old me!*' he murmured aloud, as he stooped under the table to sweep up the prized article that he had just torn from the paper. He stuffed it under his trouser leg and into his sock, just before his female neighbour stood on it with her shoe. '*Whew!*' he sighed to himself, wiping his nose, which was glistening with sweat. As he stood up, he swiftly scooped up the folders of papers and returned them to their shelves near the window. He pushed back his chair under the table with a squeal and bid the woman a polite '*Cheers*' with a purposeful nod.

Turning smartly on his heels, Nick left rapidly, just as Sidney Skillet looked up – but rather too late in wondering about what was going on. Then with a gleeful skip to his step, he tore out into the street. Gratefully, he jumped into his car and roared away with his tyres squealing... his brain buzzing alive with hundreds of questions that desperately needed answering.

His teeth tingled a little as if laced with ice. A tiny shiver ran down his spine. It was not because he was cold. Far from it... it was a touch of excitement that made even his beard stand on end. Nick felt that he was on the brink of an incredible story that needed unravelling. For instance, there were so many things to chew over since meeting that strange figure called Chance and his friend at the scene of the murder at the circus. Trained like all reporters, he felt that things didn't appear all what they seemed at first glance. He was left with a niggling feeling that the harlequin knew more than he admitted about the letters painted on the mirror in the caravan. And what about the other clues left there, including the smelly old bird and that peculiar verse?

And again, why did the name of that ancient manuscript reappear after all this time, and at a circus of all places?

And what was behind the furtive look that Chance made to his friend when they first saw what was daubed on the mirror? And what was the motive behind the little clown being murdered? Then finally, why B.C.D.? Was it some code to vex lateral thinkers? Was it a type of clever anagram, to tease the brain? His body trembled and shook with the anticipation of it all. And so, he just couldn't wait to find out what was out there. And to meet it head on before others beat him to it…

Given some patience and a bit of luck, all he had to do was to track those two colourful characters down – which shouldn't be too difficult: watch, follow and then wait… A scoop, he thought, was in the offing, as he recalled the challenge his editor threw down. He braced himself, ready for the intrigue of the chase…

Part VII

Everything in life is a riddle...

Chapter 43

BARE BONES OF THE MATTER

LIGHT WAS FADING FAST as Chance and Henry quickly made their way to rendezvous with Roland, Tim and Lotte. A definite coolness was in the air which made them quicken their pace. As they picked their way between the trailers, they suddenly noticed a tall, dark figure scurrying hurriedly towards Madame Gloop's tent. Anxiously, looking about him, he gripped a large, brimmed hat, tightly pulling it down to meet the upturn of his cloak which billowed around him, covering him from top to toe.

Without a second glance, Chance and Henry broke into a run. 'That's you know who. I'd recognise that evil creature De'Aff anywhere!' hissed Chance. 'Don't let the nasty devil out of our sight!'

But by the time they caught up, the figure had disappeared out of view. At the entrance to Gloop's tent with its adjoining trailer, Henry was forced to catch his breath – his body doubled over, his hands resting on his knees. And as he did, he noticed deep scuff marks along the grass, as if a foot had been dragged behind someone.

'I remember the lopsided way he walks,' said Henry, puffing like a steam train coming to a halt. 'You're not going to follow him in, are you?' he continued, extremely concerned for his friend's safety. He tugged at Chance's arm to restrain him.

'What do *you* think? It may be our only chance to catch and expose him,' replied Chance in a matter-of-fact voice, not wishing to alarm Henry. 'But I think you'd better stay here and keep a lookout.'

Henry's face fell at being left out from the final chase, though he still remained worried all the same about the dangers facing his friend. 'If you're not back in twenty minutes, shall I call the police, just in case?' he asked.

'If I'm not back in ten minutes, you'd better call an ambulance!' joked Chance with a straight face.

Now in order to get his bearings and to avoid falling into a trap, he looked up and down carefully for a way in. Then from the corner of his eye, he noticed a door painted in bright purple next to the trailer. He knocked loudly with the back of his fist. Nothing happened, so he gave the bottom of the door a sharp kick. After a minute or so the door creaked open. A gnarled old woman wearing a thick-laced shawl shuffled to face him. It was difficult to see her face for she was doubled over, leaning heavily on a stick. She looked up slowly, extending her neck like a turtle in slow motion.

'Madame Gloop?' Chance asked, holding her stare – more as a question than a greeting.

A flicker of acknowledgement flashed from her eyes, which were startlingly bright yellow. They gleamed inquisitively in the dark like a cat's, despite their being sunken into an extremely lined face. Shuffling at a snail's pace, she gestured them to follow her to a concealed, heavy canvas flap, which shielded the opening to the tent immediately next door. Raising her stick, she made a half-turn to face them. She pointed backwards over her shoulder and in a rasping voice that croaked from the back of the throat, said, 'Over there. They're waiting for you… over there…' as if she already knew beforehand that someone or something was expecting him.

Henry's eyes shot upwards with increasing anxiety. The back of his hand scraped his face, sensing sweat was about to break out.

No sooner had she spoken, Madame Gloop retreated to her trailer, scampering quickly this time like a startled rabbit into a burrow. However, just before she closed the door, she murmured softly, as though no longer interested in what actually happens to them once they were in there,

'Watch out, my dears. Do not disturb my little pet specimens and they'll do you no harm. But frighten the tiny monsters in their tanks… and they'll savage you to death with their razor-like fangs, make no mistake!' Abruptly, the door slammed shut in front of their faces.

'You still going in there? It sounds like a death trap,' said Henry edgily, now really scared for his friend. He grabbed Chance by the elbow.

'I've got to. I have no choice. *He's* in there! This time, Henry, there is no way of his escaping from us. Right now, it's a time of reckoning – head-on and a time of truth. So therefore, you'd better wait here.' Chance swallowed with a massive gulp. He clutched at his throat, preciously stroking his lucky pendant, pausing only for a moment to bolster his courage.

'Well, here goes. Hopefully, see you in a bit.' Chance pushed the draped canvas sheet aside and made his way into the large tent. It was pitch black. It took a minute or so to adjust to the darkness, which felt solid and oppressive in front of this face due to being completely disorientated. He felt as if he were floating in space, with no concept where his feet were, even though he held his arms outstretched in front of him in case he bumped into something he didn't quite bargain for.

As he made his way along the first part, which seemed like a long, unending corridor of sorts, the light gradually improved due to a glow from a series of tropical tanks lining the sides of the place. They threw out a diffused yellow glow from the sodium lighting which provided warmth for the creatures lolling inside their tanks and cages. The air was stifling with the damp, sticky heat clawing at his face. Air temperature was kept unbearably high, presumably to keep the creatures warm and alive. Chance felt blobs of sweat roll off the tip of his nose. Rising from the scaly bodies of the amphibians and other creatures there was a distinctive, but sickly smell. And when mixed with that of the sodden grass and sawdust, it made him retch somewhat, so he clamped his fingers to his nose.

Creeping along, feeling his way warily, Chance kept his eyes alert and his ears pinned back for any hint of alien sounds or unusual signs of movement. There were more banks of tanks and cages, about twenty in all to his left containing some very strange-looking creatures. They were all quite repugnant in features. They were swimming or creeping about in their containers menacingly, as though itching to burst out to create holy mayhem.

He threaded his way to the far end of the tent using his hands as a guide along the sides of the rough canvas, like a blind man tentatively feeling his way by touch and smell rather than by sight. And as he passed, he quickly glanced at some of the creatures, which seemed to stare back at him with heavy-lidded, malevolent eyes. Darting their blood-red tongues, they were dribbling and salivating hungrily, ogling at him. For he, the stranger and intruder, nicely chubby with rounded flesh (for so they thought), would make the perfect bait for their next fresh meal. Chance thought they all looked gruesome, if not frighteningly ferocious, which made him shudder all the more in his boots.

To the right, hidden by the folds of the tent with its supporting poles staking it to the ground, were three enormous reptiles. They were more like ancient water dragons or serpents from a far-off land. Over ten feet long, it was a type of species that he had never seen before. Slowly circling in the murky waters of their enormous tanks, they thrashed about with their fat, scaly bellies and squat-bowed legs – trapped and agitated. Flailing around with their massive tails and gnashing their teeth, it seemed that with one fell swipe they could kill a large, fit man stone dead, if provoked unduly.

An icy shiver rippled through him. He wondered just then how on earth the public paid good money to tickle them for fun. 'Gloop's Stinging Reptiles, indeed!' he murmured scathingly under his breath. Then, to stop his teeth from chattering, he forced his thoughts purposely back to the chase. 'Now I wonder where on earth that horrific creature De'Aff disappeared to so quickly...?' he mused, mystified. 'Or did that old woman deliberately lead me into a trap?'

Just then, his eyes caught sight of deep tracks, like drag marks indented in the grass just ahead of him. He squatted down to look more closely. They looked familiar. Then, he suddenly remembered the odd, weird footprints that Lotte and Tim noticed earlier with Roland. And which they thought were from someone or something they feared that had been following them shortly after arriving at the site not long after calling on Barnard.

From the end of the tent, as the light tailed off into the gloomy darkness, he suddenly heard a voice. Abruptly, he stopped dead in his tracks and immediately shrank down and hid behind a large tank of giant electric eels. From a side glance, he noticed that these creatures were squirming amongst the thick growth of aquatic plants, entangled with one another like an unruly ball of rope. Although still contained in a tank, they were still too close for comfort.

'He's late,' said a deep, muffled voice in the distance, as if talking through thick clothing.

'We'll give the fool two minutes, but not a second more,' said another voice, which was just as harsh.

'Is the trap set?'

'Yes. It has been ready and waiting... for many moons now, just waiting for the chance. We missed it the first time around. This time, there'll be no mistakes!'

Then next, he overheard disjointed words, which sounded like, '*Kill him by electric shock... throw what's left to the cannibal monsters!*' Although it seemed like an afterthought, it sounded just as frightening as before.

'But first, my friend, we must relieve him of that precious object he has hidden around his body. For where he's going, he won't need it! Remember. Our Great Master needs that piece of gem desperately. We must not fail his bidding...'

There was deep sigh and a rustling shuffle of feet.

'*And... since our funny fool arrived on this planet in a bang with nothing, then he can leave in a bigger bang with nothing!*'

An evil cackle followed that cut the heaviness of the air about them.

'By the way, why did the little one have to die? He was harmless and hurt no one,' asked the first questioner, his deep voice stilted through the upturned collar of his heavy coat.

'He saw too much, the little fool. He was spying on us. You should be grateful. Remember, he witnessed everything that went on in your trailer in the confrontation with your... you know who!' spat the other venomously. His head wriggled about in the blackness of his hood, the top of which having now replaced the large, brimmed hat – now adding to the disguise.

At that moment, Chance slowly and gingerly raised his head and peeped over the side of the tank that hid him from view. He squinted in the narrow light. But he saw only blurred shadows and hazy silhouettes rising and falling in the distance. It was difficult to make out their expressions intimately in the dark – worse because of the heavy disguises – but the awful sounds said it all, which stung his ears and shook his body. But there was no disguising the evil flying thickly through the air.

'I want out!' demanded the deep voice.

'Too late, my friend,' boomed the other savagely. 'You traded in for reward and gain.'

The figures swung round to face each other, threateningly, as if close to blows. The back of the burly one with the deep voice shielded the other from Chance's line of sight using his thick coat. In a firm grip, he grabbed the other by the shoulders of the voluminous cloak by way of reinforcing what he said. It was sinisterly emphatic.

'In the beginning, I... I only joined in to see if could help to track down those who had disappeared off the face of the earth. I was told they had gone to the Alterworld. I have been loyal to the cause. I've followed instructions faithfully to a T... And much at the risk to my reputation and my authority with the people and those around me.' He stared at his feet unhappily, still thinking.

'But that's simply not enough,' sneered the other one, snatching at his hood and cloak to get out of the grip of the other. He shrugged him off with sudden surprising strength. 'Our noble ruler, Qnevilus, *the Great King, the Worthy One*, has great plans in place and is now gathering those loyal around him to his cause. Let me also remind you that his mighty work has only *just* begun on this planet and needs unquestioning loyalty!'

'Ah, but... but, if—'

'There is *no* room for *ifs* and *buts* in what we have to do!' With outstretched fingers, he stabbed him repeatedly in the front of his chest to silence him. '*You, of all people, should remember that he – our Grand Master – will not tolerate those who desert his cause.* And he will mete out punishment appropriately of the harshest kind,' he said, pressing home the point. 'The Three Kingdoms have yet to be conquered and held securely in his power, using all the forces at his disposal. Whether by fair means or foul, it does not matter!'

He pulled his hood tighter across his face, searching suspiciously all around him – fearing eavesdroppers. He averted his face and lowered his voice. 'Remember, my friend, we are but pawns in the grand scheme of things. The followers have been waiting a long time; a very, long time, for this to happen. But never forget that rewards of untold riches, immense power and fame have yet to come to those who religiously follow his plan. To rule supreme, it is the Worthy One's – the Mighty One's destiny, I tell you.'

Bizarrely, he started to bow repeatedly towards the ground in a hypnotic rocking movement in some form of trance-like reverence, almost kissing the ground. 'And I remind you now, nothing… *nothing* must stand in his way. Those who dare will pay the price!' Narrowing his eyes, he glowered murderously, the hood around his head slipping a little.

'And this time when it happens, a savage example will be made for all unbelievers and purveyors of goodness to observe at first hand, and how we punish dissent. They will think twice, when they hear that their champion – that stupid, naïve fool, that do-gooder clown of a harlequin – has met his end. We'll soon make him laugh on the other side of his face! …*Because then, he will die… And this time horribly, I promise you, and before he gathers more support along the way!'*

With rising hysteria, his voice rose to a menacing crescendo, swelling the suffocating air around them. The other one shook uncomfortably, now nodding wearily, as though having to accept the inevitable.

Just at that exact moment on hearing this, Chance tried to suppress a gasp of horror escaping from his throat. He clapped his hand immediately across his mouth. Instead, a muffled cough spluttered out that he couldn't help. He pinched his nose with his finger and thumb, but it was too late.

'What the… What's that?' exploded the figures as they spun round, staring in the direction of the noise. 'Who's there?' they asked searchingly.

A silence greeted them. Chance ducked down into the shadows – sinking further, praying that his heart would stop thumping so loudly in case they heard it. Then, as luck would have it, one of the giant eels had slipped out of the water from the top of its tank with a splash and slithered along the floor towards them, its thick, scaly body scraping the ground coarsely.

'Bah. It's just one of that senile old woman's pet monsters searching for food in one of its wanderings!' said the heavy-coated figure, spitting on the ground after it with relief.

They turned their backs and carried on their furtive conversation in a whisper, whilst one of them tried to kick at the slippery eel with his boot, but missed. The creature slithered smoothly away under a gap at the bottom of the tent into the grassy knoll of the site, escaping to its freedom.

In the dark, Chance wiped his forehead gratefully, but his hands, wet with sweat, slipped off the frame of the tank he was leaning against when gathering his breath.

Quickly recovering his balance, he tried to recall some of Hoopy Hoopla's wise instructions. *Surprise in attack is better than defence that is too late... The power of the mind is...* So, re-inspired and re-encouraged, inch by inch, Chance crept stealthily towards them, using the shadows to conceal his tracks.

Then a whiff of pungent cigar smoke trickled towards him, as a sudden breeze from the lifting of a flap of canvas swished gently in the evening air, fanning it. *Ah, so that's who he's with*, thought Chance. *The wretched two-faced Barnard, the hypocritical rat. It is he, disguised in that heavy coat... and that evil devil, De'Aff – together like blood brothers in crime. Plotting – heaven knows what! Ah, wonderful: the two of them caught red-handed in the act! I'll soon expose the traitors for what they really are... Setting a death trap for me, were you, indeed? I'll soon teach you!* Tactically, he sized up the situation. *I'll aim for De'Aff first*, he decided.

But in that very next minute, Barnard moved slightly away, leaving his partner exposed to attack. He appeared to be staring into one of the tanks behind him. It contained a huge, repellent-looking, dragon-like creature as if from a prehistoric age, for it had huge clamp-like jaws and viciously sharp talon-like feet. He seemed mesmerised by a warning notice below the tank, which said:

"AGGROSAURUS. DANGEROUS CANNIBAL SPECIMEN DESCENDED FROM THE JURASSIC ERA. DO NOT FEED! KEEP OUT!"

Although that did not stop him from mercilessly needling the creature by prodding it with the handle of his whip just simply for the sadistic fun of it.

As it happened, Chance by now, was half-crouched like a tiger within three feet from the back of his target. Then, in one giant leap he sprang towards De'Aff and tried to rip off his cloak. But unfortunately, his grip wasn't that good due to the perspiration on his hands, for he slipped. But he still managed to hurl his two arms around his prey: one around his shoulder, the other around his chest.

'*Got you, finally!* You… you loathsome creature, Mister, Doctor of Death… you nasty, sick apology for a human being! So, planning a trap of death for me, were you?!' shouted Chance triumphantly as he gripped harder.

Unfortunately, losing his balance, he toppled over. Locked together like a breakaway boulder spinning out of control, they collided into one of the tanks with a thunderous crash. They fell to the floor, rolling under one of the trestles supporting one of the adjacent cages, smashing it to the ground. There was a terrifying noise as the two of them grappled with one another. Murderous curses rented the air.

Suddenly, Barnard tore back to help. 'What the…?' he screamed, launching himself towards the two struggling bodies which were fighting for their lives. Brandishing his bullwhip threateningly high above his head, he tried to separate the two but failed miserably. '*Ker-rack!*' The whip cracked viciously in the air above them but made little impact. He attempted a kick with his burly frame towering over Chance but missed, his boot landing into the ribs of his partner rolling on the ground. Although winded from the fall, Chance still managed to cling on desperately to the hood and cloak of his opponent beneath him, refusing to let go. Again, Barnard raised his arm, about to bring down his whip to strike. But as he did, he suddenly let out a terrifying yelp, for he abruptly collapsed and fell into a heap besides them as if he had been struck by lightning.

Momentarily, Chance stopped fighting, but still held on to his prey like a limpet. He quickly looked up and saw that Henry, against his instructions, had secretly followed him in, now leaping from the shadows. He was now reeling in his cane by its coiled silver wire, which he had from twenty paces flung like a harpoon at Barnard's skull, knocking him out in the process.

'Hen... ry. What the blazes!' gasped Chance from the side of his mouth.

'I... I had to come in to help. I was dead worried after ten minutes had elapsed,' Henry tried to explain, mouthing agitatedly. As he hovered over his friend, he wondered what to do next. 'Hold on. I'll... I'll help.'

Surprised, but grateful all the same for seeing him, Chance foolishly lost his concentration for a second, and suddenly let go of his grip as he tried to get up at the same time when bodily lifting De'Aff. But he received a thundering blow to his chin in return, which knocked him sideways. Drunkenly, he staggered backwards, when a pair of massive hands flew out from the dishevelled cloak and gripped his throat. The clamp-like grip started choking the life out of him. Henry waded in to help but received a massive mule kick in his stomach for his troubles.

As Chance's windpipe was being slowly squeezed dry, he suddenly went dizzy and limp. *I must fight De'Aff back*

with trickery, he thought. *Or I'll die by painful strangling.*
Then, automatically recalling Hoopy's advice on the noble
art of Toe Hee Do... if that was difficult – then *cheat!*
Rapidly, Chance decided to cheat. And suddenly and slyly
he managed to stamp onto De'Aff's toes with his big, heavy
boots, and then bit him on his hand.

An agonised scream followed close to his ear. In that
split second, De'Aff suddenly released Chance, who then
managed to elbow him savagely into the midriff, making
him suddenly fly like a rocket across the tent as if stung by
a thousand of volts. But as he did, Chance flung himself
after him in a flying tackle. And with the tips of his fingers
grabbed hold of one of De'Aff's shoes – which, to his horror,
came away in his hand to reveal a hairy gorilla's foot...

'Ar-argh!' screamed Henry with a blood-piercing
screech. He quickly jumped out of the way, thinking in that
split instance, *That hairy thing seemed somewhat familiar...
but where's the blood?*

And so, without letting up, Chance immediately
hurled himself like a demon possessed towards De'Aff,
and charged with his head, smashing into his chest.
Somewhat concussed, De'Aff then collided into the back
of the tank containing Aggrosaurus. His body slumped
like a sack of sand, still stunned. He slid down in slow
motion to a seating position with his back resting against
the tank. Chance leapt at him again and quickly pinned
him down by the arms, knowing the way he fought like
mule before. Despite this, De'Aff still struggled and fought
like a madman, spitting and shrieking curses from behind
a covered face. The air turned blue with unprintable
expletives.

Eventually, with Henry's help, he managed to twist De'Aff's left arm behind his back in a powerful armlock that Hoopy had taught him. Meanwhile, Henry stood on De'Aff's outstretched legs to prevent him getting up. Henry drew short, sharp gasps of breath, just a little unfit.

'I'll kill you. *I'll kill you both!*' uttered a muffled voice that snarled from behind the mask as he struggled to get free.

'Now, let's have look under this evil garb, shall we?' puffed Chance, as he spun De'Aff around. He reached forward and went to tear off the cloak and hood. De'Aff struggled like a maniac. But, like a wild ox wounded, he managed to butt Chance under the chin and wrestle him to the ground. And in his wriggling, trying to escape, the outer garment was torn off De'Aff's body to reveal, to their utter horror, the bones of *a ghostly white skeleton – complete with a skull, a dangling spine with ribs, with arms and legs attached...*

'Oh, heavens help us! What the...?' screamed Henry again, his horror exploding as he teetered on the brink of finally losing it. Instinctively, he backed away, feeling sick. As Chance clutched the outer garment helplessly in his hands, he was completely just as baffled as Henry – if not more. Then, it suddenly dawned on them! What they had exposed was an inner skin of a stage costume of a stark-white skeleton painted on black cloth... something they thought perhaps they had seen before – but couldn't quite place, where or when in the panic.

A sudden snarl was heard as De'Aff tried to squirm free. Immediately, Chance rolled on top of his chest, flattening him to the ground. His hand made a beeline for De'Aff's face. 'Let's see what you look like under this evil mask, shall we, you slimy Doctor Slatane De'Aff, you!' shouted Chance again and again, as he leant over and grabbed. But steel-like fingers shot up and tried to stop him, pulling the mask up further over his chin. So together, using all their strength, Henry and Chance wrenched the hand away... and slowly, and with trepidation, ripped off the mask...

'Oh, my G... God... it's... *not HIM after all... Instead – it's... it's Cost... Costello!*' they exclaimed, astonished. Blood drained from their faces as waves of shock replaced sudden surprise.

They both pushed their faces closer to what they saw under the mask, their noses almost touching. They simply could not believe their eyes. '*It's Costello of all people!*' murmured Chance, still stunned out of his head.

'*What on earth are you doing here?* We followed you religiously. We thought it was De'Aff creeping in here... the cloak... the hood... the large black hat...?'

Trembling with rage, Chance wiped his sleeve across his face, when he suddenly realised that, like a fool, he had fallen into the trap, hook, line and sinker, that they had so cunningly set.

'*Where is he? Where is De'Aff?*' Violently, he shook Costello by the shoulders.

'You'll never catch him, you stupid big fools! He's too clever for you... you lumbering ordinary mortals!' gasped Costello, breathing hard. 'Now, please allow me to get up, gentlemen, for old time's sake.' His eyes rolled wearily upwards, sinking deeper into his head with a tired plea for clemency.

Chance looked enquiringly at Henry, who nodded

reluctantly. 'Okay. Let him up, Henry. But *only* onto his knees, so he can't bolt. But lock his arm behind his back, in case.'

Just then, Henry's eyes caught sight of the gorilla's foot and the skeleton – the bare bones of the matter. *And suddenly it all came back to him!* Of course! Costello had worn them as props in the ring earlier on. And as for those scuff marks in the ground? Lotte's earlier suspicions perhaps were right after all...

Jabbing Costello in the chest with his forefinger, Chance demanded angrily, 'Why you? *You* of all people! Bonzo's uncle and all that!' He suddenly recalled young Bonzo's last words to him at the hospital. '*My uncle Costello. He's a good loyal man, who's kind and would not-a hurt a fly... you-a can trust him with your life...*'

'What a load of cobblers,' muttered Chance, now absolutely, livid at being taken in so easily. But even worse than that: this heartless traitor Costello must have stood by when that De'Aff had arranged the stunt that nearly killed poor Bonzo. *Being a nephew, related by blood, counts for nothing, having already been betrayed by his uncle,* Chance concluded. He was appalled at such duplicity.

Despite everything, Costello remained defiant. With false bravado, he blustered and shrieked, 'You lot are pathetic, do you know... I mean, look at you – grown men, trailing around with lost causes under the guise of doing good. And chasing foolish riddles and trying to solve ridiculous codes that are useless. Bah, you simpletons! What will it bring you at the end of it all? Eternal fame, or permanent martyrdom? You haven't a clue about the true meaning of life or how to live!'

He spat, and sneered, his face contorted out of all recognition.

Henry, seething, could hardly contain himself. And, pointedly, he began to unscrew the tip of his cane to stab Costello in the ribs to teach him a lesson...

As soon as he saw what was coming, Costello started twitching and wriggling. 'Listen,' he said, a little less arrogantly. 'Listen to me. Why risk your lives and those of your friends, especially that boy and that young girl? Send them home now, before it's too late.'

He lowered his voice into a dull monotone, as if his brain were somewhere else but there.

'But, let me tell you, there are better things over there in this other dimension. Amazing rewards and riches beyond your wildest dreams will be yours... If you come over to the Alterworld with the noble Slatane and us to join the Mighty Qnevilus and his kingdom.'

He tipped his head downwards repeatedly, as though he were bowing in deference to a higher order, and squeaked, 'Literally, there are thousands of followers like us all over the earth – just waiting for the word. Then we are to follow, when *he* takes over the Kingdoms!' His eyes shone wildly like someone deranged when talking about it, as if imminent and unstoppable. He shuffled restlessly – skidding on his kneecaps as his legs began to get cramp.

'But why throw your lot in with that sick, evil creature, De'Aff?' asked Chance, still mystified.

'He has more talent of mysteries in his little finger than you have in your whole body! That was *nothing* you saw ...hardly *anything* you tasted at his performance today!' boasted Costello sycophantically, as if he had been brainwashed. 'And just wait, he's not finished with *you* yet – not by a long chalk!'

By now, Chance was fast losing patience. He flexed his shoulders warningly. He tried again. 'Again, where is that obnoxious creature, Slatane De'Aff now?' He shook him by the arms.

'You'll never catch him now. I've given him a head start. Besides, he's too smart for the likes of you!' Costello's mood darkened. There was a madness about him, as though he were possessed.

'Why did you kill Midgy then?' demanded Henry, gripping Costello's arm.

'He saw too much. But it wasn't me who silenced him.'

'So, was it De'Aff?' asked Chance accusingly, wagging a stiff finger right under his nose. 'Did he use his poisonous serpent to slither under Midgy's door?'

'It *had* to be. The dwarf knew too much.'

'You mean the *identity* of the phantom?' asked Henry, twisting Costello's arm higher up his back. 'Come on, you treacherous leech… confess, or we'll…'

'Argh! Let me go… you're breaking my arm!' he cried, writhing in pain. 'Let me tell you something. Every… *everyone* on earth has a phantom of sorts in them at some time or other! …The one at the circus was no different!' Costello started smirking, as though it were a harmless joke.

'*And what you believe in or what you are scared of – is exactly what you see!*'

'Ah, but it was *you*, though, wasn't it… scaring the life out of everyone here, wasn't it?' Henry twisted the arm even higher, until Costello almost fainted with pain.

'It… it started as a joke… then a red herring to divert attention away from my noble master, Dr De'Aff. It was a hoax to shake up the others at Barnard's. It escalated. With Ziggarini, M'sieur Petton and the other stars in the way, I could never get top billing. They were always ahead of me as the star attractions, milking the applause.' Costello gasped as his arm went numb, for Henry dug harder with his fingers.

Chance shook his head in disbelief. 'Do you mean to say it was all down to simple resentment and pure jealousy? A trick to frighten the performers away? Then furthermore, a cynical plot to disguise the vile chicanery of that loathsome monster, De'Aff, creeping around here at Barnard's, plotting, and planning his poisonous deeds? And together with you, you worthless worm, he hatched a plot to trap and murder me, once I got on his trail?' Chance trembled with anger.

Increasingly, Henry tightened his grip. 'Who or what are the Custodians of Terror, then, if De'Aff is not the phantom at the circus?'

'Argh, steady – you're breaking my arm, you fool! Do your own snooping detective work then, you stupid, pious fools!' spat Costello, foaming at the mouth. He refused to elaborate further, as he squirmed and thrashed about, trying to break free.

'And that loose wooden stake crashing from the top of the tent which nearly killed me?' demanded Chance. 'It was you and De'Aff, wasn't it, you snake?'

Costello stared at the floor, looking guilty as charged. Then it all started to click into place… So, the previous protestations of his and his feigning disgust at De'Aff's evil plotting were all just a ruse to divert suspicion away from himself.

Just then, an awful groan was heard just behind them. When they looked round, Barnard was coming to. Suddenly, without warning, he sprung up onto his feet like a Jack-in-the-box. He swept up his whip in his hand and tore out of the place as fast as his legs could carry him.

Immediately, Henry was the first to react; he threw his harpoon cane after the retreating cowardly figure of Barnard. At considerable speed, the sharp end of the cane, like a heat-seeking missile, hit the back of Barnard's head with unerring accuracy. The deep thud was followed by a blood-curdling scream of pain as Barnard, concussed momentarily, fell forwards as he grasped the edge of the nearest tank to steady himself, but unfortunately for him, the tank held three of Madame Gloop's Giant Stinging Reptiles. The unravelling wire of the cane having rapidly wrapped tight around his legs, Barnard just could not move, although he tried desperately to wriggle free. And so, completely off-balance and disorientated in the semi-darkness, he toppled head-first into the turbid waters where the monstrous reptiles were waiting.

Not having been fed for several hours, the creatures had been salivating hungrily and immediately started to attack their human prey. Barnard didn't stand a chance as the ten-foot creatures, with their sharp, scaly claws and squat-bowed legs, stunned him dead with one thrash of their massive flailing tails. Henry ran up to see if he could save Barnard. But it was too late! Feeling sick, Henry tactfully turned his head away, refusing to witness the giant serpents going about their most-welcome meal. As they gnashed their enormous stalagmite-like teeth together in their gigantic jaws, they made massive chomping, sloshing sounds of greedy feeding that echoed graphically around the tent, Costello started screaming in horror.

Suddenly abandoned, Costello started to plead for mercy, but Chance increased his grip, whilst thinking at the horror of the savage end to the hapless Barnard. 'Please. *Please let me go*. If the others find out, they'll tear me apart, especially Willy, who was devoted to Midgy.' Rivulets of perspiration rolled off his face.

Henry and Chance were unmoved. 'What happened to Katrina? What was the significance of those ghoulish dead objects that fell from Midgy's body… the decaying bird and that ghastly verse…? *And what is the meaning of B.C.D.?*' demanded Henry, stamping on the back of Costello's bent knees.

'Ouch!' complained Costello through gritted teeth. 'How should I know? Ask Slatane De'Aff… that's if you're clever enough to find him!' He sniped sneeringly, wriggling like an eel.

'You were asked the meaning of the letters *B.C.D.* that was scrawled on the mirror in poor Midgy's caravan,' repeated Chance softly. He tightened his grip.

'Haven't you stupid idiots worked it all out? *B-arnard, C-ostello and D-e'Aff* – we, the *three* noble musketeers!' spat Costello, with a facile grin.

'You what!' said Henry stupefied. It suddenly dawned on him. 'Oh my…! How did we miss it? So Midgy was trying to tell us about you three loathsome villains!'

'But what about the other letters… How did he come in contact with… *The Oraco Dex Lo Paediac?*' snapped Henry.

'Hey. I really don't know. Perhaps it was something that nosy little parker overhead when he was spying on Barnard.

'Now I've told you everything I know, so please, have pity. You've beaten me in a fair fight. So let me go.'

'You lot didn't have pity on that poor little clown… the way he was murdered and left to die – with that scroll stuck down his throat, and frightened horrifically to death,' said Chance.

'Look. Let's shake on it. I'll never trouble you or the circus again.' Costello reached out and offered a hand with his free right arm.

After a pause or so, Chance wavered. Then he bent slightly over him, kindly. And as this happened, Costello's hand suddenly flew at Chance's throat. He then tried to snatch the precious pendant around Chance's neck in a crushing grip by smashing into his Adam's apple with the pointed nails of his fingers, but he ripped off the floppy bow tie instead. Instinctively, Chance jerked his body back sharply and quickly flicking his wrist, knocked him away using the powerful half-inch punch that Hoopy had taught him at Rousseau's. Like a projectile missile launched from the side of a battleship, Costello was flung halfway across the tent. He crashed into one of the tanks containing electric eels. The tank split open, spilling its contents onto the ground. Five large electric eels slithered and slopped onto the grass besides him, stunning him with a massive electric shock.

Apoplectic with fury, Costello lifted the frame of the broken tank with gargantuan strength and tried to hurl it at Chance and Henry. But as he did, he slipped on one of the fish, which had slithered on the grass beneath his feet. He toppled backwards and tried to save himself by grabbing hold of the top of the tank of Aggrosaurus nearby. Unfortunately, right at that very moment, the giant dragon-like monster (having been mercilessly provoked by Barnard not so long ago) leapt up and, with its gigantic jaws, snapped and trapped Costello's sleeve in its razor-sharp teeth. It started to drag him into the tank, as if he were light as a paper doll. Helplessly he toppled into the murky waters.

Screaming, Costello gurgled and choked as he was pulled under the surface. 'I can't swim... please, for God's sake... *help* me!' Briefly he resurfaced for a second, gasping for air. They rushed over to help, but it was too late. He was dragged under the water for the second time, as the monstrous Aggrosaurus stunned him unconscious with a flailing swish of its massive, rudder-like tail. Then, sickeningly, the mammoth prehistoric creature with its huge cannibal's appetite, started to swallow him whole... head-first, in three quick, easy gulps.

Averting his face, Henry felt sick in the pit of his stomach. He turned away, holding his head in horror. Chance understood how he felt, for he was equally shocked by what they had just witnessed. He put a consoling arm over his friend's shoulder. 'Let's get out of this place... and quickly, Henry. I can't stomach any more of this. We can't do anything more for him or for his rotten pal Barnard, the poor devils. Let's find Roland and the youngsters. They must be dead worried about us.

But we had better let Madame Gloop know what has happened in here so that she can contact the police. But I fear that she may not want to, because she may worry that they would automatically close her down for keeping dangerous creatures as pets without a licence!'

Henry added cryptically, 'Also, we ought to let her know that her monster pets have been already well and truly fed!' Chance gave him a hard stare whilst looking for some sign of humour or a hint of irony. But there was none.

With leaden feet, they made their way out of the maze of tanks, hoping to leave the grim smells and awful sights rapidly behind them. When they glanced back, they swore they saw Aggrosaurus give a sickening grin of reptilian contentment as he smacked his jaws happily.

'Do you think that'll be the end of the awful threat of the phantom and the Terror, now that *he's* a goner?' asked Henry apprehensively.

'I should hate to bet my life on it again, my friend, especially after all those dire warnings about it from Cecil-the-Thin at the waxworks,' said Chance with an uneasy shake of his head. 'And I daren't trust all what that slippery Costello said, after all what's happened... and honestly, that's the unpalatable truth!' He hurried Henry out of the tent by quickening his steps.

On reaching the fresh night air, they breathed in deeply to their full, hoping to blow away the cobwebs that had grabbed them. They never thought how welcome and refreshing the air was, despite how dark and gloomy the night. It seemed that time had stood still back in there... and quite horrifically too. Never had they experienced a chapter quite like this before in their lives since they met. And they hoped that they would never encounter something like this again, regardless of what happens in the future.

However, still conscience-stricken, Henry asked, 'Shouldn't we inform the authorities what's happened?' Concerned, his face was creased with worry.

'It'll be useless, Henry, there'll be no trace or evidence of the missing bodies. Who would believe us, anyway? It's up to Madame Gloop and the rest of the people at the circus. And anyhow, forensics would have a job getting close to those monsters for fear of losing their heads in their jaws. Anyway, the story's too unbelievable for words.'

Bedraggled, soaked and exhausted, the two of them hurried quickly along. Downhearted, they were still no nearer in tracking down the mysterious De'Aff or discovering his true identity. But as they reached Roland's parked taxi, they felt immense relief that they were safe... well, at least for the moment. Though what could they tell their friends right now...

That they had won the battle but, sadly, lost their prisoners... and in doing so, possibly the war.

Chapter 44

EVERYTHING IN LIFE IS A RIDDLE... A RIDDLE OF CHANCE

ROLAND HAD BEEN STARING at his watch impatiently for last thirty minutes. He got more and more agitated after Chance and Henry had failed to turn up. Like a restless animal stalking its own tail, he paced up and down, encircling the car park... just waiting. He felt giddy with worry, thinking the worst. And so, when they eventually showed up, he gave an enormous sigh of relief.

'Phew!' he gasped. 'Thank the stars, you two are back! We were dead worried about what could have happened to you.'

'Yeah,' said Tim. 'Thought you had been gobbled up by a monster or something or other,' he joked with a wry laugh.

'You're not far wrong, young 'un!' said Henry. Wearily, he climbed into the cab, thinking of the irony of what Tim had just said. He gently eased Ram's slumbering body to one side with a careful push with the outside of his foot. The dog gave him a lick of welcome and then immediately settled down with his nose deep in his outstretched paws.

'Are you all right, Chance?' Lotte asked, as he heaved himself into the passenger seat beside them. 'You look a bit down. What's happened?' She looked extremely concerned.

'Let's get the devil out of here and I'll tell you on the way.'

Giving a puzzled shrug and a sigh, Roland started the taxi. He slipped the gears rapidly and headed in the direction of Hyde Park as he concentrated on the road.

They then began to explain why they were waylaid. And what happened in Madame Gloop's tent after pursuing whom they thought at first was De'Aff. And then, they went on to describe all the horrendous things that had happened in there: the gruesome creatures, the gigantic reptilian monsters... the deadly Aggrosaurus... the terrifying fight that nearly killed Chance – culminating in the horrific end to Costello.

They described Barnard's attempt to flee from the scene earlier after being knocked out for the count... then Barnard being struck semi-conscious by Henry's harpoon cane, whereupon his legs subsequently got tangled up in the wire from the harpoon... then, when he accidentally fell into the tank of Gloop's monstrous giant stinging amphibians, only to be gobbled up by all gruesome three reptiles.

Roland and the youngsters just couldn't believe it at first, thinking that they had misheard... when Chance told them about Costello.

'You… you mean, *Cost… ello*? …Bonzo's uncle?'

'Yup. *The very same one!* Yes, the one who was supposed to be trustworthy, loyal and one in whom Chance could completely entrust his life without fear,' said Henry with a cynical, dry laugh.

'Trustworthy? *What!* …*Trusting the likes of someone like him*, my foot!' yelled Roland, exasperated. He twisted his head around angrily. 'That despicable specimen of a creature!'

'The filthy double-dealing traitor!' snorted Tim, shaking his fist. 'He deserved all he got… and more! I should have catapulted him!'

Chance grimaced painfully, as he recalled how close he got to being killed when he fell for Costello's trap. He shivered, breaking out in a sweat.

'*Timothy Needles!*' yelled Lotte, horrified at the language which threatened to get out of hand. 'But I can't believe Barnard was in on the plot to *murder* our friend Chance! He seemed quite kindly, and so concerned about the disappearance of his performers… I just can't believe it. And to die like that! Ugh! Yuk!'

'I do! I didn't trust that slippery rat from the moment I clapped eyes on him!' uttered Roland. 'He's pulled the wool over everyone's eyes. Rotten, cunning devil – just like his ghastly fiend friend, that horrendous evil so-and-so, that De'Aff creature! And Barnard really got what was coming to him! But still, what a horrible way to die, being cannibalised by reptiles!'

'But it's even *more* galling was the cunning way that Costello character had us fooled from the start *pretending* to be all innocent-like. The shifty-sly cockroach, taking advantage of honest people like us,' spluttered Roland, his temper exploding by the minute. He gripped the wheel harshly, which made the taxi slew precariously when rounding Hyde Park corner.

'Steady on, old boy,' urged Henry, alarmed, nearly sliding off the seat. 'You'll get us all killed! Anyway, we shouldn't have been so trusting and gullible in the first place.'

By the time they reached Hyde Park, it was completely dark, save for the shimmering dots of light along the still stretch of water of the Serpentine, which danced like pearls from the Lido to the bridge in the distance. Roland guided his cab alongside the northern bank of the lake and parked under the trees. He quickly cut the engine and leant forward to take in the sight. They rolled down the windows to brace the night air, which had swollen with dew that was still rising. It was crisp and refreshing and softened their mood.

'Now, tell us what else happened,' asked Roland, turning to face Chance and Henry. 'Did you report it to that Madame Gloop?'

'Yes, please tell us everything,' said Lotte and Tim together at once, as they jumped from their seats.

Chance got up to stretch his legs. He flung open the passenger door and, together with Henry, climbed out. Somewhat red-faced, Chance began to explain. 'As I said, Barnard tried to flee like a cowardly bat out of hell, when I was trying to hold on to the rat Costello. How Barnard met his horrible end afterwards we have already told you.' In front of the children, Chance didn't want to go into graphic detail more than he had already. Just thinking about it again gave him a sudden shiver.

Soon afterwards, Roland clambered out to join them on the grass verge outside. He asked, 'But why didn't you chase after him and capture him alive? He could have given you some answers about all the devious goings-on with De'Aff, Costello and the rest of that evil mob.'

Henry stared at the ground, obviously embarrassed. 'Um... but Chance had his hands full trying to fight off that maniac Costello. It was such a shock to discover it was *Costello*, not De'Aff under the disguise – and that naturally stunned and threw us,' offered Henry by way of mitigation, rather than simply a feeble excuse.

'...And especially that skeleton and that Gorilla's foot...' Henry's voice faded with a distressing shudder.

'Do you think it *was* Costello, spying on us all that time from the beginning, when we arrived?' asked Lotte. 'You know, those strange footprints dented in the grass following us...'

'Well, only if he wore those gorilla's feet all the time, in bed and outside the ring!' said Chance grimly. 'But I think it was De'Aff from the outset.'

'Well, you can hardly ask Costello now,' chirped Tim, interrupting. 'And especially if he is still inside the belly of that prehistoric monster, Aggro-what's-it! And that Barnard fella fed to those stinging reptiles like pieces of horse meat! ...Yuk. Disgusting! Can't bear thinking about!'

'Urgh. It all sounds really horrible!' gasped Lotte, all of a shiver. 'But how can such a creature as one that was on show to the public by Madame Gloop, swallow a fully grown man like Costello in a couple of gulps?'

Henry said that he had heard that a giant thirty-foot snake called an Anaconda from South America could, and often did, swallow a man or a small cow whole, in a few easy gulps. And therefore, Gloop's prized specimen was no different in its voracious, man-eating appetite after all.

'Oh, and another thing,' said Henry, scratching his chin thoughtfully, 'There's no proof that this monster had really descended from the distant past as Madame Gloop had claimed.' Though he looked uneasy when he said it, as if he couldn't quite believe it himself. 'Although in the end, what difference would it have made to Costello? He got eaten up anyway!'

'But I still don't understand why Costello went to the other side. Sure, jealousy and resentment at not being "Top dog", I can take. But why throw in your lot with a sick, evil-minded megalomaniac like De'Aff, of all people?' said Roland, still puzzled. He ran his fingers through his hair… wondering.

'Why it happens to some people and not others, I really can't explain their true motives or what's in their hearts… or even their minds, when they turn,' said Chance.

He paced back and forth his fists clenched tightly in front of him. 'Certainly, Costello was consumed by jealousy of those around him. Then, as far as I could make out, he was dying to become the main attraction. And to make his mark, he had to really do *something* that scared others witless. I think he was sucked into the plot, desperate to become a famous big fish, rather than what he felt he was before… just an obscure tiddler of little importance!' He hesitated and splayed his arms wide, shrugging hopelessly.

'But it was more than that, I fear. Like Barnard, *greed* and *power* are more usually the reasons. The attraction to follow someone like Slatane De'Aff, or the evil Qnevilus would appeal to his perverse ego. Twisted people like him want to achieve lasting notoriety by their wicked deeds. Because it is a sad fact of life that wickedness always grabs headlines and some kind of fame, whereas goodness and kindness rarely does!'

Roland reached out and placed a restraining hand on Chance's arm. He looked at him quizzically. 'But... but hang on, *you've* carried out quite a bit of kindness and some good turns recently: in fact, *three lots* of them, as part of the riddle. Wouldn't that worry you, that you might *never* achieve lasting fame? And that you will be forgotten like mist into obscurity, one day?'

'Bah!' retorted Chance, growling. 'Right now, I'm more concerned with simple survival to save my precious skin. What I did, was done as part of the deal of the riddle in order to live another day. Nothing more! Because, what's the use of eternal fame, when you are dead and buried and can't take advantage of it?'

Just then, Chance suddenly stopped pacing the ground and half-crouched against the bonnet of the cab. Gnats buzzed around amongst the overhanging foliage, nipping his hair. Irritably, he swatted them away from his face with his open hand, thinking that perhaps there were worse things to come. He continued solemnly, almost as if he were talking aloud to himself. His mind was still restless. Doubts began to fester and grow.

'But why do people like De'Aff carry on as they do, doing evil things and scaring all they come across? And coercing others, when goodness and kindness could just as well be rewarded?' asked Lotte, in disbelief. She fiddled with her hair nervously, twirling it around her fingers in knots.

'As it is, I think tyrants, such as De'Aff and others like him, are really convinced that they will be immortalised in history for their deeds of evil. It is *this* which makes them tick! For who will remember kindness? Who will remember goodness when such things fade into oblivion so quickly?' replied Chance. 'But again, people like De'Aff perhaps were *born* evil.' He stroked his chin thoughtfully and shook his head at the same time.

'But why did Costello carry on doing all those awful things, like frightening his friends and the people he worked with?' asked Tim.

Shifting his body sideways, Ram stirred gently besides his feet.

'Well, for Costello to haunt the circus by pretending to be the phantom would guarantee – so he thought – his place in history, providing he was never found out, of course. At the same time, it provided an ideal cover for De'Aff as a smoke screen. It was a perfect place and the perfect disguise to operate from,' explained Chance. 'Also, who would have suspected Costello of all people... being Bonzo's uncle, as well as an extremely popular head of a troupe of popular clowns? It was also the perfect revenge on his colleagues and friends, whom he apparently must have detested. It all boils down to a warped ego and vanity!' A deep furrow creased his face.

'However, his treachery went far deeper than that when greed and murder come into play. And together with the two-faced Barnard, they saw me as their main threat to their very existence. Then right from the beginning, it turns out that they were all in a plot with De'Aff to finish me off, and to steal this piece of gemstone. And it appears that it was on the orders of their evil master, Qnevilus.' No sooner had he said that Chance immediately felt under his collar to check that the precious piece was still safely there.

Gravely Chance winced, on thinking about Costello's savage duplicity and his collusion with the enemy. '*Mm. Wickedness and greed! Nothing in this world ever changes,*' he murmured despondently.

Thinking of this made him furious, yet depressed more than ever. Frustrated, he kicked a divot of turf into the air to vent his anger, but it did little to help his mood. After a pause, he started to calm down...

'But we're no nearer at catching Dr De'Aff or finding out his true identity, then,' said Lotte, her clear voice resonating desperately in the still night air.

'Or what he really looks like behind that gruesome mask!' piped up Tim.

'And furthermore, Costello and Barnard, the direct leads linking him and his supreme leader, Qnevilus, are now dead – and probably now mincemeat in a typical dog's dinner!' added Roland. Graphically, he gripped his throat to squeeze out his tongue in a deathly grimace, which made Lotte and Tim shriek with horror.

Wearily, Chance and Henry nodded defeat. It seemed on the face of it that their sorting out the first part of the riddle with the three good deeds had been dead easy in comparison with what was now facing them for the next part of it. But all of it, which so far had been achieved, would have been wasted if they stopped right now. The quest for the remainder of the riddle was elusive and as difficult as ever, and that troubled Chance deeply.

The solving of the gruesome clues left in the Caravan of Death still haunted him. Cursed by turmoil and doubts, what should he do now? The mysterious trail left by De'Aff was inviting him to follow... but why? And what was really behind it? Was there more to it than just the gem? Chance turned these things over again in his mind and wondered if he dared take the risks and endanger his friends. In deep thought, he started to fiddle with the pendant behind his collar as if searching for an answer. The coldness of the precious stone against his fingers gave him some strength. Although all the same, he was still worried.

Having taken on the challenge and having made promises to Zoot about uniting the Kingdoms – the animals, the people and so much more, he was committed. And what of Cecil-the-Thin's prediction that it was he – and *only he* – could do it. It was he, so he had been told, who had been chosen from the beginning to carry out these tasks so that the legend could be fulfilled. Could he still carry on under this heavy obligation and all that goes with it?

What has happened so far was all turning out to be fractious and dangerous, for it was far worse than he thought that it would be at the beginning. For yet, Chance still had to find and reach the Hidden Kingdom in the Alterworld. Even once there, he still had to track down the vile, evil leader Qnevilus in order to kill him. Then how could he ever forget what Cecil had told him at the waxworks, that he *had* to kill or be killed – whether he liked it or not!'

And what is more, the only way to get at Qnevilus was via the devious De'Aff, who was the vital link. But unwittingly, he had let De'Aff slip through his fingers after stupidly falling for Costello acting as decoy.

The road to the Alterworld was increasingly dangerous and long. Could he now cowardly abandon the cause, then live with himself? To accept defeat now, he would die anyway in a puff of smoke at the end of a hundred and thirty-five days if he didn't carry on trying. And time was running out fast.

He realised that there was no other way. He *had* to find the second piece of gemstone – *the Secret Gem of Life* – in order to survive and to carry on.

'Hey! What happens now, Chancy, me old mate?' asked Roland. He gave him a sharp nudge with his elbow, for he noticed Chance's eyes had glazed over in a kind of dull trance whilst slumped and half-leaning against the cab.

'Er… Sorry, my friend, I was miles away, just mulling things over.' Chance then wagged his head as though to clear it.

'Yes. What's next, Chance? Do we go on?' asked Tim anxiously, fearing the worst that he had changed his mind.

'What are you thinking about?' added Lotte, goading Chance for an answer. She started to get up to stretch her legs, which were getting achy and stiff from sitting for so long.

'Erm… There's so many things to take into account, my dear friends. What's happened up until now are definite warnings of dangers to come. I'm pretty certain that the terror of evil is still out there, as Cecil had warned. All of them – Costello, Barnard and that dastardly De'Aff, I think – are all part of the Custodians of Terror we were warned about. And being phantom-like, they can fade and appear as dangerous apparitions. So, I'd be a fool not to heed Cecil.

But I'm *really* worried for your safety, Tim and Lotte, as you are both young and with so much to lose.' Frowning, Chance appeared to hesitate about what to do next for the best.

As though he had itchy feet, he started to pace about again, circling the taxi, using slow but methodical steps. Everything that had happened over the last few days flashed in front of him… The discovery of the riddle, as part of the legend… The theft of the precious Gem of Knowledge from him by a young thief named Seth and its ultimate recovery. And then more recently – the ominous and deathly threats by De'Aff when they clashed in the ring… Young Katrina disappearing in the burning casket – that appeared to have levitated to another dimension… Midgy being horribly murdered… The investigation by the CID… That reporter from the paper turning up… The horrendous battle with Costello when he was nearly strangled.

His thoughts then flew back to the Caravan of Death… Finding a dead mockingbird's corpse under Midgy's body. The rolled-up piece of paper stuck down poor Midgy's throat… Now, what did it say? It came back to him in bits and pieces…

But the implications of its words were now more vivid than before – since his close encounter recently with death…

'*Oh, mocking curse, mocking curse, try not to catch me.*
Too late, you're so stupid, attempting to flee.
Per Chance you're so clever…
…oceans of treasure, so vast and so old,
Temptation… to float all of its gold.

'But, by Chance, you control the earth and the seas...
...dangers that court you with fatal disease.
...forbidden to danger, the Tree of All Life:
All you will find is curse... death and strife...'

All went quiet for a moment. It reflected the stillness of the trees along the water behind them, for the breeze had suddenly stopped...

'Have you decided to go on with the chase?' Tim asked Chance, hoping for the best. He started to root around in his rucksack to make sure that his special Rocket Catapult and his treasured supersonic-roller blades were still safe... well just in case he needed them.

Just then, Ram woke up with a start and leapt out of the cab with a yawn and a yelp. He ran into the bushes, to which Lotte assumed that he had seen a rabbit to chase. But Tim grinned knowingly, as his dog rushed in a hurry for the nearest tree trunk, scattering the birds on the way.

However, Chance was still remarkably quiet, deep in concentration. His subdued expression masking what he was really thinking, but they knew he was tussling with his thoughts. They recognised it so well from what they had been through with him these last few days. 'Er... mm... well, I don't...' he began uncertainly.

Sensibly, Henry interrupted. He stretched out an arm to stop him from marching up and down, whilst trying to get an answer from him. *'Chance has to go on. He has no choice if he wants to live!'*

'Come on, Chancy, old pal. What is it to be? Do you continue with the riddle?' cajoled Roland. Placing a firm hand on his shoulder, he spun him round to face him.

'Remember what you've faced before. Everything in life, we've been told is a riddle – *a riddle of chance...* a dice of death, so what's the odds?'

'What shall I do, Henry? What's for the best?' There was a blank expression etched on Chance's face. Hesitatingly, he pulled out the directions given him by Zoot, which had specific instructions on the bird flight paths to find Wise Black Crow in the country to help on the next part of the journey. Drumming his fingers quietly against the map, he turned it over again and again in the palms of his hands, unsure what to do.

In the very next minute, they were leaning forwards into the floor of the cab, when Roland, Lotte and Tim's eyes followed Henry, who suddenly reached into his pocket and pulled out the dodecahedron. They were intrigued...

He crouched down low, arching his back. Slowly and carefully, he handed the special twelve-sided dice-like object to his friend Chance. Unfurling his fingers, Chance licked his lips nervously. Then he wiped the flat of his hands against the sides of his trousers and waited.

'Do you remember the decisions over what to do, when we got stuck in a quandary as we did once before? In life, as always, this is not the end, but could be just the beginning,' suggested Henry confidently. 'So, for life-or-death decisions, this will help you to make up your mind – whether to continue or to turn back...'

A momentous silence fell as Chance's friends leant over him, forming a circle as they stared at the floor. Their eyes, wide-eyed, disbelieving at first when they first heard of it, were now glued and converging onto his hands. Firstly, in hushed tones, then in unison like a reverent chorus, Tim, Lotte and Roland began in a whisper. They then shouted firmly in encouragement, '*You must take a chance. Throw the dodecahedron... throw that gizmo now!*'

Chance looked helplessly at his friends, each in turn. Then, glancing upwards as if for help, he lowered his hand with the precious dodecahedron wrapped in his fingers. With a deep final breath, he loosened his grip and, slowly and deliberately, threw it high into the air. For a split second, it seemed to hover in space... And then, as they waited, holding their breath, it fell downwards with a sharp rattling clack and rolled in a zigzag fashion crisply along the floor of the taxi like a drunken crab...

The twelve-sided dice rolled onto its back and exposed all, of its almond-shaped eyes for all to see: and what's more, they were firmly shut, showing frank disapproval, which told them not to go on with the challenge.

'Oh no!' wailed Lotte. Her hand flew to her mouth in deep dismay.

'Wait. Hold on!' shouted Chance. He held them back, for the dodecahedron was still spinning on its axis, albeit now very slowly.

But before anyone could stop him, Roland gave it a prod with the side of his foot. The object spun once more in front of them. There was sharp click as it rotated on to its back before landing belly up onto another one of its facets. This time, it showed twelve – yes, twelve – of its eyes fully wide open, and with their curly black eyelashes fluttering encouragingly.

A smile of relief crossed Henry's face, as Tim punched the air, shouting, 'Wick-ed! Mag-ic! *The Riddle goes on!*'

Roland jumped into the front of his cab and started the engine. Through the open window, Ram gave a howl of defiance at the ripening moon as the taxi rapidly made its way out of the park. Passing the Serpentine, they headed southwards, leaving the city and their sudden euphoria quickly behind.

Then, without warning, not long afterwards into their journey...

'Lotte... Tim, our good young friends,' said Chance sheepishly with a solemn face. 'There's something *really important* Roland and I have got to say to you youngsters.'

There was a stunned scared look on the youngsters' faces. 'Wha... what is it, Chance?' stuttered Lotte, sensing the hesitancy in the harlequin's voice. Anxiously, she sat upright on the edge of the seat.

'Spit it out!' demanded Tim, getting worried as he glanced suspiciously towards Roland for help. Keeping his eye on the road, Roland merely shrugged resignedly as the cab headed towards the Old Kent road.

'Ahem... erm...' Chance cleared his throat. 'We adults have decided that in view of all the horrible things that have happened just recently, it would be sensible and safer to take a break to regroup, regain our strength, before we continue in pursuit of those vile people – De'Aff and his gruesome chums, not forgetting Qnevilus, their evil leader, who is still orchestrating the terror. It's going to be an arduous and dangerous journey into we don't know what, and will take time, cunning and careful planning. The Three Kingdoms cannot be saved until these evil-doers are wiped from the face of the earth.'

This was met by silence... deathly silence from the children, as if they had just been betrayed. 'You don't mean you're calling it off, are you, Chance? ...Henry?' Lotte pleaded.

Raising his body out of his seat, Tim joined in. '*What!* You're not chickening out, are you?'

Henry answered in a measured tone, but with the same gravity. 'No, my friends, we haven't got cold feet – far from it! But please let us tell you of the compromise that circumstances have forced upon us.

'Roland has arranged to take you to Mrs Chivers's for what is left of the school holidays, so that he can honestly say to your parents that you spent time at school camp. He will return and then take you home in a week's time. As it is, you will have to keep dead silent as to what has happened the last few days, so that you, as well as us, can now stop telling unnecessary white lies... I'm relieved to say!'

'Roland is that true?' wailed Lotte.

'Afraid so, Miss Lotte. It's for the best, and the less porkies and conspiracy there are, the better for everyone concerned!' As he spoke, Roland glanced backwards towards the children, confirming the new arrangements.

Henry continued quietly in case he woke up Ram, who was snoring deeply at their feet. 'Meanwhile, Chance and I have got to return to Paddington, as we have found out that Miss Saskia and her folks are returning at the end of the week from their holidays, due to Mr Goodall's work. Apparently, the parents had already spent some time in France earlier, but now the weather was also changing rapidly for the worse.'

Seeing their downcast faces, Chance then added, 'Look

you two, we *promise* that we will keep you posted about the next part of the quest. When the next term finishes there will be a long summer holiday and we promise that we will collect you.

'Honest. Cross your heart and hope to die!' demanded Tim.

'Shush! I don't think that word's appropriate in the circumstances, young 'un,' said Chance, now feeling somewhat guilty over the sudden change of plans.

'How will you let us know when you are ready in the summer?' asked Lotte.

'Zoot, our friendly woodpecker, will deliver a message to you,' said Chance, as it was the first thing that came into his head.

'Well, we will *hold* you to your promise, wont we, Tim!' said Lotte, glowering at the adults.

Tim was shuffling in his seat, still a bit surly at the sudden change of plans. 'Huh! Are you adults *sure* that this is not the beginning of a slippery way to end our friendship?'

'No, young man!' retorted Chance. 'It is neither the beginning of the end, nor the end of the beginning. *It's going to be a fresh new chapter!*'

And yet, only just some minutes before – after taking the decision with the dodecahedron, Lotte and Tim were on top of the world with joy and laughter... and then the very next minute, on hearing the news, they were crushed with disappointment and awful despair.

But, after a while from being down in the dumps, Lotte reluctantly smiled. She began to cheer up at the prospect of the next summer holidays with these extraordinary adventurers together with their magical powers on an incredible journey.

'At least you, Chance, have fought to live another day,' said Lotte. 'One hundred and thirty-nine, to be precise,' as she counted forty plus ninety-nine animatedly on her fingers.

'*No*, he's only got only a hundred and thirty-five. He's had four days already!' exclaimed Henry.

'But never mind, Chance has got his precious pendant back from that young thief as well as solving the mystery of the phantom of the circus!' added Lotte.

'Well, at least those bullies from your school got their comeuppance!' said Chance.

It was after some ten minutes or so when Tim gradually came round. 'Can we bring Ram?' he asked.

Chance nodded.

'…And my supersonic blades and my special catapult?

Chance nodded affirmatively, with a widening grin.

Lotte interrupted, so as not to be left out. 'Then I'm going to bring Brush, my robotic mouse!'

'Okay, you two. Let's not get *too* excited! Let's get some peace and quiet and some well-earned rest,' added Henry, giving them a stern side glance.

Roland shouted, conscientious as ever, 'Listen, everyone, get a bit of a shut-eye now, we'll soon be at Mrs Chivers's farm by daybreak. And then from the coast, it'll take me most of the day to get back to Paddington to drop off Chance and Henry.'

For the first time for what seemed like ages, Chance and Henry fell into a fitful sleep. Lotte and Tim went out like a light, their tired young heads lolling sideways against the back of the cab. Ram was dead to the world, his large paws covering his face as he snored like a train.

Whilst the children dreamt of the thrills of the chase they had just been through, and that of incredible adventures perhaps to come, Chance, meanwhile, visualised another journey with immense challenges ahead – though not yet set in motion. Conflicting thoughts whizzed around in his head: the promises made to Cecil and the others at the waxworks, as well as to Zoot back at the Goodall's house, and more importantly, those he had just made to Lotte and Tim. It was a monumental dilemma.

But whatever happens, he did not now dare wriggle out of them. And so, whatever dangers destiny had in store for him, he would have to face it with or without his friends, for there would be no turning back. For reassurance, he grabbed his lucky talisman hanging around his neck – the precious Gem of Knowledge to give him strength and wisdom. As weariness began to catch up with him, he lolled his head against Henry's shoulder and closed his eyes. The future was uncertain, with events around the corner that were completely unknown and not yet written; but that's another story.

EPILOGUE

Saskia Goodall

As soon as the Goodalls had returned home from France, Sassy rushed into the house to see Mudd her pet cat and more so, Chance the harlequin. She was puzzled to find that Chance was no longer looking directly out of the first-floor window where she had left him earlier to stare at number 13, opposite, belonging to Rosy Harker, because oddly, his back was now facing the window instead.

Er... mm, she thought. *I wonder if Pilar moved him in vacuuming the carpet. I must have words with her!* But when she examined the harlequin close-up, she noticed to her horror, that his clothes were matted with some dirty patches as if he had been in a fight. His hat was flattened and now lopsided. With his floppy bow tie missing and his boots splattered with mud as if he had been tramping in mud, this worried her no end. Then searching underneath his collar however, she was relieved to find that the precious pendant was still there.

However, when her attention was drawn to Henry de Poisson at the back of the room, she was even more stunned to find that his dress shirt and jacket were creased and crumpled as if they had been drenched recently. And what is more, his elegant cane was caked in soil.

Fortunately, the figure of Davinia Plum looked immaculate and pristine as ever, the haughty look of distain on her beautifully made-up face the same as before.

'Ah well,' Sassy sighed, 'must be imagining things!' Giving Mudd an affectionate stroke as the cat intertwined around her feet, Sassy murmured, 'I wonder, what's been going on while I was away? If only cats could speak, eh, Muddie?'

Lotte Pert

Four miles away, on a housing estate in the Bush, no sooner had Lotte arrived home from school camp than she was greeted by her mother, Shirley, who having returned from an overseas business trip two days earlier was overjoyed to see her daughter.

'Did you have a good time at Mrs Chivers's, my love?' she asked as she gave Lotte a bear hug.

'Oh, Mum, it was dull as dishwater as usual: the same as before, with nothing much different happening,' replied Lotte. Fervently, she kept her fingers crossed behind her back, hoping that someone up there wouldn't strike her dumb for telling a white lie.

Tim Needles

Meanwhile, as it happened in the flat next door, Joe, Tim's dad having got back from delivering goods to Germany and Greece, was at home to welcome back his son.

'Had a good hol, son?' asked Joe as he ruffled Ram's head vigorously.

'Rotten and boring, Dad! Nothing exciting at all happened! It was the same old stuff at the camp.'

'Well, boring that it might well be son, at least Mrs Pert and I know that you were safe and sound with young Lotte and the other kids there!' retorted Joe as he went into the kitchen to prepare dinner for them both.

Luckily, he didn't notice young Tim rolling his eyes to the ceiling whilst trying to suppress a surreptitious grin. He gave Ram a hug around the dog's large head and whispered into his ear, 'Lucky you animals don't tell tales out of school!' Ram just whined conspiratorially and lumbered towards the fridge looking for his usual packet of treats.

Chance and Henry de Poisson

Chance and Henry went into "suspended animation", biding their time while determined to be patient and on good behaviour... well, during the daytime at least, so as not to frighten Saskia and her parents by their finding out what really happens when they come alive.

Roland Bigglesworth

Resumed driving his taxi; thinking that the past week had all been a dream, he kept pinching himself.

Madame Grizelda

Was taken to the Tower of London by St John's Ambulance to stay with her stepbrother – a Beefeater, Edbert Tuffnut – so that she could recover from the panic attacks and her fainting at the circus on seeing the man with no eyes again – the one who had scared her witless at Glastonbury.

Katrina Belakova

Was found safe and alive hiding in a tunnel under the ring.

Seth Ropely

Now determined to turn over a new leaf: firstly, never to "borrow" another car again… and certainly not one with a body in it.

Secondly, to abandon the idea of stealing the precious mystic gem again… well at least, not immediately.

Liz and Hector Braggerley

With the rest of the gang of five, they vowed to get revenge on Lotte Pert. Later on, at school, they tried to grab hold of Lotte in order to throw her into the air to break her other leg. But however hard they tried to catch Lotte, she kept slipping out of their grasp as if she were coated in castor oil. Liz Braggerley then tried to smash Lotte on the shins at hockey, but she failed miserably as Lotte immediately jumped three feet into the air. Lotte felt that some of the harlequin's magic had rubbed off on her, and for that, she gave a secret smile.

Reverend Barbabas Quick

Returned to the vicarage, defeated, and demoralised with the shattering revelations that he had learnt about his wayward son Marcus Barnard.

Dr Slatane De'Aff

Disappeared from the face of the earth when he fled to the Alterworld of Qnevilus-the-Terrible. Kicking his heels, there he sat, seethed, and ranted – just waiting with the evil Qnevilus to seize his chance.

Nick Rossiter

Continued with his job, impatiently biding his time in seeking the "scoop and exclusive" that his editor at the paper demanded. Meanwhile, whilst this was happening, as a closet writer, he secretively began to pen a story – a story of… *A Dangerous Riddle of…*

ACKNOWLEDGEMENTS

THERE ARE MANY PEOPLE I owe a debt of thanks to, and for whom this book would never have got off the ground in the first place. I am eternally grateful to my remarkable wife Caroline for her inspirational advice and for the many corrections in the manuscript from the word go. To my ever-patient sister, Edna Crone for her constructive comments when the plot of the story was first hatched. And like her daughter Anna Green, is passionate about books – and thanks to the latter whose wonderful book design has been invaluable. Then of course, my eternal gratitude to my amazing, creative daughter Tanya, without whom the story would never have been written without her designing and making Chance, Henry-de-Poisson, Davinia Plum and the others, years ago in the first place. And to Jules Steele-Burns in Capetown for her enthusiasm for the storyline a long time ago. Many thanks to Simon Young, Lynne Stuart and Mike Fitzgerald for their comradeship and unstinting encouragement to get my work published.

I am equally indebted to the eminent agent, Patricia White for her experienced literary advice and critique of the original trilogy many moons ago. My deepest regret is that due to the out-of-sync timing, unfortunately, we were unable to work together. My enduring thanks to the late, great Michael Bond for his generous friendship and inspiration. And my thanks to my publishers, Jeremy Thompson, Philippa Iliffe, Rosie Lowe and the editorial team at The Book Guild for their faith in my work. Finally, thank you to the many people, young and old everywhere, who believe that like me, magical and mystical things can happen if you take a chance and suspend disbelief. After all, we are all children at heart that never grow up.

Frank L Ying

ABOUT THE AUTHOR

F L Ying is a retired osteopath living in London. This is his first book for young adults having been inspired by his daughter Tanya, who designed and built the main characters of the story in the first place.